Sweet As Pie

Key Lime Pie

"I had a great time following the ever-delightful Sadie as she ate and sleuthed her way through **nerve-wracking twists and turns and nail-biting suspense.**"

—Melanie Jacobsen, author of *The List*,
http://www.readandwritestuff.blogspot.com/

"Sadie Hoffmiller is the perfect heroine. She's funny, sassy, and always my first choice for crime solving. And where better to solve a mystery than the Florida Keys? *Key Lime Pie* **satisfied with every bite!**"

—Julie Wright, author of *Cross my Heart*, www.juliewright.com

"The title of *Key Lime Pie* will make you hungry, but the story will keep you too busy to bake. Even when oh-so-busy amateur sleuth Sadie Hoffmiller vows to stay out police business, life comes up with a different plan. **A missing girl, a very interesting man with bright blue eyes, and plenty of delicious recipes all create a combination even Sadie can't resist.**"

—H.B. Moore, author of *Alma the Younger*, www.hbmoore.com

Devil's Food Cake

"There's no mistaking that Kilpack is one of the best in this field and not just in the LDS market. *Lemon Tart* was good, *English Trifle* was better, but with *Devil's Food Cake* she delivers **a polished novel that can hold its own anywhere.**"

—Jennie Hansen, *Meridian Magazine*

"Throughout the book, **Kilpack offers fast-paced adventure** supplemented with well-plotted bursts of information plus several surprises to keep the reader off-balance but fascinated."

—Bonnye Good, *Suite 101,* fiction editor

"Josi Kilpack whips up **another tasty mystery where startling twists and delightful humor mix** in a confection as delicious as Sadie Hoffmiller's devil's food cake."

—Stephanie Black, two-time winner of the Whitney Award for Mystery/Suspense

English Trifle

"**English Trifle is an excellent read** and will be enjoyed by teens and adults of either gender. The characters are interesting, the plot is carefully crafted, and the setting has an authentic feel."

—Jennie Hansen, *Meridian Magazine*

Lemon Tart

"**The novel has a bit of everything. It's a mystery, a cookbook, a low-key romance and a dead-on depiction of life.** . . . That may sound like a hodgepodge. It's not. It works. Kilpack blends it all together and cooks it up until it has the taste of, well . . . of a tangy lemon tart."

—Jerry Johnston, *Deseret News*

"**Lemon Tart is an enjoyable mystery** with a well-hidden culprit and an unlikely heroine in Sadie Hoffmiller. Kilpack endows Sadie with logical hidden talents that come in handy at just the right moment."

—Shelley Glodowski, *Midwest Book Review,* June 2009

BLACKBERRY CRUMBLE

OTHER BOOKS BY JOSI S. KILPACK

Her Good Name
Sheep's Clothing
Unsung Lullaby

Culinary Mysteries
Lemon Tart
English Trifle
Devil's Food Cake
Key Lime Pie
Pumpkin Roll (coming Fall 2011)

Blackberry Crumble recipes

Download a free PDF of all the recipes in this book at
josiskilpack.com or deseretbook.com

BLACKBERRY CRUMBLE

A CULINARY MYSTERY

JOSI S. KILPACK

DESERET BOOK
SALT LAKE CITY, UTAH

To the people at Deseret Book who brought Sadie to life:
Jana, Lisa, Shauna, Rachael, and Tonya.
She'd have never been "real" without you gals.

Library of Congress Cataloging-in-Publication Data
Kilpack, Josi S., 1974– author.
    Blackberry crumble : a culinary mystery / Josi S. Kilpack.
        pages cm
    Summary: When Sadie Hoffmiller is hired by May Sanderson to investigate the death of her father, Sadie travels to Oregon and uncovers a complicated plot of greed, shady business dealings, and more than one member of the Sanderson clan with a motive for murder.
    ISBN 978-1-60641-941-0 (paperbound)
    1. Hoffmiller, Sadie (Fictitious character)—Fiction. 2. Cooks—Fiction.
3. Murder—Investigation—Fiction. I. Title.
    PS3561.I412B57 2011
    813'.54—dc22   2010045053

Printed in the United States of America
Publishers Printing, Salt Lake City, UT

10   9   8   7   6   5   4   3   2

CHAPTER 1

"Quiz me," Sadie said, straightening the row of cherry chocolate chip cookies she'd laid out on the platter. Pete Cunningham, her *absolutely-certain* boyfriend, was also laying out cookies—blueberry muffin tops to be exact. The Fourth of July had been several weeks ago, but she'd chosen the color scheme of red, white, and blue for the annual Latham Club summer picnic, which made the cookies a perfect fit.

"Okay," Pete said in his rich voice, placing a final cookie in his row—you couldn't really stack or layer blueberry muffin tops, but he was doing a wonderful job of arranging them as attractively as possible. More points in his favor, though he didn't need extra credit. Their relationship had moved to a new level the last few months, and Pete had proved himself a hundred times since then. "How many exits?"

"Three," Sadie said with confidence; that was an easy one. She popped open a plastic clamshell container and tried not to be offended by the store-bought cookies. She'd have made more cookies if she'd known the other people on the food committee weren't making their own. "Double doors straight ahead, single doors to the close left and far right. The doors behind us don't count because they lead to the kitchen, which leads to the fenced parking lot."

"Good," Pete said. "But always assume you're in the six position on a clock and specify exit locations by the hours they represent. That would make the double doors eleven o'clock, since they are slightly left of straight ahead. The single doors would then be at eight and two."

"Got it," Sadie said, a little thrill of discovery rushing through her. People might say you can't teach an old dog new tricks—and at the age of fifty-six, Sadie could certainly be considered a mature student—but she was proving the cliché wrong under Pete's excellent tutelage. "What else?"

"How many chairs are along the walls?" Pete asked. "That will give you an idea of how many people are expected to be here."

"About seventy," Sadie said, glancing quickly at the left wall and estimating that there were twenty-something chairs lined up. Two other walls had what looked like equal numbers of chairs, and the fourth wall had the tables for the food. However, since she'd helped plan the event, she already knew how many people were expected. Originally, the annual picnic-style dinner was supposed to be held outside, but Garrison, Colorado, was at the mercy of a hot spell so the event had been moved to the city hall—a former elementary school with a nice-sized gymnasium and an overzealous air conditioning system. It was 5:30 in the evening, ninety degrees outside, and yet Sadie had goose bumps since it was a chilly sixty-five degrees in the gym.

"And where are your keys?"

Sadie's head snapped to the side, and she looked at Pete in surprise. "My keys?" she asked. In the weeks since she'd started asking him to quiz her about her surroundings—honing her skills of observation—he'd never asked about anything other than the place they were at or the people they were with.

Pete glanced at her as he straightened the row of store-bought M&M's cookies someone else had brought and then wiped the crumbs off on his apron. Sadie thought he looked very cute in the apron. "If you had to leave in a hurry, you'd need your keys. Where are they?"

"Um, in my purse."

"And where is your purse?" Pete said, turning to face her and crossing his arms over his chest. His silver hair caught the light streaming in through the high windows, but Sadie was in no mind to appreciate it the way she normally would.

She had failed.

"In the kitchen," she said in defeat. "With the other half a dozen people helping with the food."

"Not to mention anyone who comes in through the back door, which is unlocked to make it easier for people to come in and out." He gave her an understanding smile, but didn't stop there. "I counted three other purses on the counter next to yours, each one of them likely holding wallets and keys. With no one specifically assigned to stay in the kitchen at all times—not that that's foolproof either—there's no one to keep an eye on those purses. They're a prime target for theft, especially since the gate is open, and Goose Park, a common hangout for transients and drug users, is right across the street."

Sadie's shoulders fell. "It's not fair," she said, suddenly petulant. "I don't have any pockets. Even if I wanted to keep my keys with me, I can't."

"Don't you have a code on the door of your car? You can leave your purse in your car where it's safer."

"That's gotten me into trouble before. I need to keep my cell phone close by."

"So keep your phone on your person."

"Pockets," Sadie reminded him, lifting the sides of her skirt to demonstrate how pocketless she was.

Pete shrugged and smiled at her. "Then wear clothing with pockets when you know you'll be unable to keep your purse with you."

Sadie narrowed her eyes at him. "Easy for you to say," she said, half-serious and half-playful. "You're a man. Everything you buy comes with pockets."

Pete grinned back at her in a superior way. "I believe, however, that men's clothing doesn't have a corner on the market."

"But some styles don't offer a pocket option," Sadie continued, reflecting on the women's clothing industry as a whole. Because of the same patriotic theme that had helped her choose the types of cookies she'd made, she was wearing what she called her Betsy Ross dress—a navy blue, cotton sundress which looked as though it had been sprinkled with white polka dots. Upon closer inspection, however, the dots revealed themselves as stars. The bodice fit well, with a wide, navy blue belt that set off her waist, even if it did make her hips look a little more prominent. Pockets on a dress like this would pad her hips even more and keep the A-line skirt from falling correctly.

"Then don't buy those styles," Pete said. He took a step closer to her, and Sadie felt the now-familiar zing as the protons between them started dancing. She loved the zing, something she hadn't felt between them for too long. But now wasn't the moment for protons.

"O-okay," Sadie said, finding it hard to stay focused as Pete moved even closer. His hand brushed her arm as he raised it to tuck her hair behind her ear. She'd been growing it out and it was now a choppy bob that was deceptively difficult to do despite its looking rather haphazard. Her breath shuddered slightly at his touch even as she felt herself leaning into him. They were alone, creating the perfect moment for him to steal a kiss . . . or three. The voices of the rest of the food committee could be heard through the door behind them; they were all in the kitchen. The scent of Pete's cologne mingled with the smell of the cookies—was there a more perfect combination than baked goods and Peter Cunningham?

"Just remember that if someone takes your keys, you're stranded, and whomever it was you were supposed to be going after is getting farther and farther away."

Shop talk or not, he was totally flirting with her, and she was completely under his spell.

When words failed her and she was feeling herself pulled into the reservoirs of his beautiful hazel eyes, he spoke again. "I've got two words for you, Sadie Hoffmiller."

"What?" Sadie breathed, thinking of all the things he could say that were only two words. *Kiss me* made the top of the list, right under *Love you*, which he'd yet to say out loud.

"Voice mail."

"What?" Sadie said, pulling her eyebrows together in surprise.

"If you can't keep your purse with you, chances are you're too busy to answer your phone anyway. Let them leave a message, and you can enjoy the peace of mind of knowing your personal items are safe."

"Oh," Sadie said, trying to hide her disappointment. "That's a really . . . smart idea."

"Well," Pete said with a sarcastic shrug and another of his adorable smiles as he tapped her nose playfully and moved away, "I didn't find my shiny badge at the bottom of a Cracker Jack box." He wiped his hands on his apron again, and in the process drew attention to the very badge he was referencing, clipped to the waistband of his pants.

At that precise moment, it caught the same light that had caught Pete's hair earlier. The metal gleamed heroically and initiated a wave of . . . envy in Sadie.

She looked away, chastising herself for being silly. She was not, nor would she ever be, a police detective. She was a retired school-teacher, for heaven's sake. And yet she'd had several adventures over the last eight months that had created a longing for . . . something. She didn't know what, exactly, but listening to Pete talk about his work—the details he *could* talk about—ignited something inside her that drew her toward his expertise.

It had also drawn her to a few websites about how to become a private investigator. She had purchased a set of lock picks online and a practice lock she sometimes played around with in the evenings, but she hadn't told anyone about those things. Instead, she peppered Pete for tricks of his trade and made him quiz her about details or procedures while she kept up with her community-oriented life as though it hadn't somehow lost some of its appeal.

The squeaking of a hinge caused both Sadie and Pete to look up as a young woman entered the room. She didn't look familiar, and Sadie had been part of the Latham Club—a nonprofit community service group—for several years. Maybe the woman was a guest, but she'd entered alone. Was that a newspaper tucked under her arm? Sadie's observation skills were getting better all the time.

A voice from behind them broke into their study of the new arrival, however. "Detective Cunningham?"

Sadie and Pete both turned toward the doors that led to the

kitchen. Glenda Meyers stood in the doorway. "I'm so sorry to interrupt, but it seems we filled the punch bowl so full that none of us can carry it. Would you mind helping us bring it out?"

"Of course not," Pete said.

Sadie sprang into action, stacking emptied cookie containers in an attempt to clear the tables. There needed to be room for the trays of lunch meat and veggies, not to mention the punch bowl, chips, and array of salads the club members would be bringing with them. Initially this was supposed to be a lunch, but after juggling the schedules, it had become a dinner . . . of lunch-type foods, since no one wanted to do much cooking—well, other than Sadie, who was always cooking something.

"Would you mind throwing these away?" Sadie asked as Pete moved toward the doorway. "Be sure to keep half a dozen or so for leftovers." There were always store-bought cookies left over, unlike her homemade varieties, which disappeared quickly. A fine argument for why being late to these types of events might be fashionable, but not wise. Pete nodded, and Sadie handed over the stacked containers. He winked at her while turning toward the doorway and the awaiting Glenda.

Once Pete and Glenda had disappeared, Sadie's eyes were drawn back to the woman who'd entered the gym . . . alone and uninvited. To Sadie's surprise, however, the woman was no longer standing at the far end of the room looking out of place. Instead she was striding toward Sadie with purposeful steps.

There were only a few yards between them, and Sadie finished assessing the woman as quickly as she could. Shoulder-length, wavy, strawberry-blonde hair tucked behind her ears, no bangs. Blue-gray eyes and a fair complexion with a smattering of freckles made her look younger than what Sadie believed to be her thirty-something years. Her makeup was minimal, and she wasn't wearing a wedding ring. The woman's jeans fit her widish hips well, and the purple tank top, while not quite the right color for her hair, went quite well with her figure, which, while full, was shapely. The woman was of average height, maybe an inch shorter than Sadie's five foot six inches. Her purse was a large, ornate, white leather number which, if Sadie wasn't mistaken, was rather high-end—making it look out of place on a woman who didn't seem particularly polished. Perhaps it had been a gift?

"Hi," Sadie said with a smile as soon as the woman came to a stop on the opposite side of the table. She put out her hand. "I'm Sadie Hoffmiller. I don't believe we've met. Are you part of the Latham Club?"

"No," the woman said. She took Sadie's hand, gave it a single firm shake, and dropped it before unconsciously wiping her hand on her jeans. She was nervous. "I came to talk to you."

"Me?" Sadie said, surprised. Granted, her name was on all the posters and fliers advertising the luncheon, but the urgency in the other woman's voice and intent of her words didn't seem to have much to do with that.

"A neighbor of yours said you'd be here," she said as she took a cursory glance at the three-dimensional, crepe-paper watermelon slices and real beach balls dangling from the gymnasium's ceiling. "I'm afraid I'm in a bit of a hurry."

"O-kay," Sadie said carefully. "What can I help you with?"

"I'd like to hire you," the woman said as her eyes snapped back to Sadie.

"Hire me?" Sadie repeated. "For what?" She looked down at the cookies. "Catering?" Sadie enjoyed helping with the food for community events, but cookies and cakes didn't seem to fit the intent of this woman. Who needed emergency catering?

"Investigation stuff," the woman said, leaning toward her and lowering her voice as though fearful she'd be overheard.

Sadie couldn't deny feeling flattered, but her attention was drawn to the newspaper in the woman's hand. It was an obvious explanation. The woman must have stumbled onto an article about one of the unfortunate incidents Sadie had been involved in. Some of the situations she'd found herself in made Sadie sound rather heroic, but there hadn't been anything written for weeks, and most of the mentions Sadie had cut out of the paper had been short and tucked between public notices and ninetieth-birthday announcements in small papers.

"I'm not an investigator. I just have really bad luck." She smiled at her own joke.

The woman shook her head. "You're exactly what I need," she said. "Someone obscure, who can help me make sense of things."

Sadie wasn't so sure that being called obscure was complimentary. "I don't understand what you're asking," she said. "I'm not . . . for hire." Though wouldn't it be cool if she were? She remembered that wave of envy she'd shrugged off a few minutes earlier in regard to Pete's badge and her own fantasies about private investigation work. Then she imagined how Pete would react if he were listening to this. He'd probably find it funny, which would make Sadie feel defensive.

"I can pay whatever it takes to make this worth your time," the woman said, keeping her eyes trained on Sadie. She was beginning to sound a little desperate. "Twice that, if I need to."

"But I'm not an investigator," Sadie explained again. "I don't know what you've heard, but it was likely overstated and—"

The woman cut Sadie off by putting the newspaper on the table.

Sadie couldn't help but look down. Her own face stared up at her. She immediately looked to the masthead. *The Denver Post*—the largest newspaper in Colorado. Sadie wasn't aware of the *Post* having run anything about her for several weeks. Where was that photo from, anyway? Her hair looked fabulous.

"I realize coming to you this way isn't exactly proper," the woman said, drawing Sadie's attention away from the newspaper. "But I don't have time to waste. I don't know if you believe in fate, Mrs. Hoffmiller, but I do. I believe in cosmic forces playing out in our lives from time to time, and I believe that this article coming out right now is no coincidence." Her voice was soft, but intent, confident, and yet not overbearing.

Right now? Sadie looked back at the paper, noticing the date for the first time. Friday, August 10th. That was *today*. She read the headline—"Modern Miss Marple: A Magnet for Murder?"—and felt a swirling heat take hold of her stomach as recent insecurities of sticking her nose in too many places it didn't belong began rising from the corner of her mind where she'd been trying to stash them.

"Mrs. Hoffmiller," the woman said, causing Sadie to look up once more. "I really do need your help." The woman's face changed in an instant, her expression falling and her eyes filling with tears. "I think my father may have been murdered."

Blueberry Muffin Tops

½ cup shortening
¼ cup butter
1 egg
1 cup sugar
1 teaspoon vanilla
1½ teaspoons lemon zest (can use 1 teaspoon lemon juice instead)
2 tablespoons milk
2 cups all-purpose flour
1½ teaspoons baking powder
½ teaspoon salt
1 cup fresh blueberries, or frozen blueberries (no need to thaw)

Preheat oven to 375 degrees. In a large bowl, cream the shortening, butter, egg, sugar, vanilla, lemon zest, and milk. In a separate bowl, combine dry ingredients. Add to shortening mixture until just mixed. Fold in blueberries, careful not to crush the berries. The batter might be a little crumbly.

Drop by teaspoonfuls (or 1-inch scoops) onto parchment or silicone-mat baking sheet (blueberries stick like crazy).

Bake 12 to 15 minutes or until muffin tops are golden brown. Cool on cookie sheet for two minutes before moving to a rack to cool. Makes 3 dozen.

Optional glaze

1½ tablespoons butter
1 cup powdered sugar
2 tablespoons lemon juice

Mix all ingredients together. Drizzle over cookies while cookies are still warm.

Note: A streusel topping might taste really good too!

CHAPTER 2

Sadie blinked at the other woman. "Murdered?" An all too familiar thrill rose up from her open-toed, navy sling-back sandals and left her spine in an all-out tingle.

The woman nodded and wiped quickly at her eyes, seemingly embarrassed over her tears.

"What makes you think he was murdered?" Sadie asked automatically. Before the woman had a chance to answer, Sadie's eyes were drawn to the newspaper again—"Magnet for Murder?" She started feeling squirmy.

The doors at the back of the gym opened again, and laughter echoed through the room as four women—all Latham Club members—entered, their heads bobbing as they talked to one another while they clicked across the hardwood floor in their heels. Sadie looked at the clock. Ten minutes before the official start.

"My name is May Sanderson," the woman said, glancing warily at the other women. She opened her purse and began rummaging through it. After a moment she pulled out a pen, then leaned forward, writing something in the margins of the newspaper still lying on the table between them. "This is my cell phone number," she said when she straightened. "Please call me when you've had time to think about what I've said. Money isn't an issue, but time certainly is." A slight pleading had entered her tone, confirming how serious she was about this.

With that, she turned and headed for the back doors, keeping her head down. The other women glanced at her briefly before returning to their discussion. Sadie's mind was already filling with questions as she glanced down at the phone number, noting that the first three numbers weren't a Colorado area code. She looked up again, wondering if she should follow May Sanderson and get more information, but the younger woman was already gone, leaving Sadie to field the questions left in her wake. Why did she think her father had been murdered? When had it happened? What would Pete say when she told him about this?

"Coming through!"

Sadie quickly stepped aside to make way for Pete, whose arms were wrapped around an enormous punch bowl, filled nearly to the brim with dark red punch. Glenda hadn't been kidding when she said it was too full for the ladies in the kitchen to carry. Pete was taking tiny steps and still the punch threatened to tidal wave out of the bowl at any moment. He began lowering his entire body, bending at the knee but keeping his back straight, so as to put the bowl down on the table without spilling.

Sadie saw the newspaper at the last possible moment, right where the punch bowl was headed. She reached for it quickly, startling Pete in the process. A wave of punch sloshed forward, splashing onto the table, the newspaper, and a cookie tray, before compensating by going backward, soaking Pete's apron.

Sadie gasped and raised a hand to her mouth while one of the women exclaimed from the other side of the table. Pete set the bowl down on the now punch-covered table.

"I'm so sorry," Sadie said as Pete stood up, revealing that his apron was completely soaked. He quickly untied it, and Sadie was dismayed to see that the punch had turned his powder-blue shirt a lovely shade of lavender. She looked around for some napkins before realizing they hadn't been set out yet.

"I'll get some paper towels," one of the women said. She came around the table and headed through the door that led to the kitchen. Pete wiped at his shirt with a dry part of his apron, but it didn't do any good.

"I'm so sorry," Sadie said again, moving toward him, feeling horrible. The woman returned with a roll of paper towels a moment later, and the other women began blotting and cleaning up the punch. Pete took a few paper towels and backed out of their way as he wiped at his own clothing.

Sadie watched as one of the women picked up the punch-soaked newspaper by one soggy corner, not even glancing at the headline, and tossed it in the big gray trash can behind the table, along with most of the blueberry muffin tops, also ruined.

"What happened?" Pete asked.

"I'm so sorry," Sadie said for a third time, embarrassed to be the cause of such a mess. "I was trying to get the newspaper out of the way."

"What newspaper?"

"The *Post*," Sadie said, her eyes going for the garbage can again. "The red-haired woman who came in before you went into the kitchen brought it." Her eyes went back to Pete. "I'm in it."

"Sadie, do you have any more of those cookies we can set out?" one of the ladies asked. The table and floor were mostly cleaned up.

Glenda walked through the doorway. "Sadie, Paul is running late with the meat trays. Has he called you?" She stopped short when she noticed the mess. "What happened?"

The women hurried to explain. Glenda looked at Sadie with surprise and disappointment. "We've got five minutes to finish setting everything up!" she said, her voice rising with every word. As if waiting for such an introduction, the back doors opened and another group of club members entered the gym.

"Um," Sadie said, trying to think of an explanation as Glenda's hands went to her hips.

"Where's the punch ladle?" someone called from the kitchen.

Sadie's head swirled as she tried to triage the situation and determine what was most in need of her attention.

Pete's hand at her elbow caught her attention, and she looked at him. His calmness helped ease the frantic feelings welling up inside of her. "I'm going to go home and change," he said, giving her arm a squeeze. "Call me if you need me to pick something up on the way back, okay? I'll help them find the ladle on my way out; it was in the box you brought from home, right?"

Oh, bless him, Sadie thought to herself as she nodded. They made such a great team.

"Good," Pete said, smiling to let her know he wasn't angry. "You do what you need to do. I'll be back."

He didn't wait around for any more discussion, allowing Sadie to turn her attention to the other expectant faces. "I have more blueberry muffin tops," Sadie said. "They're on top of the fridge, in the blue Tupperware." Glenda nodded and headed back to the kitchen. Sadie turned to assess the table. "We'll need some damp paper towels to wipe down the table so it isn't sticky. Heather and Savanna, will you take care of that?" The two women nodded and followed Glenda. "Shanna, can you help me adjust the punch bowl?" Sadie asked. "Between the two of us, we ought to be able to move it without making another mess."

Shanna nodded but stepped back as far as she could, probably to protect her cute floral skirt. They carefully adjusted the bowl, and then Sadie headed to the kitchen to retrieve her cell phone so she could call Paul and see where he was with the meat trays. He should have been here half an hour ago.

It wasn't until the phone was ringing that she thought about the newspaper article again, and about May Sanderson asking for her help. It would be a couple of hours before she could get her hands on another paper to see what the article said, but the headline flashed through her mind again, and her stomach clenched. "Modern Miss Marple: A Magnet for Murder?" What was the article about?

It took two tries to call Paul; she'd bought a new phone a few months ago, but she still didn't know how to use it very well. Finally, she got the touch screen to work and put the phone to her ear.

Paul answered and spoke before Sadie could even say hello. "I'm coming, Sadie. I swear."

"Sadie?" Glenda called from the kitchen while Paul explained about a mix-up at the delicatessen and how he'd almost run out of gas. Glenda continued, "Do we have more forks? I don't think this will be enough!"

Sadie closed her eyes and forced her brain to slow down. She simply *had* to focus on the luncheon right now. The article and May Sanderson would have to wait until later. She glanced at the clock on her way to the kitchen while Paul continued his explanation. It was going to be a long night.

CHAPTER 3

The first indication of trouble was the embarrassed smile Harriet Shub gave Sadie when she put her salad on the table. She dropped eye contact almost immediately, turning back to her sister, Leslie, who looked at Sadie with an uncomfortable expression before looking away as fast as Harriet had. Sadie adjusted the salad bowl and pulled off the plastic wrap while letting her gaze span the room. Another group was watching her and leaning in toward one another in such a way that made Sadie's stomach sink even further. Sadie knew gossip when she saw it; she was an expert on the subject, even if she preferred to call it "staying informed."

Don't overreact, she told herself. A moment later, Paul came in, and she busied herself with prepping the meat trays. Baskets of rolls appeared as though from nowhere, and then Ben Lancaster, the Latham Club president, stood up front and welcomed everyone. Sadie, as well as the rest of the kitchen crew, moved back toward the wall—out of the way, but still on hand should anyone need anything.

As she looked at the crowd, she caught the eyes of two different people, who both quickly looked away. It did nothing to calm her growing fears that there were a number of people in this room who knew something she didn't—something that wasn't necessarily complimentary. It had to be that article. She only took the Sunday paper; why hadn't someone called her if she'd been featured? She immediately answered her question. If it were negative, people would be hesitant to tell her about it. Her stomach sank further.

Ben droned on and on while Sadie continued experimenting with eye contact. Several people smiled back when she held their eye, helping her feel better, but there were a few who pretended not to see her.

Finally, Ben finished speaking, and people began to line up at the food tables. Sadie was unsure what to do and decided to retreat to the kitchen. Maybe she could call Pete and ask him to get another paper on his way back so she'd know what she was up against.

Smiling tightly, she was just stepping over the kitchen threshold when someone saying her name in conversation caused her to come up short. The open door blocked the room from seeing her, but didn't protect her in any other way.

"Sadie and that locksmith?" Glenda's voice said, tsking. "And here she's going around as though she's a good Christian woman."

Instant heat overtook Sadie's chest. The locksmith—Eric Burton.

"It's a new world," a voice Sadie didn't recognize said. "Even so-called conservatives are embracing more and more liberal lifestyles. I heard she told the women at church she'd visited a roommate that weekend."

"And we all fell for it," a third voice said as Sadie's whole body seemed to catch fire. "I can tell you one thing, she's not going to be the speaker at the youth campout this summer if I have anything to say about it. No way am I having her stand up in front of my daughter and voice her opinions on taking the moral high ground."

Sadie was too stunned to notice the voice drawing closer to the doorway until Brenda Norton was suddenly in front of her. Brenda's eyebrows went up and for a split second her expression showed embarrassment, but almost as quickly her face settled back into one of judgment. "Excuse me," she said in a perfectly polite tone.

Sadie was the first one to look away, which she feared made her look guilty, but she *felt* guilty. She stepped aside, letting Brenda leave before she entered the room. Glenda and the other woman, Jackie something, looked at her with embarrassed surprise.

They know about Eric, she said to herself, feeling her heart rate increase. *They know I didn't visit a roommate.* Sadie's eyes focused on her purse by the door, and she hurried toward it. She had to get a copy of that article!

She dialed Pete's number, despite her stomach being in her shoes. "Pete," she said when he answered. Her voice cracked, and she took a breath, turning away from the other women in the room, who were silent as they went about finding serving spoons for the salads.

"I'm in the parking lot," he said. "Come out for a minute."

Sadie searched his tone for anger. Did he know? Had someone called him? But she didn't ask. She just hung up, put her phone back in her purse, and went outside, glad for a reason to distance herself from whatever was happening.

The heat nearly knocked her over after the too-cold air conditioning in the gym; she felt as though she'd walked into the stream of a massive blow dryer. Pete got out of his car as soon as the kitchen door closed behind her, and gave her a sympathetic look. Her eyes went to the newspaper in his hand. He'd bought a copy without her having to ask. Was that a good thing or a bad thing?

Whatever it was that was initiating the gossip was fifteen feet away and getting closer with every step she took. Ten feet, eight, five, two. Pete held out the paper, and she watched his face as she took it from him. Being unable to read his expression was not new to Sadie—he was a police detective, after all—but it hurt her this time. She wondered what he was hiding.

She took a deep breath and looked again at the headline of the paper: "Modern Miss Marple: A Magnet for Murder?" by Jane Seeley, feature reporter.

The evening sun was as unrelenting as the words on the page. Sadie could barely note the impending heatstroke, however, as she read the article. Instead, she was numb, and the lump in her throat threatened to strangle her at any moment. When Pete's hand touched her arm, she jumped and looked up, finally aware of the sweat gathering under her arms and down her back.

"Are you okay?" he asked.

"How can I be?" she whispered. "I—I don't even know how to process this." The things Jane said weren't true—well, mostly. Sadie *had* gone to Florida, and Eric Burton *was* there, and she *had* become involved in a missing person's case, but the other things were just . . . wrong. She hadn't gone *away* with Eric, a Garrison resident she'd met several months ago, for some romantic weekend despite being in a relationship with Pete. She hadn't misled Florida police and shown "no regard for the law" as stated in the article. And those were only things Jane had said about what had happened in Miami. She'd also pointed out each of the other murder cases Sadie had been involved in, presenting the information almost as though Sadie had been a . . . cause of those tragic events.

Her eyes went back to the byline: Jane Seeley. Jane was a very unfortunate acquaintance of Sadie's, whom she hoped would never cross her path again. Apparently that had been wishful thinking. Whether the motive was revenge or simply Jane's disregard for people when a story was on the line, Sadie didn't know. Didn't really care. What mattered was that Sadie had just been libeled on the second page of *The Denver Post*.

Pete's hand was still on her arm. Sweat beaded on his forehead, and Sadie was disappointed to see that his expression was still guarded. She wanted to ask if he believed any of this; if he thought what she'd told him about the Miami trip was an attempt to hide the truth. But even if *he* believed what she'd told him months ago—when all this had happened—it didn't change the fact that she was *his* girlfriend, which meant anything said about her would affect him too. How unfair.

"I'm sorry," Sadie said.

Something jumped in Pete's eyes, and she realized that her apology sounded like she was admitting to the things Jane had written. She hurried to repair it. "It's not true. Well, I mean parts of it are, but the other stuff . . . It's not true, I swear."

"You *did* let people believe you were visiting a roommate," Pete reminded her.

"I didn't let *you* believe that," she said, before remembering that wasn't entirely true either. "Not for long anyway." Besides Sadie's best friend, Gayle, Pete was the only other person who knew the whole story, but neither Pete nor Gayle had actually *been* there. They had taken her at her word. How hard was it for them to imagine that she'd lied about it? Especially when a very different version of the story was printed in black and white?

Pete looked away from her, and she noticed that he'd changed into a yellow polo shirt. It was a cheerful color, and completely incongruous with the mood between them. "I believe you," he said, but something was missing from his tone, and Sadie felt as though the last three months they'd shared were being sucked into a vortex.

"No, you don't," Sadie whispered, feeling the tears rise in her eyes.

She pulled her arm away, suddenly reliving the other times when Pete had questioned her integrity. She would be the first to admit she hadn't always given him reasons to trust her completely, but she'd thought they'd moved past it. She thought they were heading to a new point in their relationship—one where they would use a certain four-letter word that started with "L" and ended with "E." The current climate between them, however, didn't seem to support that level of intimacy, and she wondered about their stability.

"Of course I believe you," he said, a flash of irritation crossing his face. "Let's talk about this later." He offered her a reconciliatory smile as he pulled on the collar of his shirt. "I'm melting out here, and staying in this heat isn't going to do either of us any good. I just need a little time to process everything, that's all."

Without waiting for her to answer, he moved toward the back door of the city hall building. Sadie stood rooted in her place. Pete didn't look back, and the door shut behind him with a soft *oooph.* A few moments passed before Sadie managed to gather up her shattered courage and go back inside.

Glenda was in the kitchen when Sadie entered, and she paused in refilling the platter of cookies. She looked away from Sadie, then took a breath and looked back, smiling in a careful way that made Sadie stiffen.

"I'm sorry if you overheard something," Glenda said. "I'm usually very careful about what I say."

"I know you are," Sadie said, noting that Glenda hadn't apologized for saying it, just for being overheard. Sadie lifted the newspaper she was still holding and shook her head for emphasis. "It's not true."

"Of course it isn't," Glenda said quickly, too quickly for it to be anything other than the *right* answer. It's what she was supposed to say, and it broke Sadie down even more. She'd known Glenda for years and had always had an easy friendship with her. Sadie's eyes drifted to the doors that led out to the gym. She could see people through the window; they weren't looking at her, but were they talking about her? Whispering about her lack of virtue? Wondering if she was somehow a catalyst to the murders that had been happening around her? A lady looked up and saw her, then took the arm of the person she was talking to and pulled her to the side, out of Sadie's range of vision.

Suddenly the idea of heading out there and pretending she didn't know or didn't care about the accusations being made about her seemed impossible. Sadie could smile through many things, but she'd never had to smile by way of her own defense. She didn't know how to do it, and her feet were frozen in place as though they too knew that entering the gym was something they were ill prepared to do. It didn't help that in the months since Miami, Sadie had interrogated herself as to her motivations for the things she had done. There were still a few questions she couldn't answer as comfortably as she wanted to, and Jane's accusations made those things pulsate in Sadie's brain.

"I think it would be a mistake for me to stay," Sadie said to Glenda, who was lifting the now-full tray of cookies. She wondered if Glenda would argue. After all, Sadie was head of the food committee, and dinner had just started. If Glenda tried to convince Sadie to stay, maybe she could. Maybe all she needed was someone to tell her to keep her chin up and stick up for herself by not retreating.

"Maybe that would be best," Glenda said, sounding both sympathetic and relieved. "We'll be fine."

Sadie stood for a moment, absorbing both what Glenda had said, and what she had not said. After a few seconds, Sadie nodded her understanding that Glenda didn't want her there. It was impossible to think that anyone else felt differently. She didn't bother saying good-bye to Pete or retrieving her dishes. She didn't even take a plate of her own cookies. She simply grabbed her purse, noted with relief that no one had stolen her keys, and slipped out the back door. She tried to talk herself out of the heaviness she was feeling. What was it they said, the pen was mightier than the sword? She felt chopped into a million pieces as she slid into the front seat of her car, a head-ache coming on thanks to the stress and the heat of the last several minutes.

Sadie drove straight home, kicked off her shoes, and climbed into bed with her dress still on. She hoped that silence and rest would bring clarity. Was she overreacting? Were her feelings justi-fied? She'd never dealt with anything like this and had no way of knowing if her reaction was reasonable. The whole town would know she'd lied about her trip to Florida. And how would she ex-plain her reasons for that?

She pulled the covers over her head, questioned everything she'd done on that trip to Miami three and a half months ago, and racked her brain for ideas on how to make things better.

CHAPTER 4

The phone on her nightstand started ringing half an hour later. It was Pete, asking where she'd gone. She explained the headache, assured him she was fine, and cut the conversation short. The next call was from Jack, Sadie's younger brother. She had a similar conversation with him—she was afraid to ask how he'd heard about the article—and again ended the call quickly.

The third call, twenty minutes after Jack's, was from a number she didn't recognize. She didn't answer. As the minutes ticked by, all Sadie could think about were the stories she'd seen on television where media crews camped out on the street, drooling over a potential interview.

When the phone rang yet again, she pulled the covers over her head. When the ringing stopped, she took the receiver off the hook. Was it too much to ask for a little silence so she could focus on how to best recover?

Gayle called her cell phone around eight o'clock. Sadie let it go to voice mail, then sent a text explaining that she was tired and going to bed early. Just before hitting send, she decided to send it to Breanna and Shawn as well in case they heard about the situation before she had time to talk to them. Breanna was in London, working at the London Zoo in a temporary position while she determined the status of her current romantic relationship, and Shawn was in Michigan getting ready for his junior year of college. She would take this night to pull herself together before discussing it with them . . . or anyone else for that matter.

Bases covered, she turned off the volume on her cell phone, ignoring the vibrations as text messages came in. She just needed a little time to figure things out. However, as evening slid into night, she found it harder and harder to pull herself out of the embarrassment. It was difficult to imagine how she could set the record straight due to the complexity of what was truth and what was not. What happened in Miami had barely made the news there, let alone anywhere else, and after coming home, she'd held her breath those first few weeks, hoping nothing would connect her to the case. When a month had passed, then two, she had concluded that her story about visiting a roommate had done the trick. Her complacency was now working against her.

Around midnight, she plodded into the kitchen and chose to eat the last of the blueberry muffin-top dough; she hadn't had any dinner. The red light blinking on her wall phone meant that she had new calls—which meant she had voice mails waiting for her, but she dreaded listening to them. They could wait until she felt stronger. She peeked out her front window, relieved to see that there were no news vans at the curb, but she didn't discount the possibility that they were waiting around the corner.

She took the cookie dough to her favorite chair in the living room and stared at the blank television screen while she ate in the dark. In the back of her mind, she tried to make herself feel better by saying the numbness couldn't last forever. Then she remembered the article. She retrieved it from the kitchen, sure she could be more objective now. All she needed to do was properly compartmentalize the comments and come up with a way to counter each one of them effectively.

After turning on the lamp by the chair and reading the article again, however, she realized numb wasn't so bad. *Romantic tryst. Cover story. Disregard for proper procedure.* The words stabbed through any reasonable thoughts she'd come up with.

In its place, anger took hold. This was so unfair! Yes, she'd lied about why she went to Florida, and yes, she'd been involved in yet one more murder investigation down there, but Jane had twisted things—turned them into something they weren't. Sadie didn't deserve that. She'd never been malicious to Jane and had done nothing to earn this kind of treatment. Yet, she was the one holding a leaking reputation, having to figure out how to explain it. And what *could* she explain? The case in Miami hadn't gone to trial yet, and she'd been told not to talk to anyone about the particulars of the case until the FBI, or whoever, took over and had gathered all their information. Even if she wanted to explain it to people, her hands were tied. She couldn't defend herself without jeopardizing everything she'd uncovered.

"Jane Seeley," she growled, stabbing her spoon into the half-empty container of cookie dough and scooping out a huge bite. She shoved the whole spoonful into her mouth and chewed it up, the sugar gritty between her teeth even as the blueberries both sweetened and soured the overall taste. What she wouldn't give to be in a room with Jane Seeley right now.

The sugar rush kept her up until two o'clock; but the closer Saturday morning came, the more her weekend to-do list began dominating her thoughts. She had to go grocery shopping, and clean the carpets, and get her tires rotated. Finally, she did her yoga breathing and meditation until she felt her body began to relax. Then she climbed into bed and hoped that morning wouldn't come for a very long time.

The next thing she knew, it was bright outside her window. Rather than popping out of bed, however, she pulled the blankets back up to her chin and rolled over. It was 8:46, and she needed to build herself up before she could imagine going into the world and facing the same looks she'd encountered at the dinner.

The anger had given her some oomph last night, but had faded in the morning sun. Nine o'clock came and went; Sadie couldn't remember the last time she'd stayed in bed past nine. Even when she had the flu she puttered around the house. At 9:10 she got a text from Gayle, asking if she was okay.

She ignored it.

Breanna had texted as well, asking if Sadie was okay and lamenting that she was on the other side of the world. Sadie assured her daughter that she was fine, even though she'd give just about anything to have Breanna come home for the weekend. Shawn, who knew Jane almost as well as Sadie did, called her a bad name in his text, and Sadie had to chastise him for it—via text, of course; she didn't want to talk to anyone yet.

At ten she finally got up and showered, not bothering to do her hair. She simply towel dried it and brushed it away from her face. A hint of gray was showing at the roots, meaning she needed to make an appointment to get her burnished brown with natural-looking highlights redone, but even that simple errand felt overwhelming. Going to a salon full of people who might believe those things from the article—she didn't think she'd survive it. Maybe it was time to follow Paula Deen and embrace going silver.

As she climbed back into bed, it did not escape her notice that after hours and hours of lying around, waiting for a plan to come to mind, she still had no idea what to do.

Around noon, someone knocked at her door. She imagined a hulking reporter with hungry eyes thrusting a microphone into her face. "Why did you lie to your entire community about your trip to Florida? Don't you think they deserve to know the truth? What else have you been hiding from your unsuspecting neighbors? Are you really dating a Garrison police detective? What does he think about the other man in your life?"

Her mind went back to the article as she closed her eyes and snuggled further down into the blankets, grateful that it was illegal for reporters to break into her house and wishing, again, that everything would just go away. Far, far away. A second knock sounded, and she wrapped the pillow around her head. Even when the knocking stopped she didn't unwrap the pillow from her ears, wishing she could fall asleep and wake up when this was all over.

"Sadie."

Sadie jolted and her eyes flew open. Gayle stood at the foot of her bed, looking at her with concern.

Relieved it wasn't Barbara Walters, but wishing she hadn't told Gayle where she hid the spare key, Sadie forced a smile. "I'm okay," she said, hoping she sounded casual. "I . . . I've been up all day cleaning and just laid down for a nap."

"Right," Gayle said, putting her hands on her hips and cocking her head to the side. "That's why there are dishes in the sink."

Sadie squinted at her, not ready to be rescued. Gayle wore her hair short and had just enough natural curl to keep it full and hip-looking. Her hair was as red as ever—not fake red, but a color that

29

was actually believable—and it made Sadie think of May Sanderson, the redhead who had first brought the article to Sadie's attention.

"I'm fine," Sadie said, waving one hand through the air. "I'm just . . . tired."

"Pete's here," Gayle said.

Sadie pushed herself up and began smoothing her hair, which was still damp in some places from the shower. She was sure it looked atrocious. "Oh, please tell me you're kidding," she whined. "I don't want him to see me like this."

"Like what?"

"Like this," Sadie said, annoyed that Gayle was being difficult. "Undone."

"We're worried about you," she said as she sat down on the edge of the bed.

Sadie fiddled with the satin trim of her bedspread while avoiding Gayle's eyes.

"It's a stupid article written by a woman who makes a menace of herself," Gayle continued. "It's not worthy of this kind of unraveling."

"You don't understand," Sadie said, giving up the pretense that she was all right. She leaned back against the headboard and held her pillow in her lap. "She attacked every part of me. She made me sound like a hussy and a criminal. No one has ever said things like that about me."

"Then you were due, sweetie," Gayle said, her tone soft as she squeezed Sadie's leg beneath the blankets. "We all have our moments, and after the last several months, didn't it ever cross your mind that someone somewhere just might try to capitalize on it?"

Sadie hadn't thought about it that way, but it didn't make her feel any better. The memory of people whispering about her and summarizing her character still hurt, and she shriveled away from it all over again. Then she thought of Jane, and her stomach started to burn.

Gayle continued. "You're Sadie Hoffmiller, and people love you, even if they have a momentary lapse of judgment. The best way to convince them that Jane Seeley is a rat-faced, self-serving, manipulating tramp is to be the Sadie this town knows and loves, not the one Jane Seeley is trying to sell."

She made it sound so easy.

"And Pete's still here," Gayle said, reminding Sadie of that fact.

"But my hair," Sadie whined, raising her hands to her hair again, which had dried into a horrendous state of hills and valleys. "Can you tell him I'll call him later? I really don't want to see him."

"He wants to see *you*," Gayle said, a different softness to her voice that caused Sadie to look up at her. The look they shared filled in the blanks left behind by Gayle's tone, and Sadie was reminded that at one point her friend had been interested in Pete. Sadie had given her blessing for Gayle to date Pete before quickly realizing that had been a mistake. Gayle hadn't gotten upset when Sadie had renewed her relationship with Pete, but Sadie knew she still had a soft spot for him. Luckily, it wasn't nearly as big as the soft spot she had for Sadie. Remembering how easily Gayle had accepted Sadie and Pete being together again caused any other arguments to fizzle in her throat. After all of that, Gayle was here, pulling Sadie out of the mire. Surely Sadie owed her a little compliance.

"You've got two minutes," Gayle said, patting Sadie's ankle and shooting her a look that communicated her expectation for Sadie to follow her instructions. She stood up and left the room, clicking the door closed behind her.

Sadie sat there for nearly a minute before finally getting out of bed, accepting her fate. She changed into the white-and-pink, polka-dotted pajamas her daughter Breanna had sent her for this last Mother's Day. They were silky and lightweight. Sadie didn't wear them very often because she was afraid she would spill something on them. But she wanted to present two things to Pete and Gayle, and the pajamas would help her do that. First, that she was okay; and second, that she wasn't leaving the house yet. She did hurry to the bathroom to spritz and gel her hair, using her fingers to tease it into some semblance of style. She still looked awful, but at least she didn't look like a drowned rat anymore.

Pete and Gayle both stood up from where they'd been sitting around the table when Sadie entered the kitchen, feeling foolish and conspicuous in her cheery jammies. Pete pulled out a chair next to him and waved her toward it. She sat and Gayle pushed a bowl her direction. Sadie's stomach rumbled as she looked into the bowl before looking up at her friend.

"You made me potato salad?" Sadie said, her voice soft with gratitude. Gayle made the best potato salad in Garrison, and she knew Sadie loved it.

"The ultimate comfort food," Gayle said. "Well, at least when it isn't soup weather."

Sadie had Gayle's recipe in her Little Black Recipe Book, but she only made it for family events, not wanting to take credit for it around town. "Thank you," she whispered before taking her first bite and savoring the perfection of texture, taste, and good old carbohydrates.

"So," Pete said after Sadie had eaten most of the potato salad, "how are you doing?"

"Umm, can we start with something else?" Sadie asked, using the spoon to scoop up a final bite.

"No," Gayle said. "Your behavior isn't healthy."

"I know," Sadie said. "But I need a little time to pull myself to-gether."

"That's called wallowing," Gayle said. "And it's the worst thing you could be doing right now. Hiding out only gives credibility to the things Jane wrote. You've got to get out there and prove she was wrong."

"She's not wrong," Sadie mumbled, painfully aware of Pete's presence next to her. While part of her wished he wasn't there, maybe it was better that he was. Sadie took a breath. "I mean, yes, she's exaggerating some parts, of course, but I did go to Florida in part because I was . . . curious about my feelings toward Eric. And I did lie about visiting my roommate. And I did withhold information from the police and—"

"Solve the case," Pete finished.

Sadie was so surprised to hear him not only speak, but speak defensively, that she couldn't come up with a reply.

Pete continued. "Jane Seeley obviously got ahold of someone who gave her bits and pieces of the story, and she glued them to-gether any way she wanted to."

Sadie looked at him. "You believe that?"

"Of course I do," Pete said, holding her eyes. "It would be really nice if you'd give me a little more credit. I said I needed some time to process it, and then you disappear while I'm defending you to the people at the dinner."

"But you were so mad."

"I was *upset*—not mad, upset. You would have been too if there had been an article like that about me, twisting my words and ac-tions the way Jane did yours."

Sadie felt tears in her eyes. "Really?" she whispered. He smiled and reached for her hand, making her question her earlier doubts. Maybe they weren't so far off track as she thought.

"So, anyway," Gayle cut in. "What are you going to do now?"

Sadie reveled in Pete's warm hand wrapped around hers and lifted her other hand to wipe at her eyes. She looked at Gayle sitting across the table and sniffed slightly. "I don't know," she said honestly. She meant it when she said she'd never faced anything like this. She'd never had to find a way to defend herself to an entire state full of people.

They started brainstorming. Gayle suggested a letter to the editor of the paper, and Pete said she had grounds to request a retraction, but they all agreed that a few sentences buried in Monday's paper wouldn't do much. And it didn't solve the problem of Sadie being unable to explain a lot of the details associated with the case. They all agreed that was a definite roadblock.

"Maybe it will just go away," Gayle said after it felt like they'd exhausted all their possibilities.

"Maybe we just have to find a way to live with it," Pete countered. "It's not that bad. I mean, it was in Friday's paper, for heaven's sake. Everyone knows that's the least-read paper of the week, and it was on the second page."

Sadie knew that was true, but she also knew that it only took a few people reading the article to start the story going, and in a small town like Garrison, where the next biggest news was rezoning the agriculture space on the north end of town, it was just too tempting not to repeat.

Gayle's cell phone rang, and she excused herself from the table before putting it to her ear.

"Sadie?" Pete said, squeezing her hand.

She loved the sound of her name on his lips. She looked up at him, feeling sheepish, and attempted a smile.

"You're a good person," Pete said. Sadie fidgeted with her spoon. He reached over and touched her chin, causing her to look up at him. "You are a *good* person."

Sadie felt tears come to her eyes again, wishing she didn't need to hear that right now. But she *did* need to hear it, especially from him. If Pete could believe her and support her through this, then surely she could believe in herself. Right?

The moment was interrupted by the unexpected sound of the television.

Sadie and Pete turned toward the TV in the living room. Gayle stood in front of it, blocking Sadie's view, the phone still to her ear. She shook her head. "I better go," she said into the phone, looking over at Sadie as she lowered the phone and turned it off.

"What?" Sadie asked, though her voice was almost a whisper.

Gayle didn't say anything as she stepped aside, showing the television screen. The weekend anchorman for the noon news sat at his desk with a small picture of Eric Burton, the ill-fated companion of Sadie's now-legendary trip to Miami, hovering above his left shoulder.

"Turn it up," Pete said, pushing away from the table and striding into the living room. He planted his feet and crossed his arms over his chest. Sadie stayed in her chair, hiding behind her potato salad bowl as the newscaster continued talking.

"While details are sketchy, pending ongoing investigation, the involvement of not one but two Garrison, Colorado, residents has been confirmed by the Miami police department. Hillary Martin has more."

The screen flashed to Eric's face, and Sadie felt herself sinking in her chair as though she could hide from whatever was coming next.

"It was a very difficult time," Eric said, sounding sympathetic before saying a few sentences about his daughter's disappearance three years earlier and how that had factored into his coming to Florida.

"And the other Garrison resident—Sadie Hoffmiller—how did she get involved?"

"Well, Sadie and I had been . . . close for quite some time, and when push came to shove, she was there for me. She was a real asset, no matter what that article said."

"It's been reported that she told friends she was visiting a roommate that weekend. Were you aware of that cover story?"

Eric shrugged and smiled like it was no big deal. "Sometimes the ends justify the means. Sadie is a phenomenal and . . . *passionate* woman."

Sadie clenched her eyes shut and let her head drop to the table with a thunk as Eric went on to basically confirm everything Jane had said.

She should never have gotten out of bed after all.

Gayle's Potato Salad

10 fist-sized red potatoes
10 eggs
¼ teaspoon salt
1½ cups chopped dill pickles
1¾ cups mayonnaise
1½ tablespoons to 2 tablespoons mustard (to taste and consistency)
2 tablespoons to ¼ cup pickle juice (to taste and consistency)
½ cup finely diced green or white onions (optional; Jack insists that the onions are NOT optional)

Salt (to taste)
Pepper (to taste)

Wash potatoes well and boil (with skins on) until a knife cuts through the potato easily. Drain, refill pan with cool water, and set aside. Potatoes can be cooked the night before, drained, and refrigerated.*

Put eggs in a 2-quart saucepan. Cover with water and add ¼ teaspoon salt. Cook eggs on high heat until the water comes to a boil. Boil eggs one minute. Remove pan from heat, cover, and let sit for 9 minutes. Drain pan and refill with cool water. Repeat after two minutes. (This will cool the eggs quickly and keep them from getting the green layer around the yolk, which is due to overcooking.) When cool, peel the eggs. (Eggs can be boiled in advance and refrigerated, but don't peel them until ready to use.)

Mix pickles, mayonnaise, mustard, pickle juice, onions, salt, and pepper together in a small bowl.

Dice the cooled, unpeeled potatoes and place in a large bowl. (Use a small knife and cut them carefully in your hand over the bowl; boiled potatoes are messy on a cutting board). Dice the cooled, peeled eggs and add to the potatoes. Add pickle and mayo mixture. Use a large spoon or rubber scraper to mix potatoes, eggs, and mayo mixture together.

Adjust flavors and thickness of sauce by adding more pickle juice (don't be shy with the pickle juice if the sauce needs it). Salt and pepper to taste. Refrigerate until serving. Serves 10 to 14.

*Gayle always flavors her potatoes first: Drain the potatoes on a dish towel to absorb most of the water. After dicing the potatoes, pour additional pickle juice directly on them so they absorb the juice and have an even better flavor.

CHAPTER 5

Neither Pete nor Gayle said anything about Eric's interview; instead, they insisted Sadie make herself presentable and go to dinner and a movie with them. Sadie tried not to cast glances around the restaurant, but it was so hard. When the lights went down for the movie—something with Sandra Bullock in it—she felt herself relax for the first time. No one would know she was there. She could hide for at least ninety minutes.

Sadie had talked to both of her children between the news and the dinner, but Breanna texted her halfway through the movie. Sadie stepped out into the lobby and spent another twenty minutes reassuring her daughter and pretending that everything was fine. She wished she believed it herself.

When they returned to the house, Gayle gave Sadie a parting hug and left Pete and Sadie together on the front steps. The night was still warm, but significantly cooler than it had been during the day. Pete walked her inside and left her with a goodnight kiss that went a long way to repairing her still-crumpled self-confidence.

"Call me in the morning," Pete said, squeezing her hand before heading out the front door.

"I will," Sadie said, stepping out after him. She watched as he got into his car, drove around the cul-de-sac, and disappeared. She wondered if there would ever be a point where he wouldn't go home at night. They'd be married by then, of course. Despite Jane's accusations, Sadie really was a woman of virtue. But thinking about the future of her relationship with Pete made her worry a little bit. Despite all he'd done for her today, she worried about what effect this situation might have on their relationship long-term. She thought of what he'd said about being upset about the article rather than mad: "*You would have been too if there had been an article like that about me.*" Pete was right; she *would* be upset. Would she also distrust him a little bit?

She locked the door behind her and was beginning her nightly routine when Shawn called. Sadie loved her mountain of a baby boy, but she was exhausted and wished she could put off this conversation another day. But it was her son, and he was worried about her. She answered the phone.

"Hey, sweetie."

"I found the online version of that article. Jane Seely is such a—"

"Reporter," Sadie cut in, saving both of them from whatever word Shawn was about to use. She went on to repeat Gayle's opinion that it was only a matter of time before someone like Jane capitalized on the sensational nature of the last ten months of Sadie's life. Like she'd done with Breanna, she tried to pretend it was no big deal, but the more they talked about it, the harder it was to keep up the pretense.

"So, you're not mad about this?"

"I'm totally mad," Sadie said before remembering she was supposed to be taking the high road—or at least giving that impression to her children. Too late now. "She twisted things to make the story more exciting, and I can't even properly defend myself because of the pending trial." It felt good to vent.

"I think I should slash her tires," Shawn said. "Or sneak into her house and put limburger cheese on all her light bulbs—that stuff stinks to high heaven when the heat starts cooking it."

Sadie chose not to ask how he knew that particular fact and changed the subject. "So, are you ready for school?" Fall semester started in about two weeks. Shawn was on probation in regards to his scholarship; he seemed to be losing interest in the academic side of the sports medicine program, despite having completed two years of it already. He'd stayed in Michigan for the summer because he'd gotten a job working with the city parks and recreation last fall and didn't want to give it up. He loved the job. School? Not so much.

"Aw, man, do we have to talk about this?"

Within five minutes, Shawn managed to end the call, and Sadie had something new to worry about while she washed her face and finished up the day's dishes. She usually watched the ten o'clock news, but now she looked at the dark television screen warily. Did she trust it? Her eyes went to the phone still holding her messages and blinking to tell her people had been trying to reach her. She decided she wasn't ready for either of them.

Instead, she took a long, hot shower, put on her polka-dotted pajamas, and climbed into bed with a heavy sigh. What. A. Day. Tomorrow she had a Sunday School lesson to teach and had offered to bring appetizers for the Woman's Group meeting that afternoon. Should she act like nothing happened, or should she try to explain herself? She fell asleep amid attempts to visualize a positive result that, despite herself, seemed rather unrealistic.

A little after three o'clock in the morning, her eyes snapped open, the name May Sanderson heavy in her still dream-drugged mind. She searched her brain for why May's name had come to mind right now, but whatever the dream had been, it had slipped away from her. But the name stayed.

For hours.

All the questions she'd started to ask herself after she'd met May Sanderson came back, and she added more to the list. Why had such a negative article caught May's attention? What made the woman think her father was murdered? Sadie remembered May had written her phone number on the newspaper that minutes later had been drenched in punch and then thrown in the garbage.

At five-thirty, Sadie finally got up, put her feet into her slippers, and shuffled into the kitchen. The sun was coming up over the eastern mountains, and the morning was peachy-pink. Gayle had left some potato salad in the fridge, and Sadie smiled to herself as she dished up a bowl. It was potatoes and eggs—people ate that for breakfast all the time. She sat down at the table to eat while the house began absorbing the morning light, but her eyes were drawn to the computer across the room. She had learned a lot about the World Wide Web in the past few months. And wouldn't finding May Sanderson be the polite thing to do? If only to let her know Sadie hadn't ignored her situation. May had said something about fate and cosmic forces. Sadie didn't want to interfere with May's spirituality by ignoring her impressions completely.

She took her bowl with her across the room and settled into the computer chair, fully aware that losing herself in this task could help her block out everything else that was still rubbing her raw inside. She was hungry for the distraction.

First, she went to Google and simply typed in *May Sanderson*.

Within seconds, she had 621,000 links to sift through. On another day, at another time, it might have seemed rather daunting to begin a search for one woman with only a name to go on. But it was five-thirty in the morning on a day Sadie was dreading. What else did she have to do?

CHAPTER 6

A fter clicking on random Google links for ten minutes, Sadie got serious. She logged on to Peoplefinder.com, a website she'd learned about from her daughter months earlier. She had her own account for it, though she'd told no one that she used it. So far, she'd only played around with it, mostly looking up family members to see how much information was available through the program and researching the City Council members just for fun. She hadn't really discovered anything she didn't already know—other than the fact that Jeffrey Headstrom had been married three times, not the two he claimed—but researching people was more fun than playing Solitaire. Unfortunately, she needed more than a name in order to get additional information about a person. Just knowing the state May was from would help, but she didn't even have that.

The area code! Sadie had glanced at May's number on the news-paper and remembered it wasn't from Colorado. But she couldn't re-member what the numbers were. She closed her eyes and squinched her brow. It started with a two—Sadie was pretty sure about that, but the rest of the numbers wouldn't come. She Googled area codes that started with a two, but nearly every number between 201 and

299 was an area code somewhere, and as she scanned the list, none of them stood out right away. So much had happened in the last thirty-six hours since she'd glanced at that phone number, it wasn't surprising that she couldn't recall it. Still, it was disappointing. She imagined that real investigators had impeccable memories.

Border states. Lots of towns close to the border between states offered news from both the state they were in as well as the state close by. Garrison was in northern Colorado, so their news, for instance, often overlapped with news from Cheyenne, Wyoming. Unfortunately, not a single state that bordered Colorado had an area code starting with the number two. Undaunted, Sadie pulled a notebook out of the top drawer of the computer desk and opened an Internet browser window with a map of the United States. Researching the bordering states of Colorado's bordering states didn't make as much sense—they wouldn't have Colorado newspapers— and yet she had to start with some kind of criteria. She looked at the map and started making a list.

After crossing off the states without an area code beginning with two, Sadie began the tedious task of looking for May Sanderson in the white pages of the first few area codes. It crossed her mind an hour and a half later, as she began searching Modesto, California— she could imagine May being a California girl, even though there were two full states between California and Colorado—that she ought to plan out what she was going to say to Ms. Sanderson if she found her. Was she going to ask questions about the things May had told Sadie about her father being murdered? After the way Sadie's last case had just exploded all over the media, she wanted nothing more than to hide in her closet for a few months. Getting involved in another murder mystery was not high on her list of priorities. So why was she putting so much effort into this?

I'm just going to explain why I can't help her, Sadie told herself as she stared at the results on the computer—no May Sanderson in the Modesto area. She changed "May" to "M." There was the chance that May was married, but she hadn't been wearing a wedding ring.

A new listing came up, and Sadie felt her jaw drop. There were more than three hundred listings for M. Sanderson in Modesto, California.

"This is crazy," Sadie said, pushing herself away from the desk. Three hundred listings! And that was in only one of dozens of area codes. "You're being ridiculous," she told herself as she stood and turned her back on the computer, irritated at both the time she'd wasted and the impossibility of the task.

Sadie glanced at the clock; it was after eight o'clock. She'd just wasted almost three hours on a futile task. Church didn't start until ten, but she needed to get ready and at least work on the cream-cheese layer of the crab dip she was taking to the Women's Group afternoon meeting. She pulled the cream cheese out of the fridge and left it to warm up on the counter while she showered for the third time in twenty-four hours, annoyed and not looking forward to going to church. She couldn't stop reviewing the looks and whispers from the dinner on Friday, the humiliation of it all. She could only hope church would be better than that. It was *church*, after all. The thought of attending the women's meeting was even less appealing, but it was imperative that she stick to her routine and act as though nothing were bothering her. Besides, she'd said she would attend, and they were counting on her being there. Now more than ever she needed to keep her word.

She was ready to go by 9:30, even though she'd been even more meticulous of her appearance today, worried that people would be paying her extra attention. She called Pete and they chatted for a few minutes. He seemed distracted, which reminded Sadie that she'd totally hijacked his Saturday. She felt bad and ended the call earlier than she'd planned to so that she wouldn't ruin his entire weekend.

Once off the phone, she opened the cream cheese and began humming while she spread it on her nicest crystal platter in hopes of brightening her mood. While she worked, however, she could feel the computer screen calling to her, tempting her to try again. The information she needed was somewhere online, she was sure of it, and just knowing that made it seem silly not to keep looking. It was all about finding the right questions to ask.

When she finished spreading the cream cheese, she covered the platter with plastic wrap, put it in the fridge to finish later, and then turned to eye the computer—the screen yawning at her, sucking her in.

Well, I have ten minutes. She smoothed her skirt beneath herself and sat back down at the computer. There was nothing else to do, right? She began scrolling through the listings and finally admitted to herself that if her intent was simply to apologize for being unable to help May, she wouldn't be going to all this trouble. After everything that had happened this weekend, the thought of getting involved with another case should have been abhorrent. Instead, Sadie felt the same thrill run up her spine as when May had first mentioned her suspicions about her father's death.

Easy Crab Dip

1 (8-ounce) package cream cheese, softened
¼ cup cocktail sauce
1 (4.25-ounce) can lump crab meat
Lemon juice (to taste)
Crackers
Celery sticks

Place softened cream cheese in the middle of a medium-sized dinner plate or similarly sized platter. Using the back of a spoon, smooth cream cheese evenly across the surface of the plate. Spread a layer of cocktail sauce over the cream cheese.

Open canned crab meat, drain, and use a fork to fluff the meat. Spread crab meat evenly over the cocktail sauce.* (Drizzle lemon juice over crab for additional <u>yumminess</u>—but use sparingly!)

Use a firm cracker or celery stick to scoop up the layered dip.

*Breanna likes this dip with a drained can of tiny shrimp instead of the crab.

CHAPTER 7

By the time Sadie left for church, she was once again telling herself she was crazy. One person among millions? How could she believe that finding May Sanderson was even possible? If only she could remember that area code.

She pulled up to the gray stone church and parked her car. She sat for a minute, enjoying the car's air conditioning before she had to step out into the heat.

She really, really didn't want to be here today.

Eric's words from the TV interview came back: "*passionate woman.*" Her cheeks burned all over again. How would people interpret that? What would she think of it, if it had been said about someone else? After another minute, she took a deep breath and headed inside while putting her best fake smile on her face. She made it through the parking lot and most of the hallway before her luck ran out.

"Sadie!"

She felt she had no choice but to stop and turn in the direction of the voice. She didn't want people to believe she was immoral *and* rude. Her smile tightened as she recognized Bertie Mayer. There was a joke that circulated under the breath of many of her fellow parish-ioners that if anyone knew anything about anyone else, it was be-cause a little Bertie told them about it. As far as Sadie knew, Bertie was unaware of such comments, and yet she seemed to take an un-natural amount of pride in being the holder of so much information. It was important that Sadie play this well. "Good morning, Bertie."

Bertie turned her head to the side, looking at Sadie with one eye—like a chicken. Her dusty gray hair was in a bob that ended in a sharp curl beneath each ear. Her body was long and thin, and she always leaned forward slightly, as though not wanting to miss a word someone might say in her presence. "There was an article about you in Friday's paper, did you know?"

"Yes, I knew," Sadie said, hoping none of the tightness in her chest showed on her face.

"It said some really . . . surprising things."

"Yes, it did," Sadie returned in her super-polite voice. "Freedom of the press can be a double-edged sword."

Bertie nodded slowly, contemplating each word of Sadie's an-swer. "I felt just awful for you," she said, putting her hand to her chest. "And I said, that poor Sadie—how unfair that she would have someone make up such things about her. I mean, a woman of such character, like yourself, must have taken that very hard."

Oh Bertie! Did she honestly think Sadie didn't feel the barb be-hind her words? "It was quite a shock," she said out loud.

Bertie clicked her tongue and lowered her chin, looking at Sadie over the top of her glasses. "I'm surprised the paper would print such *obvious* lies."

Sadie noticed Brother Leverage standing a few feet to the left. He was looking out the window, but Sadie couldn't help wondering if he was standing close enough so that he could overhear what they were saying.

"I was surprised as well," Sadie said, looking longingly toward the chapel doors. She needed to make her escape. She was not up to sparring with the likes of Bertie Mayer after all.

"Especially when they talked about that locksmith," Bertie continued. "My cousin Faye lives by him, you know. She remembered seeing you there once or twice—rather late in the evening. Of course, I *assured* her you were the picture of virtue and that she must be mistaken."

Sister Maureen Morne walked by and gave Sadie a look Sadie couldn't quite decipher. Was it sympathy for having been caught in Bertie's net? Or was it something else? Would she pull Bertie aside after their congregational meeting to ask her what Sadie had said? Suddenly it felt as though everyone was talking about her or thinking about her—just like Friday night's dinner. She should have stayed home, but it also made her angry that she wasn't safe at the one place she should be.

"Thank you, Bertie," she said, noting the stiffness in her voice but not expecting that Bertie would. "I appreciate your thinking so well of me. Now, if you'll excuse me." She turned, pretending not to see Bertie's bony hand reaching for her arm as she headed for the chapel doors. Bertie's fingers barely brushed her elbow, but Sadie didn't stop.

She usually sat in a front pew next to Sister Ruth and Sister Leanne—other women who came to church by themselves—but today she sat on the back row for fear that her friends would expect a rehashing of all that had happened. She pretended to study the church newsletter in order to avoid making eye contact as people filled in the empty spaces. Bertie patted her head—her head!—when she walked by, and Sadie fought the urge to slap her hand away. She'd always found Bertie to be a nuisance—even if she was the most amazing seamstress in town—but had never been on the wrong end of information with her before. As much as she didn't like the comparison, Sadie couldn't help but think of the times she had imparted information about people. She wasn't hurtful about it and always categorized it as a "healthy interest in other people's lives," but had she made someone feel the way she felt now? She sincerely hoped not.

Pastor Donald stood at the pulpit as the prelude music ended, allowing Sadie to breathe normally again. No one would try to converse with her during the sermon. *How long am I going to feel like I'm beneath Garrison's microscope?* she wondered as she turned to the opening hymn.

Sunday School was better; she taught the nine-year-olds, and as long as she gave them treats—miniature candy bars this week—they were putty in her hands. After all the meetings, she hurried to her car, not wanting to be caught by anyone else. It was perhaps the first time she'd ever not stayed to help put up chairs or visit with her friends. The heat outside was intense, and the seat of her car burned the backs of her legs when she slid inside, causing her to gasp. She couldn't wait until this heat spell was over. As she drove through the parking lot, she read the marquee on the front lawn: "For by grace are ye saved through faith—Ephesians 2:8."

Something rushed through Sadie, and she stopped to read the marquee again. Grace, of course, always impressed her—the concept of someone else making up for all that she lacked was one she loved—but the numbers were what held her attention. Two and eight. Something was familiar about that sequence. She closed her eyes and pictured the two numbers, then tried to imagine the numbers May Sanderson had written on that ill-fated newspaper. Had it been the same sequence?

She was sure that it had.

But what came after the eight? she asked herself, really digging into the recesses of her gray matter. What was the third number?

Someone honked behind her, reminding her that she'd stopped in the middle of the parking lot. She lifted her foot from the brake while going through the possible number combinations in her head.

281.

282.

283.

It clicked.

"Two eighty-three," Sadie said under her breath and felt herself sincerely smile for the first time in several hours. She repeated the number in her head. *Two eighty-three. Two eighty-three. Two eighty-three.* That was it! That was May's area code. She pressed too hard on the gas, squealing the tires as she left the parking lot, but she didn't even glance behind her to see how many people had looked up, wondering who was hot-rodding it out of church.

She had to get back to her computer. She had to find May Sanderson, and she had the area code. She needed the success of discovery more than ever.

Grace—that was the pastor's message on the marquee this week. Interesting.

CHAPTER 8

Sadie was so excited to get to her computer that she didn't bother pulling all the way into her driveway. As she stepped out of her car and headed toward her front porch, she noticed a little red sports car parked across the street. The driver's door on the car opened, and Sadie's steps slowed as a tall woman with blonde hair spiked at the crown of her head unfolded herself from the front seat. She smiled at Sadie, her red lipstick too bright for her plain features.

Jane Seeley.

The hair was a different color, but it was still Jane: tall and thin, but almost masculine-looking in the angles of her face and shoulders. She was dressed in black, skinny jeans that hugged her already slim legs and a charcoal-gray T-shirt featuring some band Sadie had never heard of. She wore Converse sneakers, and a few inches' worth of rubber bracelets trailed up her arm. The dark ensemble drew the eye to Jane's long, bright green fingernails. It was an odd color combination, but nothing less than Sadie would have expected. Jane was weird. And she was the reason Sadie was uncomfortable at church, the reason she hadn't gotten her tires rotated yesterday, the reason May Sanderson offered the possibility of redemption.

"Sadie," Jane said in her low voice as she crossed the cul-de-sac and adjusted her sunglasses. Her long nails reflected the sunlight. "I was hoping I'd catch you."

The bad name Shawn had used yesterday for this woman came to Sadie's mind, and she nearly said it out loud but pressed her lips together instead. Afraid that opening her mouth would release the offending word, Sadie turned away and headed toward her front steps again.

Jane ran the last few steps and grabbed Sadie's arm.

Sadie immediately pulled out of her grip, glaring at Jane. "How dare you come here," she said, taking another step away, which put her at the bottom of her stairs. All she had to do was keep going and disappear inside her house, but she couldn't walk away from this opportunity to have her say. "How dare you say those things about me and then show up at my home. What more do you want? Was humiliation and false accusations not enough for you?"

Jane's eyebrows lifted from behind her dark lenses. Sadie couldn't see, but thought Jane looked amused more than anything else. Typical. "You're mad?"

Sadie felt her hands balling into fists involuntarily. "Yes, I'm mad! You lied about me to the whole city, the whole state." She flung her arm up to emphasize the vastness of her ruined reputation.

"Lied?" Jane said, giving Sadie a mocking grin. "Are you saying it's untrue?"

Sadie clamped her mouth shut. Jane had gone for the jugular. Was it true? Could Sadie honestly say that it wasn't?

Sadie realized she should have gone inside instead of saying anything at all. She was simply feeding this woman's fire just as she'd fed Bertie's at church. She stepped up onto the bottom stair as Jane grabbed her arm again. This time Sadie twisted away fast enough that Jane stepped back in surprise.

"You are not welcome here," Sadie said with as much calmness as she could force into her tone. "And you're not to touch me, talk to me, or write about me anymore, is that understood?" Remaining on the bottom step put her at eye level with the other woman. "I'll be filing an official complaint with the *Post* in the morning. I want you off my property."

"Sheesh," Jane said, shaking her head as though Sadie were being silly. "I just came to see if you wanted to explain things better, lay any assumptions to rest." She lifted her shoulders in a patronizing shrug. "But have it your way, if you insist."

Sadie's jaw hurt from clenching it so hard, and she forced herself to relax. "As if I can trust you to print what I say," she said, her eyes narrowing. Beads of sweat had formed on her forehead and upper lip; she needed to cut this short and get out of the sun. "You forget that I know how you work, Jane. You've thrown me under the bus before. Why on earth would I stand next to you on the curb now and wait for the next bus to come into view?" Sadie turned and headed up the steps, fishing for her keys in her purse, hyperaware of Jane watching her every move. Could she call the police when she got inside and charge Jane with trespassing? Sadie liked the image of Jane behind bars.

"Has a woman by the name of Sharla-May Sanderson contacted you?"

Sadie's hand touched her keys and she froze. *Sharla*-May? It was a few seconds before Sadie realized she still hadn't moved, which would certainly catch Jane's attention. She moved her hand around inside her purse, pretending to still look for her keys and hoping Jane would add more information.

"I have no idea what you're talking about," Sadie said.

"She called me," Jane said. "Friday morning. She asked a lot of questions about you. Said she'd called your house and needed to get in touch with you."

Sadie didn't know what to say, so she settled for a shrug. It was time to go inside. She had the area code and May's real name. Jackpot. But her mind was spinning. It had been nearly six o'clock in the evening when May had found her at the Latham dinner. And, Sadie realized with a jolt, she'd been gone most of that morning and afternoon setting up. Could May have tried to call before she had found Sadie in person? Would she have called Jane when she couldn't get a hold of Sadie by phone? She thought of the blinking "new call" light on her home phone that she'd been ignoring all weekend.

"She seemed quite intent on reaching you and was irritated when I wouldn't give her your cell phone number," Jane continued.

Sadie inserted her key into the lock, thinking about her caller ID and the fact that May's number might be on it.

"Who is she, Sadie?" Jane said. Her voice sounded a little more frantic, desperate for answers. Of course, Sadie was all the more determined not to give her anything. "Is she a client? Are you doing investigations on the side?"

Sadie looked over her shoulder as she twisted the doorknob, liking the annoyance in Jane's voice. She kept her own voice properly schooled. "You give me far too much credit, Jane. I'm not a detective, a private investigator, or a woman of easy virtue. I'm afraid your story is nothing but a fairy tale. Now get off my lawn before I call the police."

She stepped inside before Jane could respond and shut the door with a snap, ensuring she got the last word. Jane's words rang back to her: *"Are you doing investigations on the side?"* Sadie couldn't help but smile. It was just Jane—someone Sadie respected little and trusted less—but she obviously thought Sadie capable of investigation work. Sadie liked that a lot.

Before going to the phone, she closed the blinds on the living room window and pulled the curtains closed in the kitchen, not wanting to give Jane any opportunity to see what she was doing. Then she hurried to the phone in the kitchen, took a deep breath to calm her tingling nerves, and began reviewing all the incoming calls her caller ID had recorded over the last three days.

When she saw the 283 area code, she gasped out loud and covered her mouth. May's number had been there all along, only a phone call away. Sadie picked up the handset, the patterned dial tone alerting her to new messages. What on earth was she going to say to this woman? Why was she trying so hard to find her if she was simply going to tell her no?

Chapter 9

Sadie found herself in the middle of a full-fledged quandary as she paced back and forth across the living room, glancing at the phone every few seconds. She'd called her voice mail and written down May's number. May had left messages Friday morning and afternoon, asking Sadie to call her. The other messages were mostly from friends, though two different reporters had called, making Sadie cringe. How would this all go away if people kept writing articles about it? She pushed everything but May from her mind and considered her options.

The sensible decision was to tell May she was flattered, but she wasn't an investigator and, due to her current circumstances, she was unable to help. Imagining those words coming from her mouth was a bitter fantasy. The other option was to agree to help May any way she could. Would that be misleading May, though? Would she be setting up the other woman to expect more of Sadie than Sadie might be able to give? The very idea of getting involved after the fallout of the last few days made Sadie question her own sanity. The argument and justifications were at a fever pitch in her head when the phone rang.

She shot toward the phone. Was it May? If so, it was most definitely a sign that Sadie was meant to take this job. It could be the fate and cosmic forces May had talked about!

"Hello?" she said, a little breathless. "This is Sadie," she added.

There was a pause. "Well, I hope so since I called your house."

Gayle.

Sadie relaxed, feeling guilty for being disappointed that it was her friend on the phone instead of her first potential client. "Oh, hi. How are you?"

"I'm good," Gayle said. "How are you? You sound a little . . . intense."

"Jane Seeley was waiting for me when I got home from church," Sadie said, happy to blame her mood on Jane.

"What!" Gayle nearly yelled. "She came to your house?"

Sadie launched into a play-by-play account of the entire exchange. She might have exaggerated Jane's frustration a little bit, and she might have made herself sound a little more articulate than she really had been, but she knew Gayle practically expected that. In retelling the story, she got herself all worked up again—her heart rate increased and her head tingled.

"That woman," Gayle said in a huff when Sadie finished. "Is she still there?"

Sadie turned toward the closed blinds. "Hang on, let me get the cordless phone so I can check."

She hurried to the bedroom for the cordless, then hung up the wall phone after verifying that Gayle was still on the line. Then she went to the living room and twisted the wand to open the slats. Her eyes were immediately drawn to Jane's little red car still parked across the street.

"You are kidding me," she grumbled. "Her car is still there."

"Is she waiting for you to come out?" Gayle asked, and Sadie could picture her friend pacing back and forth in her living room.

Sadie leaned forward to get a better look at the driver's seat. "She's not in her car," she said, scanning the empty street. Where had she gone?

She carefully opened her front door and peered around her yard. "I don't see her anywhere," she said into the phone, trying to make sense of what Jane was up to. "Oh, no," Sadie said as she hurried back up her front steps, her neck sweaty from just the few minutes she'd spent outside. "What if she's talking to the neighbors?"

"What for?" Gayle said, but she sounded as upset as Sadie was.

"I'll call you later," Sadie said. As soon as she'd hung up with Gayle, Sadie called her next-door neighbor and sister-in-law, Carrie. Their relationship had been strained since the murder of their neighbor, Anne, ten months earlier—not that it had ever been particularly good to begin with.

"Hi, Sadie," Carrie said automatically—caller ID.

"Hi, Carrie." Sadie looked through the kitchen window, scowling at the black walnut tree that blocked her view of the cul-de-sac. "I was just wondering if a reporter had come to your house."

"I sent her packing."

So Jane *had* gone to the neighbors. The woman was relentless!

"Did she ask about me?" Sadie asked.

"Yep," Carrie said. "She's the one who wrote that article in Friday's paper, right?"

"Yes, that's her."

"She's a viper."

For whatever reason, hearing Carrie call Jane names made Sadie feel better. "Thank you," Sadie said, even though that wasn't really what Carrie's comment had invited. "Did you see where she went after she left your place?"

Carrie was silent.

"Carrie?"

"Mindy's," Carrie said.

Sadie's heart was seized with instant panic at the mention of her motormouth of a neighbor, Mindy Bailey. If there was one person in the circle Sadie didn't want talking to Jane, it was Mindy.

"How long has she been there?" Sadie asked, horrified by the implications.

"I think she's been at Mindy's since I told her to get lost."

Sadie was just about to hang up when she remembered something from her conversation with May. "Did another woman come looking for me on Friday? With red hair?"

Carrie was silent for a moment. "She wasn't a reporter, too, was she?"

Sadie was relieved. "No, she just said a neighbor had told her where I was."

"I hadn't heard about the article yet," Carrie said sheepishly. "If I had, I'd have been more suspicious."

"It's not a problem," Sadie said, feeling unexpected tenderness toward her sister-in-law. "Thanks for your help." It was just one little mystery solved, but it gave Sadie confidence.

She hung up the phone and reset her priorities. After a few seconds of thought, she marched straight to the cupboard, pulled out the Tupperware that served as her cookie jar, and began loading a plate with the leftover cherry chocolate chip cookies she'd made for the Latham Club dinner on Friday and had been saving for dessert tonight. This was serious stuff. It was time to act.

Cherry Chocolate Chip Cookies

1 (10-ounce) jar maraschino cherries (chopped, should yield ¾ cup)
½ cup butter
½ cup shortening (Breanna uses butter-flavored shortening)
½ cup sugar
¾ cup brown sugar
1 teaspoon vanilla
3 tablespoons reserved cherry juice
2 eggs
2½ cups flour
1 teaspoon salt
½ teaspoon baking powder
¾ teaspoon baking soda
¾ cup mini semisweet chocolate chips*

Preheat oven to 350 degrees. Drain jar of cherries but reserve the juice. Chop cherries and set aside.

Cream butter and shortening, add sugars and beat until fluffy. Add vanilla, cherry juice, and eggs. Mix well. Add flour, salt, baking powder, and baking soda. Mix until combined. Add chopped cherries and chocolate chips. Mix until combined.

Drop by rounded teaspoons (or use a 1-inch scoop) onto an ungreased cookie sheet. Bake 8 to 12 minutes or until the edges begin to brown slightly. (The center of the cookie may still appear uncooked.) Cool on pan for 2 minutes before moving to cooling rack. Makes 3 dozen.

*Milk chocolate chips work, too, but they have a higher tendency to scorch, so don't overcook. I prefer white chocolate chips; they keep the cherry flavor center stage.

CHAPTER 10

Sadie could hear Mindy talking a mile a minute when she reached the Baileys' house. The front door was open, with only the screen serving as a barrier. She stepped into the shade of the porch and sighed with relief. It was maybe eighty yards from her house to Mindy's, and she was already sweating. She took a deep breath, prayed for calmness, and then rang the doorbell. Mindy's voice got louder but didn't stop as it approached the door.

" . . . So then I said, what did you think I was calling you for, you're a plumber right? And he goes, Well, lady—but I didn't even let him finish. I said, Don't call me lady when you're treating me like some stupid teenage girl who doesn't know a floater from a wax ring. I mean, really." She pulled open the screen door while she paused for breath. Her frizzy blonde hair was pulled up into a high bun on top of her head, and her cheeks were flushed. Sadie suspected it was due to the thrill of having a new set of ears to fill with her babble.

An instant smile lit Mindy's face when she recognized Sadie, reminding Sadie that while Mindy could be annoying, she meant no harm. Sadie just hoped she didn't accidentally *cause* any harm. The woman could have easily told Sadie's entire life history to Jane in twenty minutes.

"Oh, hi, Sadie, how are you doing? You brought me cookies?" She pushed open the screen door. "You shouldn't have, but you know we never say no to your treats. I honestly don't know how you find time to bake with everything else you do in a day. My kids are lucky to get a store-bought cake on their birthdays, that's how often I bake anything around here." She took the plate, not seeming to realize that Sadie had yet to speak a single word.

"Speaking of birthdays, did you know Gina turns fifteen on Thursday? Fifteen—as in a full decade and half of another decade. That is just cra-zy! Do you remember when she was born?"

"Anyway," another voice cut in. Sadie looked past Mindy and glared at Jane, who was coming toward her. "Thanks for your time, Mindy. You've been very . . . informative."

Sadie scanned Jane's face for sarcasm, but took smug satisfaction in the wide-eyed look on her face that held none of her usual, arrogant superiority. Go Mindy.

"Oh, are you leaving already?" Mindy said, turning toward her guest with her eyebrows raised. "You should stay for some cookies. And milk, of course. You can't have cookies without milk. When I was a little girl, my mother made cookies twice a week and kept the leftovers in an old bread bag so we could have cookies after school every day."

Jane smiled and nodded as she reached the door. "Yeah, that sounds great. I better go though."

Sadie stepped back, giving Jane a pointed look as she passed her on the porch.

"Well, at least let me get you a baggie of cookies to take back to Denver with you. I always love to have something to snack on when

I have to drive long distances, which is probably why I had to buy a size sixteen the other day. I've never been a size sixteen in my life. Well, other than when I was pregnant. I found that buying larger sizes gave me more variety of styles than if I just settled for maternity clothes."

Jane was on the sidewalk, waving over her shoulder. Mindy came out onto the porch as well, still working her magic. "And cheaper, too. I couldn't believe how expensive maternity clothes were. I mean, you only wear them for a few months."

Jane reached the road and practically sprinted across the cul-de-sac. Sadie watched her with a smile, then gave Mindy a hug, cutting her off just as she was launching into her regrets of not saving those size sixteen clothes since she fit into them now.

Mindy went quiet and looked at Sadie in confusion when she pulled back. Sadie didn't think she'd ever hugged her neighbor before. But had she had a good enough reason before now?

"Mindy, you are one of a kind."

Mindy pulled her eyebrows together, thoroughly confused. And, for once, entirely speechless.

"Did she ask about me?" Sadie asked, glancing over her shoulder to see Jane fumble for her keys as she neared her car.

"Um, I don't remember," Mindy said, scowling slightly. "I'm afraid I didn't give her much time to talk. It's kind of a problem I have."

Sadie grinned at the understatement.

Mindy took the smile as an invitation. "Like this one time, at work, my boss said I talked to the patients on the phone too long, so I decided to time myself and at the end of the week reported that the average phone call lasted only four and a half minutes. He said they should be less than a minute. Less than a minute? Honestly, can you believe that?"

Jane's engine started up, and Sadie listened to her car drive off before turning her full attention back to Mindy. She could listen to Mindy for twenty minutes as a thank-you for running Jane off, even though knowing May's number was on her caller ID made it harder than usual.

Sadie hoped Jane wouldn't come back; yet as Mindy jumped from talking about work to her mother-in-law and then Sea World, Sadie thought back to why Jane had come. Did she really think Sadie wouldn't be upset about the article? Or was she curious enough about something—May, perhaps—to come all the way up to Garrison in hopes of getting information?

But Mindy wouldn't have information about May. What was it Jane wanted? Denver was a long way away to come for some-thing that wasn't important. Granted, Jane must have known Sadie wouldn't have talked to her over the phone at all, so driving up was her only option. But still, what was Jane trying to find out? What had she hoped Mindy knew? It was an unsettling thought, and one Sadie was determined to ponder as soon as Mindy stopped talking.

It might be a while.

CHAPTER 11

It was nearly an hour before Sadie returned home, leaning her back against the door and letting out a breath. Even after so many years, it amazed her how much Mindy had to say. Sadie found herself less annoyed than usual, however, simply because Mindy had managed to run Jane off. That took skills.

Sadie lined up the wall phone in her sights. The moment had arrived; it was time to call May Sanderson. In the time it took to cross from the front door to the kitchen phone, Sadie tried to come up with what she was going to say, mentally debating the options for what felt like the hundredth time.

It was a chance to prove that, like Mindy, Sadie had skills of her own.

It was ridiculous to encourage May to put her faith in Sadie, who was not, after all, an investigator, professional or otherwise.

May contacting her was a sign that Sadie was *supposed* to pursue this.

May contacting her was a temptation sent by the devil himself.

She was reaching for the phone when it rang, causing her to jump about a foot in the air. Just like with Gayle's call an hour earlier, her first thought was that it was May. She was so caught up in her assumption that she grabbed the handset before the caller ID registered.

"Hello," she said, a little breathless.

"Sadie? It's Karen. Are you coming to the women's meeting? I need those handouts you made of the new committee chair people."

Sadie spun around to look at the glowing numbers on the oven clock. It was 3:14. The women's meeting started at 3:00. "Oh my goodness," Sadie said, horrified to have forgotten. "I am so sorry. Yes, I'm on my way. I'll be there in five minutes."

As soon as she hung up, Sadie ran for the fridge, only to realize that she hadn't finished putting the crab dip appetizer together. Thank goodness the *easy* part wasn't simply a clever title. However, it still took another ten minutes to spread the cocktail sauce and crab meat over the cream cheese and cover it with plastic wrap again. She dumped a variety of crackers into a basket, grabbed the handouts and her keys, and flew out the door at 3:26—with hardly a moment to be frustrated that despite having May's number for more than an hour now, she still hadn't managed to call her back.

It was 3:38 when she appeared in the doorway of the fellowship hall. Two dozen women continued eating their meals while Sadie tried to catch her breath, the appetizer that was no longer necessary in her hands. Karen stood up from her place at one of the tables and hurried toward Sadie, a brilliant smile on her face. Karen was an eighty-year-old grandmother in the body of a thirty-year-old woman; she was full of grace, kindness, and boundless energy.

"Oh, this looks delicious, Sadie," Karen said, taking the plate and leading Sadie toward the buffet, drawing everyone's attention to her tardiness in the process. "Everyone, Sadie brought her cream-cheese crab dip, so be sure not to miss it."

A few sincere smiles helped ease the sting of the polite ones as Karen arranged Sadie's appetizer between a half-eaten pasta salad and a picked-over veggie tray. Sadie gave Karen the handouts and then began filling her plate, wondering if she should just go back home. How could she have forgotten about this meeting in the first place? Sadie never forgot. In fact, she was usually the first one to these meetings—force of habit after having been president for six years. By the time anyone showed up, she'd have the chairs arranged, the tables covered, and the napkins laid out in a fan design.

She slid into a seat between Sister Maxine and Sister Tana; Karen's table was full. Everyone smiled a hello, and Sadie turned her attention to her food so as not to interrupt the ongoing conversations. The topic under discussion was timeshares, which was something Sadie knew nothing about. She picked at her meal and tried not to look as out of place as she felt, counting the minutes until she could go home and wondering if anyone was going to bring up the article.

Bertie sat at another table, but Sadie swore she could feel it every time the other woman looked at her. Annie Samulson's famous triple-berry salad was, of course, divine—a perfect summer salad for a hot day—but it didn't distract her as much as she'd hoped.

After most of the women had finished their meal—and Sadie had helped herself to another serving of the wonderful salad—Karen stood and updated them on last month's project of care. The school bags they had put together for children in Kosovo had been a huge success, and Karen read a thank-you card from the head of the organization. The women's group chose a service project each month, so, following the update, Karen introduced this month's project—baby quilts for the YWCA.

"As always, I need two women to head up the project. Do we have any volunteers?"

Sadie slunk down in her seat and tore off a piece of her roll before stuffing it in her mouth. She'd overseen this project the last two times they'd done it. She wasn't an expert quilter by any means, but baby quilts were easy, and since she already volunteered at the YWCA on a regular basis, she made the perfect liaison. In fact, she had been the one who had brought the project idea to the woman's group in the first place. But the last thing she wanted was to stand up in front of these women and take some position of authority right now.

"Sadie?"

Her stomach dropped as she looked up to see two dozen sets of eyes looking her way. She straightened in her chair and opened her mouth to accept, despite how much she didn't want to—she always said yes—but very different words came out. "I can't do it this time, Karen. I'm sorry."

The room was silent, each of them as surprised to hear "no" as Sadie was to have said it. Karen blinked while Sadie tried desperately to analyze her feelings. At the other table, Bertie leaned over to her neighbor and whispered something in her ear. The two women looked at Sadie quickly, then looked away again.

Sadie felt her cheeks heating up and wondered how so many things had changed so quickly. Service projects had been a priority for her for years; they made her feel connected to her church and her community. Yet, even before the dreaded article had been written, something had begun to feel different. She was unsettled, almost . . . bored with the very things that had given her meaning a few months before. And yet, until right now, she'd still done them. She'd gone above and beyond anytime anything was asked of her. What had changed?

Jennie Owen raised her hand after several silent seconds. "I can oversee it this time, Karen," she said, casting Sadie a quick look of understanding. Jennie had assisted with the project before, and Sadie knew she'd do a good job.

Sadie shoved another bite of roll into her mouth and chewed slowly while using her fork to line up the rigatoni noodles of the somewhat bland pasta salad on her plate.

"Wonderful," Karen said, quickly repairing her expression. "We still need another helper. Keep in mind you won't be doing all the work yourself, just making sure it gets done."

Tana Mills, sitting to Sadie's left, raised her hand. "I can do it if no one else can."

"Thank you, Tana," Karen said with relief. Sadie could feel everyone looking between herself and Tana, their gazes shooting across the room, hitting her like darts.

She felt her face heat up again, but this time it was as much with anger as it was with embarrassment. For years Sadie had taken meals to the new moms, made cakes for every funeral, helped with fun runs, blood drives, and food collections. She was glad to have helped these organizations, and she took pride in having been part of so many good causes, but here she was facing a personal crisis and, other than Gayle and Pete—and Carrie, sort of—not one person had stepped up to assure her that they knew her better than some reporter with an ax to grind. Some, like Karen, had ignored the situation, but not a single woman in this room had come up to Sadie and told her that she was more important than some juicy story they could dissect over the back fence.

The thought actually brought tears to her eyes. She may never have expected to have her reputation questioned, but she'd unconsciously assumed that the people she knew and loved, the people she had served with for so many years, would reach out to her and lift her up rather than avoid her, ignore her, or talk about her behind her back. For the first time *ever*, Sadie felt as though she didn't fit here, that she was a liability rather than an asset to this group of women.

Discussion filled the room on how they would execute the quilting project. Sadie waited until a few ladies stood to get dessert, then she blended in with them, picked up her mostly untouched appetizer—no one wanted crab dip now that the desserts were ready—and headed through the doors, not looking back. She was sure her exit didn't go unnoticed. Bertie, especially, would love that Sadie had left early, but Sadie didn't care about that as much as she did about the need to get away.

She turned on the car, and a gust of musty air blew out of the vents as the air conditioner came to life. She looked at the church in front of her, at the melting crab dip on the passenger seat, and at her own eyes in the rearview mirror. The last forty-eight hours of her life had not been enjoyable in the least. Tomorrow was Monday, the start of a new week. Would Jane run another article? Would Eric do another interview? Would she keep smiling as though none of this bothered her? Or would she step out of her self-pity and do something?

She was a proactive woman, and she needed to be as proactive as she could. Maybe she couldn't make this go away, but maybe she could make it better.

Take the job, a voice inside her head said. It might have been her own voice, she didn't rule that out, but she absorbed the possibility. If she took the job, she'd have something to distract her from the muckraking. She'd also physically remove herself from the situation, which would be a relief in itself. More than both those reasons, however, was the chance to prove that she didn't simply get in the way of serious work. Helping to solve those other cases hadn't happened by accident. She'd put together clues the police had missed, uncovered family secrets, and righted wrongs that had gone on for years and years without resolution. May was offering Sadie her first actual job as an investigator. If Sadie took May up on her offer, and if she solved this case as she had the others, maybe she could redeem a little bit of her tarnished reputation.

The idea filled her stomach with butterflies. It was such a *big* decision, yet the fact that she was considering it—and considering it strongly—meant it wasn't *too* big. She didn't know anything about the case, so there was a very real possibility that she was jumping the gun by even thinking about it so much. She took a deep breath and blew it out, trying not to get ahead of herself. There was only one person she could think of who could help her with this decision; one person she trusted to help her determine what her next step should be.

But that simply doubled the swarm of butterflies already wreaking havoc in her digestive organs.

What would Pete think?

Annie's Triple-Berry Summer Salad

¾ cup candied walnuts
⅓ cup sugar
Salt
5 cups (6 to 8 ounces) baby spinach
2 cups fresh berries of your choice (blackberries, boysenberries, blueberries, sliced strawberries, etc.)
½ cup red onion, sliced thin (Jack likes lots of onions on his salad)

1 cup of your favorite sweet dressing (poppy seed, raspberry
  vinaigrette, etc.)

To candy walnuts, preheat frying pan on medium-low heat. Add
walnuts and cook for about 3 minutes, until you start to smell them,
stirring constantly. Sprinkle sugar and a dash of salt over the nuts.
Continue to stir quickly until the sugar melts. Toss nuts until sugar is
no longer grainy and nuts are coated in the melted sugar; about five
minutes. (A little smoke is normal, but be careful not to burn them.)
Once the nuts are coated, spread them out on a sheet of wax paper
and let cool while you assemble the rest of the salad.*
  For the salad, toss together all ingredients except the dressing.
Add cooled walnuts and dressing. Toss to coat salad. Serve
immediately. Serves 6 to 8.

*Gayle insists that candied walnuts are impossible to make at
home, so she uses walnuts straight from the bag.

CHAPTER 12

"Sadie?" Pete's eyebrows went up in genuine surprise when she stood on his doorstep ten minutes later. "What are you doing here?"

"I've got a situation and I could use your advice," she said, eager to get the words out. What a blessing it was to be able to talk about these things with him! "Remember that redhead we saw come into the gym before you went to help with the punch on Friday? Well . . ." It took her about ninety seconds to fill in all the details, carefully scrutinizing every word to make sure she didn't miss anything. "So I have her number and need to call her, but I don't know if I should take the job or not." She took a deep breath, nearly lightheaded from the rush of words she'd just delivered.

Only then did she realize that Pete seemed rather tense and distracted. They were silent for a few beats. Sadie waited for him to ask a question or make a comment or . . . something.

"Is everything okay?" she asked when he didn't respond immediately.

"Yeah, sure," he said, flashing her a smile before his eyebrows pulled together. He looked past her shoulder. Sadie craned her neck to see what he was looking at, but nothing stood out to her.

"Can I come in?" she asked. Despite it being almost five o'clock, it was easily eighty-seven degrees, and she was in full-sweat zone. She worried that her dress was starting to smell bad. The car had just started to cool off when she'd turned into Pete's driveway. The crab dip would be a loss.

"Um . . ." Pete glanced into the house.

"What's wrong?" she asked, starting to wonder why he was acting so strange.

"Nothing," Pete said, forcing a smile that Sadie knew was fake. "Nothing's wrong."

"Then can I come in?" She knew she was sounding pushy, but her radar was up. She also identified the smell of lasagna in the air. Pete was cooking?

Pete looked past her to the street again, and she realized he had been expecting someone. Someone who wasn't Sadie. Her heart dropped. She looked past him and noticed that the dining room table was set—for two. Her eyes snapped back to his. "Who's coming over?"

Guilt flashed behind his eyes, and Sadie winced inside. This was not happening! When Pete didn't answer, she spun on her heel and headed down the steps, her mind in a whirl. First an article that put everything she stood for into question, and now Pete was seeing someone else? In the months they'd been dating, she'd never been past the foyer in his home—they always spent time at Sadie's. She hadn't minded much; she had better food at her house. But she minded now—a lot—but didn't know what to do about it.

Pete called her name, but Sadie didn't look back. Who was he seeing? That blonde police officer she knew had a crush on him? Or maybe Mona Lennar, who lived down the street and brought him cinnamon rolls the first day of every month. She caught her breath. *Not Gayle*, she prayed. *Please not that.*

Moments later he caught up with her on the sidewalk and stepped in front of her, forcing her to stop. "It's not what you think," he said quickly, putting his hands out, palms facing her. He reached for her hand, but she put them both behind her back. She looked up into his face, for once hoping her hurt and anger were showing as keenly as she was feeling them.

"Usually when people say something isn't what it looks like, it's *exactly* what it looks like," she said. She was instantly reminded of the article and clamped her mouth shut. The article didn't count; and it didn't change her feelings, it only made her feel more foolish. "Are you seeing someone else?"

Pete's eyebrows shot up. "No," he said, shaking his head as though to further convince her.

"But someone's coming over," Sadie said, crossing her arms over her chest. "You . . . cooked."

Pete took a breath, then let it out slowly. "My daughter Brooke is coming in from Fort Collins for dinner—just the two of us. I heated up a frozen lasagna."

Sadie felt mildly sheepish until Pete glanced at the street again. She frowned. "You don't want her to see me here, do you?"

"Look," he said in a gentle tone. He reached out and placed a hand on her arm, creating sparks along her skin. She ignored those sparks with everything she had. "It's been less than three years since Pat . . . died. The kids have had a hard time. Surely you can understand that."

Sadie was almost offended that he would insinuate that she *wouldn't* understand what it was like to heal from such a loss.

However, she latched onto something else. "You haven't told your kids we're dating?"

A slight pink lit up his cheeks as he shook his head and dropped his hand back to his side. "I've been trying to ease them into it, but then the article came out and . . . "

That was the one part of the article that hadn't given Sadie ulcers—the part about her and Pete dating. She'd had confidence in that *one* detail—but apparently she was the only one.

Pete continued. "Jared and I talked on the phone this morning." Jared, Pete's only son, lived in Massachusetts. The girls, Brooke and Michelle, were both in Fort Collins. "I'm meeting Michelle for breakfast tomorrow morning."

Sadie blinked. She suddenly felt like the other woman; it was a horrible feeling.

She looked past Pete at the sound of a car engine approaching. A gold minivan began slowing down as it approached the house. The sun reflected off the windshield, but Sadie could see a brown-haired woman in the front seat wearing sunglasses. Brooke.

Sadie tried to decide how to react. She understood the complexities of their relationship, and though she respected Pete's need to handle things carefully with his children, they had been dating for *nine months.* Sadie's children were asking her when she was going to set a wedding date, and Sadie was waiting for him to verbalize his feelings for her. Pete, on the other hand, hadn't even told his children about her yet. Was that why Sadie had never spent time at his house? Had Pete been hiding her from his family all this time? Keeping her at arm's length from the rest of his life? The disappointment was sharp and brittle in her chest. Apparently their relationship hadn't moved forward as much as she'd thought.

The minivan pulled into the driveway, and Pete closed his eyes.

There was always the option of playing out the brokenhearted girl-friend and throwing a tantrum. Or she could march up to Brooke and force an introduction. But neither of those options were in Sadie's nature. Pete hadn't tried to hurt her.

"I'm sorry for making things so hard," she whispered under her breath.

"It's not that," Pete said, but Sadie could feel the hyperawareness of his daughter opening the car door behind him.

"I'll follow your lead. You can introduce us, or I can just go. What do you want me to do?" Sadie whispered again.

Pete vacillated, but it was obvious he couldn't just have Sadie leave now that Brooke was here. He nodded and turned toward the van, putting his professional detective smile on his face.

Sadie prepared herself for an awkward introduction, quickly smoothing her hair behind her ears. Moments before Brooke stepped out of the car, however, Sadie leaned toward Pete and whispered, "I came here to make a decision about that case—thanks for your help. I'm going to take it."

His head snapped to the side, his eyebrows pinched together. "What?" he asked in a tight whisper.

Sadie forced her most sincere smile as Brooke approached them, a look of polite discomfort on her face. Sadie ignored how hurtful it felt to be looked at that way and put out her hand. "You must be Brooke," she said, feeling like an idiot for so many reasons. "I'm not staying, but wanted to say hello."

CHAPTER 13

As it turned out, *making* the decision to take the case was harder than executing the choice, which Sadie took as a sign that this was what she was supposed to do. As soon as she returned home, she called May.

"Mrs. Hoffmiller?" May said as soon as she answered the phone. "I've been praying you would call."

Sadie felt a rush of . . . anxiety, eagerness, maybe anticipation, wash through her at the other woman's excitement. "Well, uh, I guess it's good that I called then, isn't it?"

"It's wonderful!" May said. "But maybe I'm jumping to conclusions. Are you going to accept my offer? Are you going to help me?"

Sadie took a deep breath, then let it out slowly. "Yes, I'm ready to help."

There was silence on the other end of the line and then a slight sniffling. "Oh, Mrs. Hoffmiller, you have no idea what this means to me."

Instantly, Sadie felt calmer than she had in three days. This was the right thing for her to do, she was sure of it. This woman needed her help, and circumstances had come together for her to find Sadie.

"I'm glad to be a part of this," Sadie said. "And I'm committed to helping you uncover the truth."

The rest of the conversation consisted of May's offer to take care of Sadie's flight arrangements and the basic details about her suspicions concerning her father's death. May had been traveling from Ohio to Portland, Oregon, where she would be packing up her father's house, when she'd stopped in southern Wyoming. That was where she'd come across the newspaper featuring Sadie. She'd gone a few hours out of her way to talk to Sadie personally when she couldn't reach her by phone. It was thrilling to hear May's relief and excitement to have Sadie's help, which increased Sadie's confidence tenfold.

Just like that, the phone call was finished, and Sadie had two pages of notes, which she skimmed through to ensure she was familiar with the basics. May's father, Jim Sanderson, had died suddenly, and May was certain that his former business partner, Keith Kelly, was involved. Sadie had names and dates to pursue, and it was so very Perry Mason that she couldn't help but grin as she committed the information to memory. She was eager to do as much research as possible before she left for Portland, where she would get more details.

As soon as Sadie finished studying her notes, she called Gayle and gave her the rundown of all that had happened since they'd last spoken. Gayle caught the spirit right away and agreed to take Sadie's place at the March of Dimes fundraiser if Sadie wasn't home by Saturday. After that, Sadie went online and ordered *Investigating for Idiots* to be shipped overnight. It was guaranteed to be delivered by ten o'clock Tuesday morning, which is why she'd told May to book an afternoon flight. After that, she went to the website for Powell's bookstore, a famous Portland staple she'd always thought would be a fun place to visit. She typed in "Investigating" in hopes of finding another book on the subject and quickly had more than seven thousand titles to chose from. Overwhelmed, she closed the tab and made a note to go to the store in person if she could find a few extra minutes after she arrived.

It was 4:00 in the morning in London, so she simply texted Breanna about her plans and began mentally preparing for the conversation with her daughter that would take place tomorrow when they were both awake. Breanna would not be thrilled, but Sadie hoped her daughter would at least be supportive once Sadie explained the entire situation. For the first time, she wasn't stumbling on to something; she had a plan and a guide and a chance to take her abilities to the next level.

Shawn hooted and immediately asked if he could come—which Sadie said wasn't such a good idea. By the end of the call, he was pouting as only a two-hundred-and-eighty-pound, twenty-two-year-old man-child could. Part of Sadie liked the idea of having him with her—he could be Watson to her Sherlock Holmes or Robin to her Batman—but it seemed like an irresponsible allowance on her part. It was hard enough keeping him in Michigan and focused on the upcoming school year as it was. He didn't have room for distraction, whereas Sadie was looking for something to keep her mind off her problems.

She was pulling clothes out of her closet that night and planning out the next two days of preparation for the trip, when the phone rang. The caller ID told her it was Pete, and she took a deep breath as she lifted the handset and put it to her ear. They exchanged rather formal hellos, then sat in silence for a moment before Pete asked if she was really going to accept the job. She recited to him a shortened version of what she'd told Gayle and Shawn.

Pete listened for nearly a minute before he broke in. "Sadie," he said. "You're not a private investigator."

The words made her stomach tighten, and although she'd been on the defensive since she'd picked up the phone, she felt the walls go up even more. "You're right," Sadie said. "But I've had some pretty good hands-on training for the position."

She could tell Pete was struggling to keep from going into lecture mode as they both sat there in silence. Finally, Pete spoke again. "You really don't care what I think about this, do you?"

That made her heart shudder just a little bit. "I do care what you think," she said, her tone softer than she expected it to be. "That's why I came to your home to discuss it, only to realize that I've obviously put more weight into our relationship than you have."

"That's not fair, Sadie," Pete said. "My circumstances are complicated."

Ouch! "Do you have any idea what it's like to feel like a complication instead of a partner, Pete?" Sadie said, tears threatening. At least she was alone; no one would see her break down. She hurried to speak again before Pete could respond. "Why have I never been invited to your home?"

"You've been to my home," Pete defended.

"I've only ever stood in the foyer while you grabbed your coat." Sadie paused. Pete was silent. "Your children knew nothing about me, and while I don't discount the pain all of you have had since Pat's death, you *have* moved on, Pete. You *have* developed feelings for me, but you've obviously gone to great pains to not let me cross into territory you're not ready to address. Only I didn't know that. I thought we were going somewhere that I'm not sure you've ever considered. I feel very foolish right now." *More foolish by the second.* She wiped at her eyes and tried not to sniffle.

The silence stretched even thinner over the phone line. "I don't know what to say," Pete said.

"How about wishing me luck," Sadie said. She wouldn't mind some reassurance of his feelings either, but wasn't going to beg.

Pete let out a heavy sigh. "You don't know what you're getting into with this job, Sadie. You're looking into a possible murder, and where there's a murder, there's a murderer. You don't know this woman, and you don't know the specifics of this case. There are right ways and wrong ways of gathering information."

Did he think Sadie didn't know the difference? Being instructed by him right now set her teeth on edge, especially when he flipped to shoptalk in order to avoid the emotional things she'd brought up.

"I need to go," Sadie finally said.

"I'm just worried about you," Pete said.

Was that as close as he was going to get to sharing his feelings? It wasn't much, but it triggered the tears again. Without realizing it, Pete had given her one more thing to run away from, one more reason she didn't want to be in Garrison right now. "I'll be okay."

The silence dragged on much longer and heavier than before. Finally he let out a breath. "At least get all the information before you go. Don't let yourself get blindsided."

It was likely the most support Sadie could hope for. "I'll be fine," she said. The fact was that she didn't have time to get *all* the information before she left. But she wasn't about to say so.

When Pete spoke again, his tone was resigned. "Call me when you get there, okay?"

Despite herself, her girlish heart fluttered at him wanting her to call him; at wanting her at all. "I will."

Sadie hung up the phone and let her hand rest on the receiver, mourning the relationship she'd thought they had a few hours ago and not sure what they had now. They had felt *together* lately, and she liked that so much. Would their relationship—such as it was—emerge from this experience better or worse? Even feeling the way she did right now, Sadie found it difficult to imagine not having Pete in her future.

I guess we'll see, Sadie thought as she turned back to her suitcase and put a layer of tissue paper over her underthings before adding a pair of linen capris on top so as not to perpetuate more wrinkles than necessary. She tried to ignore the heaviness pressing upon her chest. She was more eager than ever to get away, more determined to prove herself. She tried very hard not to think about Pete at all. Real private investigators stayed focused on their work. She needed to figure out how to do that. She also needed to figure out how many pairs of shoes to bring. What was the weather like in Oregon in August anyway? Would her hair be okay?

CHAPTER 14

Tuesday afternoon, Sadie waited for her suitcase to come out of the baggage claim at the Portland International Airport. To quell her anxiety, she pulled the notebook out of her purse, turning to the instructions May had given her. There was just so much to take in. Rather than read through everything, she looked at the first few things she'd written down.

Pick up rental car.
Drive to Mark Spencer Hotel downtown.
Call May after checking in.

It wasn't that the instructions were difficult, or that real detectives didn't do this kind of thing all the time, it was just . . . different. Every other time she'd been part of an investigation, she'd been on the inside. This time it felt as though she were circling the situation, poking a stick through gaps in the fence to see if she hit anything. She'd bought a pocket organizer to put all her receipts in, and she'd even searched the Internet and found a simple business contract she'd adjusted so as to be official, but it all felt very strange. The fact was that she *wasn't* licensed, and she didn't *really* know what she was doing. The closer she got to Portland, and the farther she moved away from Garrison and all its reasons to leave, the more she questioned herself. Was she up to this? Did it even matter, since she was too far in to turn back now?

Her blue suitcase with the orange poppy painted on the front for easy identification slid down the angled baggage conveyor, and Sadie stepped forward in anticipation of retrieving her bag. Every little detail was getting her closer and closer to the actual work.

"Mom, are you sure about this?" Breanna had asked when they finally talked Monday morning—late afternoon in London.

"Yes, Bre, I am," Sadie had replied with a confidence she was having a hard time holding onto right now. She hadn't said anything to Bre about Pete, even though she wanted to. By the end of the call, Breanna was supportive, but still concerned. Sadie hated giving her daughter more things to worry about; Bre had plenty on her plate without the mama-drama Sadie had stirred up. It was supposed to be parents worrying about their children, not the other way around.

It took another twenty minutes before Sadie had the keys to her rental car and was headed out the doors that would take her to the parking lot.

The heavy air hit her when she exited, not as heavy as Florida humidity, but the dry breezes of Colorado were a distant memory. Luckily, the temperature wasn't above seventy-five, which made the humidity bearable. She pretended more confidence than she felt and walked toward the attendant waiting for her. He led her to a light brown Sentra—she'd requested a nondescript car at the desk because that's what her new book recommended—and minutes later, with the GPS she'd affectionately named Dora programmed with her hotel's address, she was watching Portland whisk past her window while trying to keep her eyes on the road.

So many trees, she thought, overwhelmed by the green as she slowed down to follow Dora's instructions and make a left-hand turn, taking her into what must be downtown Portland. It was unlike anything she'd ever seen before. There was an eclectic mix of old homes and modern buildings. Space was at a premium and yet everything seemed to fit. She slowed down for a light and read a huge sign stretched across the brick wall of a building that read "Keep Portland Weird." A bicyclist pulled up alongside her car, putting his hand on the hood as he waited for the light. He had what looked like a turban on, but which, on closer inspection, turned out to be his hair, formed into dreadlocks and twisted up on his head like a beehive. The light changed, and he pushed off from her car, giving her a little wave. She waved back, even though he was several feet away, and then checked to make sure her doors were locked.

"Turn right in point-two miles," Dora said. Her tone didn't sound nearly as intimidated as Sadie felt. She passed a few more people on bikes and noted food cart after food cart on the sidewalks. Tacos, gyros, and . . . Belgian waffles? It was all she could do not to get lost in the personality of the city around her.

She missed two turns, which sent her on an extended tour of the city before she spotted the Mark Spencer Hotel: two tall, square buildings that shared an entrance squeezed in between them. May had insisted Sadie stay downtown once she'd learned Sadie had never been to Portland before. It took Sadie a minute to realize she would have to park across the street. She didn't like having to pay for parking, but once inside, the charm of the place eased her ruffled feelings. The hotel was beautifully decorated without being too fancy, and the girl at the desk was very nice. Sadie checked in smoothly and then headed to her room, impressed once again when she walked into the retro-decorated room complete with vintage fixtures and soft colors.

She inspected the bathroom and the view of a building across the alley before finally turning to the task at hand. Now that she was here, it was time to call May. She pulled her phone from her pocket. "Here goes nothing," she said as she pushed number nine on her speed dial; she'd saved May's number into her phone as soon as she had accepted the job.

As the phone rang, the faces of Jane, Bertie, Eric, and Pete flashed through her mind, and she was surprised at how calm she felt. She'd written a strongly worded e-mail to *The Post* Monday morning about Jane's article; it felt good to have her say, and she felt twenty pounds lighter just being out of Garrison.

"Mrs. Hoffmiller?" May said into the line after the third ring, sounding excited. "You're here?"

"I'm here," Sadie said, rifling through her purse for the notebook where she'd already been jotting down notes. "You can call me Sadie."

Let the games begin.

CHAPTER 15

May had suggested they meet at Karri's Restaurant, a few blocks from the hotel. It was off the main street and tucked between a record store and an old house that had been converted into a law office. Sadie suspected the restaurant had once been a home as well, but it looked as though multiple owners had put their own touch on the building until it looked a little cut-and-pasted together. The front of the bungalow-style house had a wide porch, but the brick had been covered with some kind of metal plating, and the porch covering had been removed so as to facilitate the sign to the restaurant, which looked like it had been painted by a tag artist.

Inside was one big, open room with pillars supporting the high ceilings and what looked like yard-sale furniture arranged in mismatched sets throughout the dining room. Sadie saw May seated on the far side of the room and waved as she made her way across the room. Once at the table, she pulled out a wicker chair with a gingham chair pad; May was already seated on a wooden chair painted with black-and-brown stripes.

Any oddness of the décor was forgiven due to the amazing smells wafting in from the double doors on the far side of the big room—and the fact that the music was playing softly rather than blaring. After the two women exchanged hellos, May handed Sadie a piece of paper that Sadie quickly realized was the menu. It had the day's date written at the top. Written! The whole menu was in handwriting rather than type, though it looked like a copy. May seemed to notice her inspection. "Karri does a new menu every day," she explained. "She makes copies before the restaurant opens. She says she never knows what she's in the mood to make until she comes in."

"That is just delightful," Sadie said, scanning the handwritten menu. There were a few salads that sounded interesting, and a corn burrito—whatever that was—as well as gluten-free spring rolls and asparagus soup. Impressive. At the bottom, it said in small letters, "We make every attempt to use locally grown produce. Visit our website for details on the local farms we support!"

"You had a good flight?" May asked once Sadie had finished reading all the items and succeeded in not drooling all over the paper. May's voice reminded her that eating was not her main reason for being here.

"Yes, thank you," Sadie said with a smile, focusing on her new employer. May looked very much like she had at their first meeting. Her light red hair had a wave to it, parted on the side, and just brushed her shoulder. Her side-swept bangs framed her big blue eyes really well. Minimal makeup made the most of her natural coloring and gave her a fresh look. She wore a lime-green, buttoned-up shirt that emphasized her eyes and denim capris that still allowed her shape, while full-figured, to be appreciated.

"And I absolutely love the hotel," Sadie continued, casually sliding the contract she'd printed off the Internet into her lap, waiting for the right moment. Asking May to sign it so soon seemed awkward, like maybe Sadie didn't trust their verbal agreement, but she was trying to handle herself as professionally as possible, and she was pretty sure professional investigators had their clients sign contracts.

"I'm glad you like it. It's a bit of a landmark, and I wanted you to have the whole Portland experience while you're here."

"It's lovely," Sadie said, touched by May's thoughtfulness. "So many trees—even downtown."

May looked out the window, partly covered by a Japanese maple. "It is beautiful. There's no other city in the world like Portland."

Sadie heard the regret laced in May's words and saw the wistful look on her face. "Did you grow up here?" she asked.

"In Lake Oswego," May said, turning her attention back to Sadie and smoothing her expression. "Ten or twelve miles south of the city."

"Is there really a lake?"

May smiled, a dimple showing on the left side of her chin. "Yes, there's a lake, but we didn't live on it—only so many houses will fit on the shore, you know."

Sadie smiled. "What took you to Ohio?"

May shrugged and looked at the menu, but the movements weren't casual. "Oh, you know, leaving the nest and all that grown-up stuff. Ohio has lots of trees, too, so it feels a little like home." She laughed and smoothed her shirt front. Her smile was determined, and Sadie moved on, despite knowing there was more to this story.

"I, um, brought a contract," Sadie said, sliding the paper across the table. May seemed to want a shift in topic as well, and it made sense to get it signed and taken care of before they discussed more specifics. May barely skimmed the document before pulling a pen from her purse and signing it with a flourish.

That was easy, Sadie thought as she signed her name as well. "I'll make copies and get one to you as soon as possible."

May waved the idea away with a swish of her hand. "I'm not worried."

"Good," Sadie said, putting the contract back in her purse. "Then I guess we're ready to get to work."

May clasped her hands together and put them on the table between them. "What do you want to know?"

Where to start? Sadie wondered, skimming the notes she'd made in regard to what May had already told her, which wasn't much, and what she'd discovered on her own, which also wasn't much. After a few seconds of deliberation she determined her starting point. "When we spoke on the phone, you mentioned a former business partner of your father's, Keith Kelly. He's the one you're suspicious of."

May nodded. "I know he had something to do with Dad's death. I just know it."

"What else can you tell me about him?" She found a pen in her purse and within moments was primed and ready to write down every bit of information May gave her.

The waitress stopped at their table, setting down a pair of water glasses. "Are you ladies ready?" She nodded toward the photocopied menu Sadie had all but forgotten about.

"We'll need another minute," May said. The waitress tapped the table with her hand and said she'd be right back. May nodded and turned to the white shoulder bag she'd brought with her—the same one she'd had when she came to Garrison. She removed a manila folder and handed it to Sadie. "My father and Keith Kelly went into business together in 1985. They'd met in college years before that; my dad was getting his degree in engineering, and Keith was getting his MBA."

"Different majors," Sadie said, scribbling notes as quickly as she could. "Were they roommates?"

May shook her head. "Not roommates, but they shared a passion for golf and lager."

"Beer?" Sadie asked, wanting to make sure she was following. She opened the folder but only glanced at the papers inside, not wanting to divide her attention between what May was telling her, what she needed to write down, and what was printed on pages she could read later.

"A distinctive beer," May continued. "I know, being a beer connoisseur in college—especially in Oregon—is far from unique, but lager has a cleaner taste and ferments at cooler temperatures, I guess; it's considered high-end, especially for college kids. Anyway, they became good friends, and after working for awhile after graduation, they came together and started their own fire suppression company; Dad had worked for a company that manufactured system parts."

Sadie nodded. "So Keith and your dad formed SK Systems in '85?"

May looked at her in surprise. The name of their company wasn't a detail Sadie had received from May.

"I did a little poking around after we talked on Sunday," Sadie explained. "Both Mr. Kelly and your dad mentioned SK Systems in their website bios."

"You're on the case already," May said with an enthusiastic grin. "I love that!"

Sadie shrugged but was pleased to have impressed her. "But they both went on to establish their own suppression companies in 2000. Was there a falling out between them?"

May nodded, her expression sobering. "In the fall of 1999, Keith wanted to make changes to the company."

Sadie didn't look up from her notebook, writing fast. "What kind of changes?"

"Well, my brother, Hugh, was working on the manufacturing side of things when Keith suddenly didn't want him as a supervisor anymore. Hugh didn't have a degree, and Keith felt they should hire someone who did in order to maximize their growth potential, or something like that." She huffed slightly. "Hugh had been involved with the company since he was fifteen years old. He grew up in the shop. He knew the business backward and forward—he knew a lot more than any college graduate. My father stood up for Hugh, but Keith was insistent. Over the course of a few months, Dad's relationship with Keith soured completely. Twenty-plus years of friendship wasn't as strong as they'd thought. It was a really hard time for my dad—for all of us, really."

Sadie's notes consisted of random words: *Beer, Hugh, degree, market potential, hardship.* She hoped she could make sense of it later. Maybe she should have bought a voice recorder.

"You were, what, in your early twenties when this happened?" Sadie asked, pausing to flex her hand in hopes of warding off an impending cramp.

May nodded. "I handled all the customer billing for the company. Jolene, my sister, was doing accounts payable part-time, and Hugh was working full-time in the shop with Dad. We all had a stake in the company, which is what my father had always wanted. Keith had wanted the same things—his kids were involved as well—but for some reason, he wanted to take that away from Hugh.

"After things really started to crumble between them, Keith came to my dad with a proposal to split the business—this was in early 2000—and Dad agreed. They spent a couple months splitting assets and operations. My father had always been more involved in the manufacturing side of things, while Keith had focused on sales and marketing. By the time they had divided things up, I thought they might even preserve their friendship. My father was led to believe that Keith would continue buying from him and that he could focus on manufacturing without Keith's interference."

"Led to believe?" Sadie repeated. "I'm assuming that isn't what happened."

May's eyes narrowed slightly. "Weeks after the split—I guess it would have been February 2000—Keith landed a huge contract with one of the largest commercial contractors in northern Oregon: C-Spec Development. His portion of the initial deal was nearly half a million dollars, an amount that he and my dad would have shared if they were still in business together. There's no way Keith negotiated that contract in so short a time, and we all suddenly realized why Keith had wanted to split in the first place."

"To cut your dad out?"

"Exactly," May said with a sharp nod. "They'd been building up this company for fifteen years and only just begun the commercial side of things, which is where the big money is. It had been slow going. The commercial market is competitive, and the contracts are notoriously complicated. Keith had likely worked the C-Spec contract for several months. When Dad confronted him about it, Keith denied it—of course. Whatever relationship they had managed to salvage while splitting the company was gone. Keith didn't use Dad for the manufacturing; he built himself a new office and began marketing for commercial contracts."

"And your father? How did he do with his new company?" Sadie asked, even though she knew from the website that S&S Suppression was a much smaller company than the new Kelly Fire Systems.

"Without a sales arm, Dad struggled. I moved to Ohio, and the company shrank down to just him, Hugh, Jolene, and a couple other employees. It was tough, especially when Keith seemed to do better and better every year. Eventually, Dad made some connections to other sales companies and began doing well for himself again. And then he . . . died."

"Suspiciously," Sadie added. This is where her attempts to gather information online had come to an end. Public records indicated nothing out of the ordinary about Jim Sanderson's death. He died of a heart attack a month ago, nothing more.

"I think so," May said. She opened her mouth, but closed it when the waitress approached the table.

"Are you ladies ready to order?" the young woman asked. Sadie scanned the menu while May gave her order—something called a turquoise salad.

"What's this salmon and mushroom pasta?" Sadie asked, pointing at the last item on the menu.

"Today's special. It's pasta with salmon and mushrooms in a cream sauce."

"Is it good?"

"If you like pasta, salmon, and mushrooms it is." The waitress shrugged one shoulder. "Personally, I have fungus issues."

Sadie held back a smile but threw a look toward the double doors that she assumed led to the kitchen. She wondered what Karri would say about her employee's issues with fungus.

"Well," Sadie said, "I'll eat just about anything as long as it tastes good. I'll take it."

The woman shrugged again as if to appear nonjudgmental of Sadie's liberal eating habits and gathered the menus. Sadie was determined to eat as many new things as possible while on this trip; now would be a perfect start.

"Sorry," Sadie said, turning her attention back to May. "Where were we? Oh, right, you said you think your father's death was suspicious?"

"Right," May said with a nod toward the folder she'd handed Sadie a few minutes earlier. "I put a copy of his death certificate in the folder. It came yesterday. It *says* he died of a cardiac event."

"And your father didn't have heart problems," Sadie assumed, opening the file.

"Well, he'd recently had an angiogram that showed some buildup that his cardiologist was worried about, but it wasn't bad enough for a heart attack. Dad was in great physical health—well, except for the forty pounds he'd put on over the last ten years or so."

Sadie kept her expression neutral. An overweight man with heart issues having a heart attack wasn't much of a smoking gun. Sadie thought back to her husband, Neil, who had died of a massive heart attack more than twenty years ago. He didn't have diagnosed heart problems and wasn't overweight. He'd been having a little chest pain the weeks prior, and Sadie had bullied him into making an appointment he thought was unnecessary. The doctor's office had called to remind him of the appointment two days after the funeral.

Shaking off the painful memories, she shuffled through the papers until she found the copy of the death certificate. The exact date of his death was July 16. "What makes you think he was murdered? That's a pretty strong accusation—that someone killed him."

May rested her crossed arms on the table and leaned forward, her expression intent. "Last year, my dad secured a patent on a new low-pressure atomizer he'd spent four years designing."

"What's an atomizer?" Sadie asked, writing furiously and having serious thoughts about her ability to read her own handwriting when the time came to review these notes.

"It's the nozzle part of a suppression system that the water sprays through," May said, pointing at the ceiling.

Instead of the spur-looking sprinklers Sadie was used to seeing, these were little metal mounds on the ceiling with a hole in the middle and painted the same color as the ceiling.

"Dad designed Karri's system a few years ago," May explained, looking at the atomizers as well. "The new atomizer got a lot of attention in the industry. Dad and Hugh were barely able to keep up with orders. But when Kelly Fire Systems tried to place an order, Dad refused to sell to Keith. Dad told me all about it because it was the first time he'd been in the power position since the split."

"I'm sure it was very personally satisfying," Sadie said, thinking Jim's decision was also rather smug. "But it doesn't seem like a wise business decision. A buyer is a buyer."

May didn't seem to get Sadie's point. "Keith was probably already getting them from another company Dad *would* sell to. At least, that's what Hugh thinks. But since Keith was the only supplier Dad refused to sell to, even if Keith bought them from someone else, he'd pay more than anyone else. Keith doesn't like to lose, and Dad was sticking it to him."

Sounded a bit like poking a sleeping bear to Sadie. "And so you think that Keith thought if your dad was gone, Hugh *would* sell to him?"

May furrowed her brow as though she hadn't thought of that. "Maybe," she finally said, but Sadie could hear the discomfort in her voice. "Or he's just a homicidal maniac who finally had reason enough to take out someone who had become his arch nemesis and *finally* beaten him at something."

Sadie made a note about May having a dramatic bent; it would be an important detail to remember. However, dramatic bent notwithstanding, Sadie began piecing together a *possible* scenario in her mind: Keith tries to smooth ruffled feathers in order to shore up his own business, Jim refuses, and *bam*, he's dead! It wouldn't be the first time someone took out the competition. Sadie's notes were still illegible; she'd have to rewrite them completely as soon as she got back to the hotel. "Had Keith made some kind of threat against your father?"

May shook her head. "Not that I know of."

"Perhaps Keith met with your dad personally and tried to sway him?"

"I'm sure Dad would have told me about that if it had happened."

Sadie tried not to show her disappointment. Sadie's imagined scenario was still possible, but killing Jim Sanderson without threats or attempts at a reconciliation seemed . . . far-fetched. Surely May had some solid reasoning to feel the way she did, right?

May continued, "At least, Keith never attempted to push the issue one way or another *before* Dad died."

Sadie pricked back up. "But he did something afterward?"

"He wrote us a letter a week and a half ago," May said. "We were all starting to get over the shock of everything, and then all three of us kids got a certified letter from the *illustrious* Keith Kelly." She pointed to the manila folder again, and Sadie shuffled pages until she found the Kelly Fire Systems letterhead. The sound of chirping birds caught her off guard, and she looked up to see May pull her cell phone from her purse—or rather, a Blackberry. Sadie thought they were too big to be convenient but realized she was in the minority.

"Sorry," May said, pushing a button to cut off the chirping. "I'll call them back."

"You can take the call," Sadie said, curious as to who it was.

May shook her head and dropped her Blackberry into her purse. "It's not urgent." She waved toward the folder, and Sadie looked back at the letter.

Dear Jolene, Hugh, and Sharla-May,

I was deeply saddened to hear of the death of your father. Despite our differences, I have always had a very high opinion of him and was sorry to hear of your loss. With his death being so unexpected, I thought perhaps I could assist you in determining how to continue his pursuits by offering to purchase S&S Suppression. Without him at the helm, I can see how continuation would be difficult. I would like to help. Please contact my attorney directly to discuss the situation. He is fully versed on my intended offer and is prepared to handle all aspects associated with the purchase.

Sincerely,

Keith Kelly

CEO/Owner Kelly Fire Systems

"Wow," Sadie said, scanning the letter a second time in search of some emotion. "It sure is . . . professional."

"Exactly," May said, her tone showing her disgust. "He's always been so arrogant and opportunistic, but he didn't even have the decency to let us deal with Dad's death before he swooped in, ready to *save* us from the best thing that could ever happen to *his* company."

Sadie looked at May and suppressed her desire to give motherly advice. Putting May on the defensive would not work in her best interest, but not challenging some of the information wouldn't help her build a solid foundation for her investigation. So far, this was all very circumstantial, and even that was shaky. "Is there anything else that makes you think Keith's a murderer?"

"Like I said, the timing is just too perfect." May's certainty made Sadie uncomfortable. May was hurting and might very well be looking for someone to blame for her pain. Sadie thought back to Pete's advice that she get all the information up front before she accepted the job. Perhaps she should have listened. "Keith had access to all kinds of chemicals used in suppression systems. Couldn't some kind of chemical be used to induce a heart attack?"

That was a good point, and Sadie nodded, reading over the death certificate again. Cause of death was listed as sudden cardiac death—or a massive heart attack, just like Neil. The significant condition contributing to death was listed as heart disease. James Earl Sanderson had been sixty-eight. Another person may have thought that was old, that he should be retired and playing golf all day, but Sadie was fifty-six and could keep his age and ambition in the proper perspective. "Did they do an autopsy to confirm the cause of death?"

"No. Because he had a history of heart disease and there was no evidence of it being anything else, his doctor was able to certify his death without one. I guess that's typical in older people under a doctor's care."

"It was an unattended death," Sadie said, not asking, just reading the information on the certificate. "At his home?"

May nodded and pursed her lips together. Sadie could practically read her mind—she didn't like that her father had died alone. For some reason, that was hard to think about when you lost someone you loved. Sadie wondered where May's mother was. Were May's parents divorced? Had Jim been a widower?

"And you didn't request an autopsy?" In Colorado, you could request an autopsy even if a death was certified as natural causes.

May shook her head. "I didn't suspect anything until I got Keith's letter—certified—two weeks after Dad's funeral. Then I—"

The waitress approached with their meals, and May fell silent and moved her hands off the table to make room for their plates. They both fiddled with their meals, salting and peppering to get the flavors just right. The turquoise salad ended up being named after the colored tortilla strips on top, but it was Sadie's meal that held her attention. Sadie concentrated hard on the first bite of the pasta dish. She'd expected an Alfredo-type sauce, but it didn't have a cheese base. It was good and didn't overpower the subtlety of the mushrooms or salmon.

She was on her third bite and already composing the recipe to duplicate the dish at home when May spoke, causing Sadie to look up and remember she wasn't alone. Food had a way of monopolizing her attention sometimes.

"I mentioned my suspicions to Jolene and Hugh, and they think I'm crazy. A lot of things changed between us when I left Portland. We weren't raised religious, but I've found great comfort in my faith since then. I attend a community Christian church in Ohio, and my family isn't sure what to think of that. And, I mean, we've lived in different states for a long time. I'm the baby sister." She shrugged. "I don't think they like that I think I know better than they do."

Sadie swallowed her bite. "So how do they feel about me being here?"

May squinched up her face. "Well," she said carefully, "I told them a friend of mine was coming to help me get Dad's house packed up. We've decided to sell it and split the proceeds, which was one of the options Dad gave us in his trust. It makes the most sense."

Sadie set down her fork and looked at May closely. "You don't want them to know my real reason for being here?"

"Not yet," May said, looking down at her salad. A moment later she lifted her head, an apologetic look in her blue eyes. "I know that makes things a little awkward, but they are both dealing with so much that I really don't want to bother them about it until I have some proof."

"I had really hoped to talk to them in order to flesh out the details," Sadie stated, feeling bold. She took another bite of her meal. She was distracted by this newest detail May had thrown at her, but not *that* distracted.

"I'm giving you full access to Dad's business files at the house," May said. "And I'll introduce you to Hugh and Jolene as my friend, but I'd rather they not know what you're really doing here until, like I said, I have something to back up my suspicions."

Sadie frowned, and May seemed to pick up on her disappointment.

"If at some point you feel like you have to talk to them, I'll explain things," May said. "I'd just rather wait a little while." She paused. "I have to know if Keith is as desperate for Dad's new atomizer as I think he is." She went back to her salad, but her face was tense. "I really think that's the key to all of this."

Sadie might see holes in May's reasoning, but May was sincere in her feelings and clearly hadn't made the decision to hire Sadie lightly.

"Um, I did want to tell you that, although I've been involved with this sort of thing before, I don't usually get paid for it." By *usually* she meant *ever*.

May looked up at her, confused. Sadie continued. "I'm not an official private investigator," she said, feeling rather small. "I mean, I'm working toward it, but . . . "

"That's okay," May said, shrugging slightly. "I'm fine with all that."

"Well, good," Sadie said, relieved to have addressed that issue. She twirled pasta on her fork again.

They both ate in silence for a few minutes, then May leaned forward, her eyes pleading. "You have to understand, Sadie, that Mr. Kelly will hurt people if it means getting what he wants. He's done it before and not lost a night's sleep over the lives he's destroyed. I think he wanted Dad's creation, and I think I'm an orphan because of it."

"Lives?" Sadie repeated. What was May not telling her? Orphan?

May picked up her fork and knife, cutting the salad into smaller pieces. It was really just stalling, which Sadie found interesting.

"We were all affected by what Keith did to Dad when they split the business. After all these years, Dad had something Keith wanted, and when he couldn't get it, he killed my father. I hired you to find the proof I need to show the world that Mr. Kelly is the slimeball I've always known him to be."

Sadie opened her mouth to ask more questions, like how, exactly, was May affected, and why did she leave Portland, and when had her mother died, but the words dissolved on her tongue as the waitress leaned over with a dessert tray in her hand. Sadie laid down her fork in reverence as she looked between cheesecake and apple crisp and a four-layer chocolate parfait with chocolate shavings on top.

"Did you ladies leave room for dessert?" she asked. "We do have our seasonal desserts right now." She pointed to what looked like a cobbler. "The blackberry crumble is particularly good."

Whatever Sadie had been about to say was lost as she contemplated the juicy berries and crumb topping, which meant that whatever thoughts she'd been about to share must not have been all that important in the first place, right?

Salmon and Wild Mushroom Casserole

1 (12-ounce) package wide egg noodles
½ cup butter, plus 2 tablespoons butter, divided
1 (14-ounce) can salmon*
1 onion, chopped
5 celery ribs, diced
4 to 8 ounces wild mushrooms (oyster, shiitake, etc.), washed and
   sliced (quantity should be based on how much you like mushrooms)
½ teaspoon salt
6 tablespoons flour
1 teaspoon double mustard powder
1 cup milk
1 (14-ounce) can chicken broth
1 cup crushed oyster or saltine crackers

Preheat the oven to 350 degrees. Butter a 2-quart casserole dish. Cook the noodles according to package directions (don't forget the salt). Drain, then return to the pot and toss with 2 tablespoons of butter. Set aside.

While the noodles are cooking, open and drain the can of salmon. Remove any round bones and discard them. (Other bones are soft enough to mix with the fish.) Mash the salmon meat with a fork. Set aside.

Melt 6 tablespoons of butter in a large skillet over medium-low heat. Add the onion and celery and sauté until translucent, about 3 to 4 minutes. Add the mushrooms and salt. Cook, stirring often, until the mushrooms give up their juices, about 4 minutes.

Add flour to the skillet and stir well. Add mustard powder. Stir until combined. Cook 2 minutes. Slowly add the milk and chicken broth, stirring constantly (remember to scrape up any browned flour on the bottom of the pan for more flavor). Stir until mixture is thick and bubbly. Add the salmon. Turn off the heat. Salt and pepper to taste.

Pour the vegetable-salmon mixture over the buttered noodles and mix until well combined. Pour into buttered casserole dish.

Melt remaining 2 tablespoons of butter and toss with crackers. Spread buttered crackers over the top of the casserole dish. (A little garlic salt tossed with the oyster crackers is yummy, too.) Bake 30 minutes. Serves 6 to 8.

*Could use canned chicken in place of salmon.

CHAPTER 16

Both of them decided on the blackberry crumble—how could they not?—and the contrast between the tart berries and sweet crumble topping was perfect. Nothing beat a fresh berry dessert; Sadie's own recipe for blackberry crumble was similar to this one, though Karri's version had a hint of lemon and the crumble was more like a big oatmeal cookie on top of the fruit. How fortuitous that Sadie had been able to come to the Pacific Northwest during berry season. Another good omen, right?

It wasn't until she and May had parted ways that she realized they'd left some of the details of the case undone. But she had taken good notes—up until the food arrived—and knew May's goal was to determine whether or not Keith Kelly killed her father. Despite Sadie's reservations, she really, really wanted to help May and that fueled her determination and quieted her concerns.

On the way back to the hotel, she veered off course when she saw a sign for Camera World—she'd heard about that place. It was supposed to be the largest camera store in the country, and here she was in need of a camera! However, it took only a few minutes to realize they sold much more than cameras. Half an hour later, she was offering a twenty-dollar tip if a stock boy would help her take her purchases back to the hotel. It wasn't until she'd started looking at the all the gadgets that she realized how many she needed. A laptop computer—her desktop was a dinosaur anyway—a wireless printer, a voice recorder, and, of course, a camera that could record video as well as take still shots. It was exciting to invest in so many tools of her new trade, even if she couldn't carry them all herself. The employee who helped her told her about various places he swore were a must-see—Voodoo Donuts and the International Rose Test Garden, for starters.

Once she'd thanked her helper and given him the well-earned tip, however, her excitement at being so well-outfitted quickly led to intimidation at figuring out how to use it all. After attempting to read three different sets of easy set-up instructions, and finding them all rather taxing, she decided to follow up on her promised call to Pete in hopes it would give her technology-inspired feelings of intimidation some time to even out. Plus, she'd promised she would call, and it had lingered in the back of her mind ever since her plane had landed.

"So, how are things going?" Pete asked after he said hello and asked about her flight.

"Things are good," Sadie said, trying to sound bright and cheery but professional all at the same time. "I've determined my starting point and met with . . . my client." It seemed strange to say that, but in a good way . . . she hoped.

Pete was quiet for a moment. "You know I can't help you with this, right?"

Sadie straightened slightly and put her free hand on her hip as all the defensiveness came rushing back. "Help me?" she repeated. "Did I ask you to help me?"

"Well, no, but, you know, based on some things I've done for you in the past, I just need to make sure you understand that this is different."

"Because I'm getting paid?" Sadie asked, trying not to be annoyed by his assumption that she needed his help. The annoyance helped cover her disappointment that he was going to the effort of letting her know he wouldn't be available for her. Not that she needed him or anything.

"Because you're working without a license or training," Pete said. "I know you see that as a trivial detail, but it isn't. For instance, if you break into someone's house, it's a crime."

"I'm not planning on breaking into anyone's house."

"Did you bring that lock pick set?"

Sadie froze. How did he know she even had that?

"You left the shipping receipt out on the counter a few weeks ago," Pete explained as though reading her thoughts through the silence.

"Well, I sometimes lose my garage key," Sadie said, defending the purchase. "It's not the same lock as the house."

Pete actually chuckled. "You do not lose your key," he said, calling her bluff. "It's on your key holder with a label like all your other keys. You've been teaching yourself how to pick locks. What are you up to—double or triple pins?"

"Five pins, thank you very much." She nearly slapped her hand over her mouth when she realized she'd fallen right into the trap he'd made for her by giving her a chance to brag.

"Don't pick any locks," Pete said, his tone serious again. "And don't impersonate anyone who needs a badge or a degree."

"I'm not going to do anything stupid," Sadie said.

Pete didn't answer, which she took to mean that he already thought she'd done that.

"Licensed investigators have a little more leeway, but are also under more obligations to uphold certain—"

"Colorado doesn't require a license," Sadie said in a haughty tone.

"Are you in Colorado?"

Shoot, she hadn't thought about it like that. "Look, I don't even think I'm going to charge her," she said, justifying herself even more. "But I did a contract and everything to keep things on the up-and-up. This is just my practice run, Pete, to see if I want to pursue this further. I'm not going to break any laws."

"Or ask me to give you information?"

From his tone, she could tell that he thought there was no way she could do this *without* his help. She was even more offended. "You've made yourself quite clear," she said. "And I don't plan to come running to you for help. But, just to clarify, you *offered* to help me in the past. I didn't ask you do anything you were uncomfortable with."

"I didn't say you had asked me to do anything previously," Pete said, and his tone sounded a little defeated but as determined as ever. "I just need to be sure you understand my boundaries on this one."

"As I said, you've made yourself *very* clear." Even Sadie could hear the icy tone in her voice. "Would you prefer that we not talk until I'm finished here?"

"Actually, I was hoping we could really talk, now that we've both had a few days to think about things. But maybe this isn't the right time." A touch of insecurity had entered his voice, and Sadie knew he wasn't referring to the case anymore.

She was silent for a moment, trying to shift gears. "Talk about us?"

"Yeah," Pete said. "Us." The conversation had taken a 180-degree turn in two sentences—a turn Sadie wasn't ready for.

Sadie gathered her thoughts and then pushed forward. "I don't want this to sound wrong, Pete," she said, carefully. "And I don't want to give the impression that 'us' isn't important, but I've spent the last few days getting ready to come up here and take on this case. I haven't had the time to think about 'us' much. I think you're right that now might not be the right time to discuss it."

"I see," he said. The disappointment in his tone cut like glass.

"I would like to talk when we can both focus," Sadie said. She wanted to offer him an olive branch of her own humility. "And I think it would be better in person when I can keep my thoughts centered on us and not be pulled in half a dozen different directions."

Pete paused a moment as he considered that. "How long do you think you'll be there?"

"A few days," Sadie said, relieved that he'd accepted her suggestion to talk about their relationship later.

She wanted to give him the list of what she was going to do, starting with surveying Keith's home and business, then moving into a basic background check. Those things were necessary to really know the kind of man he was. But she also planned to go deeper and learn all about the fire suppression industry and see where that took her. She was eager to get started and eager to tamp down the feelings of insecurity Pete had ignited. Of all people, Pete would understand those feelings, could even give her advice, but he'd drawn the line and she wasn't about to cross it.

"I'll give you a call when I get back to Garrison," she offered, trying to sound casual. They had spoken or seen one another nearly every day for months, and she hated the separation, but didn't want to have this conversation every day either.

"I miss you."

Sadie startled at the quickly spoken words from the other end of the phone. They weren't the three words she'd been hoping to hear from him, but they softened her all the same and helped renew at least a little bit of her confidence in their future. "I miss you too," she replied, turning to sit on the bed and feeling all squishy inside. She'd needed assurance that all was not lost between them.

"I really am worried about you, Sadie," he said, sounding vulnerable. He paused for a breath. "You've found yourself in some pretty difficult situations these last few months."

"And I've been fine."

"You've been hurt," Pete clarified.

"And I've healed." Sadie took a breath, rolled the shoulder she knew Pete was referring to, and softened her tone. "Pete, I don't know if you can understand this—it probably sounds very silly—but I believe I'm supposed to be here right now. I believe I'm supposed to help this woman find closure to her father's death. It's not like the other situations I've found myself in. I'm not working against the police or caught in the middle of the action. I'm on the sidelines hunting for information—not people. I appreciate your concern, I do, but I'm going to be okay, and I'm not going to do something stupid."

"It's not stupidity I'm worried about, it's . . . ignorance, I guess."

Sadie's hand tightened around the phone, and all those soft feelings he'd inspired went out the window. She stood up from the bed. "Well, I'm glad to know where you stand. I think—"

"I don't mean it like that," Pete hurried to say. "I just meant that—"

"I know what you meant," Sadie snapped. "I know that you don't think I'm capable of this. Maybe you're right, but either way I'm going to find out for myself. I'll call you when I get back to Garrison. We can talk about all this, and we can talk about us and decide what kind of future we have. For now, however, I need to get to work. I have a *client* waiting on me. Bye, Pete."

She pulled the phone from her ear and pushed the END button without feeling at all guilty about hanging up on him. Well, maybe she felt a little guilty. But she felt a lot mad! Of all the arrogant, demeaning . . . She took a deep breath to calm herself. *He was only trying to help,* she told herself, but she couldn't stop herself from thinking he didn't know her as well as she thought he did. How was that face-to-face meeting going to work out when she returned to Garrison? The very idea made her clench her eyes closed, dreading it already.

In serious need of a distraction from the phone call, she turned back to the bed and surveyed the equipment she'd bought. She picked up the compact camera, grateful for the photography class she'd taken in college thirty-five years ago. She knew how to take a decent picture; it was the downloading and technological details that were overwhelming. Now was not the time to start questioning herself, however.

With her purpose in mind, and even more determination to prove herself after talking to Pete, Sadie shoved the camera into her purse, put batteries in the new voice recorder she was going to use for notes from here on out, and fixed her hair before heading out the door.

Chin up, purse over her shoulder, and keys in hand, she marched out of her room and into the role of Sadie Hoffmiller, PI extraordinaire!

CHAPTER 17

Dora led her through downtown Portland and over one of the eight bridges of the city before winding around until Sadie had no idea where she was in relation to her hotel. Once she arrived at the offices for Kelly Fire Systems, she drove around the building—unobtrusively, of course—and took thirty-one photos of the office, the parking lot, the cars parked in the parking lot, and the UPS man who was making a delivery. That took about ten minutes, which then left her sitting in her car across the street doing absolutely nothing for nearly an hour. It was so boring!

She had her investigating book with her and read through the section on stakeouts, which left her feeling a bit concerned that she had no goal, which, the book had pointed out, was essential. Sure, she would learn Keith's routine by watching him, but it would take days of observation to establish reliable patterns and that wasn't really the point of her coming here. She was trying to prove he was a murderer—how would sitting in her car and determining what time he went to lunch every day help her with that?

Was it her imagination that she was not only looking for a needle in a haystack but didn't know which haystack to even start with? She let out a long, labored breath and tried to talk herself out of her negativity, but it wasn't easy. She tried to reassure herself that the newness of this whole thing was the reason she felt intimidated, but that just made her more insecure.

The dashboard clock told her it was 5:52. The workday was coming to an end. Then what would she do? Stake out his house, and wait for him to come outside with his hands up? There had to be a better use of her time than this. She flipped through the pages of the book, hoping to find some new ideas, and ended up reading a couple more chapters on finding information online, but the minutes dragged by as though tied to the back of a turtle. It was agony.

After what felt like forever, she caught movement out of the corner of her eye—a man walking toward a car in the parking lot. He was young and tall and wore a baseball cap—not Mr. Kelly. A woman left a few minutes later, tapping her way across the parking lot in really cute brown pumps that matched the brown patterned skirt she'd paired with a red shirt. She was laughing on her cell phone. *Secretary*, Sadie guessed.

The next man to come out of the building, however, headed for the white Mercedes she'd already determined was probably Keith's. It was the most expensive car in the lot, and from what Sadie had learned about him, he was the kind of man who liked expensive cars and would park them by the road so they could easily be seen by people driving by.

Sadie sat up straight and scrambled through the papers on the seat to find the picture of Keith Kelly she'd printed off the Internet. She looked from the black-and-white photo to the full-bodied version, lining up the round face and full head of gray-white hair. She noted the double chin was more pronounced in real life—Photoshop strikes again—but the basic details were spot-on. A surge of adrenaline rushed through her as he got into his car and started the engine. She suddenly felt so obvious—like he was going to see her and know she didn't belong here, know she was watching for him. She shifted her own car into DRIVE and then picked up her cell phone, pretending to talk on it so that she would look occupied as Keith came out of the parking lot and passed her on the road.

"I know, right?" she said into the phone, nodding and smiling. "It's about time something happened!"

Keeping the phone to her ear, she put on her left blinker and looked over her shoulder before pulling into traffic behind him, hanging back as far as she dared. Her heart was pounding, which she found rather pathetic since she was simply following him. What was she afraid of?

"This is silly," she said into her silent phone. "But what choice do I have? Who knows—maybe I'll get lucky, and he'll lead me to his secret lab where he concocts various toxins, and one vial will have the name 'Jim Sanderson' written on it in his handwriting. Maybe this isn't his first kill and he keeps a death journal I'll find when he accidentally leaves his car unlocked!"

Keith was a couple of car lengths ahead of her as they turned left, then right, and then went over another bridge—not the same one she'd crossed on her way here. Crossing the bridge, however, meant she would be back in downtown Portland. She could feel her curiosity bubbling up, her sense of adventure and desire for justice taking hold once again. What a relief!

And then she glanced in her rearview mirror to see a police car pull up behind her and turn on its lights. Even then it took her a few seconds to realize *she* was the car being pulled over.

CHAPTER 18

"Y ou've got to kidding me," she said, setting her phone down as he put on his blinker, telling her to pull to the right. She was going twenty-five miles an hour! What could he be pulling her over for? She looked ahead as she pulled to the curb; Keith's car was in the turning lane. She came to a stop, and the officer approached on the left side of her car. Sadie put on the smile that had gotten her out of countless tickets over the years and rolled down the window.

"Ma'am, do you know why I pulled you over?"

"I'm afraid I don't," Sadie said. "I was under the speed limit, I believe, and my seatbelt is on." She pulled on the strap across her chest to prove it.

"You were talking on your cell phone," he said, looking at her with an expression that seemed both annoyed and horribly bored.

"And that's a problem?"

"It's against the law."

It is? Sadie had never heard of that. Everyone talked on their cell phones when they drove in Colorado. Granted, it wasn't all that safe, and Sadie avoided it out of determination to be a good example to the other drivers who might not have the same ability to multitask as she did—but against the law?

"License and registration, please, ma'am."

Sadie sighed and reached for the glove compartment, trying not to panic. "I'm not from Oregon," she said, handing over the rental car registration. "I didn't know it was against the law to talk and drive, and I wasn't really talking into the phone, just pretending. That's not against the law, is it? To pretend to talk on the phone?"

"Right," he said slowly, nodding. "I'll give you credit for originality, lady, but we're zero tolerance around here."

"Zero tolerance?" Sadie said. Not only had she lost her quarry, but she was going to get her first ticket in twenty-five years for not-really-talking on a cell phone. She glanced back to the officer, her confidence waning quickly. "But I'm from out of state, and I wasn't really talking."

"Like I said, zero tolerance. Your license?"

It was a good fifteen minutes before Sadie put the pink ticket in her purse and pulled away from the curb, still aware of the police officer watching her, and trying not to feel absolutely humiliated. At least she didn't know anyone here, but it still stung to have a piece of paper certifying that she was a lawbreaker; she'd only recently come to terms with her other confrontations with the law. To avoid too many self-recriminating thoughts, she turned at the same intersection as Keith had, but after driving several blocks, she admitted that she'd never find him. How frustrating. This was her first day as a real investigator, and although she couldn't expect things to go perfectly, she hadn't expected to get a ticket. Pete would love it when he found out she had, in fact, broken the law. *Biscuits!*

Sadie pulled onto a side street and parked at the curb. She punched Keith's home address into the GPS and waited while Dora calculated the route. Twenty minutes later, she arrived at the address in West Hills, where the homes were increasingly larger and more spread out the closer she got to Keith's home. She pulled over to the side of the road across from his driveway and studied his particular residence.

It wasn't the largest home in the neighborhood—some were monstrous—but the Kelly home was no sore thumb. It had to be at least six thousand square feet—three thousand per above-ground level—and was made of a dark brick, with even darker trim and shutters. It was set a few dozen feet back from the road, making it impossible for Sadie to get a good look around without leaving her car and crawling through the numerous trees and shrubs that surrounded the property. There was no guarantee he was even home, though, since he had a triple-car garage where the Mercedes might—or might not—be.

Surveillance would be difficult, and, Sadie noticed, there were no cars parked on the street, making hers conspicuous. It was 7:45, but the sky was still bright. A jogger passed her window, startling her. And then a lightbulb went on in Sadie's mind.

Fifteen minutes later, she huffed her way up the hill toward Keith's home and wondered how that jogger had managed to run up the incline when Sadie was struggling to walk the same distance. Portland was much lower in elevation than Garrison, which gave her more oxygen, but she didn't like to think about that because it made her strain harder to justify.

As per Pete's instructions, she'd been working on making it a habit to put her keys in her pocket—there was nowhere else to put them anyway since she'd left her purse in the car—but they kept jabbing against her thigh, which didn't improve her mood. She'd rolled up her capris to look like knee shorts and hoped no one would notice that she was wearing sandals instead of sneakers. As for who might notice a woman out for a walk—she'd already passed half a dozen people walking their dogs, as well as a couple of women about her age walking together and another jogger.

When she reached the Kelly home, she slowed down and looked for an opportunity to get closer. The dog walker she'd been trailing turned the corner, and she quickly scanned the street. She was alone for the moment.

It took walking past the home entirely before she decided exactly what to do. After she passed the home, she darted behind a tree to the side of Keith's house. She took a breath and then ran to the next tree. The wooded lot had made surveillance from the street difficult, but it sure was helpful now that she had gone from stakeout to stalking her prey.

Her heart thumped in her chest, but the thrill of actually doing something was enough to keep her going from tree to shrub and from tree to tree, veering toward the east side of the home. Finally she found herself with her back against the brick wall of the house. She took a deep breath, grinning at her success, and then moved toward the backyard, grateful that there were no fences or dogs. She spotted two windows and peeked inside, but only saw darkened rooms. Though it was still light outside, the trees cast most of the house in shadow, which was good for Sadie; she was trying to be as shadowlike as possible.

As she rounded the corner of the house and began moving along the back side, she heard the first signs of life and felt a shiver run through her. A television was on. Keith was home, which meant all this subterfuge was not in vain. She crouched down as she approached the next window, which had a light on, and then carefully peeked inside, her heart rate increasing once again. She inhaled sharply and ducked—Keith was mere feet away, pulling open the microwave door with his back facing her.

After taking a deep breath, she lifted her head again, stopping when her eyes just cleared the windowsill. He was still in his business attire: a white shirt and slacks. He turned around, and she pulled back slightly, but he didn't look in her direction. While watching his every move, she lined up what she knew about the man.

He was obviously successful; he still worked hard despite being in his late sixties. Since he hadn't left the office until almost seven o'clock, she could probably deem him a workaholic. Was he married? Divorced? May had mentioned that Keith had children who had been involved in the company when he and Jim Sanderson had finally split. He was alone right now, which seemed odd if there was a Mrs. Kelly in the picture. Was she at a book group or red-hat club meeting? Or did he live in this big, beautiful home all by himself?

Keith stopped at the counter and put down whatever he'd taken from the microwave. After fiddling with it for a moment, he peeled back the plastic layer. A TV dinner.

He was definitely single. No woman with any self-respect would expect a man of his caliber to eat a TV dinner. After retrieving silverware from a drawer, he moved toward the television at the other end of the room. Sadie tried to ignore it, but a little ping of sympathy knocked around her stomach. Keith was a powerful and successful man, but he ate TV dinners alone at night.

Taking small steps, Sadie moved along the back wall, carefully skirting a large plastic box of bright plastic pails and a few sports balls pushed against the back of the house. Grandchildren, she assumed. Pete had a similar setup on his back porch, and she sincerely hoped to have a box like that herself some day; though with the direction Breanna was going, her grandchildren would live in England and say words like *brilliant* and *chum*.

When she reached the edge of the sliding glass doors, she crouched down between the cement steps and the toy box, trying to ignore her aching quads. Keith was watching CNN, but changed the channel every time a commercial came on. *How predictable*, she thought. Was there a man anywhere in the world who sat through commercials outside of the Super Bowl?

Five minutes passed, and she sat down on the patio, keeping her back against the brick and her head turned so she could still see the back of his head where it stuck up above the couch. Another five minutes passed. And then another. This was as irritating as sitting in her car across the street from his office, *and* she'd left her camera in her purse in her car so as to complete her disguise as a woman taking a leisurely walk. What was she supposed to discover by sitting here in the increasing dusk while sweating through her cotton blouse, thanks to the humidity that wasn't going away with the sunlight?

After nearly twenty minutes, Keith finally moved, and although he simply stood up from the couch, Sadie was on high alert. She pressed her back against the wall as hard as she could, willing him not to see her, only breathing when he'd passed the sliding glass door. Returning to her quad-screaming crouch, she crept back to the first window—skirting the box of toys again—and watched him turn a small glass bottle upside down and stick a needle through the lid.

She watched as he drew back the plunger, pulled the needle out of the bottle, and pushed the plunger up slightly, causing a tiny spurt of whatever was in the vial to push through the needle. Her first thought was steroids, which she knew could lead to psychosis in some people, but he didn't look as though he worked out, never mind that serious bodybuilders would never eat a nitrate-infested TV dinner. Keith pulled the tails of his shirt out from his pants, pinched his skin at his side, and then deftly plunged the needle in with his other hand. He didn't wince, but Sadie did. It didn't look as though he felt it at all.

Within moments, he withdrew the needle and then opened a cupboard to throw it away. In a Sharps container, she hoped. She moved slightly to get a better view, and saw a black leather case and what looked like a small cell phone on the counter near the glass bottle. She squinted, trying to make out details and then realized what it must be.

"Insulin," she said under her breath. Keith was diabetic. He really should have taken his insulin before he ate instead of after—hadn't his doctor told him that?

She was processing how this detail could be important when she realized Keith wasn't in the kitchen anymore, although the paraphernalia was still on the counter. She leaned even closer to the window in order to see if he was heading back to the TV when she heard the click of a lock from behind her.

He was coming outside.

CHAPTER 19

By the time she heard the first footfall on the steps, she was curled up in a corner against the far side of the toy box, holding her breath and mentally chanting, *oh please, oh please, oh please.* The patio was fully shadowed now that the sun had fallen behind the trees, but it would not be hard to spot a woman hiding next to a box. She began a panicked race to come up with a reasonable explanation should he spot her, but absolutely nothing came to mind. There was no legitimate reason for her to be here—well, other than the fact that she was investigating him. Chances were good that *he* wouldn't find that very legitimate. She kept her eyes closed, not because she thought he wouldn't see her if she did, but because watching him made her anxiety worse. She heard some quiet clicks and moments later smelled cigarette smoke.

At least he hadn't come outside because he'd seen her through the window. However, a man with insulin-dependent diabetes had no business smoking, especially when he took his insulin after a meal. The man was a walking death wish. She kept her eyes shut while she delivered her nonverbal lecture. At least he didn't smoke cigars, though. Her father used to get one every Christmas, and it would take him hours to smoke it.

It took about seven minutes to smoke a cigarette—she'd learned that in *Reader's Digest*—and she began counting the seconds. At one point she couldn't stand it and opened her eyes, half-expecting to find him standing there watching her. But she couldn't see him at all from where she was, and she wasn't about to unwrap herself in order to get a better look. She clenched her eyes shut again and kept counting.

She heard a creak and assumed he'd sat down in one of the lawn chairs. Two more minutes passed, then three. Sadie took no comfort in the passing of time. At some point, he would finish his smoke and head back up the steps, coming within ten feet of her impromptu hiding place. She knew from experience that there were no guarantees when trying to hide from trouble. But it had worked before. She could only hope this would be another one of those times.

Finally, after what she assumed was eight full minutes—she might have to write to *Reader's Digest* about that—she heard another creak of the chair. She scrunched down even tighter and held her breath as she listened to his feet move toward the door and then pause.

Oh please, oh please, oh please, she begged in her mind. When she heard the door close, she finally exhaled. She waited another thirty seconds before daring to lift her head to make sure the coast was clear. Maybe another investigator would stay and watch some more, but Sadie's whole head was tingling at the close call.

Forcing herself to use caution, she left the same way she'd come—darting between trees and bushes, though her retreat was much faster than her advance had been forty-five minutes earlier. When she reached the street, she looked back for only a moment before running down the hill toward her car, sandals or no sandals. Her head was still buzzing, and she could barely breathe when she slid into the heat-intensified interior of the car and began fishing through her purse. She found the voice recorder and brought it to her mouth.

"Insu—lin after dinner and . . . he . . . lives alone, I think. . . . Grandkids."

She pushed the stop button and let her hand fall to her lap. Perhaps it would be better to take notes after she could breathe normally again. She leaned back against the seat and couldn't suppress a smile, despite the fear still stabbing her insides. She'd done it! She'd sneaked up on her target and learned details May hadn't been able to tell her. Now, to take all those details apart, bit by tiny bit, and turn them into information that really meant something. As she drove back to the hotel, she felt a little like a real investigator. She liked the feeling. A lot.

CHAPTER 20

"Hi, this is May Sanderson. Please leave a message, and I'll get back to you as soon as possible."

Sadie waited for the beep. "May, I was up half the night researching. I'd love to share some things with you. Please call when you have the chance."

She clicked off the phone and stared out the window of her hotel. Even a view of the strip mall and freeway was beautiful here, especially in the early morning sun. Sadie felt invigorated! Apparently nearly being discovered gave her a strange rush of adrenaline.

She picked up the top paper in a rather large stack of things she'd printed off the computer and read the title, "Death by Insulin Overdose." The thrill that had carried her through the late-night hours diminished as reality took its place. Discovering a possible cause of death was bittersweet. She returned the paper to the stack and tried not to let her emotions get the best of her. In addition to insulin-related deaths, she'd researched chemicals used in fire suppression systems. Oy. Who needed to die in a fire when you could inhale ammonium phosphate instead by trying to put it out? It was hard to pinpoint which of those chemicals could induce a heart attack without leaving any other evidence to tip off a coroner, which is why insulin had eventually captured her attention. Apparently, in people with heart disease—like Jim Sanderson—an insulin overdose could cause Acute Respiratory Distress Syndrome, which could trigger a heart attack. However, insulin wouldn't appear in a toxicology report if it had been in the patient for at least eight hours.

She'd also learned everything she could about Keith Kelly himself. What she'd found, paired with what she'd seen last night, had led her to determine that he wasn't a happy man. His grandmother had raised him—Sadie didn't know why—and he'd been married and divorced three times. He had a son and a daughter with his second wife. Sadie knew nothing about the daughter, but the son worked for the company—at least, the Chief Financial Officer was named Richard Kelly, so Sadie assumed he was some kind of relation. Keith had been divorced from wife number three for nearly five years. While marriage hadn't been a talent, working had. He was doing very well for himself, and his home was worth more than a million dollars, according to the most current tax appraisals in his area. In addition to Kelly Fire Systems, he owned a separate billing company and was part owner of a metal fabricating company. He had a few traffic tickets, and had been cited by the labor commission after apparently refusing to pay a couple of employees over the years, but other than those things, he seemed to be a relatively upstanding citizen.

It seemed unfair to assume that any of these things somehow supported him being a murderer, but the fact was that Sadie had uncovered details she needed to relay to May. She hoped May would call her back soon.

In the meantime, it was time to stake out the office one more time. She'd slept a little longer than she'd planned to—seeing as she'd stayed up so late—so it was nearly ten before she pulled out of the hotel parking lot, still mulling over everything she'd learned.

She'd chosen her white denim, wide-leg capris and multicolored-striped polo shirt for today's adventures, but she'd strapped on her running shoes. Her arches were still aching from wearing sandals on last night's job. Typically, Sadie was against running shoes with short pants, but on the way out of her hotel room, she saw a woman wearing what looked like a purple leather top with orange-and-red leggings beneath an earth-toned skirt. Surely Sadie could get away with her own fashion faux pas of wearing the wrong shoes.

When she arrived at Keith's office, she parked in a different spot than she'd been yesterday, further from the building but still with a clear view of the parking lot. Once settled, she opened her book and started reading about public databases and how to use them while glancing up now and then to make sure nothing was happening. Keith's Mercedes didn't leave the lot, not even for lunch.

At two o'clock her phone rang, but she scowled at the number. The Denver area code could only be one person: Jane Seeley. That woman did not take a hint. Sadie rejected the call, but was a little disappointed when Jane didn't leave a message. As much as she disliked the woman, she was curious as to why she had called.

For the next ten minutes, she kind of hoped Jane would call back, but she didn't. Sadie's stomach growled; the complimentary breakfast at the hotel had been good, but it was definitely time to eat. She walked to the Burger King half a block away for a bathroom break and to grab some lunch, glad for the chance to restore circulation in her legs.

After a quick bite, Sadie returned to her car and her book, settling back into stakeout mode. When she finished the book at four o'clock, a long, dull headache pounded at the base of her skull. The information was interesting, but she was *so* bored, and Keith hadn't come outside even once. The excitement of discovery she'd felt that morning had completely petered away.

She laid her head against the headrest, in hopes that it would relieve her headache, and closed her eyes, just for a minute.

When her phone rang again, she snapped up in her seat and looked around, momentarily disoriented. Instinctively she fumbled for the phone and clicked it on, only giving herself a split second to realize it was May.

"Hello?" she said, blinking quickly to clear the sleep out of her eyes.

"Hi, Sadie," May said. "Sorry it took me so long. We were meeting with Dad's lawyer all day, working on the second disbursement and other estate stuff, ugh." She let out a long sigh. "I still can't believe this is happening."

Sadie sobered quickly and rolled her shoulders as best she could. She looked at the dashboard clock, dismayed that she'd slept for forty-five minutes. Immediately, she scanned the parking lot and relaxed when she saw that Keith's Mercedes hadn't been moved. She turned her attention back to May. "I'm so sorry," she said sincerely. It had only been two years ago that Sadie had been in the same situation, listening to her father's life be reduced to black words on white paper. Even though she'd known his passing was coming, it was still a shock to face life without him. "These are such hard things."

May sniffled on the other end of the phone. "Harder than I expected," she said in a whisper. Then she took a breath, and when she spoke, it was obvious she was trying hard to seem unaffected. "You said you learned something?"

"I did," Sadie said. She took five minutes to explain everything she'd found, ending with a disclaimer that she certainly hadn't proved anything, just determined a possible scenario of how Keith Kelly could have caused Jim Sanderson's death. Like Sadie, May latched onto the insulin idea right away.

"I had no idea insulin could cause a heart attack," she said. "And it would be so easy, wouldn't it? How much insulin would Dad have to have been given?"

"Well, it depends on the type of insulin," Sadie said, shuffling through her papers. "I have some info here somewhere." Half the stack fell to the floor on the passenger side. "Oh, biscuits," she breathed as she leaned forward to pick them up.

"What?"

"I just dropped some papers," Sadie said, trying to pick them up with one hand while still talking on the phone. "How about I bring them to the house and show you?"

"Oh, uh, that's probably not a good idea."

"I'm out and about, and it will only take a minute." Not to mention saving her from this miserable stakeout.

"Well, Jolene and her husband are coming over for dinner," May said. "How about tomorrow morning?"

Sadie frowned. Wasn't this more important than dinner with her sister? She quickly remembered, however, that May hadn't been to Portland in quite some time—other than for the funeral—and it had been a taxing day for her. "Tomorrow is fine, if that's better for you," Sadie said. "You'd mentioned that I could have access to your dad's files. I'd like to look up his past contracts with Keith and see if anything stands out."

"Oh sure," May said, perhaps sounding more agreeable than normal due to guilt at putting Sadie off for now. "That would be great. How about eleven?"

That was hardly morning in Sadie's opinion, but she didn't want to argue. The idea of staking out the office again tomorrow made her ill, but maybe she could find something else to do with the extra time. "Sounds good," Sadie said. "I'll see you then."

"Okay, good," May said. "And let me know if you find out anything else. I'm ready to see this guy burn."

The severity of the comment took Sadie off guard. It's not as though she'd been unaware of May's goal in hiring her, but there was something so caustic in her final comment, and the words teetered back and forth in Sadie's mind. "Tomorrow, then," she said.

May said good-bye, and Sadie hung up the phone, staring at it for a moment. She looked up in time to see Keith's Mercedes pull out of the parking lot. She startled, but quickly recovered, throwing her phone on the seat while shifting into drive. If he went home again, maybe she could get close enough to find out what kind of insulin he used.

Two blocks later, however, he turned in a different direction than Dora indicated; Sadie had programmed his address into the GPS in case she lost him again. She took the same turn he had and followed at a discreet distance while Dora kept trying to reroute her. Sadie turned off the GPS.

After a few blocks, he slowed down and pulled into the parking lot of a restaurant tucked—like everything else in downtown Portland—between two other buildings with limited parking. She circled the block while deciding that, since she'd come this far and she needed food, she might as well follow him inside. Who was he meeting? What would he order? Would this restaurant have as good a dessert tray as Karri's?

CHAPTER 21

Ten minutes later, Sadie stepped into the restaurant and scanned the tables from behind a ficus tree in the lobby. It was 5:20 on a Wednesday night, and business was slow; Portland struck her as a nightlife kind of town. She spotted Keith at a table on the far side of the restaurant, near the bar. There were three other men with him; one had his back to Sadie.

"Can I help you?"

Sadie looked through the plastic branches to see the twenty-something hostess looking at her strangely. The girl had unnaturally yellow hair and a teal scarf tied around her forehead, the ends trailing down her back. She had those gauge-earrings in her ears, which allowed Sadie to see through her earlobes. It was very strange, and Sadie sent up a little prayer of thanks that neither of her children had ever explored that type of statement. Sadie stepped out from behind the ficus tree but turned away from the group of men, pretending to scratch her face and forcing the hostess to walk around her in order to look her in the eye.

"Are you all right, ma'am?"

Sadie put on her best smile. "Of course, but I would love a quiet little table if you've got something available."

"Sure," the hostess said, giving Sadie a careful smile. "For one?"

Would it look suspicious if she were alone? "I have a friend who might be joining me."

"O-kay," the hostess said. "Follow me."

Sadie followed directly behind the young woman so as to remain undetected, still scratching that invisible itch and keeping her face averted. The girl kept going and going until, finally, Sadie couldn't take the chance of getting any closer to Keith's table. She slid into a booth several tables away from the group of men, but with a good view of them. She couldn't hear them talking, but she could see them across the table from where she'd popped herself down.

"This is perfect," she said.

The blonde walked back to the booth. Sadie kept smiling. "I like the view from here," she said, waving toward the windows obstructed by two different pillars. She hurried to validate her excuses. "Any closer to the windows and I'll get a headache—too much light."

"Oh," the girl said, nodding slightly. "Um, I'll get you some silverware."

She disappeared, and Sadie shrank down so that she could just see over the opposite seat. Without taking her eyes off the four men, she reached into her purse and fished around for the voice recorder.

She put her mouth as close to the microphone as possible and used clear, crisp words. "Keith Kelly eating at the Gallery with three unidentified men at 5:23, Wednesday evening. Late for a business meeting, but too early for a guys' night out." She clicked off the recorder and looked up to see the blonde hostess standing next to the table, two silverware sets in hand and a downright worried expression on her face. Sadie smiled again and sat up straight, though she pulled into the corner of the booth. "Grocery list," she said, waving the voice recorder slightly. "Everyone should use one of these—I never forget anything!"

The hostess smiled politely, set a place for Sadie and one for her "friend," told her the server would be with her shortly, and left. Sadie brought the voice recorder back to her mouth and slumped in her seat. "Keith Kelly sits at the three o'clock position. I can only see the back of the man seated at six o'clock, but he has dark, slick hair and is wearing one of those blue oxfords with a white collar and white cuffs—fancy. The man in the nine o'clock position is dressed in a dark-green polo, has a full beard and longish hair; mid-forties is my guess on age. The man at twelve is facing me. He has a receding hairline and the rest of his hair is cut short—probably in his mid- to late thirties. He's also in business attire and looks . . . contemplative. No one is laughing or joking around. Must be business related."

Someone cleared their throat, and Sadie looked up to see a young man with overly tanned skin and overly blond hair watching her. She gave the same grocery list excuse as she slid the recorder back into her purse, and he gave her the same polite smile the hostess had bestowed.

"Are you ready to order?" he asked. "Today's special is the loaded bread dip or our couscous pepper chicken salad with lemon caper dressing."

The salad sounded horrid, but the other special caught her attention. "Loaded bread dip? Is that an appetizer?" Sadie asked.

"It can be. But many people like it as a meal too. It's a hollowed out artesian bread loaf filled with cheesy bacon dip and baked. You eat it with the bread previously scooped out."

"That sounds fabulous," Sadie breathed, contemplating the joy of her palate. Her stomach growled, and she snapped the menu shut too loudly. Looking quickly at the table of four men, she cringed as the man facing her took notice of the sound. She ducked her head as much as she dared and casually lifted the menu so that it blocked her face. "I'll take the bread dip," she said quietly. "Thank you."

"You bet," he said, taking the corner of the menu Sadie was attempting to hide behind. Sadie's grip tightened until she realized that wrestling the menu would only draw more attention. She let go, smiled, and watched the server walk away. Luckily, receding-hairline-guy wasn't looking at her anymore, but she still pulled into the corner of the booth again, hoping she'd blend in with the burgundy vinyl of the benches. The men continued to talk, and it took a full four minutes before Sadie started tapping her foot in boredom.

Pictures! That's why she'd bought the camera in the first place, right? And it would be good to have a record of the people Keith was with—just in case. She carefully fumbled around in her purse until she found the camera, zipped up in the new case. She carefully moved it into her lap and unzipped it, glad for the muted conversations in the restaurant that hid the sounds she was making.

Once the camera was out, she made sure to disable the flash, then slid to the edge of her booth, holding the camera in such a way as to take a picture of the men without having to lift it to eye level and risk their notice. She made sure no one was looking and lined up her shot as best she could before clicking the button. The picture itself was almost silent, and Sadie smiled at her own ingenuity. Glancing sideways at the view screen, she zoomed in and had snapped two more pictures before she noticed a woman at another table watching her. She lifted the camera and made a show of slapping it in her hand and looking at it closely, as though trying to make it work. When she glanced up again, the woman was taking a sip of her wine and looking adoringly at the man across from her, but Sadie chided herself for getting carried away. She slid the camera back in her purse and was trying to decide what to do next when her meal came.

Steam swirled up from what looked like soup in a bread bowl as he slid the plate in front of her. She brought her hands together and leaned forward, inhaling the divinity of the meal—garlic, cream, cheese, and bacon. One of these days she would have to go on a low-fat cooking spree to make up for the rich meals she kept finding herself confronted with. But not tonight. "Oh, this smells wonderful." She hoped her compliments were repairing her reputation among the staff a little bit in case talk about the crazy lady talking into a recorder was getting around the kitchen.

"It tastes even better," her waiter said and set down an additional plate filled with chunks of bread for dipping. "Is there anything else I can get you?"

Sadie had already picked up her first piece of bread as she shook her head. "Not right now," she said, inhaling again. "Thank you."

"Great, I'll check in on you in a few minutes." He walked away, leaving Sadie alone with the meal. If it tasted half as good as it smelled, her day had just gotten significantly better.

She dipped the bread into the thick sauce and lifted the first bite to her lips, blowing on it a few times before determining it cool enough to eat. The flavors were magnificent! The subtle sweetness of onions, the clean, salty texture of bacon, and the blending mellowness of just the right amount of cheese along with the texture of the soft bread was as good as she'd hoped it would be. Sadie groaned softly and dipped in for her second bite. For the next five minutes, she was lost in her dinner.

It wasn't until movement from the direction of Keith's table caught her eye that Sadie realized she'd forgotten why she was sitting here eating dinner in the first place. All four men were standing, shaking hands across the table while depositing the fabric napkins on their chairs. Wasn't that a rather fast meal? It wasn't even 6:30 yet.

Sadie had to ignore her meal completely in order to take in the details of the parting. The man in the green polo shirt looked even more out of place now that she could see he was wearing jeans while the other three men were in business casual. He smiled nervously and nodded at each of them, but he looked ill at ease and stuck his hands in his pockets as soon as he could.

"Is your friend still coming?"

Sadie looked away from Keith and his party to the face of her waiter. "My friend?"

"The hostess said you might have a friend joining you."

"Oh, right, yeah. She, uh, couldn't make it," Sadie sputtered, trying to see past him as the men headed toward her table. It would be a perfect chance to get a close-up photo—assuming she could do it without being noticed—but the waiter was blocking her potential shot.

"Are you ready for your check, then?"

The four men passed behind the waiter, and Sadie looked at her meal, debating whether she should follow them immediately or finish eating. They couldn't have talked for another five minutes?

"Ma'am?"

"Yes, my check would be great," she said, trying to smile but knowing it didn't look sincere. She hated leaving food behind.

"I'll be right back."

Sadie pretended to scratch her neck in order to look over her shoulder for a glimpse of the men as they left the restaurant. After debating a moment, she pulled a twenty-dollar bill out of her wallet and laid it on the table, took three quick dips of her dinner, and then headed for the door, slinging her purse over her shoulder.

Keith's Mercedes was pulling out of the parking lot as Sadie pushed through the heavy glass door. Sadie hurried to her car, which she'd parked at the far side of the lot, and pulled her keys from her pocket—she hadn't even remembered putting them in her pocket. By the time she started the engine and inched out of her spot, Keith was gone. Two other cars—presumably belonging to his dinner guests—pulled onto the street in quick succession, one turning left, the other right.

"Shoot," Sadie said, stopping halfway in and halfway out of her parking stall, not sure what to do next. She tapped her thumbs on the steering wheel. There was nothing to do but go to Keith's home and finish her assessments of his lifestyle and business. She scrolled through Dora's memory banks and chose his home address again. It took a minute to calculate the route, which Sadie immediately began following.

Not feeling in any hurry—she had officially determined that she truly hated stakeouts—Sadie saw a sign advertising photos printed while you wait. Although she appreciated the innovation of digital photos, there was something far more substantial about a printed picture. Shaving twenty minutes off the inevitable sitting around didn't worry her and being able to inspect and categorize the photos while she "staked" made the decision for her.

Luckily, the attendant knew more about her camera than she did, and only ten minutes later, she slid into the driver's seat of her rental car, turned the air conditioning back on, and began thumbing through the pictures she'd taken already. The main door of the Kelly Fire Systems office building; the back door; the side windows; a close-up on the sign, address, and mailbox. The UPS man was at least nice to look at. She knew she was being thorough, but right now it felt more like amateur hour.

She finally saw the photos of the men at the restaurant—her best chance at discovering something of importance, though she didn't know what. Her angle was a little odd, taken from the side of her table like it was, but considering her circumstances, she was pleased with the results. Maybe May would recognize someone. She wasn't sure how it would really help the case she was trying to put together against Keith, but at least it showed she wasn't wasting her time. The first two pictures from the restaurant showed each of the men clearly, given her angle. When she saw the last picture in the stack, however, she gasped.

The man with the receding hairline, the one she'd been facing while at the restaurant, was looking right into the camera.

Loaded Bread Dip

1½ cups mayonnaise
1½ cups sour cream
1 cup grated Parmesan cheese
½ onion, diced
1 clove garlic, mashed
1 cup cooked, crumbled bacon
3 cups shredded cheddar cheese
1 round loaf artisan bread*

Preheat oven to 350 degrees. In a large bowl, combine all ingredients except the bread. Hollow out a round loaf of artisan bread, reserving the bread removed from the center. Spoon the dip into the bread and bake on a cookie sheet for 40 minutes.

When done, use the bread you removed to eat the dip. Serves 4.

*Use smaller rounds of bread for individual dips.

CHAPTER 22

Sadie gasped and stared at the photo, feeling her body tingle. He'd known she was taking a picture of them! She hadn't seen him look in her direction at all other than when she had made the racket with her menu. But his blue-gray eyes stared back at her in the photo, his expression hard to read. Was he angry? Curious? Confused? If he knew she'd taken his picture, why hadn't he confronted her? Who was he? Did he tell Keith what he'd seen?

Shaken to the point of being completely ineffective, Sadie programmed Dora to take her to the hotel. She needed to think this through and determine what to do about it, assuming she could do anything at all. She hadn't even been in Portland two days and she'd blown her cover. Some investigator she turned out to be. As she followed Dora's instructions—the beauty around her completely lost—she wondered if she should tell May.

What if that guy called the police? She already had a ticket, what would they do with a report of . . . voyeurism, or whatever they would call her taking the pictures. Was it against the law to take pictures in a public place? Paparazzi did it all the time, right?

When Dora finally directed Sadie to the hotel parking lot, she grabbed her things and hurried to her room, wanting to hide under the covers with a pint of ice cream. Shoot. She didn't have any ice cream!

She let herself in with the credit-card key, then leaned back against the closed door. She looked at the photo again, feeling her cheeks heat up. She bit her bottom lip and shook her head before sitting on the bed and flopping backward, her arms outstretched. What was she supposed to do now?

Someone knocked.

In an instant, Sadie's thoughts went from self-recrimination to panic. She propped herself up on her elbows and stared at the door. The only person who knew her room number was May, but why would she stop by unannounced? May had made it clear she didn't want to see Sadie until tomorrow anyway. Maybe the knock was meant for another room.

Sadie got to her feet and approached the door carefully. She was inches away from the peephole when the knock sounded again, causing her to jump a full two inches off the ground and raise a hand to her throat to keep her heart from popping out of her chest. It took several seconds before she pulled herself back together and looked through the peephole. The same eyes from the photo looked back at her. Sadie's heart began racing all over again. The man from the restaurant stood in the hallway.

Sadie pulled back, took a breath, and then looked through the peephole a second time to make sure she wasn't seeing things. It *was* him! There was no mistaking it.

"What do I do?" Sadie whispered. Pretend she wasn't there? Call the police? Or should she find out what she could learn from him?

Her heart started racing again, but for a completely different reason. He'd seen her at the restaurant and had obviously followed her to the hotel. What did he want to know? What could he give her in exchange? Was he dangerous?

"Who is it?" Sadie asked, impressed with how strong her voice sounded.

"My name is Richard Kelly. I'd like to talk to you."

Richard Kelly, Sadie repeated in her mind. At the restaurant, she'd pegged him to be in his thirties, a reasonable age for Keith's son who was CFO for the company but didn't have a photo on the website. She swallowed. "What do you want?"

"I could ask you the same thing," the man replied, not necessarily angry but not joyous either. "I'd like to talk to you."

"I'm not letting a strange man into my hotel room."

"Fine," he said with a snap in his tone. "Meet me in the lobby. Two minutes."

She kept her eye to the peephole and watched him walk away without waiting for a reply. He disappeared almost instantly; peepholes offered little peripheral vision. Sadie stepped back from the door and took a deep breath while turning back toward the bed. She picked up her purse and moved the voice recorder into the front pouch normally reserved for her cell phone. She was halfway to the door before she considered the possibility of an ambush.

After slipping on her jacket—which she certainly didn't need in this heat—she pulled a thin, black stick from the side of her suitcase. It was about eight inches long and made of a dense plastic. The website through which she'd purchased it called it a blackjack, and she'd felt it was the wisest weapon of choice for her. She'd seen one in action before, and since her purchase, she had watched several YouTube videos that taught her the basics. She slid the stick up her left sleeve, ready to pull it out at the slightest provocation. A girl couldn't be too careful.

With her back straight, her purse over one shoulder, and the blackjack up her sleeve, she opened the door and cast a wary glance down the hall as she made her way to the lobby. She spotted the man sitting at one of the small tables used for the free continental breakfast. The desk clerk was on the other side of the wall, but within screaming range.

Sadie hoped she looked calm as she slid into the seat across from Richard Kelly and put her purse on the table, cell phone pouch facing him and the voice recorder already on. It was trickier than she'd anticipated to adjust the position just right due to the fact that she had to hold the blackjack in her sleeve the whole time. Maybe he would think she'd had a stroke and her arm was crippled.

As soon as the purse was situated, she dropped her hand into her lap and turned her full attention to the man in front of her. "So," she said simply. "You said you wanted to talk."

"Why are you following my father?"

A good answer to that question didn't readily come to mind, so she said nothing, hoping he would fill in the awkward silence.

He did.

"You were asleep in your car at the office this afternoon, then you followed him when he left the office. I saw you taking pictures at the restaurant, and I saw you hurry out behind us. What do you want with my father?"

He'd seen her asleep in the car? How embarrassing. A good answer still eluded her, so she lifted her chin slightly and said, "I don't think it's any of your business."

"Not my business?" he said, almost laughing—although he didn't smile even a little bit. "You're taking pictures of a private meeting, and you think it's none of my business?"

"A meeting?" Sadie pulled out, hating that he was getting upset and yet reminding herself that it was her best chance to get information. "Is that what that was?"

Richard clamped his mouth shut. "Who sent you—Jepson?"

Sadie had no idea who Jepson was, but she shrugged and made a mental note to find out. "A man with nothing to hide, hides nothing."

"Meeting at a public restaurant isn't hiding anything," Richard said. "But we're tired of you guys messing with us, and if you don't cut it out then the deal is over and done, do you understand?"

Sadie's head was spinning. Deal? Messing with them?

Richard pushed away from the table but kept his hands on the edge. Sadie ran through all the information she'd learned about Keith Kelly and his company, grasping at anything she could say that would prolong this meeting.

"Do you have the authority to decide when a deal is over and done?"

She both saw and felt the hit Richard took at her comment and winced a little bit for him as she realized she'd touched a tender spot. But she couldn't let go of it just yet. "I didn't think so," she said. "And if you ask me, that's the biggest mistake Keith Kelly has ever made."

Richard froze, halfway between sitting and standing.

He looked vulnerable and unsure of himself, which was a golden opportunity for Sadie. She wondered how much she dared say, and then pictured herself sitting outside of Keith Kelly's back door again tonight and outside his office all day tomorrow. Good investigators went with their gut—it even said that in the book—and Sadie's gut was telling her to not let Richard get away. But that meant she had to show her cards—at least one or two of them.

"I want to know about the Sanderson deal," she said.

For the second time, Richard Kelly was taken off guard. "The Sanderson deal?" he asked. "What about it?"

"Why your father's sudden interest in S&S?"

"That's what this is about? You think that's going to affect your position?" He finally sat. "It's nothing—peanuts."

Sadie shrugged, putting two and two together and concluding that Jepson was either interested in buying Kelly Fire Systems or Kelly Fire Systems was interested in buying Jepson. She didn't really understand a lot about buyouts and mergers and things, but that's what this sounded like. "It doesn't feel like peanuts," she said, then stepped even further over the line. "It feels . . . personal."

Richard eyed her carefully. "Like I said, it has nothing to do with our deal."

"Then you won't mind telling me more about it."

Richard considered that for a moment, but must not have felt threatened. "Jim Sanderson and my father were business partners several years ago. They split and Dad took sales and Jim took manufacturing. Jim passed away recently, and Dad's trying to help out his kids by buying back that arm of the business."

Help out the kids? Sadie repeated in her mind. Oh, brother. "So, it's purely philanthropic?"

"Not entirely," Richard said. Sadie could sense his confusion. What he was telling her didn't seem guarded, but he was clearly unsure of why she wanted to know it. Sadie didn't mind his confusion. So far it was working in her favor. "Jim Sanderson is a . . . *was* a brilliant engineer. He's responsible for several advances in piping and placement technologies, not to mention what he's done with atomizers over the last several years. His ideas would be a huge boon to Kelly—and therefore to Jepson by association."

"And the children—they want to sell?"

Sadie knew she'd crossed the line when Richard's eyebrows came together. "Who are you?"

She didn't want to lie to him, so she didn't answer directly but tried to formulate another track of questioning. "What caused the two companies to split in the first place?"

He narrowed his eyes even more. "You're not with Jepson," he said under his breath. "You're with . . ." As his voice trailed off, his face suddenly relaxed. It was such a quick transition that Sadie found herself fingering her blackjack and pressing herself against the back of her chair. When he spoke again, his voice was a whisper. "You're with . . . May."

CHAPTER 23

The way he said May's name was so sweet that Sadie forgot about holding the blackjack all together. It fell out of her sleeve and clattered on the tile. The sound caught her attention, however, and she quickly picked it up and slid it under her legs. It was uncomfortable, but she tried to ignore it in hopes Richard would too. She was in luck—he was completely oblivious to the weapon she had stashed so non-discreetly.

Richard leaned across the table. "How is she?" he asked, oozing tenderness that made Sadie feel as though she were part of an intimate moment of some kind.

"She's fine," Sadie said, then clamped her mouth shut. She'd just revealed the name of her client, or employer, or whatever May was. What was she doing?

"Is she really?" he asked. "Is she back here, in Portland? I'd heard she was coming to help settle the estate, but is she here already? Is she staying at the house?"

Sadie didn't know what to say—she felt like she'd already said too much—and bit her tongue to keep from giving this man what he wanted. There was no doubt in her mind that Richard Kelly had strong feelings for May Sanderson.

"How do you know May?" Sadie finally asked. She was too far in to pretend she wasn't, and her curiosity pulled her forward. May had given her very little background to work with; maybe Richard would give her more.

"She didn't tell you?" Richard asked, those intense blue-gray eyes looking hurt as he leaned back against the chair. "I guess she wouldn't," he said, looking at the tabletop. He closed his eyes and ran his fingers through what was left of his hair. "Oh, May," he said in a remorseful kind of growl.

Sadie watched him for several seconds, touched by his reaction. She tried to stay on her side of the table and wait him out, but she couldn't. The torment was coming off him in waves. She reached out and put a hand on his forearm, causing him to look up at her.

"I knew she'd freak out about this."

"Why?"

"Because she hates me . . . us."

"And why is that?" Sadie remembered the flares of anger she'd seen when May talked about Keith Kelly.

"Who are you?" he asked. But beneath his confusion was something else, something . . . longing and hungry.

It was the second time he'd asked the question, but she wasn't willing to tell him anything more than she already had. She was saved having to answer by the ringing of Richard's cell phone. Normally, she found it rude for people to answer their phone while with another person, but she was grateful for the interruption this time.

He unhooked his phone from his belt. He looked at the screen, then up at Sadie as he pushed a button and lifted the phone to his ear. "Hi, Dad," he said, staring straight at Sadie.

She froze. Would he give her up?

"I had to stop and pick up some things for the kids."

Kids? Sadie's heart sank. Was he married and yet still pining for May? She looked at his left hand, relieved to see it was ring-free. She looked back at his face; he was still watching her. She could see that he knew exactly where her thoughts had taken her. He wasn't embarrassed, but she was a little bit.

"I'll be another forty-five minutes," he said. "I know. . . . I know. . . . Right. . . . I know, Dad." His voice didn't tighten; it didn't show frustration or anger or anything. "You'll have it first thing in the morning. . . . I know. . . . I know." He went quiet, and Sadie could hear the snappy tone of the voice on the other end of the line—lecture mode was hard to hide. Richard looked down at the table while throwing in a few more "Okay"s and "I know"s before finally finishing the call. He put the phone on the table between them.

"I didn't tell him about you," Richard said.

"I noticed," Sadie said. "Why not?"

"Because he's the reason I lost May the first time."

Sadie absorbed every word and weighed them while simultaneously remembering what May had said—that the whole Kelly family was arrogant and opportunistic. That Keith Kelly had ruined her life once and she wasn't going to let him do it again.

"You're in love with her," Sadie said, wondering how on earth this story was going to play out.

"Have been since I was fifteen years old," Richard said without hesitation.

"You have children," Sadie added—this was no boy-meets-girl fairy tale.

He nodded, but offered little. "I do."

"Are you married?" If he was, Sadie wasn't saying another word about May. Proving a murder was one thing, meddling in marriage was something else entirely.

He shook his head. "Not anymore."

"What happened between you and May, then?" Sadie asked, relieved that there wasn't a Mrs. Kelly wondering where her husband was.

Richard's gaze was intense, and it was all Sadie could do not to look away. She was suddenly grateful for the boring car trips of her youth when she and Jack would have staring contests. "I'll tell you everything," he said in a low tone. "I'll answer every question you have about my father, but I need you to promise me something."

"What?" Sadie asked, reeling from the magnitude of his offer.

"I need to be face-to-face with May at some point."

That shouldn't be too difficult, Sadie thought, though she was hesitant to make promises. She had a pretty strong sense that May would want nothing to do with Richard.

"Promise me," Richard said. "Promise me you'll help me see her. It won't be as easy as it sounds."

A tingle of trepidation spread through Sadie's spine. "Why? Is she afraid of you?"

"Yes," Richard said slowly. "No one has hurt her the way I did."

Sadie backed up. "Hurt her?" She had sudden visions of some sociopath using her as a gateway to reach a prior victim.

"I broke her heart," Richard clarified, "to the point that I don't think she'll ever forgive me for it, but I have to tell her how wrong I was and how truly sorry I am for everything."

Sadie was nearly bursting with curiosity. "And you need me to help you find that opportunity?"

Richard nodded. "I'll tell you everything you need to know if you'll promise me five minutes with May." He stretched his hand across the table, and Sadie regarded it carefully before looking up into those intense eyes again. *Trust your gut,* she told herself. And her gut was telling her to trust Richard. She reached out her own hand and grasped his tightly. They shook one time before pulling their hands away.

"So," Richard asked, "what do you want to know?"

"Did your father kill Jim Sanderson?" Sadie asked, almost without thinking.

His body visibly shook and his eyes went wide. "Is that what May thinks?"

Oops, Sadie had not only given away her employer, now she'd given away what she was investigating—and yet had it really been on accident? Sometimes it took a little shock value to take someone off guard enough that they would give up information they wouldn't otherwise. But giving up so much so fast didn't sit well with her either. This investigating stuff was a lot harder than it seemed at first, but Sadie quieted her concerns in order to take advantage of the situation she'd just created by revealing May's suspicions. Richard still looked stunned, but Sadie could see that he was forcing himself to be objective.

"It's interesting timing," Sadie said, grasping for something she could say that wasn't in direct conflict with what she was supposed to be doing. "Jim Sanderson dies shortly after inventing a new automat-icator."

"Atomizer."

"Right. He died shortly after inventing a low-pressure atomizer that he wouldn't sell directly to Kelly Fire Systems, and then Keith Kelly solicits a purchase of the business shortly following the funeral. It looks fishy."

After a few seconds, Richard said, "And May hired you to prove that my father had something to do with *her* father's death?"

"I can't confirm or deny my terms of employment," Sadie said, hoping she sounded professional.

Richard took a deep breath and leaned back in the chair. "I don't think Dad killed Jim," he said in a very calm, very reasonable tone. "But then again, Dad's done a lot of things I didn't think he could do. What do you need from me? How can I help?"

CHAPTER 24

A lot could happen in forty-five minutes—or, at least, a lot could
be learned.

They had abandoned the lobby for the famous Voodoo Donuts,
a twenty-four-hour, cash-only donut shop unlike anything Sadie had
ever seen before, though it'd already been recommended to her at
least once. Sadie had passed over the Miami Vice Berry and the
chocolate cake doughnut topped with Cocoa Puffs cereal and gone
with the basic buttermilk bar, but Richard had ordered the Voodoo
Doll, a donut made to look like a person, complete with iced facial
features and a pretzel stake through its jelly-filled heart. While Sadie
had always struggled with things like biting the heads off gummy
bears or chocolate Easter bunnies, she could appreciate the creative
genius behind such a thing.

"So, after the company split, you and May broke up?" Sadie
was struck by the casualness of her own question. The tension that
had been part of the first portion of their meeting had slipped away
the longer she'd listened to Richard's recounting of the split of SK
Systems. It was a more detailed version of what May had already
told her, but from the Kelly side of the table. In this version, Hugh

Sanderson was stealing from the company and making huge over-sights, which led to the collapse of the partnership. Sadie took it all with a grain of salt and hoped she could find the truth amid both perspectives she'd now been given.

Richard pulled the pretzel stick out of his donut, and Sadie tried not to look at the jelly that oozed out. "May and I both hoped that when things blew over, we could make things work." Richard paused and stared at the tabletop. It was nearly nine o'clock at night, but whoever thought donut shops were for breakfast had never been here—the place was hopping. Luckily, Sadie and Richard had found a relatively quiet wrought-iron table outside of the impossibly small, brick-walled café that had no inside seating. Even outside, Sadie had to lean toward Richard in order to be heard over the continual chatter of people waiting in line or eating donuts or accessing the highly vandalized ATM. It was hard not to get lost in the atmosphere.

Richard continued. "It wasn't until Jim accused my dad of having stolen the C-Spec account that things trickled down to May and me." He put the pretzel in his mouth and bit it in half.

"You didn't think your dad had taken his advantage with C-Spec?"

"Not at the time," Richard said once he'd swallowed. He pinched off the last remaining arm from his donut. "In hindsight, my support might have had more to do with the fact that he bought me a Land Rover and offered to pay off my student loans if I came to work for him instead of graduating. He needed someone he could trust to serve as Chief Financial Officer of his new company, and he didn't want to wait."

"You didn't graduate from college?" Sadie asked, surprised. She'd assumed he was a CPA.

Richard glanced at her. "I almost did. But the only reason I'd gone to school in the first place was because Dad wouldn't let me work for him unless I was as good as the next guy he could hire. After four years—and with one more year to go, thanks to the fact that I had spent more time with May than I had studying—he offered me the job and a car and the get-out-of-debt free card." He paused and shook his head. "At the time I thought I would be a fool not to do it."

"And now?"

"I *know* I'm a fool to have fallen for it." He let out a breath while Sadie nibbled at her donut. "I think he sensed that I was considering other options for when I graduated. The division between our families—May's and mine—was getting bigger. He knew I'd choose May, so he started tightening the screws on me, manipulating the situation. He knew that I would have little value outside of Kelly Fire Systems without a degree—but I didn't see it—and my going to work for Dad was the beginning of the end for May and me."

"How so?"

"We had planned to get married when I graduated from college. Then I dropped out, and Dad demanded a lot of my time those first few months. I also defended my dad when the accusation came up about the C-Spec account. May and I tried to ignore the contradicting opinions, but they ate at us. Little problems turned into big ones. Dad didn't help, constantly making little references to the Sanderson family, talking about ways Jim had burned him over the years.

"One day May came to the office, and she and I ended up arguing about something. Eventually everything that had been building up between us and our families came out, and Dad stepped in and then it was both of us against her. She didn't stand a chance, but returned fire as long as she could before storming out of the office. Dad turned to me and told me to choose my destiny—a hotheaded girl who didn't trust my decisions, or a stable future and the chance at a life I'd only ever dreamed of. He flat out told me I couldn't have both anymore, that life has a way of forcing the issue. He said she was a liability for me and, therefore, for Kelly Fire Systems. If I chose May, I'd lose all the incentives Dad had offered me, and I'd be a twenty-five-year-old kid without a degree and without my father's generosity." Richard stopped and shook his head.

"You chose your father," Sadie summed up.

"May wouldn't talk to me after the fight, so I sent her an e-mail and told her that she was a liability to my future." He lowered his voice. "I didn't realize how much that must have hurt her until a couple of weeks later, but I never spoke to her again. She blocked my e-mail, she didn't answer my calls, and a few months later, I heard she'd moved out of state. I haven't seen her since."

"How long after the breakup did you get married?" Sadie asked, making the point that *he* had moved on with his life.

Richard got the hint and wilted. "About eight months. Leslie was the daughter of one of Dad's friends from the country club. She was an *asset* to me—that's how Dad had said it, and it was hard not to see it that way. I was hurting over all that had happened with May and wanted to prove I didn't need her, I guess. But Leslie and I weren't a good match. She got the house and primary custody of our two boys in the divorce; I got alternating weekends and another reason to feel sorry for myself."

"Do you blame your dad for all that?" Sadie asked.

"I blame myself, but I know I wouldn't have done what I did without his encouragement. He and I had it out a few years ago, and he came right out and told me that he owned me—that I was bought and paid for and that I should be grateful he rescued me from a life I thought I wanted. I started to wonder what could have been if I'd been more of a man and less of a Daddy's boy. I found May online—she was living in Ohio—and I wrote to her, but she never responded. After a few unanswered e-mails, I got the point and let it go."

"And yet you still work for your father," Sadie reminded him. "Despite all that."

"Dad pays too well for me to quit. At the same time, he struggles to keep employees long-term because he's just such a . . . jerk. He needs me to hold things together for him. When I read May's name in Jim's obituary, I started to ache all over again, started to wonder if there might be a second chance for us."

"I'm guessing your father wouldn't like that," Sadie suggested.

Richard shrugged. "Would I be here, telling you all this, if I cared what my father thought anymore?"

"What about your job?" Sadie said. "You just told me you can't make the kind of money you make with him somewhere else. You pay alimony and child support, right?"

"And, like I said, he needs me. I'm willing to risk it."

Sadie couldn't help but be a little suspicious. Several of the people she had trusted early on in other investigations had turned out to be far less trustworthy than they'd appeared. While the other situations Sadie had been involved in had given her confidence in a lot of areas, determining who was telling the truth and who wasn't had not turned out to be one of her strengths. She mentally backed up, not wanting to get too emotionally involved in his story.

"So, May changes *all* of that?"

"Yes," he said without a flinch or a pause or even a stutter. She waited for him to expound. He didn't, and she chose to change the subject in order to keep him talking.

"You don't seem to have a very high opinion of your father," Sadie said.

Richard shook his head. "He's a good businessman, and I admire what he's accomplished, but that's about the only credit I can give him. I grew up mostly with my mom—his second wife—which might be part of the reason I jumped so quickly when he offered me what sounded like a partnership. I've spent most of my life waiting to have a real dad, you know, until I finally gave up."

"A few years ago, when you two had it out?"

"Yes. Our relationship wasn't all that good before, and now we're more like colleagues than blood relatives. I'm tired of trying to get something from him that he's not prepared to give."

"Love?"

"And respect, and appreciation. It's all about the money to him; nothing else matters."

"Would he kill for money?" Sadie asked. "Would that be enough motive to murder Jim Sanderson?"

She felt Richard tense before he seemed to force himself to relax. "It's not really Dad's style," he said slowly.

Sadie leaned forward. "But you aren't ruling it out?" She could hear the surprise in her voice. She hadn't expected Richard to answer so easily.

"Dad prides himself in outsmarting, outworking, and outselling the competition—not in cheating. Killing Jim would be cheating."

"He cheated Jim out of the C-Spec account."

Richard shook his head. "He would consider that outsmarting Jim and shoring up his interests. Getting rid of the competition is a totally different game."

"But he *does* want to buy S&S," Sadie reminded him, pushing ahead even though she really wanted a break where she could process everything she had learned so far.

"Oh, don't get me wrong, he's opportunistic, but for all his faults, I have a hard time believing he's a murderer." He looked thoughtful before letting a long breath out through his nose. "May was devastated when we broke up. I've no doubt that her accusations against my father are tied up in what I did to her."

Hadn't May said the entire Kelly family couldn't be trusted? Hadn't Sadie suspected there was more to May's nostalgia about Portland than she claimed? Could it be Richard? Could this all be some kind of hunt to find something to pin on the two men who together broke her heart and shattered her future?

"It's been ten years," Sadie said. "That's a long time to carry a grudge."

"It feels like yesterday for me. I can imagine it feels that way for her too, especially after losing her father. They had a very special bond, and he was the one person she thought would never abandon her."

"Who else has abandoned her? I mean, other than you."

Richard looked surprised at the question. "She didn't tell you? I guess you don't know May very well, do you?"

"I'd, uh, like to hear your side of it," Sadie said with a sharp nod.

"Well, May's family has one of the strongest histories of cancer I've ever heard of. In fact, they were part of a university study on genetics several years ago. May's mother, Leena, was diagnosed with breast cancer the first time when she was thirty-five."

"She died?" Sadie asked, glad to have that blank filled in, though the information was very sad.

"Not then," Richard said with a shake of his head. "She made it eight years after the first diagnosis—during which time *her* mother, two aunts, an uncle, and an older brother all died of some form of cancer. Leena's cancer came back with a vengeance when she was forty-three; she didn't beat it a second time. May was a sophomore in high school when her mother died. It was devastating."

Sadie could only imagine, and she felt the heaviness of May's loss in her heart.

Richard continued. "May had two surviving aunts when her mother died, Carla and Marie, but Carla was dead within five years of Leena. By the time May was twenty-two, every close relative on her mother's side, except Marie, had died of some type of cancer. To lose her father—who wasn't on the cancer-gene side of the family— must be horrible for her. He was the one she thought would always be there."

They both fell silent. It explained so much, including why May had gone to such pains to have Sadie help her, and why she didn't want to make a big deal to Hugh and Jolene about what Sadie was really doing. Sadie took advantage of the silence to take a few more bites of her buttermilk bar and ponder on her role. She was May's employee, hired to prove that Jim Sanderson's death was not a result of natural causes. But maybe the real reason she was here—the ethereal and higher-plan reason—was simply to help May find some peace. With her father's death, yes, but perhaps with Richard's abandonment as well. May couldn't be more than thirty-five years old; there was a lot of life left for her to live. Maybe Sadie could be part of that process. The more she let those thoughts pour into her head and heart, the more *right* they felt.

"Could you help me prove your father had nothing to do with Jim's death?" Sadie asked after a little more thought.

"How?"

"I'm not really sure," Sadie said, wishing she were. "I'm still trying to adjust to all this information myself. Jim died of a heart attack, but there are chemicals and medications that can induce a heart attack—including insulin."

Richard considered that, the crease in his brow getting deeper. "Did the police find Jim's death suspicious?"

Sadie shook her head and frowned. "No."

"But May's convinced," he summed up, rubbing his chin with his thumb and forefinger. "If we could prove Dad had no opportunity, that might be a starting point."

"Jim died on July sixteenth. Could you find out where your father was that day? What he was doing?"

Richard crossed his arms over his chest and nodded thoughtfully.

She held his eyes. He'd already given her an awful lot of information, and she was worried he had reached his limit.

"What color is May's hair?" he asked abruptly.

"What color is her hair?"

Richard nodded. "She was a redhead in high school, then a brunette in college. She felt it made her look more mature. Not long before things came to an end for us, she became a blonde—I hated it. I've wondered a hundred times since then what color her hair is. Did she stay blonde just to spite me?"

Sadie's insides melted, and she couldn't help but wonder if Pete ever thought about her hair color. It was ten o'clock, Colorado time. He'd be getting ready for bed; probably reading the morning paper he never got to in the mornings.

"She's a redhead," Sadie said, keeping herself in the present. "She's beautiful."

Richard smiled and took the last bite of his donut, taking ten years off the lines around his eyes in the process. When he finished, he stood up, digging into his pocket for a couple of one-dollar bills to leave as a tip, although Sadie wasn't sure a tip was required for a donut shop when they hadn't even sat inside. She suspected someone would take the money off the table before an employee noticed it was there and save themselves from having to use the ATM, but she still gave Richard credit for making the effort.

They waited to talk until they were back on the sidewalk and heading for Sadie's hotel. The streets were packed despite it being so late.

"Dad's secretary keeps an online calendar for him, but he also has a planner he takes notes in," Richard said.

They passed a man playing a saxophone, and Sadie threw a dollar into his open case. He stopped playing and wished her a great gift from the Universe of Love. It sounded good to Sadie.

She smiled at the musician before turning her attention back to Richard. "Do you have access to those things?"

Richard frowned and shook his head. "There's no reason for me to," he said, shoving his hands into his pockets. "But I think I can *find* the access." He stepped to the left to let a couple holding hands pass between them. When they met back up on the sidewalk, he continued. "You've given me a lot of motivation. I help you clear my father, and you help me clear myself."

Sadie was unable to deny the sincerity of his desire to talk to May. It was very touching, and she nodded. "I appreciate it."

Richard looked down and said under his breath, "Not as much as I do."

CHAPTER 25

Sadie took her time the next morning. She typed up all her notes, looking over all the information she'd collected, and wondered if she'd ever dare give them to May. It made her nervous to consider admitting to May that she'd talked to Richard, but hopefully things were coming together in a way that May would see all of this as a good thing.

Needing to relieve her anxiety, Sadie spent an hour walking the Portland streets even though most of the boutiques and shops weren't open yet. Window-shopping was fun, though, and when she saw that Powell's bookstore opened at nine o'clock, she ducked inside to see the landmark for herself. It was amazing, but equally overwhelming. Her head spinning by 9:30, she had to force herself to leave for fear that if she stayed much longer, she'd never find her way out again. It would take a three-day trip all by itself to see the whole store, though she did grab a romance novel on her way out so she could say she'd bought something.

She bought a Belgian waffle from a food cart on her way back to the hotel—it was delicious—and was crossing the lobby when the desk clerk called out to her.

"Mrs. Sadie Hoffmiller?" The man was tall and thin, with a smile too big for his face.

"Yes?"

He held out a small, manila-colored bubble mailer. "A package came for you in this morning's mail."

Intrigued, Sadie took the package and headed to her room, where she quickly opened it. Maybe it was a clue, like some voice tapes Jim had made about what to do if he died suddenly. Or maybe the key to a locker at a bus station! Unfortunately, it wasn't either of those things. When Sadie dumped it upside down on the bed, a slim, black wallet fell out, along with a folded-up piece of lined paper. She picked up the paper and opened it.

MOM,

CONSIDER THIS MY CONTRIBUTION TO THE CAUSE. I'VE LEARNED A THING OR TWO IN MY GRAPHIC ARTS CLASS! ARE YOU SURE I CAN'T COME?

LOVE YOU ANYWAY,

SHAWN

Sadie chuckled and shook her head as she opened the wallet with trepidation. What would he have gone to all the trouble to send her? As it turned out, it wasn't a wallet at all, but a badge holder. And right where an ID was supposed to be was something that looked a little bit like a driver's license, only with the words "Private Investigator" printed in big blue letters. It had a photo of Sadie, her home address, and some type of phony—but still official-looking—seal in the bottom corner. Sadie shook her head and pulled her phone out of her purse, pressing number 3 to speed dial her son.

He answered on the second ring.

"You made me a bogus ID and mailed it all the way to Portland?"

Shawn laughed. "It looks awesome, doesn't it? I spent hours getting it just right."

"Yes, it does look awesome, but it's still a fake."

"I know, but you have to admit I have skills."

"Have I ever doubted how highly skilled you are?"

Shawn didn't answer right away and a split second before he spoke, Sadie knew where this conversation was headed.

"Please let me come, Mom," Shawn begged. "I can tell my work it's a family emergency. They'll give me the time off. I'll even pay for my own ticket."

Sadie took a breath and sat on the edge of the bed, where, for the next fifteen minutes, she explained frontward and backward why Shawn couldn't come. School started in two weeks, this wasn't a family emergency, he couldn't afford a ticket, and Sadie was already pushing things by doing an investigation in a state where she wasn't licensed. She let him argue for awhile and then ended the discussion as only a mother can do sometimes. He was not happy, but she thanked him a final time for the badge before they hung up. She hoped he'd let it drop now. There was no way around the fact that it was not a good idea for him to come.

After ending the call, Sadie went to put the badge in her suitcase when she paused. She opened up the leather cover again and smiled. It was a very sweet gesture on Shawn's part, and since she'd never seen a real investigator's license, it looked legitimate to her. After considering it for a few more seconds, she put the badge in her purse instead. Just in case.

It was a quarter to 11:00 when Sadie parked in front of the light-gray rambler with white trim and a real estate sign in the front yard. She double-checked the address she'd typed into Dora fifteen minutes earlier. Yes, she was at the right place.

Jim Sanderson's house was tucked into a sprawling and beautiful neighborhood; kids were riding their bikes, a man was mowing his lawn, and a pair of women were speed walking around the block. She loved how many people always seemed to be out and about.

Sadie let herself out of the car and took a deep breath, inhaling the earthy smell. No wonder Oregonians were so environmentally conscious; they had a lot to lose. As she headed for the front door, she slipped her keys in her pocket as Pete had taught her to do. She hoped she'd be able to manage this meeting without revealing all the things she'd learned since she'd spoken to May on the phone yesterday, but the words seemed to be bursting inside of her. She worried about her ability to keep them to herself. It was imperative, however, that she didn't give things up before she heard back from Richard about his father's whereabouts the day Jim Sanderson died.

Her foot was on the first step when the front door opened and May slipped out, pulling the door shut behind her. Her hair was twisted up into a crude French knot, a few tendrils of hair framing her face. She gave Sadie a nervous smile while twisting the hem of her oversized T-shirt in her hands.

"Good morning," she said.

Sadie stopped at the top of the stairs. "Good morning," she said back. "What's wrong?"

May bit her lip. "Jolene stayed here last night," she said in a low voice. "She had a treatment yesterday, and Gary had a lot to do today; she didn't want to be alone."

"A treatment?" Sadie asked. "Is she sick?"

May blinked at her, her expression confused. "Did I not tell you about Jolene?"

Sadie shook her head. "She's your older sister and does the books for S&S. That's all I know."

"Oh," May said in a dull voice. She looked back at the house, then headed down the stairs. "Let's take a walk. I don't want her to overhear us."

Sadie fell in step beside May and adjusted her purse on her shoulder as they reached the sidewalk that followed the curling streets. Most of the sidewalk was covered in blessed shade. May waited until they had crossed the property line before she spoke.

"Jolene has cancer," she said simply.

Sadie's heart sank. "I'm so sorry," she said sympathetically, looking to the side, trying to read May's expression. She was watching the sidewalk and not looking at Sadie at all. "What kind?"

"Breast," May said simply, then took a breath—the kind Sadie imagined soldiers took before going into battle—and looked up. "She's beating it, but the treatments take a lot out of her."

"Does she have a family?"

Another pained expression flitted across May's face. "Her son, Bryce, is at the University of Washington in Seattle. She and her husband, Gary, live in Hillsboro, which is about half an hour from here." May paused. "Dad would help take care of her when she didn't feel up to making the trip home after her treatments at Providence, and, well, now I'm here instead."

Sadie put her hand on May's arm, causing her to stop. She turned to Sadie, her expression cautious. "I'm so sorry, May," she said. "Losing your father at a time like this must be even more devastating." Thanks to Richard relaying some of May's family history, Sadie knew just how horrible this really was.

Quick tears rose in May's eyes, but she took another of those strengthening breaths and faced forward, walking again. Sadie quickly matched her pace. They didn't speak for nearly a minute.

"You said she's beating it," Sadie said. "That's good news."

"She looks awful, though," May admitted, her gaze on the sidewalk. They had looped around to the point where Sadie had no idea where they were in relation to the house. "I mean, I know the treatments are designed to get you as close to death as possible without killing you in an attempt to kill off the cancer cells, but it's hard to watch, hard to believe she'll get better."

"Hard to believe doesn't equal hopeless," Sadie pointed out.

May shrugged. "You can see why I don't want to upset her, why it's important that you're just a friend helping me get Dad's house ready to sell and not someone who is going to give her any reason to worry about anything at all."

"I understand," Sadie said, nodding. "I'll be careful."

"Thank you," May said with a smile. "I appreciate your understanding."

She stopped, and Sadie realized they'd looped back to the house. The sidewalk was a full circle; they hadn't crossed any streets. May continued. "I'll show you to the study. Her room is on the opposite side of the house, so I don't think we'll disturb her too much; I just didn't want her to overhear us."

Sadie followed May through a living room decorated in the soft pinks and blues of the early eighties. She'd always liked that color scheme herself; too bad it hadn't remained popular. The floor plan of the house was such that the living room was the center of the home, with the kitchen off to the side. A hallway stretched toward the back of the house and another one stretched to the right of the living room. May led Sadie down the back one, but Sadie looked over her shoulder at the one they hadn't taken, counting three closed doors.

Bedrooms, she assumed. Maybe a bathroom as well. Jolene was behind one of the doors.

"Here it is," May said, standing to the side of an open doorway. Sadie walked past her and took in the floor-to-ceiling bookshelves on one wall and the white-painted paneling on the other walls. There was a large desk flanked by bone-colored filing cabinets. The desk was quite tidy, with a computer taking up most of the desk space. There were no pictures on the wall or plants or anything that would be called decorative, attesting to the fact that this had been a man's office for a long time. A shrink-wrapped stack of flattened file boxes lay in the middle of the floor.

"The filing cabinet on the right of the desk is business related," May said, coming into the room and closing the door behind her. "I'm pretty sure all the original contracts between Dad and Keith are in there. If you don't mind boxing them up while you go through them, that would be great." She waved toward the file boxes on the floor. "To, you know, keep up appearances."

"Sure," Sadie said. She faced May and ignored most of what she wanted to talk about, which was Richard and cancer and the holes left in May's life by both of them. "Do you happen to have a copy machine?" she asked, looking around the office but seeing only a small printer. "I don't want to hold on to originals, but I might want to take some papers back to the hotel to look over later."

May frowned. "I didn't think about that," she said. "There's a copy shop a few blocks over, though. I've got some errands to run, so I can make whatever copies you need."

"That will be great," Sadie said with a smile. They both stood there, looking around.

"Well, I guess I'll leave you to it," May said.

Sadie nodded. "Sounds good."

May left the room, closing the door behind her, and Sadie got down to business. May had said the cabinet on the right was business related, which meant the cabinet on the left was likely personal. She glanced at the door, and then moved to the left side of the desk. It was reasonable to want a glimpse at the man who was the reason she was here, and May hadn't told her *not* to look. Besides, she would only spend a few minutes before she moved on to the business contracts.

CHAPTER 26

The top drawer of the filing cabinet was full of household information—home repair invoices, old bank statements, and personal files. Sadie fingered through the alphabetized files and pulled out the one marked "Leena." Richard had said Leena had died when May was fifteen years old, and the death certificate from 1990 seemed to confirm that. Behind the death certificate were pages and pages of what looked like test results, medical reports, and the like. Sadie wondered why they were all still here; it had been twenty years since Leena had died. But she knew that sometimes it was hard to let go of people, of proof they were once alive. She wondered if she might still have similar things of Neil's tucked away back home.

Sadie reverently placed the file back in the cabinet drawer and moved on through home warranties and tax files that held years' worth of receipts.

When she came upon a file titled "Will—Legal Trust," she pulled it out and opened it. There were five thin, professional-looking folders, each labeled "Will and Testament" with a date printed on the front and a notarized seal. The first folder was dated 1982, with the other folders dated roughly every four or five years after that. The last file was dated just a few years ago and the title had changed to "Living Trust."

Smart man, Sadie thought as she extracted the trust documents. Her brother, Jack, managed her financial affairs, and he had recently suggested she consider replacing her will with a legal trust. Per Jack's explanation, Sadie would essentially create a trust which would then hold all her assets: home, stocks, bonds, certificates, and so on. She'd already decided that she'd probably appoint Jack as her trustee since he handled such things already.

The trustee, under the supervision of an attorney, would manage the trust, and upon Sadie's death, which she expected would be a long time from now—knock on wood—the trustee would then execute whatever wishes she had stipulated to happen when she died.

Her late husband, Neil, had had a will, but because they owned everything in joint, she was able to avoid probate, and settling his will was fairly simple. When Sadie's father was first diagnosed with colon cancer, Jack had him draft his own living trust, and due to Jack's insight, they had avoided a lot of the legal and emotional toll of settling his estate as well. She was relieved to know that despite the heavy loss Jim Sanderson's children were shouldering, he had taken care of so many details, saving them what could be months of trying to put his affairs in order without him there to help.

Sadie skimmed through the first parts of the trust, which explained the way assets would be managed while he was alive, until she finally came to the "On Death" portion of the document. She was surprised to see it was written in first person, as though Jim himself were speaking to his heirs. It was a nice touch.

On death, all assets of trust, both business and personal, are to be divided equally among my three children, Jolene, Hugh, and Sharla-May. They will each receive equal amounts of all insurance settlements and account balances after expenses are paid, and will become equal partners in S&S Suppression. Should any of the three want to take full ownership of the house on Poplar, they are to receive three appraisals and go with the median assessment amount, buying out their siblings legally and fairly.

In the event that I outlive any of my heirs, their portion is to be divided equally between those remaining, except in the case of my daughter Jolene. Her portion of my personal assets and balances will revert directly to her only living child, Bryce G. Tracey, to be held in trust until he reaches the age of twenty-five. Inheritance is not subject to reassignment to spouses.

In the event of Jolene not inheriting, Hugh and Sharla-May will absorb her portion of S&S Suppression and be 50/50 partners. All distributions and reassignment of rights and titles are to be executed by Rylin, Schow, and Freeburg, attorneys at law.

If liquid assets allow, the first cash amount shall be distributed within thirty days of my death, after funeral expenses are paid, and is not to exceed $10,000 dollars each.

That's where the expensive purse had come from, Sadie thought, thinking back to May's white handbag. It also helped explain how May could afford to pay for Sadie's services.

Jim's wishes of what should happen to his estate upon his death didn't present anything unique, but Sadie deduced that Hugh, like May, was childless and without anyone to inherit in his place at the time this trust document had last been revised. She found that rather sad. Jim Sanderson had three children who should have netted him several grandchildren by now. Instead, he had only one. It was one of Sadie's greatest fears that she'd be denied the opportunity to be a grandparent, and she felt for Jim. She hoped he had enjoyed Jolene's son as much as he possibly could.

As she returned the file to the cabinet, she wondered if May planned to have children at some point. If she was in her early thirties, there was time yet to have a family, assuming she found the right man to make a family with.

Richard Kelly had been that man once upon a time, and while Sadie didn't want to let her romantic notions get too far ahead of her, she wondered if perhaps he might still be May's happily-ever-after. She shut the drawer with a snap and was ready to open the next drawer down when the study door opened. She quickly pulled her hand away from the cabinet and turned around.

"How's it going?" May asked from the doorway.

Sadie was well aware that she was on the wrong side of the desk but hoped her smile would cover her guilty conscience. May looked from Sadie to the unwrapped package of file boxes still on the floor.

"I'm just getting my bearings," Sadie said, desperately scanning for an excuse as to why she hadn't even opened the business filing cabinet yet. Her eyes landed on the bookshelf a few feet away from the cabinet she *had* been looking through. "Your dad was very well-read," she said, stepping forward and skimming titles, looking for a book that would explain her interest. Unfortunately, at first glance all she could see were titles related to physics, operational systems, and obscure topics such as the density of alloys and mathematical theories related to the universe.

"He had an amazing mind for science," May said, but she sounded a little flat, as though she knew something wasn't quite right. "I wondered if you wanted a drink or anything."

"A glass of water would be great," Sadie said, heading to the right-hand filing cabinet as though satisfied with her inspection of the bookshelves. "Thank you."

May smiled and left the room, leaving the door open. Sadie winced at her own lack of professionalism and reminded herself that this job was not about satisfying her personal curiosity. By the time May returned, Sadie had assembled two file storage boxes and was pursuing a file marked "Partnership SK—Original," hoping she looked studious. May put a glass of ice water on the desk, along with a wicker coaster—the glass was already sweating—and asked Sadie if she needed anything else.

"I think I'm good for now," Sadie said, scanning the page with her best concentrating-teacher expression. "I'll let you know."

"Okay," May said with a quick nod. "I'll, um, be in the kitchen."

She left a moment later, again leaving the door partially open. Sadie couldn't help but wonder if she wanted to keep a closer eye on Sadie. She hated having given May a reason not to trust her and was more determined than ever to meet the woman's expectations.

"Focus," she whispered to herself. Then she took a deep breath and did just that, determined that the next time May checked on her, she'd have no reason to worry about how Sadie was using her time.

CHAPTER 27

It was a little past noon when Sadie took a final sip of her water. The remaining semi-melted cubes clattered around the bottom of the glass as she returned it to the coaster. She surveyed her work and smiled at her progress. She had two file boxes partially filled. One held files with no mention of Keith Kelly, while the other contained all the files with any information about Jim Sanderson's former business partner, but which didn't seem particularly important. Sadie wanted easy access to them if she needed to go back.

In addition to the boxes, she had a stack of nearly a dozen files with documents she wanted personal copies off. They included business contracts, loan pay-off documentation, and a few letters of correspondence between Jim and Keith that took place after they had split the company. Sadie had only skimmed the papers, wanting to get as much work done as possible before taking the time to focus on individual details. That's why she needed copies. But she also needed a break. And food.

She'd enjoyed the hotel's continental breakfast, but was in need of an actual meal. She wondered if May would be opposed to her throwing something together. Being in berry country during berry season made Annie's triple-berry salad an absolute must, so long as May wouldn't mind Sadie running by the grocery store when she went out for copies. She'd already determined to make the copies herself since it would be difficult to lay out exactly what she wanted May to copy for her. The more she thought about Annie's salad—which she hadn't been able to fully enjoy at the ladies' auxiliary meeting due to her unhealthy stress level at the time—the better it sounded.

"May?" Sadie asked quietly as she approached the kitchen, files in hand.

May was wrapping wine glasses in newspaper and putting them into a specially designed moving box with cardboard partitions that created twenty-four smaller squares to keep the glasses separated.

"I'm going to head out and make some copies," she said, holding up the stack of files. She moved to the far side of the kitchen so as not to get in the way of May's tasks at hand.

"Did you find anything?" May asked hopefully.

"Maybe," Sadie said, keeping her answer ambiguous. She didn't want to raise or lower May's hopes too much. "I'd like to go over them in more detail, though. And I wondered if you had plans for lunch? My friend Annie has a recipe for a triple-berry salad that is just calling out to me, and I thought it would make a wonderful lunch for the two of us—really keep the energy up."

"Well, I didn't pick up much when I went to the store," May said. Her tone was still a little flat for Sadie's taste. Maybe some of Sadie's yummy salad would help their relationship get back on track. Everyone knew that people who made salads were of good solid character.

"I could go grocery shopping after I make copies," she suggested.

"Well, I guess it is about lunchtime and—"

She was interrupted by a knock at the kitchen door.

"Just a minute," May said, turning to the door and pulling it open. The door blocked Sadie's view, but she heard a woman's voice saying that she was glad she'd caught May at home. Sadie casually moved to the other side of the island so she could get a look at the visitor.

The woman at the door was older than Sadie by at least fifteen years and had starkly dyed black hair done in the typical, old-lady-ratted hairdo that looked like black cotton candy. Her eyebrows were penciled, her shoulders and arms thin, but her skin was tanned, her eyes were bright, and her dentures were shining in the summer sun-light. She was wearing denim shorts that came to the tops of her wrinkled knees, flip-flops Sadie suspected were orthopedic, and a T-shirt that said "Read My Lipstick."

Sadie liked her immediately—even before her eyes were drawn to the plate of muffins covered with plastic wrap the woman held in her hands. Muffins would be a perfect complement to the triple-berry salad. What luck!

"Lois," May said, releasing the door and stepping into an em-brace with the woman, who was a few inches shorter than May, probably no taller than five foot two. Lois slid the plate of muffins onto the counter in order to hug May back properly. If she weighed a hundred pounds it would be because she had quarters in her pockets and cement in the thick soles of her sandals.

May stepped back, both women holding the upper arms of the other and drinking each other in. "It's been a long time," May said. "You look wonderful."

Lois made a coy face, glancing at the ceiling briefly and letting go of May's arms. "Oh, go on," she said, fanning herself as though overheated, while she batted her sparsely lashed eyes. "I'll pay you a quarter for every nice thing you can say about how good I look."

May laughed, the first genuine laugh Sadie had heard from her. "You'll send me to the poorhouse if I do that." She looked at the muffins and raised her eyebrows. "Are these what I think they are?"

"I couldn't come over and say hello empty-handed, now could I? Blueberry walnut—isn't that your favorite?"

"Of course," May said, and she seemed lighter. "Thank you, that was very sweet of you. But you don't have to bring me offerings in order to stop by, you know that."

"Yes, I do," Lois said with a nod. "And don't try to change me because—"

"You're too old and set in your ways," May finished. "You've been telling me that for thirty years." She laughed at the memory of what was obviously a shared joke between them.

Lois laughed too, raising a hand to her mouth, probably to make sure her dentures didn't fall out. Sadie had seen that happen before at the nursing home. It wasn't pretty, but unless someone could afford new dentures every year or so, it was difficult to have a perfect fit with those things.

Once Lois recovered from her giggling, she continued, "I've been dying to say hello ever since Jolene said you were coming, but I was sailing out by Waldport 'til this morning. How are you, my dear?"

"Come inside," May said with a smile, waving Lois inside and shutting the door. She headed back to where she was wrapping glasses, which said volumes about her relationship with this woman—absolute comfort.

Lois looked at Sadie, who smiled a hello, which Lois returned before following May to the counter and pulling a piece of newspaper off the stack. She grabbed a glass out of the cupboard.

"I sure wish one of you kids would keep the house," Lois said, wrapping the glass and sliding it into the box. "It won't be the same without a Sanderson living here."

May smiled and looked regretful. "I thought maybe Hugh would take it, but he said he can't afford it, and he seems to like his little condo in Old Town. Jolene, well . . . They aren't making a lot of big changes right now."

"Poor Jo-Jo," Lois said softly. She put a hand on May's and gave it a sympathetic squeeze. "Poor May."

May glanced at her quickly and smiled, but looked embarrassed by the attention. "We had estate stuff all day yesterday," she said, changing the subject. "Dad hadn't redone the trust for a few years, so there were some things we had to work out, but it's coming together pretty well."

Lois pulled her hand away and shook her head. "It just breaks my heart to see you all going through this again."

She carefully rolled another fluted glass in the paper, pausing to fold the corners into the bell of the cup.

Again, Sadie noted. May had said she'd grown up here, so Lois would have known the family when Leena passed away. She watched for May's response to Lois's comment, which began with a thoughtful silence, then a sigh. "I certainly wasn't expecting it," she said in a soft voice that sounded hungry for validation. "I can't believe I spent the last ten years of his life so far away."

Lois put the wrapped glass in the box and placed a hand on May's shoulder. Sadie noted it was the third time she'd demonstrated affection through touch; she was definitely a touchy-feely type of neighbor. Sadie wondered if perhaps she'd even filled the role of a mother figure for May after Leena had died.

"Your dad never held your leaving against you, you know that, right? He understood the need for distance," Lois said.

May nodded, but in the process of looking up seemed to realize Sadie was still there. Sadie smiled, not the least bit bothered by having been forgotten. Being a fly on the wall for this conversation had helped to verify some of the things Richard had said, or at least support them.

"Oh, Lois, I forgot to introduce you. This is my friend, Sadie Hoffmiller. Sadie, this is Lois Hilbert. She's a very good friend of the family, going on some thirty years. She lives across the street."

Sadie stepped forward and put out her hand. "In the champagne-colored house? The one with those trellised peace roses?" Sadie had noted the home the moment she'd pulled up. It was bright and well-tended, an English cottage-style home painted a light-peach color that offset the pink-tinged yellow roses perfectly.

Lois raised her penciled eyebrows in surprise. "Yes," she said with a small laugh. "That is my home. You know roses?"

Sadie hoped her smile didn't seem too arrogant, but she took great pride in the fact that Pete's lessons seemed to be working. She was noticing details she didn't even mean to notice. The two women shook hands and Sadie shrugged. "My mother grew peace roses. They were her very favorite."

"Then she was a softhearted woman," Lois said with a nod. "And had excellent taste."

"If you do say so yourself, right?" May laughed.

Lois put a wrinkled hand to her chest. An emerald ring glittered on her right hand—a birthstone? "Who better to make the judgment than someone so equally bestowed with good judgment?"

All three of them laughed that time. "It's a pleasure to meet you, Lois," Sadie said, trying not to look at the muffins again. Lois had called them blueberry walnut, but they looked like they were bran as well. Double prizes—delicious and packed with fiber!

"Sadie, you were going to run some errands, right?" May asked.

Sadie was surprised at the change in subject, but it served to put her back in her place. She wasn't really May's friend; she was an employee, and she had work to do. She kept her smile sincere and nodded. "I am," she said, hoping the hurt of being dismissed didn't show too much. "I'll grab those salad fixings as well. It will go great with the muffins."

"Sure," May nodded. "Dad's grocery bags are there." She pointed to a fabric parcel wedged in the gap between the fridge and the wall. Sadie pulled out the parcel and found it to be four reusable bags rolled up into one.

"Do you need anything else while I'm out? Bread, eggs—you have real butter for those muffins, right? I don't mean to be rude, but I do not compromise on butter."

Lois laughed and came over to Sadie. "This is my kind of woman!" she said, putting her arm across Sadie's shoulders and giving her a squeeze with her spindly arm before going back to wrapping glasses.

May smiled. "I've got butter—my mother was a purist, too—but we could probably use some more milk. I've been surviving on cereal and coffee."

"Oh, that reminds me!" Lois said, touching May's arm again. "Did you get the flier about the summer picnic? Once I learned you were coming home, I put it on the back door so you'd see it when you arrived. I meant to say something when I got here, and it completely slipped my mind."

"I got it," May said. Her smile was instantly more polite than it had been. "That was very sweet of you to invite me but—"

"Not just you," Lois said. "All of you." She waved her hand. "Jolene and Gary come every time, you know, and Hugh's stopped in a time or two as well. I know Jo-Jo isn't up to it, and I don't know about Hugh." She gave May's arm a squeeze. "But you must come and represent the Sandersons."

"Well, I don't know," May said, grabbing another cup and another piece of newsprint. "It seems . . . wrong, what with Dad gone and Jolene so sick." She flicked a look at Sadie, reminding Sadie she'd been told to leave. Sadie kicked herself back into gear and dug her keys out of her pocket, though she would have much preferred to stay here and learn more about the things in May's life she hadn't told Sadie.

Lois was having none of May's excuses. "Your dad would love for you to go, you know that. And Jolene is all about people living their lives."

"I don't want her to be alone," May said.

Lois was shaking her head before May had finished talking. "Isn't Gary picking her up around six tonight?" She cocked her head to the side as Sadie headed for the front door, not making a production out of her exit. "Sharla-May, I insist."

May let out a breath, remaining unconvinced. Sadie put her hand on the doorknob and gave it a twist as May continued. "And I suppose the pitchforks will come out if I don't show up with bacon ice cream, right?"

Sadie whipped her head to the side. "Bacon ice cream?" she exclaimed without thinking.

Both women turned to look at her, and Sadie felt her cheeks heat up from her outburst. "I'm sorry," she said. "I just . . . Did you really say bacon ice cream?"

"My dad made it every year," May said, though her tone and

expression were reticent. She clearly wanted Sadie to leave, and Sadie would . . . in just a minute.

Lois continued when May didn't volunteer anything more. "Jim didn't like fruity desserts. Naturally, at a summer picnic in Oregon, every dessert that shows up is berry-related. That's why we age so well, you know"—she made an exaggerated flip of invisible hair—"all those antioxidants. So, anyway, after a couple years of berry desserts, Jim and Leena showed up with bacon ice cream, of all things."

"It was supposed to be a joke," May added. The nostalgic memory seemed to have granted Sadie a stay for the moment. "A real *man's* dessert, you know, and about as different from fruit as anything could be."

"Lo and behold, everyone loved it," Lois said. "We all begged them to make it again the next year. After Leena died, Jim made it himself. He's been making it for every summer picnic since."

"Bacon ice cream," Sadie repeated again in wonder, releasing the doorknob and walking back toward the island. "I've never heard of such a thing. And it's good?"

"Amazing!" Lois said.

"Fabulous!" May said at the same time. They both laughed. "Which is why showing up without it just seems wrong."

"Can't you make it?" Sadie asked. She could well understand May's hesitancy. It would be hard enough to go to the picnic for the first time in a decade and without her father, but without his signature dish, it would be even more uncomfortable. But Sadie was a great cook. And if it worked out, she would be able to eat something she'd never even heard of before today—how often did *that* happen?

"I can barely butter my own toast," May said. "Hence my living on cereal these last three days. You have to, like, glaze the bacon and stuff. And don't even get me started on making ice cream from scratch."

"But there's a recipe?" Sadie asked.

"Sure," May said, shrugging one shoulder. "But, like I said, I don't cook."

"I do," Sadie said quickly. "If there's a recipe, I can make it." She sent Lois a pleading look, begging for support.

Lois picked up her cue immediately and winked at Sadie before turning to May—they were now officially in cahoots! "That's perfect," Lois said, clapping her hands together. "Your friend can make the ice cream, and we can all pay tribute to Jim one last time." She clasped her hands together and held them beneath her chin, a perfect match to the pouty look on her face. "You'll come now, won't you?"

The glance May flashed at Sadie didn't look entirely pleased, but Sadie hoped she wasn't entirely displeased either. "I'm not sure how I can say no."

"You can't," Lois assured her, wrapping her arms around May's shoulders. "I brought your favorite muffins, remember. I think that's officially called a bribe around here."

"If you've got that recipe, I can pick up what we need when I go to the store," Sadie offered, now feeling rather eager to leave. "The salad will come together in a jiffy, and then I can work on the bacon ice cream." It would mean the files and things would have to wait, but if she hurried, she could still get in a few more hours of work before the picnic.

May smiled and nodded, but didn't make eye contact as she retrieved the recipe from the recipe box in the cupboard above the stove and handed it over. They discussed which store to go to—May insisted on organic everything—and how long Sadie would be.

Lois was back to wrapping glasses by the time Sadie said good-bye and stepped out the front door. She paused on the porch, scanning the recipe with butterflies in her stomach. There were few things quite as exciting as discovering new ways to enjoy food, and bacon ice cream was something she'd never even thought of.

And, while the seduction of such a recipe was a prominent motivation, Sadie also wanted to meet Jim Sanderson's neighbors and get a feel for the people in his life. You never knew who might have seen something or heard something that might help her case. Sadie would make sure to tell May that as soon as she had the chance. For now, however, she was on a mission!

Bacon Ice Cream

6 slices of bacon
2 to 4 tablespoons brown sugar
2 quarts heavy whipping cream
1 teaspoon vanilla extract
2 to 4 cups sugar, to taste
Milk to the fill line, about 4 inches from the top of the ice cream container

To candy the bacon, line 6 slices of bacon on a jelly-roll pan covered with either aluminum foil or a silicone mat. Sprinkle approximately 1 teaspoon brown sugar on each bacon slice, keeping as much sugar on the bacon as possible (or put bacon and sugar in a zip-top bag to coat).

Put pan in a cold oven and set heat to 325 degrees. Bake for 25 minutes. While the bacon is cooking, prepare ice cream base (see below). After 25 minutes, turn bacon over. Continue turning bacon every three minutes until bacon is crispy and the brown sugar gives it a candy coating.

Remove pan from oven and move bacon to a cooling rack, if using foil. (Bacon can cool directly on the silicone mat.) Once cooled, chop bacon into very small pieces. Store chopped bacon in refrigerator or freezer until ready to add to the ice cream base.

To prepare ice cream base, use a standard 4-quart ice cream maker.* Add whipping cream, then sugar. (You want it quite sweet, since the sweetness will mellow as the ice cream freezes.) Add milk to the fill line of the container (usually 4 inches from the top). Add more sugar if necessary. Mix and chill in the refrigerator for about an hour.

When bacon has cooled, add the chopped, candied bacon pieces to the chilled ice cream base. Freeze according to ice-cream maker directions. (Adding the bacon a few minutes before the freezer is finished will keep the "candy" from dissolving into the base as much.) Final result should be a soft, toffee-flavored ice cream with bits of bacon, which give it a salty flavor and are similar in texture to bits of toffee. Serve immediately.

*Adjust ingredients accordingly if your freezer has a different capacity.

CHAPTER 28

S adie was back to May's house within an hour. Her adrenaline
was rushing, and she couldn't wait to get to work in the kitchen.
Despite the neighborhood being very suburban, there was a strip
mall only a mile or so away, complete with a copy store and super-
market that sold genuine Oregon blackberries!

May wasn't in the kitchen when Sadie let herself in the side door
after a light knock, but Sadie felt funny about hunting her down,
so she simply got to work in the kitchen—starting with her salad.
Candying the walnuts took a few minutes, but while they cooled, she
mixed everything else together, and in fewer than ten minutes after
entering the kitchen, she had finished the salad.

She made up her own plate, adding a muffin to the side. It
hadn't been officially offered to her, but there were half a dozen, and
it was downright unwise for May to eat all of them, seeing as how
they were bran and everything. Sadie had hoped to eat with May,
but she was starving and so decided to eat alone.

After settling onto a barstool, she picked up her fork and dug
into what, in her opinion, consisted of a fabulous lunch. It was as
good as she'd hoped and the muffin was delicious, not too heavy,

but not too light. She made a note to ask Lois for the muffin recipe before she left. She was halfway through the salad—the blackberries and walnuts were wonderful together—before she started looking around the room, noting what had been packed and what hadn't.

There were boxes everywhere, some full and some empty, and an overall disorganized order to everything, which was typical of packing. For the first time, Sadie noticed a large family photo over the mantel in the living room. She picked up her plate and walked over to get a better look. The picture was outdated, but Sadie assumed it was the last family photo taken before May's mother had died. Leena Sanderson had strawberry-blonde hair and soft brown eyes. She sat next to Jim, their three children standing behind them. Sadie took in the features of each one of them, smiling at the 1980s version of adolescent Sharla-May. She had big red hair, a metallic smile, and huge hoop earrings. She looked so young and so happy—a moment frozen in time.

The longer Sadie stared at the picture, reflecting on how much had changed since it had been taken, the heavier her heart felt. She finished her salad and returned to the kitchen to put the plate in the sink and get a start on the bacon ice cream, leaving her heavy sympathies behind.

She'd never glazed bacon before, but the recipe—written out by Leena Sanderson, Sadie assumed—explained the process in detail. Bless conscientious cooks! Within minutes the bacon was coated with brown sugar and spread out on the foil-lined pan. She slid the pan into the cold oven and set the timer and temperature according to the recipe. Sadie then turned her attention to finding the ice cream freezer so she could mix up the cream and sugar portion of the recipe.

"You're back."

Sadie looked up. She'd been so intent on looking through the cupboards for the ice cream freezer—though the chances of it being stored in the average-sized kitchen were slim—that she hadn't heard May approach.

She smiled as she closed another cupboard door. "I was looking for the ice cream freezer. I can mix up the base, then let it chill until it's time to add the bacon and get it mixing. What time is the picnic?"

"Seven," May said, looking uncomfortable. "I'm really not sure it's a good idea to go."

Sadie saw her chance to assure May why it was important to be there. "You're father died at home, right?" she asked, keeping her tone even.

May furrowed her brow, but nodded.

"And if Keith were a part of that, he could have come to the house. The only people who might know if he did are your neighbors. I have a list of Keith's cars, as well as a photo of him. Should the opportunity arise—and I will be very careful about not blowing my cover—your neighbors might have some information about that night. In addition, it sounds like your dad was relatively close with Lois, and perhaps some other neighbors, too. Maybe he said something that will support what we're looking for. Without him here, it's up to those people around him to put the pieces back together."

May wasn't convinced and shook her head to emphasize her lack of faith. "If anyone had seen anything, they'd have told me before now."

"Unless they didn't know that what they saw was important," Sadie reminded her. She came around the island and stopped in front of May. "Look, if you really don't want to go, or don't want me to go, I'll respect that—I'll even help you come up with an excuse.

I didn't mean to make you feel cornered. And you're right that there may be nothing of value for this case at the picnic. But there might be something, even a small something, and"—she paused and smiled—"you have to eat more than just cereal, young lady. With all the stress you've been under, you're ripe for catching some horrible virus that will send you to your bed, and you don't want that, do you?"

May didn't soften as much as Sadie had hoped she would, but she did nod. "Okay," May said. "But I really don't want anyone to know who you are. Everyone has accepted Dad's death as tragic, and no one suspects anything other than a natural death. They'll all think I'm crazy if they find out why you're here."

"They won't find out," Sadie said. "I'm very good with people, and I won't endanger you or what we're looking for in the least, okay? But we need more than paper," she said, waving toward the stack of files she needed to return the office. "And people often know things they don't realize they know."

The oven dinged to indicate that it had reached the correct temperature, and Sadie let May ponder on what she'd said while she peeked in on the pan. It still looked like raw bacon coated in brown sugar. May crossed behind her to the fridge, where she took out a yogurt and a Diet Coke. Sadie moved out of the way so May could get a glass out of the cupboard.

"I've got the salad right here," Sadie said, pulling open the fridge and removing the plastic-wrapped bowl of salad. "It goes great with Lois's muffins."

"This is for Jolene," May said, setting her items on the counter. "I'd love some salad and, of course, one of Lois's marvelous muffins." She glanced at the plate and seemed to notice there was one missing.

"Sorry," Sadie said, embarrassed. "I couldn't resist."

May smiled. "No one can."

"And that's another reason we need to go tonight, I need to sweet-talk that recipe away from Lois."

"Mom had a copy of it," May said, nodding toward the cupboard that housed the recipe box. "You're welcome to copy it down; Lois doesn't guard her recipes."

"She is a good, kind woman," Sadie said almost reverently, thrilled to get the recipe so easily.

May gestured to the yogurt and Diet Coke again. "Jolene says she feels like she could eat something—that's a good sign. The first few days after getting chemo are brutal, so I'm relieved she's feeling well enough to eat. She could use a few pounds."

Sadie felt the sympathy brimming in her chest as she thought about what Richard had said, that May's dad was the one person May thought would never leave her. Sadie wondered how sick Jolene was. How would May cope if she lost her sister so soon after losing her dad? "Is there anything I can do to help?"

May shook her head and seemed to be working hard to keep her expression neutral. "Thanks, but we're okay. It's kind of nice to be taking care of someone again. I haven't had anyone but myself around for so long that I forget what it feels like to be connected, you know?"

"I know exactly what you mean," Sadie said, hoping May believed her. She leaned back against the counter and crossed her arms over her stomach. "After my kids left home, I realized how much I needed to be needed. It's hard to adjust to those changes sometimes. I'm sure Jolene appreciates you being here too. I bet she's missed you."

May shrugged and frowned while pouring the Diet Coke into the glass. "I don't know about that." She pulled open a drawer and removed a bendable straw, which she put into the glass. "We've never been particularly close. I know most sisters are, but it was just never like that with us." She pulled open another drawer and hunted for a spoon. "It's nice to be getting along now. Better late than never, right?"

Sadie wasn't particularly close to her own sister, but she kept that to herself. "Relationships can be complicated," she said, trying not to be too pushy now that May was opening up a little bit.

May let out a breath. "Can they ever."

Sadie busied herself with making May's lunch plate while May finished putting together the simple meal for her sister. "I'll be back in a few minutes," May said.

"Sure," Sadie said with a nod, refolding the cloth grocery bags as May left the room. Once she was alone, Sadie pulled down the recipe box. There were blank cards at the back of the box. Sadie removed two and then fingered through the "Breads" cards until she found "Marvelous Bran Muffins." She pulled it out only to realize there was another recipe stuck to it—a common kitchen problem. Sadie gently pulled the secondary recipe off of the back, intending to re-file it appropriately.

"Second-Chance Baked Potato Soup," she read out loud, smiling at the clever title. A quick skim through the ingredients and instructions made her wish she wasn't full and that she had half a dozen leftover baked potatoes on hand. The soup sounded delicious, and after quickly determining that should she ask, May would likely be fine with her copying down this recipe as well, she pulled another blank card out of the box. As she wrote it out, she reflected on the title again. Second chance. She thought about Richard and May— one across town in his office, the other only a few rooms away—and wondered if a second chance was really possible between the two of them. She hoped so.

It took four minutes to copy down the recipes. Then Sadie slid the cards into her pocket and went back to work, completely pleased with how the day was going. Three new recipes in one day—fabulous! She eyed the recipe box as she worked, wondering if there were any other treasures in there.

Sadie turned the bacon over and was putting the pan back in the oven when she heard the sound of an engine pulling into the driveway. She stuffed the grocery bags back between the wall and the fridge and stepped to the sink to peek out the window at whoever had pulled up.

A little green truck—at least fifteen years old and probably not washed for almost that long—had pulled in behind May's car, which meant it was someone comfortable with the house and with May, or otherwise they wouldn't block her car. A man stepped out of the driver's seat wearing a baseball cap and sunglasses. Was it another neighbor? Jolene's husband coming to pick her up early?

She was about to drop the curtain, anticipating him coming to the side door, when he surprised her by heading down the driveway toward the street. She craned her neck and watched until he turned the corner of the house, and then she hurried into the living room to peek out the side of the window closest to the driveway to see where he was going. Sadie was a little disappointed when he just headed for the mailbox.

He approached the silver mailbox and pulled open the door, giving Sadie a chance to get a closer look at him—for all the good it did her. The hat and sunglasses covered most of his face, but she could see that he had a mustache and goatee. There was something familiar about him, but Sadie couldn't place it and chalked it up to her *wanting* something about him to look familiar.

He pulled a stack of mail out of the mailbox and began scanning it on his way to the front door. He paused at the bottom of the porch steps, taking one of the envelopes and deftly tucking it into the waistband of his khaki shorts.

Sadie felt her heart race just a little. He was stealing mail. Didn't he know that was a federal offense?

He continued up the steps and, thrown off her game, Sadie headed for the kitchen instead of the front door. She checked the bacon, and not a minute too soon. It was nearly done. She grabbed the hot pads just as she heard the front door open. The mail thief had let himself inside the house!

"May?" he called, causing Sadie to jump as she crossed to the oven, unsure of what to do as she heard him approaching. Mere moments before he appeared, she decided to use her "What do you mean I'm not supposed to be here?" façade. Ignorance was such a blessed disguise sometimes.

The oven door hinge squeaked as she pulled it open. She used the hot pad to lift the pan and turned to find the man standing on the threshold of the kitchen, staring at her. He'd taken off his sunglasses, and without them, Sadie realized why he looked so familiar. She'd seen him before and felt her heartbeat increasing as she flashed back to Keith Kelly's dinner guests from last night. Richard and Keith had met with two unidentified men—one of whom had been wearing a green polo shirt and seemed the least comfortable at the table.

He gave her a tentative smile, and she could only hope he hadn't seen her at the restaurant or that her expression now hadn't betrayed her surprise. "Hi, you must be May's friend, Cindy."

"Sadie," she corrected him, taking her time to place the hot pan on a trivet she'd already put on the counter.

"Sadie, right, sorry." He put the stack of mail down on the counter. Well, most of the mail; there was still the matter of an envelope tucked in his shorts.

"Happens all the time," Sadie assured him, trying to stay calm. She wiped her hands on the dish towel hanging from the oven door handle and put out her hand. "And you are?"

"Hugh Sanderson," he said with a nod, giving her hand a quick shake. "May's brother."

Marvelous Bran Muffins

3½ cups All-Bran® cereal
1 cup boiling water
½ cup butter
1 cup white sugar
½ cup brown sugar
2 eggs
2 cups buttermilk
2½ cups flour
2½ teaspoons baking soda
2 teaspoons cinnamon
½ teaspoons salt

Preheat oven to 350 degrees. Line muffin cups. Soak 1 cup of All-Bran cereal in 1 cup boiling water and stir until evenly blended. Set aside. Cream butter and sugar. Beat eggs in one at a time, then add buttermilk and soaked bran. Mix. Add flour, baking soda, cinnamon, and salt. Blend just until batter is moist. Fold in remaining All-Bran cereal. (If desired, mix in up to 2 cups of suggested additions.*)

Spoon batter into muffin cups, filling each to the top. Bake 30 to 35 minutes, or until cake tester comes out clean. Makes 2 dozen.

*Suggested Additions

Mix-and-match up to 2 cups of any of the following ingredients:

1½ cups blueberries (fresh or frozen)
1 cup chocolate chips—any type
½ cup chopped walnuts or pecans
1 cup Craisins®, raisins, or dried cherries
1 cup chopped dates
1 cup chopped fresh cranberries
1½ cups chopped apples
½ cup coconut
1 cup pineapple tidbits, drained

CHAPTER 29

Sadie felt her eyebrows go up slowly and her smile become a little plastic as she put the pieces together and tried to look unsurprised. When she spoke, she stuttered. "O-oh," she said as though firing bullets. "I-it's wonderful to meet you." He probably thought she was touched in the head.

Desperate for a moment to compose herself, she turned back to the oven and took a deep breath while she turned it off. There were probably several perfectly reasonable reasons May's brother was having dinner with Keith Kelly last night. The problem was that Sadie couldn't think of a single one.

"Are you making Dad's ice cream?"

Food. Thank goodness. *That* was a topic she could always talk about.

Sadie schooled her thoughts and her expression and turned to face him. "Yes," she said. "May didn't dare show up at the picnic without bacon ice cream, so I'm trying my hand at it. It's unlike anything I've ever made before."

Hugh's smile was polite, but he stared at the bacon with an almost nostalgic expression. She wondered if her making his father's signature dessert made him uncomfortable, but wasn't sure how to ask about it.

"Hey, Hugh."

May came out of the hallway and entered the kitchen. She set the half-full yogurt container on the counter and put the spoon in the sink. So much for Jolene's appetite. Sadie watched for the siblings to embrace or something, but they kept their greeting rather cool. There was no way to know if it was because they had already had several days to become reacquainted or because they simply weren't close. Sadie sensed it was the latter.

"Hey, how's Jolene?"

May shrugged. "She ate about a tablespoon of yogurt." She flicked her eyes up to meet Hugh. "It's hard to say that's progress."

"Try organic unsweetened applesauce next time," Hugh suggested. "The chemicals in those store-bought yogurts aren't good for her, and her body is probably rebelling against them."

Ah, Hugh was a health nut.

The room was silent; May caught sight of the bacon and forced a smile. "Candied bacon," she said, seemingly eager to change the subject. "It's been a long time."

Hugh's tight expression caught Sadie's eye. "Not long enough, if you ask me."

May sighed. "Let's not go there right now," she said under her breath, pulling open the cupboard beneath the sink and throwing away the unfinished yogurt. "We're making the ice cream one final time in Dad's memory."

"If you ask me, *going there* when he was still alive might have made all the difference."

Sadie looked between the two of them, but was hesitant to insert herself. May, however, caught her eye and took pity on her position of ignorance in all this. "My father had heart issues," she reminded her.

"And ate things like bacon ice cream," Hugh added.

"Once a year," May countered.

"And pasteurized eggs for breakfast every morning, and homogenized milk three times a day that came from cows fed all kinds of antibiotics and chemicals," Hugh continued, getting more worked up by the minute. "He knew better. Making this in his place is morbid, if you ask me."

"Well, I didn't ask, did I?" May said in a tired voice. She put one hand on her hip and raised the other to massage the newly formed lines on her forehead. Hugh didn't seem to bring out the best in his little sister. "Lois wants you to come to the picnic too, so consider the invitation officially extended."

"I have some things to finish up at the shop," Hugh said in a neutral tone. Maybe he'd realized how he was coming across. "I'll come by if I can."

"I'll tell her," May said. She picked up the plate Sadie had fixed for her and lifted the tone of her voice in what Sadie assumed was a desire to get along with her brother. "Did you want to look in on Jolene? Is that why you stopped by?"

Hugh paused for a moment, then nodded, heading down the hallway.

Sadie watched him go but wondered if he really wanted to check on his sister, or if he'd stopped by specifically to steal the mail. As soon as he turned the corner, May gave Sadie an embarrassed smile. "Hugh's a vegan and only eats organic," she explained, getting herself a fork and sitting down on the same barstool Sadie had when she'd had her lunch. "And he thinks everyone else should too. He's convinced that the hormones in traditionally processed meat and dairy cause cancer, and it made him crazy that Dad didn't buy into it."

"Sounds like you don't buy into it either," Sadie suggested.

"Everything and nothing causes cancer," May said, using her fork to spear a blackberry, a strawberry, a spinach leaf, and a candied walnut to make a perfect bite. "You're either going to get it or you're not, and other than avoiding the obvious—like smoking and asbestos and radiation—there's not much you can do to prevent it if you're in the crosshairs." She took a bite and chewed quickly.

"You have a pretty strong opinion of that," Sadie said, leaning against the counter.

May focused on putting together her next bite. "My mother did all kinds of weird things to keep from getting cancer, and then to keep from dying from it—coffee enemas, liquid diets, homeopathic stuff. Nothing worked for her, or her sisters, or . . . anyone else I've ever known."

Sadie watched her, waiting for her to confide more information; this was the first she'd heard about May's mother's cancer from May herself.

May took another bite and smiled up at Sadie. "This is really good," she said. "Thanks."

"You're welcome," Sadie said and refrained from giving the woman a hug. She looked as though she could use one, but an uninvited hug didn't seem appropriate. Sadie was trying to decide whether to tell May about the stolen mail when Hugh returned.

"I'm back to the shop," he said, tapping the pile of mail he hadn't put into his shorts. "I brought this in." He looked between the two of them and might have smiled for a split second, it was hard to tell. He pulled his keys from his pocket, and Sadie couldn't help but notice the bright blue-and-red poker chip with a hole drilled through it that served as the key ring. He jiggled the keys in his hand as he turned toward the door. "I'll catch you later."

"Nice meeting you," Sadie said on the heels of May's "Bye." Hugh said good-bye and left through the front door, pulling it closed behind him with a snap.

"Hugh seems quite a bit older than you," Sadie finally said, hoping to keep May talking about her brother without touching on anything too sensitive.

"Five years," May said. "Jolene is two years older than he is."

"Quite a gap," Sadie said. "Is that one of the reasons why you aren't close?"

"One of them," May said simply. She took the last bite of her salad and swallowed. "You wanted the ice cream freezer, right?"

Sadie nodded, willing to let May off the conversation hook. They went out to the garage and eventually found the ice cream freezer, a 1970s model with a bucket made to look like a wooden barrel. Sadie thought of the hand-crank unit her parents had years and years ago. It was hard to imagine the determination it took to make ice cream back then, and she was grateful Jim's ice cream freezer had a motor.

In the kitchen, Sadie washed all the parts and laid them out on a dishtowel to dry while May ate her muffin and went through the stack of mail with her free hand, sorting it into piles.

"What's the criteria?" Sadie asked, nodding at the three stacks of mail.

May held half of the muffin aloft. "One for bills, one for junk, and one for everything else. Dad's attorney is taking care of the bills for us, so that's one thing I don't have to worry about."

"And Hugh's running the business, right?" Sadie asked.

May nodded and took another bite as she finished sorting.

"Is Jolene still doing the books?"

May shook her head. "Dad hired a gal last year when Jolene was diagnosed. She does all the books and office management stuff. Hugh does the rest."

"Quite a lot on Hugh's shoulders all of a sudden," Sadie said. "Is he doing okay having to do it all himself?"

May looked up at Sadie and held her eyes for a moment. "I don't mean to be rude," she said in a hesitant tone. "But I really prefer not to talk so much about my family."

She might not have meant to be rude, but Sadie was a little stung by the comment nonetheless. There were soft parts to May's personality, but she had an edge to her as well, and Sadie didn't like that part. Sadie shrugged and looked away. "I wasn't trying to be nosy, but knowing about your family helps me get a better feel for your dad and his life."

"I can see that," May said. "I just want to make sure we both keep our focus. Quite frankly, my family is dealing with so much that I don't want to violate their privacy right now. I also want to get things figured out as quick as possible, and spending time investigating my family isn't what I hired you to do."

"Of course," Sadie said, forcing a smile that wouldn't show her hurt feelings. Hurt or not, May was right; Sadie wasn't here to learn about May's family. If Sadie would stay on track, she wouldn't need reminders. "Speaking of which, I'd better get back to work until it's time to make the ice cream." She glanced at the bacon and decided it would be fine on the counter for a little while.

"The salad was wonderful," May said again, standing as Sadie headed out of the kitchen.

"I'm glad you liked it," Sadie said. She could hear the clip in her own words but doubted May would pick it up. She didn't know Sadie well enough to translate her tones.

Sadie picked up the stack of original files she'd made copies off—the copies were in her car—and headed toward the study. As she methodically sorted and stored, her thoughts kept returning to Hugh Sanderson. What had last night's dinner been about? Was it possible May knew about the meeting? She had seemed so incensed by the letter from Keith, it was hard to imagine she wouldn't care about Hugh meeting with him. What about the felonious mail theft? Maybe Hugh received some of his mail at the house. It was possible, but then why tuck it away like he did? The more she thought about things, she more she realized she needed to know. Things weren't lining up.

But May didn't want Sadie digging into family matters. As hard as it was to admit, May's resistance simply equated to increased curiosity on Sadie's part. Was May trying to hide something? It didn't make much sense for her to hire Sadie to investigate Keith Kelly if there was something suspect within May's own family. That line of thinking only brought Sadie back to needing to take May at her word—she wanted Sadie's focus on Keith Kelly and no one else. Not talking about her family was simply part of keeping Sadie from becoming too distracted. Still, it didn't settle right in Sadie's mind, though she tried to tell herself it was fine.

Nearly an hour passed before Sadie took a break from the files to work on the ice cream some more. May was on a stepladder, emptying the top cabinets. When she saw Sadie enter the kitchen, she offered a smile. "I was rude, wasn't I? About not wanting to talk about my family."

Sadie looked away and headed for the ice cream freezer parts she'd laid out. "I understand—you want me to focus. It's okay."

"I get a little sharp sometimes," May said, focusing on the cupboards and giving Sadie the impression that she didn't apologize easily and wanted to keep her hands busy.

"No big deal," Sadie said, committing to let it go since she was acting as though she was far less bothered than she had been. She pulled a paper towel off the roll and wiped it along the inside of the ice cream canister, hoping to accelerate the drying process. She hadn't considered that the humidity made drying dishes on the counter less effective than she was used to.

"My parents lived here for almost thirty years," May said, lifting a stack of plates from a high cupboard and taking careful steps down the ladder. She set them on the counter. "It makes for a lot of years to pack up."

"Yes, it does," Sadie said, putting the canister back on the counter and heading to the refrigerator for the milk and cream.

"What is it you do back in Ohio?"

"I'm a receptionist," May said. "For a research and development company."

"And you don't want to move back to Portland?" Sadie asked, hoping that asking questions about May wasn't as touchy as asking questions about her family.

"I'm not sure there's enough to come back to," she said, climbing the ladder again. "Now that Dad's gone, and with Jolene sick, I just . . . I don't know that there's more here than there is in Cleveland."

Sadie wanted to ask more questions, but didn't since the questions were about Jolene and Hugh and whether May would have much of a relationship with them once she left. It was sad to think she wouldn't.

"So, have you found anything else out about Keith? I haven't even asked you about yesterday's surveillance."

"It was pretty boring," Sadie said, and that was true . . . for the first eight hours. The last two hours, however, had been pretty interesting. She wasn't ready to tell May about that, yet. Sadie doubted May would take Hugh's dinner with the Kellys well right now. She chose to focus on something else. "From what I've read in your dad's files, I don't think he trusted Keith, even when they were partners. The contracts were so fastidious and to the letter; they don't read like an agreement between friends." Yet even as Sadie talked about Keith, her thoughts were on Hugh and his secrets. The fact was that right now, Hugh was far more interesting than Keith.

"Really?" May said. Sadie could see her mentally picking apart the comment as though searching for some kind of validation in it.

"Just a gut reaction on my part, of course," Sadie said. She reached for the cutting board propped up against the wall behind the sink and put it on the counter before transferring the bacon to it and extracting a chef's knife from the butcher block.

"I wish I'd paid more attention," May said. "I didn't until things fell apart, and, of course, everything seemed suspect after that."

She asked for details from the files, and Sadie relayed what she could remember while she finished mixing the ice cream, then put the base in the freezer to chill.

May's Blackberry rang with those chirping birds again, and she stepped outside to talk to whoever was on the other end. After the side door closed, Sadie wondered if Lois might be a good resource for family information. She'd known the Sanderson family for a long time, after all. Maybe Sadie could find a way to talk to her at the picnic tonight. And then Sadie remembered the personal filing cabinet. There might be information about Hugh in one of the files.

The ice cream was chilling, May was distracted, and there were drawers full of information only a few yards away. It couldn't hurt to read up on what parts of Hugh's life Jim had held on to. Maybe she could get more of a feel for him that way.

She walked quietly to the side door and leaned close enough to hear May talking, though the words didn't come through. Whoever she was talking to was getting an earful, though. Sadie had the perfect opportunity. She hurried toward the study and closed the door quietly; she'd only need a minute to swap Hugh's file with a business one that she could then take to the hotel with her. May wouldn't miss it until tomorrow—if at all.

She headed directly for the family filing cabinet. She wrapped her fingers around the slender silver handle and pulled. Nothing happened. She pulled again and only then did her eyes drift to the lock at the top of the cabinet. Between now and the time she'd first looked at the contents of this cabinet, someone had locked her out.

CHAPTER 30

Sadie immediately thought of her lock pick set. She knew from her research that filing cabinet locks were pretty easy to pick because they used a wafer system to raise and lower the single pin. Sadie hurried to the kitchen and retrieved her purse. May was just coming inside, so Sadie pretended she was looking for gum.

"I better get a shower before the picnic," May said, still holding her phone. "I've been packing up stuff all day. Are you okay for a minute?"

"Absolutely," Sadie said, finding a lone piece of Trident in the bottom of her purse. She unwrapped it and popped it in her mouth. It was rock hard. "I'll jus be in du stuhy," she said, trying to bite through the gum. Rather than attempt talking again, she smiled instead.

"Okay," May said. "I'll only be a few minutes."

Sadie tucked the petrified gum into her cheek. "No rush," she said innocently. "Take your time." She headed back to the study while May headed down the other hall, but slowed her steps as she neared the door. As soon as she heard a door shut in the other hall, she turned and tiptoed quickly back to the kitchen and grabbed her whole purse.

Once back in the study, with the door shut, she spit out the gum, removed her lock pick set, and went to work. She pulled open one of the business cabinet drawers so that it would look like she was working on those files, then went to the other cabinet and took a breath. This was the first lock she'd picked for real rather than for practice. It was a little intense. She hoped filing cabinet locks were as easy as the website promised.

After two minutes, she was sweating bullets and getting more and more anxious. How on earth would Sadie explain why she was digging metal sticks into the filing cabinet lock? She could feel the pressure she needed to lift, but felt as though she was already pushing too hard. She knew from experience that pin locks jammed rather easily, but the only thing she could think of to do was apply more pressure. She wondered why she'd never practiced on her own filing cabinets at home.

She pushed a little harder, then harder still, and was about to give up for the sake of her blood pressure when she finally felt the snap. For an instant, she thought she'd broken the pick, but when she pulled the handle, the drawer slid open. She smiled to herself and then looked quickly at the door.

No way could she risk May coming in now. She closed the drawer and opened the study door a crack.

"May?" she called.

There was no answer, so she closed the door and ran for the cabinet. Bingo. A file marked "Hugh" was right between "Homestead Insurance" and "Internet Info." Sadie shut the drawer and swapped the contents of Hugh's file with the contents of one of the business files she'd already put in a storage box. She quickly grabbed a couple more business files and stacked them on top of Hugh's. Then she took a deep breath, checked the hallway again by calling for May, and returned to the filing cabinet to relock it.

She came up short. She knew how to pick a lock, but unpicking it? How did that work? Her heart immediately started racing. If the filing cabinet wasn't locked, May would be suspicious. Why hadn't Sadie thought of that earlier?

Desperate for her own self-preservation, she put Hugh's file folder—now holding commercial tax rate information—back in its place in the personal file and shut the drawer. Maybe May wouldn't remember locking it, but it was pretty obvious she'd locked it to specifically keep Sadie out.

Maybe she wouldn't check for a couple of days, but that seemed too much to hope for. Where did they keep the key? Sadie went to the desk drawer and fumbled through the contents. It wasn't there. Next she looked through a pottery dish that held an assortment of odds and ends—nothing there either. She could sense she was running out of time. May had been in the shower for at least ten full minutes.

She'd have to jam the drawer shut for now—but how? There were several binders in the bookcase, and Sadie grabbed one. She was about to wedge it on top of the files in such a way that when she pushed the drawer closed, the binder would raise up and prevent the drawer from opening, when she noticed another file in the drawer, not far from Hugh's fake one. "Key duplicates."

Could it be that easy? She grabbed the file and opened it to find a piece of cardstock with five keys taped to the page. Scrawling handwriting identified them as house, garage, car door, and car ignition. At the very bottom, looking rather pathetic next to all the real keys, was a small, silver key about two inches long with the words "filing cabinet" written beneath it.

Bless your heart, Jim Sanderson.

Sadie took the filing cabinet key off the paper and promptly returned the rest of the keys to the folder before snapping the drawer shut, locking it up, and stashing the key in the desk drawer. May wouldn't think to check the file to look for the key, would she? Sadie wiped sweat from her forehead; this was a little too much anxiety. She needed to take a break, and maybe have another muffin. Hoping she looked calm, and would *feel* calm in a few minutes, she picked up the stack of files from the desk. She was halfway across the room when the door opened, causing her to startle.

"Sorry about that," May said as she entered. She'd changed into jeans and a black, V-neck T-shirt that was quite flattering. Her hair was wrapped in a pink towel. "Everything okay?" She scanned the office and seemed to let her gaze linger on the personal filing cabinet a little longer than anything else.

"Everything's fine," Sadie said, hoping her breathing appeared normal. She held up the stack of files. "I found a few more papers I needed to make copies of."

"Right now?" May asked. She glanced at her watch. "Isn't it about time to finish up the ice cream?"

Sadie looked at the clock on Jim's desk. It was almost six o'clock. Time flew when you were afraid of being caught. "I guess it is," she said, not sure what to do.

"You can take the files with you after the dinner and make copies before you come back tomorrow," May suggested.

Sadie wondered if the offer was evidence of May feeling a little guilty for locking the personal filing cabinet in the first place. May seemed to make spontaneous decisions she thought better of later.

"That would be great," Sadie said. "In that case, let me just finish this one file drawer, and I'll be right there."

"Okay," May said. "I'm going to look in on Jolene—Gary should be here any minute—and finish getting myself ready."

Sadie smiled and nodded like the good girl she was pretending to be, but it was hard for her to meet May's eyes as the guilt set in. May left, and Sadie reflected on the fact that she was going against May's wishes. But it felt equally wrong to ignore her concerns about Hugh. She prayed it wouldn't explode in her face.

She left the files on the desk and went into the kitchen to work on the ice cream. May returned ten minutes later, her hair still damp but drying into soft waves. She had her makeup on and black flip-flops on her feet. She smiled hello at Sadie before heading back to work on another cupboard.

Sadie's phone rang as she was pouring ice and salt into the ice cream freezer. May looked at Sadie's purse.

"I'll call them back," Sadie said. "I'm not in a good stopping place." She added a layer of ice, a layer of salt, and than another layer of ice before the bucket was full. Her phone chirped to indicate she had a message. Sadie plugged in the freezer. The sound of the motor was horrible, and she turned it off immediately. "That's loud," she said.

"My dad always ran it in the garage," May said.

"Oh, good idea," Sadie said, though the ice would definitely melt faster out there. "I'll take it out and check my messages."

May nodded, and Sadie slipped her phone in her pocket before picking up the now very heavy ice cream freezer. She took slow and careful steps down the back stairs and into the garage; her arms were shaking by the time she put it down. She plugged in the freezer and then stepped out of the garage, pulling the door closed and effectively muting the horrible grating of the motor.

She retrieved her phone to see who'd called, but as soon as she saw the number, her eyes narrowed. Jane Seeley again. This time, however, she'd left a voice mail. For a moment, Sadie considered deleting the message without listening to it, but, no, there was no way she could *not* listen to what Jane had to say.

She quickly called her voice mail, bracing herself for the worst. "Sadie? It's Jane. You'll be pleased to know that I got written up for the article I wrote, and as part of the deal, I've been asked to write a retraction. It will be going into tomorrow's paper." A long pause atypical for messages ensued. When she spoke again, her voice sounded different. "On a personal note, I would also like to offer you an apology. It really wasn't my intent to make things difficult for you; in fact, I thought you would be flattered by the attention. If there's something I can do beyond the retraction to make up for whatever harm I've caused, I hope you'll let me do so."

Sadie nearly snorted at the idea of going to Jane for help. The retraction was nice, and she was grateful she'd taken the time to lodge the complaint about it, but she didn't trust Jane's assertion that she wanted to make it right. She couldn't help but reflect on Pete's comment about a retraction being buried in some obscure section of the paper. How many people would read it? And of those who did read it, how many would be able to pretend they'd never read the original article?

She hoped she'd never hear from Jane again, though the apology did make her a little more sympathetic. The retraction would hurt Jane professionally even if she didn't understand the moral damage she'd done to Sadie's reputation. It would be nice if there was some solution, but life didn't work that way. Choice meant consequence—you couldn't control the latter unless you controlled the former. Sadie deleted the message, glad to feel a sense of finality about the whole situation.

"Sadie?"

She looked up from where she was standing in the shade of the garage. May was at the back door. "I need to get down some platters that have probably been up here for more than ten years. They're kind of heavy, and I'm afraid I might lose my balance. Could you help me?"

"Of course," Sadie said, slipping her phone into her pocket. "I'd love to." May asking her for help was a good sign.

CHAPTER 31

"Hi, Lois," Sadie said, coming up while Lois made a fan of multicolored napkins on the table that ran along the far side of Lois's fenced yard. She'd helped May with the platters, and then assisted her with a couple more cupboards before it was time to go to the picnic. May had been grateful for the help, and Sadie was glad to have the earlier tension softened between them.

"What a party!" Sadie added, scanning the beautifully landscaped backyard. There were trees around almost the entire perimeter, offering plenty of shade, and rose trellises here and there, interspersed with what Sadie thought were tomato plants, though you wouldn't guess it right away because they blended with the flowers so well. There were two barbeque grills sending up smoke signals on the other side of the patio and clusters of people sipping drinks and chatting with one another while they waited for the meat to finish cooking.

"Isn't it great?" Lois said, looking around as well, a satisfied smile on her over-lipsticked lips. "Some of my favorite people in the world are here." She looked at May, and her smiled turned from satisfaction to contentment. The difference was subtle, but Sadie could tell how pleased she was that May had come. "Did Gary take Jolene home? I was hoping he'd stop in for a minute."

Sadie frowned. "He called and said he was running late. Jolene apparently insisted May come anyway."

"Typical Jo-Jo," Lois said with a smile. "Always thinking about everyone else."

Sadie appreciated the optimism. "May wrapped the ice cream container in an old mohair blanket to keep it insulated until the dessert bar opens."

"Oh, good," Lois replied. "She put it on the dessert table?"

There had been two other blanket-wrapped containers when May had set hers down. "As soon as her arms were free, she was hugged and swept up in 'I haven't seen you in ages' conversations."

"Excellent," Lois said. "That's exactly what I had hoped would happen."

Lois fussed with the napkins. Sadie looked for something else to say to keep the conversation going with the only other person she knew at this party besides May. "Your muffins were amazing, by the way. I hope you don't mind that May let me copy the recipe from Leena's file."

Lois looked up from her napkin arranging. "Are you kidding? I'm flattered you enjoyed them so much." She leaned toward Sadie and said conspiratorially, "They're deceptively easy to make, aren't they?"

Sadie nodded. "Which makes them even better."

Lois beamed. "Thank you for your help in getting May to the party. We just love that girl, and I keep hoping one day she'll come back home for good."

Sadie's gaze flickered to May, who seemed to be relaxing now that they were here. Connecting with old friends was always good for the soul. "It's good for her to get reacquainted," she said. "Other than the funeral, it's been a long time since she's been here, hasn't it?"

Lois nodded, placing the last short stack of napkins on the table and cocking her head to the side. She made a final adjustment. "It certainly has been," she said, frowning.

"It amazes me how she can smile through it all."

"Well, that's May," Lois said brightly. "Leena used to say that we didn't need as much sunshine as the rest of the world because we had May in ours. Of course, as much as I hate to say it, she's lost some of that brightness that came so easy when she was young."

"I guess life has a way of doing that."

"Yes," Lois said. "I suppose that's true."

"I take it you and May's mother were close," Sadie said, hoping to learn more family information from this woman who obviously knew the Sandersons very well.

Lois nodded. "Bart and I moved to the neighborhood a few years after Jim and Leena. May's mother was my very best friend."

"It must have been very hard when she passed."

"The hardest," Lois said, thoughtfully. "I've lost two husbands after long illnesses, which wasn't any easier, but there's something about a young mother leaving children behind that . . . " She cleared her throat. "That makes it twice as painful. I've done everything I can to take those kids under my wing since then."

"That's wonderful," Sadie said, tears rising. She didn't know these people very well, but it broke her heart to hear about the trag-edies May's family had experienced. She was glad they had people like Lois to help try to fill the void left behind.

A man with an apron that said "Kick the Cook" brought over a platter of hamburgers. "I think we're ready to get dinner started," he said, putting the platter in the space Lois made between the potluck dishes. It was affirming to know that, though she was far from home, there were familiar rituals that made Sadie feel so comfortable with these people. "The veggie burgers still need another couple of minutes." Well, not everything was familiar.

Lois signaled to one of the men lording over the barbeque grills, and he emitted a shrill whistle that made Sadie jump. However, it did the trick, and the conversations muted as everyone automatically turned to Lois. Clearly, they'd done this before. A man in his thirties appeared at Lois's side and helped her step up onto a wooden chair. He stayed close by, for which Sadie was grateful. Women Lois's age shouldn't stand on chairs; it wasn't safe. But it was effective in that she set herself above the crowd, if only barely, due to the fact that she was so petite.

"I am so thrilled to see so many of you here tonight," Lois said once she had her balance, clasping her hands in front of her chest. "This is the highlight of my summer, and we are so lucky to have so many wonderful friends living close by." A murmur of agreement wove through the crowd.

Sadie nodded right along with them, even though she was a stranger. The good-neighborliness was contagious.

Lois continued. "I would like to especially welcome our own Sharla-May." Heads turned to look at May, who ducked her head and smiled. "We all miss Jim so very much." A blanket of sorrow fell on the crowd. "But we are so happy to have part of him here with us tonight, and not just in Sharla-May." The tone of her voice lifted, and the mood seemed to follow it. Lois had power with these people. "She brought Jim's famous bacon ice cream." A cheer went up, and Lois grinned. "Well, enough of this talk. Let's eat—just remember to hold off on the desserts until after you've had dinner." She wagged her finger at the group and closed one eye. "I'll be watching."

Everyone laughed, and the man who'd stood guard helped Lois down from the chair.

Within seconds, people were dishing up hamburgers and salads, laughing with each other, and commenting on Dorothy's famous three-bean salad and Sherri's homemade mustard pickles. This really did seem to be a highlight of the summer, and it made Sadie miss her own neighborhood get-togethers. Thinking about home caused her smile to falter a bit, though. She hoped that things would return to normal when she got back to Garrison, but the hope didn't quiet the fear completely.

Rather than get lost in her thoughts, however, Sadie stayed on the edges of May's conversations, speaking when spoken too, but mostly just listening to May give updates about her life to people she hadn't seen for a long time. It was informative, though Sadie didn't learn much beyond what she already knew. Quite frankly, May didn't have much in her life other than her work, which wasn't particularly interesting. She didn't talk about a boyfriend or hobbies, and Sadie became certain that May's life in Ohio was a rather lonely one.

They continued eating and chatting, but as soon as Sadie saw Lois uncovering desserts at the dessert table she excused herself.

"Can I help serve?" Sadie asked Lois. She put her empty plate in the trash and wiped her hands on a napkin.

"Oh, certainly." Lois pointed at one of the ice cream canisters. "We need to take off the blankets, and then we need a server for each ice cream flavor. We can't let people serve themselves or half the group ends up without anything at all."

By the time Sadie had removed the blankets, May had taken her place behind her dad's ice cream freezer. Sadie smiled at her and settled in behind what looked like strawberry ice cream just in time for another shrill whistle and Lois's invitation for people to now swarm the dessert table.

Sadie smiled at the people waiting for her scoop, introducing herself when needed, and looking into all these faces in hopes she could remember them to make notes later. She'd belatedly remembered her reason to be here was to talk to the neighbors about what they might have seen the night Jim died. It was hard to focus with so much going on. It wasn't until her container was half gone that she realized May wasn't at the dessert table anymore. Instead, her canister and lid sat alone on the far end of the table. A teenage boy hurried to it, looked inside, and frowned. The bacon ice cream was gone, and Sadie kicked herself for not getting a scoop. She'd really wanted to try it.

"Well, the crowds are thinning," Lois said from behind Sadie. "We can just put the tops on and let people serve themselves from here on out. Thanks for your help."

"Of course," Sadie said.

"So, what's your poison?" Lois asked. "And don't tell me you're on some kind of diet. We all agree that there are no calories allowed at the summer picnic."

Sadie laughed. "Calories would be tragic," she said, looking at the freezers. "I think I'll just stick with this one," she said, indicating her own container. Mostly she just didn't want Lois to serve her. Despite the older woman's obvious vitality, she'd been running at full throttle all evening. Sadie dished herself up a bowl of strawberry while Lois chose a bowl of peach. Sadie might try that one next. She'd need to be sure and satisfy herself, otherwise she'd pine for the bacon ice cream all night. Once Lois had served herself, and Sadie had filled a plate with the picked-over desserts, the two of them mutually retired to a row of chairs at the edge of the patio.

"I met Hugh for the first time this afternoon," Sadie said, watching Lois carefully. She wasn't disappointed. The slight tightening around Lois's eyes betrayed that she was not quite as fond of Hugh as she was of May. Rather than supply a direction for the conversation to follow, Sadie took a bite of ice cream and hoped Lois would pick up the thread of conversation for her.

"I hope he was polite," Lois said.

"I suppose he could have been worse," Sadie said. "I've been trying to figure him out ever since. There's something . . . evasive about him."

Lois flicked a look in Sadie's direction, and Sadie felt her heart rate pick up a little bit. Lois agreed with her. Sadie could only hope she'd confirm it out loud.

"That sounds about right," Lois said, taking a small bite. "He cloaks his weaknesses in piety and complains when other people judge."

"Piety?" Sadie repeated. "Religion?"

"Not that kind of piety," Lois said. "He's one of those vegan people," she said with a wave of her hand and a roll of her eyes. "He can't sit down to a meal without trying to convert you. If you ask me, however, if I'm ever going to convert to anyone else's way of doing things, they'd better convince me that it makes them happy. Life is too short and too fraught with road hazards for me to do something on purpose that makes me miserable."

"I'll eat to that," Sadie said, lifting her spoon as though making a toast and taking a bite of ice cream. That very philosophy was why Sadie hadn't crumbled after Neil had died, and why she didn't really mind the extra twenty pounds on her backside. Life was meant to be enjoyed, and when it wasn't, then something was wrong.

"I'm interested to see how he'll manage with the whole business in his lap now," Sadie said.

"Especially without Jim there to save him anymore."

Ding, ding, ding. Sadie was on to something. "Exactly."

Lois took another bite and looked at Sadie carefully. "Did May say something about the handouts?"

"Not much," Sadie said. "Mostly, he just didn't strike me as the kind of guy I'd want overseeing my interests in the company, that's all."

Lois took a few bites. "I've had the same concerns," she finally said. "But I don't want to burden May with borrowed trouble."

"Of course not," Sadie said. "She's in no position to carry more than she already is. I'm just trying to get to know May's family, and I'm curious about Hugh. If he can't manage his life, well, that says a lot about him. And if Jim was willing to bail him out, that says a lot about Jim."

Lois considered that, but soon enough Sadie saw her let down her guard. Lois liked to tell a story, and Sadie was all ears. "That boy has cost his parents so much money," she said. "Jim became more tightfisted those last few years, though."

"Oh," Sadie said, unsure whether Lois was for or against Jim's actions. "With that kind of financial history, do you think Hugh can run the business?" Sadie said, jumping to conclusions and hoping that Lois would revise them.

"He knows the business," Lois said, stirring her ice cream slowly. "I won't argue that, but, well . . ." She looked to where May was talking to an older couple. "Hugh's always been rather high maintenance."

"That's what I figured," Sadie said, though she didn't really understand what Lois meant. She tried a different tack. "I heard he was part of the reason for the fallout Jim had with a business partner a few years back."

"He wasn't just *part* of it," Lois said. "He was ninety percent of the problem. What did May say about it?"

"That Jim's partner didn't want Hugh to be a supervisor because he didn't have a degree." Sadie realized that was the same reason Keith had told Richard to go to school, at least until it worked better for Keith for his son not to have that degree. Interesting hypocrisy. "I sensed there might be more to it than that."

"Did May give you that impression?" Lois asked intently, forcing Sadie to tell the truth.

"No," Sadie said, studying Lois as casually as possible in hopes it would guide her forward. This was a fragile conversation, and she needed to proceed with caution. "May only mentioned the degree and Mr. Kelly's lack of character as the reasons. After meeting Hugh, though, I found something a little distrustful in him and wondered if the issues the business partner had with him were more than educational. But, then, if that were true, why wouldn't May know about it?"

"Jim didn't want anything coming between his children," Lois said, but Sadie sensed more.

"I see, but you knew the real reason for the company split? Or at least Hugh's part in it?"

Lois shrugged and leaned toward Sadie. "Don't tell anyone, but I'm a bit of a busybody so I know more than even Jim thought," she said in a whisper, though her tone showed how pleased she was to have this tidbit to share. "The fact is that Jim took out a second mortgage on the house to pay off Hugh's debts."

"No!" Sadie said in hushed tones, playing up the shock factor.

Lois's eyes sparkled, and she nodded quickly. "He used my son-in-law's title company, and a little peek here and there laid it all out for me. Jolene and May never knew a thing about it, though it might have come out in settling the estate, I don't know." She sat back in her chair looking pleased.

"She hasn't said anything about it to me," Sadie said, shaking her head. "A second mortgage." She tsked. The debts must have been too high to simply work out a payment plan. "How did Hugh manage to get into that much debt? He would have been in his late twenties back then, right?" She didn't suppose that Hugh had a shoe obsession, which was the only debt-creating vice Sadie feared falling into herself.

"Chips and sips," Lois said.

Sadie frowned. What did that mean? Lois noticed and explained. "Gambling and booze. A dangerous combination."

"Absolutely," Sadie said, remembering the poker chip on Hugh's key chain. "Is he still drinking and gambling?"

Lois raised an eyebrow. "You met him—what do you think?"

Good point, Sadie thought as she reflected on Hugh's demeanor and obvious tension each time she'd observed him. "Isn't that kind of weird? I mean, a vegan alcoholic gambler?"

Lois laughed and patted Sadie on the knee. "If you lived in Portland, you wouldn't ask that kind of question. Hugh is who he is. The drinking and gambling is one thing, but I think his food issue is all caught up in the fear of dying. We all have it—some worse than others. He's got a lot of holes he's trying to fill up. He's just more creative than most on how he fills them. Don't get me wrong, I love that boy like my own son, but he worries me a great deal too."

They ate a few bites before Sadie spoke again. "So, Jim got a second mortgage to pay off Hugh's debts, which was the reason he split with his business partner. I'm guessing that wasn't the only time Jim bailed out Hugh, though, right?"

Lois shrugged. "I can't be sure. But little things Jim and Jolene have said over the years make me think Hugh still has financial issues. Did you see his truck? He's been driving it since high school. Anyone who could afford it would have bought a new one by now."

"I think May needs to know about these concerns," Sadie said. "Maybe she can get some safeguards in place."

Lois let out a breath. "I don't want to make this a heavier burden on her; she's already carrying so much."

"Better now than after things go south," Sadie said.

Lois shrugged, but obviously didn't love the idea, so Sadie decided to drop it. The sun was going down, casting a stillness over the evening. Lois had white Christmas lights wrapped around the beams of her covered porch, and they flickered on, though it was bright enough outside that they didn't stand out like they would in another half an hour. The mosquitoes were out too, and Sadie slapped at one hovering by her ear.

"I'm curious," Sadie began after lining up her next items of interest. "After the fallout of SK Systems, did Jim ever talk about Keith Kelly much?"

Lois shrugged. "Now and again, but not often. It was a painful split, and Jim didn't like to revisit it."

"So, he hadn't talked about his former partner recently?" Sadie asked, hoping she still sounded casual.

"Not to me, but, well . . . I looked out for Jim in little ways—taking him bread, letting in service people when he needed repairs done on his house—but I'm much closer to his children, and none of them have said anything about Keith other than the letter he sent them." She shook her head. "He's like a shark going after blood in the water."

"What about Richard Kelly? Has anyone talked about him lately?"

She suddenly had Lois's full attention, which made her a little uncomfortable. "Richard Kelly?"

Sadie nodded and hoped she wasn't blowing her cover by asking too many questions.

"Jim hasn't mentioned him for years, and no one else would bring him up," Lois said. She was watching May again, and Sadie followed her eyes. "He's the reason May left Portland, you know. The thought of running into him was more than May could take. No one talks about him; I can't remember the last time I even heard his name, really."

"She really loved him, didn't she?"

"He was her moon and stars," Lois said softly, looking into her ice cream as she reflected on the memory. "Richard was there for May when Leena died. He helped give her the stability she needed as her family defined themselves again. After he ended the relationship, she was just . . . lost. Jolene was the same way, you know, which is why Gary was such a great match for her; he kind of bridged that gap between the before-Leena-died and after. Of course, I did my part as well, but Jolene and Gary were a good match. May never found out if things could have been that way for her and Richard, so she never really got closure."

Lois looked up and sighed, and Sadie glanced over at May again. May was holding someone's baby, and Sadie was so struck by the expression on her face that she momentarily forgot the line of conversation.

May ran her finger along the hairline of the sleeping infant—no more than a few months old, if Sadie wasn't mistaken. May's smile was reverent, her eyes heavy with . . . longing? Sadie felt her own heart tighten. She knew the feeling reflected on May's face—knew it well. The woman sitting next to May said something, causing May to look up. May pulled the bundle even closer to her chest as though afraid she was going to be asked to give it back to its mother. Instead, the woman pointed to the dessert buffet. May nodded eagerly and was left alone with the baby, that same soft look returning to her face.

"How could she have thought the relationship would work after the company fell apart, though?" Sadie asked. "With the animosity between Keith and Jim, it would be practically impossible for May and Richard to ever really make things work."

"I told her that once, too, but she felt sure that she and Richard could heal the gap." She rolled her eyes. "Us old ladies know better, but those kids still thought love conquered all. When that crashed, May did too. I had hoped she would find someone in Ohio, but I guess she didn't." She turned to look at Sadie. "Is she seeing anyone?"

"Not that I know of," Sadie said honestly. "Maybe she never really got over him."

Lois nodded, a sad expression on her face. "Maybe she gave up."

"On love?"

"On a lot of things," Lois said. Her ice cream was gone, but she balanced the empty bowl on one knee, which was crossed over the other one. "When Jeremy died about a year before the company split, she took it hard, just like the rest of us."

"Jeremy?" Sadie repeated, scanning her brain for the name.

"Jolene and Gary's younger son," Lois said, her face reflecting her confusion. "Didn't May tell you about him?"

"No," Sadie said with conviction. "She hasn't said anything about him."

CHAPTER 32

Sadie listened carefully to Lois's story about Jolene's second child. Her older boy, Bryce, was at school in Seattle, and the one mentioned in the legal trust, which had specifically mentioned Jolene's *living* son. Jeremy, on the other hand, had developed leukemia at the age of nine and had died two years later after all treatments had been exhausted.

"That poor family," Sadie said when Lois finished. "How do they stand it?"

Lois shook her head. "Everyone finds ways to cope. Jolene and Gary had Bryce and each other, and me and Jim. Maybe May's coping mechanism was to not create those connections because they hurt when they break."

"If that's true, it's tragic," Sadie added. "I cannot imagine my life without my children. They are my life's greatest accomplishment."

"You and me both," Lois said. "And it would be a shame if May never experienced that joy because of her fear of the unknown. She would make a wonderful mother. I wish she could accept that we have more choices then we think we do when things get hard. We don't have to suffer through our trials, and the people we love don't have to suffer with us. After every tragedy, it seems there's a rebirth of some kind—a new awareness or an appreciation for the person they lost. It's really rather beautiful, if you ask me."

Sadie reflected on that. "Yes, there is beauty in overcoming sorrow. But if you get stuck in the heartache, it feels as though the sun will never rise. I can see how someone like May might feel that way."

"Me too," Lois said, uncrossing her legs and setting her empty ice cream bowl on the table. "I just wish there was a way to fix it. But I won't be the one to ask her about it. I hate bringing up any of those tender topics with May."

Sadie nearly said "Me too," but then realized she might have to ask about such things at some point so she ought not rule it out. They were both watching May now, who was reluctantly relinquishing the baby back to the arms of its mother, when Sadie's phone rang, startling her. She fumbled to pull it from her pocket, her heart skipping a beat when she saw the name—Richard Kelly; she'd programmed his number into her phone last night. She immediately turned the screen away from Lois so she wouldn't see the name, counting on the other woman's elderly eyesight more than her own quick reflexes.

"I've got to take this," she said, standing. "If you'll excuse me."

"Of course," Lois said, standing up as well. "I need more ice cream anyway."

Sadie hurried toward the fence line and put the phone to her ear. "Hello," she said as she took the last few steps, keeping her voice low despite being fairly isolated. "Richard?"

"Yes," Richard said. "I was able to get the password to Dad's online calendar."

A thrill swept through Sadie's body. "Oh, wow," she said,

immediately jumping to what her next step should be. She couldn't think of anything. "Um, what should we do now?"

"Well, since it's online, I could meet you somewhere, and we could look at it together. Do you have a computer?"

"I do," Sadie said. "How about my hotel"—she looked at her watch—"at nine o'clock?" That should give her time to finish up at the picnic as well as review the copies of both Keith's files and Hugh's before she met with Richard. She could use the transition time.

"Sure," Richard said. "I'll be there."

"Great," Sadie said. She hung up, then turned back to the group, eager to leave. It certainly hadn't been a wasted evening. She'd learned a lot from Lois, but having access to Keith Kelly's appointment book was big, too. She hoped that May wouldn't ask too many questions too soon about what information she'd been able to get from the neighbors. The only person Sadie had really talked to was Lois, and Lois hadn't given her what May would want Sadie to have received.

Sadie worried it would be hard to leave May so quickly, but when Sadie said she was ready to head back to the hotel, May chose to stay at the party. Sadie said her good-byes to Lois and the few people she could remember names for, and then headed back to May's house to collect the files she'd left behind.

She let herself in through the kitchen door and headed back to the study, coming up short when she realized the study door was closed and the light was on. In the darkened house, the light bled through the cracks around the doorway. Sadie approached with tentative steps. She'd had no need for the lights to be on when she'd been sorting through files that afternoon, and she'd left the door open when she'd left for the picnic. Hugh's file was sitting on the desk; she couldn't leave without it.

She pressed her ear to the door and listened carefully. She could hear tapping—typing, maybe—but little else. If there was more than one person in there, they would probably be talking. She continued listening while debating her options. She could go in and confront whoever was in there, which was her first inclination, or she could wait for them to come out. This wasn't her house, so she had little authority to make a complaint, but that led her to the realization that this wasn't *anyone's* house. She, therefore, had as much right as anyone else to confront an intruder.

Weapons. She knew from previous experience it was unwise to face confrontations of this nature unarmed. She tiptoed back into the kitchen and considered ways to arm herself, wishing she'd thought to bring her blackjack. A knife was out of the question because she couldn't imagine stabbing anyone if it came down to it. Blunt force, however, she could live with. She carefully pulled open drawers, frowning when she found the marble rolling pin— too heavy and brutal for Sadie's tastes. She would have to settle for something else, but what? A cookie sheet? Perhaps a glass mixing bowl? The unwillingness to use knives limited her options. She was weighing out the merit of the pan versus the bowl—literally, which was easier to wield—when she heard shuffling footsteps in the hallway. She looked up in time to see what at first appeared to be a very old woman turn the corner of the kitchen. She came up short when she saw Sadie standing there, a cookie sheet in one hand and a large mixing bowl in the other.

"Oh," they both said in unison.

They then both paused in unison as well. It took Sadie only a moment to realize she was likely looking at Jolene, who was supposed to have been picked up by her husband well over an hour ago. While Jolene looked older than Sadie, she realized, upon further inspection, that Jolene's appearance was deceptive due to her illness. She wore a scarf tied over her head, and her skin was pallid and her face had an emaciated look to it. Wireless glasses balanced on her nose, and she pushed them back against her face with one hand. Her thin shoulders pulled inward, causing her to appear somewhat hunched. Though Jolene was probably in her forties, Lois exuded more health and well-being than this woman did; she did not look to be on the road to recovery. Oh, this poor family.

Sadie lowered the pan and bowl, grateful beyond words that she hadn't stormed into the study with either one of the kitchen items raised over her head in attack. She didn't imagine that would be a healthy event for Jolene. "I'm Sadie. May's friend."

"Is May here?" Jolene said, making a cursory scan of the kitchen.

"She stayed at the picnic," Sadie said. "I was going to head back to my hotel, but I needed to get my things."

Jolene looked at the cookie sheet and mixing bowl with confusion.

"And . . . I was putting away some dishes," Sadie added before doing just that, sliding the cookie sheet and the mixing bowl in the cupboards from where she'd removed them. "Um, I'm assuming you're Jolene?" Her voice raised at the end, making it a question.

Jolene nodded. "I had to walk around a little. I've been in that bed all day and couldn't stand it anymore."

Sadie smiled sympathetically. "I can imagine," she said, wondering if she should share her sympathies. It seemed out of place, since they'd only just met. "Can I get you something?" she asked.

Jolene waved the offer away and took a step toward the hallway that led to her room. "Oh, I don't mean to bother—"

"It's no bother," Sadie assured her. "Truly. I could make some scrambled eggs, maybe, or open a soda for you."

Jolene hesitated, and Sadie hurried to the fridge, pulling open the door. "We've got grapes, some yogurt, and some Jell-O cups." She looked at Jolene over the door of the refrigerator. "Do any of those sound good?"

"Is there any red Jell-O?"

Sadie nodded and reached for a cup. "One red Jell-O, coming up." She pulled off the foil lid and found a spoon, placing the cup on the counter as Jolene slid into one of the three barstools pushed up against the overhang of the island. Sadie turned to the cupboard, only to realize all the glasses were packed away. No matter. She went to the closest box and unwrapped a glass before rinsing it and then filling it with water from the fridge. Hydration was an important element of healing. She set the glass down in front of Jolene and watched as Jolene raised a spoonful of gelatin to her mouth.

"Can I get you anything else?" Sadie asked, busying herself with wiping down the counter so that Jolene wouldn't feel like Sadie was hovering.

"This is fine," Jolene said. "Thank you." Sadie wiped the counters some more until Jolene finally broke the silence. "It's sure nice of you to come up here and help May. I wish I had more to offer."

"It's no trouble at all," Sadie said. "My dad passed away a few years ago, so I understand the difficulty of . . . putting . . . things . . . in order." She swallowed and berated herself for talking about death to a woman who was sick.

Jolene peered at her from behind her glasses, a knowing look in her eye. "Please don't abridge conversation on my account," she said. "I know it doesn't look it, but I'm actually beating this thing. The doctors are very optimistic."

"Really?" Sadie said, then cleared her throat when she realized she sounded a bit too surprised. "I mean, I'm so glad to hear that."

Jolene smiled, creases capturing her mouth in parenthesis. "Me too," she said. "I'm sure May's filled you in on our family's up close and personal relationship with cancer."

Well, *May* hadn't, but everyone else had, and Sadie assumed that counted. "I honestly can't imagine it," she said quietly. "Your family has been through a lot. I'm relieved that they won't have to go through it again with you."

Jolene looked away. "Not soon, anyway," she said. "In fact, my husband and I are going on an Alaskan cruise next month; it's something we've been planning for a long time."

"I've heard that's a fabulous cruise. Did you know they have midnight buffets on cruises? Can you imagine? All the food you can eat, all day and night?" Sadie shook her head in wonderment at the whole thing. "Incredible."

Jolene smiled. "We're really looking forward to it."

"So, um, your treatments will be finished by then?" Sadie asked.

Jolene looked into her Jell-O and nodded. "I'm actually done with this round. I should be feeling a lot better in a few weeks." For some reason, her tone didn't match the optimism of her words, but maybe that was just because she felt so lousy right now.

"Enough about all that," Jolene said. "Tell me about you. You live in Ohio with May?"

Oh biscuits. Sadie hated having to make up details. She skimmed over the pretended place of residence and instead talked about her life and her children.

"You never remarried," Jolene commented when Sadie finished her brief explanation. "Why not?"

Something in the way Jolene asked the question caught Sadie's attention. This was a married woman who, though apparently on the road to recovery, had faced her own mortality and the inevitableness of her spouse continuing on. That made this question of particular importance, despite what seemed like Jolene's intent to ask it as casually as possible. Pete flashed through Sadie's mind, and yet Pete had nothing to do with Sadie's feelings for Neil.

Giving Jolene the answer she deserved required Sadie to dig deeply into her convictions and the feelings she kept in the dusty corners of her past. "Neil was my soul mate, if you believe in that kind of thing," she said with a tenderness that didn't necessarily surprise her. Rather, the act of saying it out loud reminded her all over again of just how well suited they had been for one another. "He was everything I had ever hoped for in a partner, and the years of our marriage were the very best years of my life. I've found his influence particularly difficult to replace."

Jolene blinked at her, appearing almost stunned by Sadie's words. Perhaps she hadn't expected such a personal answer from a woman she'd just met. Sadie smiled to cover up the vulnerability she felt at having been that honest, while ignoring the ache those words had ignited in her chest. She missed Neil on a regular basis, but sometimes the pain was more intense than others. Certainly, it was intense tonight.

"What a beautiful thing to say," Jolene said, smiling slightly. "I can relate, you know. I mean, not to having been widowed, but to everything else." Her face softened even more. "Gary and I will have been married twenty-four years in November. Sometimes it feels as though I didn't start living until he entered my life."

Sadie felt her throat thicken at the sentiment as Jolene's comments added another layer of grief to the situation. She hoped with every ounce of her being that Jolene's doctors weren't feeding her false hope about her future.

"He's a lucky man to be loved that much," Sadie said, meaning every word. She was reminded of Pete again, about a particular conversation they'd had in regard to the good marriages they had had and the fact that it honed their goals to find something similar in each other. She couldn't help but wonder where she was with her relationship with Pete. He'd clearly been disappointed with the decision she'd made to take this case. But then he'd withheld their relationship from his children, so she was questioning him as well.

"I'm a lucky woman to have Gary," Jolene said. "We've experienced so much together, but we've had each other through every twist. I can't imagine life without him." She looked at the clock above the stove and squinted, making Sadie wonder when she'd last had an eye exam. Did cancer treatments affect eyesight? "I wonder where he is," Jolene said. "He called after you guys left and said he'd be by to get me around 7:30."

Sadie looked at the clock as well. It was almost eight o'clock.

"Would you like me to call him?"

Jolene pushed herself off the barstool, albeit slowly. "I have my cell phone in my room; I'll call him myself. Thank you for the Jell-O."

She'd only taken that one bite and hadn't taken a single sip of water. Sadie smiled. "You bet. If you need anything else, just let me know."

"I thought you were leaving?"

"Oh, right," Sadie said. "I guess I am. You're okay here until May comes?"

"Gary will probably come first," Jolene said. "How long will you be staying in Portland?"

Sadie shrugged. "I have to admit I'm a bit bewitched by the place," she said with a chuckle. "Maybe I'll never leave."

Jolene smiled. "You wouldn't be the first. I hope I'll see you again."

"I hope so, too," Sadie said with sincerity. "I enjoyed getting to meet you."

Jolene headed toward her hallway with slow steps.

Sadie looked after her and let out a breath. Life was not fair sometimes.

After a few more contemplative seconds, Sadie headed toward the study for the files she'd left on the desk. Only then was she reminded of Jolene having been in the study, something Jolene had not mentioned and probably assumed Sadie didn't know.

The study light was off and the door open just as Sadie had left it. Sadie flipped the light on and surveyed the room. Nothing looked out of place. She stepped into the room, realizing it was likely impossible for her to determine what Jolene had been looking for in here.

The files still sat in the same tidy stack where she'd left them. Her eyes moved to the computer monitor. There were no lights on the display, but when she looked at the computer tower under the desk, a green light was on. Only the monitor was turned off, and she'd heard tapping when she'd been on the other side of the door. She pushed the power button on the monitor, and it flickered to life, showing the desktop.

Sadie slid into the desk chair and opened an Internet browser window. She went to the line where she would normally type in the website she wanted to find, but clicked on the arrow next to it instead. A list of websites that had been visited appeared, but didn't say when. She clicked on the most recent URL.

Hillsboro Hospice. A community of caring.

Hospice?

Sadie blinked and tried to make sense of the conflicting information she'd been given. Jolene had had a treatment yesterday, and she'd told Sadie minutes earlier that not only was she beating the disease, but she and her husband had a dream vacation planned for next month. Was her research on a hospice only Jolene's way of being proactive and making sure she had her ducks in a row should things take a turn, or was she not as convinced of her recovery as her doctors were?

Sadie bit her bottom lip, trying to imagine how May would cope with Jolene's death if, in fact, she was sicker than the doctors said. A heavy breath escaped her lungs as she lamented again the pain this family had experienced that seemed to have no end in sight.

CHAPTER 33

H ello? May?"
Sadie looked toward the door of the study and pushed away from the computer. The male voice was coming from the front of the house, and she didn't think it was Hugh. She was partway down the hall when she realized it must be Gary, Jolene's husband, coming to pick her up. She turned the corner to see a man sending a text message on his iPhone.

He glanced up at her and smiled before finishing his note and then sliding the phone into his pocket. He immediately put out his hand and moved toward her. "Gary Tracey," he said easily, not seeming the least bit surprised to find a stranger in the house.

Sadie took his hand and tried to return his firm shake with one of equal confidence. "Sadie Hoffmiller." His hand was warm and, if she wasn't mistaken, manicured. Few men had such soft hands, and she was instantly aware of her own tendency toward dryness. "May's friend."

"That's what I figured," Gary said. He smiled widely, revealing unnaturally white teeth. Considering the teeth and the fingernails, she guessed that his hair was not only colored but also highlighted to make it look more natural. His face was pleasantly tanned, his brown eyes bright, and his overall physique well tended, other than a bit of a belly that pushed against his department-store polo shirt. He was likely in his mid-forties, but could easily pass for late-thirties if he tried. Sadie wondered if he ever did. The only thing missing was a gold chain around his neck. "Is May around?"

"She's across the street at the summer picnic."

Gary nodded. "Right. Too bad I wasn't able to get away in time to make an appearance. I hear she was taking Jim's bacon ice cream."

"It went fast," Sadie said, still disappointed not to have even had a taste.

"I wish I could have found the time to stop in," Gary said. "Long days at the office, you know."

"What is it that you do?" Sadie asked. Unable to stand still, as usual, she went to the sink and began rinsing dishes—all four of them that had already been rinsed twice. Gary followed her into the kitchen.

"It's hard to pin me down with a title," Gary said, chuckling slightly at the comment. He rested his hips against the counter a few feet from Sadie. "I have ownership in a few different businesses. I suppose you can call me a jack-of-all-trades because I do whatever it takes in whatever arena I find myself in to get the job done." His smile sparkled.

Sadie smiled back, but she found herself hesitant to form a positive opinion about him. There was something about him that screamed "used car salesman." Plus, he was supposedly here to pick up his sick wife, but he hadn't asked about her at all. Instead, he was chatting up a friend of May's whom he'd never met and had little reason to think he'd ever meet again.

"What kinds of businesses do you own?" Sadie said, feigning more interest than she felt.

"Well," he said, smiling again and moving around the kitchen island in order to slide onto a barstool. "I'm part-owner in a thriving direct-mail company, and I also serve as CEO for a car dealership in town."

"A car dealership," Sadie repeated, keeping her expression from showing her smugness at having correctly determined why he came across the way he did.

"But mostly, I handle investments."

"Like financial planning?"

"Exactly," he said, giving her a good-girl smile for having properly figured it out. If she leaned forward, she felt sure he would pat her on the head. "I help people capitalize on their financial futures by building upon their current financial foundations, which allows them to one day attain the freedom from the day-to-day money worries that so many of us are plagued with."

Sadie had no doubt that he rattled off that speech a few times a day. She continued to nod and appear interested.

"For instance, what do you do for a living? If you don't mind my asking."

"I'm retired," she said.

Did she imagine the sudden straightening of his posture, the increased focus in his eyes?

"Oh, surely you're kidding," he said, dropping his chin and raising his eyebrows. "No way you're old enough to be retired."

Oh, he oozed with salesmanship, but she saw no reason not to play along. She might not yet have formed an opinion about him, but he was definitely intriguing.

"Nearly thirty years with the school district." She almost said "in

Colorado," but stopped herself. Admitting she was from a different state than May would blow her cover. "I taught second grade." She lifted her shoulders as though to indicate that she couldn't figure out how it was she was old enough to retire either. In all actuality, she'd taken an early-retirement window and had therefore only worked twenty-four years, but it didn't seem an important detail to bring up right now.

"So, you're drawing a pension."

Sadie nodded.

"Excellent! That's a perfect scenario. What's your percentage— three-quarters of your outgoing salary?"

"Two-thirds of my median income based on the last five years I taught," Sadie said. She turned off the water, dried her hands, and leaned back against the counter, suspecting that her interest would simply encourage him to continue.

He shook his head and tsked. "I'll keep to myself my personal views on how the education systems of our country *ought* to reward those committed to the cause of future generations." He smiled at Sadie in reverence for their shared connection to the virtue of education before continuing. "Besides, we play the hand we're dealt, right?"

"Absolutely," Sadie said, checking the sarcasm in her tone before realizing he wasn't catching any of it anyway.

"So, you're given two-thirds your outgoing salary to live on for the rest of your life. What if I were to tell you that there was a way to double that amount?" He looked at her eagerly, perhaps waiting for her to clasp her hands together and gasp in astonishment.

"How?" she asked simply.

"Through the intricacies of compounding interest, maximization of real estate values, and some savvy investments on your part, this time next year you could be bringing in twice the income you're pulling now. Not only would your quality of life improve exponentially, but you'd have the kind of security that no pension could offer you."

"Wow," Sadie said. "That's really amazing."

He winked at her. "And that's only the beginning," he said slyly. He pulled a card out of his pocket and handed it to her. She noticed the corners were bent. The logo consisted of a crown sitting above the words "King Me!"

"'King me'?" she asked, looking up at him.

He was still grinning. "Like in checkers. You make it to your opponent's side and your stature doubles. That's exactly what I can do for you, Mrs. Hoffmiller. You and I having this discussion qualifies as you having made it across the board."

"But I don't even live in Oregon."

"Doesn't matter," he said with a confident shake of his head. "With King Me on your side, the world is your oyster, and all the pearls belong to you. It would only take a few hours to work out the details, and you would be on your way to the real American dream."

"Which is?"

"Financial security," he said simply. "That's what we all want more than anything in the world—the promise that we will be cared for regardless of what challenges we might face."

"And that's what you're selling," she said, almost biting her tongue when she realized how antagonistic that sounded.

He didn't notice her tone. "Exactly. So, do you think May will let you out of packing long enough to explore the possibilities with me?"

"Um, well, I'd have to ask her," Sadie said, backpedaling quickly. "And talk to my brother, of course. He's an accountant and has managed my financial affairs for years."

Gary's smile faltered only a little bit. "But they are *your* financial affairs, right?"

"Of course," Sadie said. "But he'd need to be involved since he's far more aware of where I stand than I am."

"Well, sometimes—and I mean no disrespect to your brother—but sometimes those trained in the more rote methods of finance, such as the training expelled through most educational institutions, have a difficult time thinking outside of the box in regard to opportunity. Certainly talk to him, that's only fair, but be wary of him dismissing the idea out of hand. It wouldn't hurt for you and me to sit down so I can show you the opportunity first and prepare you for that discussion; put you two on equal ground, so to speak. There's also the added consideration that—and again, I mean no disrespect—but sometimes things as petty as jealousy can get in the way. Relationships are often based on a hierarchy, and if he's the brother who takes care of his retired sister and that role becomes threatened, well, that's something to consider."

Sadie nodded and kept her thoughts to herself. Jack would laugh his head off when she repeated this pitch to him. "I see your point."

"So, what do you think, tomorrow? I could even make room for you on Saturday if you'd prefer."

Sadie happened to glance at the clock, shocked to see it was already 8:10. She was meeting Richard in less than an hour. She held up the business card. "I'll let you know," she said before putting it in her back pocket. "I'm actually on my way back to my hotel, though. In fact, I'm running late."

"Well, maybe you could give me your cell phone number, and I could follow up with you tomorrow."

He had his phone out of his pocket within moments.

"Oh, well, I—"

He reached out and put his hand over her own. She looked down, noting that he most definitely had had a manicure recently, and then back up at him. "With all you're doing to help May right now, the least I can do is take one more worry off your shoulders. Let me give you a call tomorrow, and we can set up a time."

Sadie had a sudden desire to run his name through some of the sites her new book told her about. He was slick as oil on a rain-washed street, and she wondered what a basic background search on him might bring to light. "Sure," she said, then gave him her number after he pulled his hand back.

"Well, until tomorrow then," he said, tipping an imaginary hat in her direction. "I suppose Jolene's in her room?"

Ah, he'd remembered his wife. How sweet. Sadie nodded.

"I'll go look in on her," he said, heading toward the hallway. He paused and turned back, "Unless you'd like me to see you to your car?"

"No, of course not," Sadie said, waving the idea away. "Jolene was eager to see you, and I monopolized you long enough."

"Until tomorrow then," he said, apparently forgetting he'd used that line already.

He disappeared, and Sadie rolled her eyes before grabbing her purse and the files she was taking with her—only one of which she really needed. She fished for her keys as she headed toward the rental car parked at the curb. Gary Tracey was definitely someone she wanted to learn more about, but not at the risk of being unprepared for her meeting with Richard.

It wasn't until she was halfway back to the hotel that she remembered the wording of the On Death stipulations of Jim Sanderson's will. It said point-blank that none of his children's spouses were to inherit in their place. Jolene was the only married beneficiary, meaning that Gary was the only person in Jim Sanderson's circle who had, essentially, been cut out.

CHAPTER 34

It was 8:45 when Sadie opened the door of her hotel room. Her eyes were immediately drawn to the two beds—one still filled with newly purchased equipment and the other calling to her in a seductively soothing voice. She was tired. Her back hurt from all the bending and lifting, and she was unsettled by many things that were hard to define. But the day wasn't over yet. Richard was coming in fifteen minutes, and Sadie felt a rush of nerves. After having Lois confirm the details of Richard's relationship with May, Sadie wondered how May would react if she knew Sadie was meeting with her ex-fiancé. And what about the promise Sadie had made to put May and Richard in the same room? Why had Sadie promised such a thing that, after talking to Lois, sounded like a really bad idea?

Still, she needed what Richard had to give her and had to focus on that right now. She freshened up a bit and then headed to the common area of the hotel with her laptop and the files she'd copied, as well as those she hadn't made copies of yet. It wasn't until she'd set up her computer on a nearby table and sat down on one of the couches in the lobby that she realized she'd left her purse in her room. She grunted, not wanting to pack her stuff back up in order to get her phone and knowing it was inappropriate to leave it here while she checked. After a momentary debate, she decided not to worry about her phone. She didn't want anything to interrupt her meeting with Richard. If for some reason he didn't show up, then she'd have a reason to get her phone and see if she could track him down.

She opened Hugh's file and flipped through the contents: a copy of Hugh's birth certificate, Social Security card, school transcripts and a variety of programs, report cards, and childhood artwork that seemed brittle after so many years. As she looked through everything, she was reminded that despite who Hugh was now, he'd once been a child, a teenager, and a young man who'd lost his mother tragically. She needed to remember that as she moved forward.

After fingering though the proof of his earlier years, Sadie came upon several contracts between Jim and Hugh. She guessed Jim had typed up the financial contracts himself—they didn't look official at all. One, dated 2001, was about Hugh repaying a $10,000 loan. In 2002, there were two contracts: one for a loan of $2,500 and another one for $4,000, in addition to $1,300 still owing from the prior loan. In 2004, there was a contract for $7,000, as well as $3,600 from the prior total. And then there were no more contracts. Did that mean Hugh didn't borrow any more money, or had Jim stopped expecting to be paid back and therefore hadn't bothered with contracts anymore?

At the back of the folder was an envelope. Sadie opened it and removed a letter.

Dad,

I know you're tired of hearing this, but I'm sorry. I don't know what's wrong with me, or why I can't get this under control. I'm going to kick it, though, I am! I'm going to make you proud of me, and I'm going to prove to you that I can be trusted again. You're the only person who really loves me. I'll make good this time. I swear it.

Love,

Hugh

Sadie swallowed the lump in her throat as she refolded the letter and put it back in the envelope. There was no date on the letter and the envelope hadn't been postmarked, so she had no idea when the note had been written. Hugh sounded sincere, though, and Sadie had no doubt that as he had penned those words, he'd meant what he said. If only recovering from an addiction was solely dependent on desire to do so. She thought again about his poker-chip key chain. It was a blatant display; there was nothing being hidden. She didn't imagine that many recovering alcoholics carted a beer around with them, and the fact that Hugh was advertising his passion made it difficult to believe that he'd left his vice behind.

"Mrs. Hoffmiller?"

Sadie startled and looked up to see Richard Kelly standing a few feet away. She'd hadn't heard him approach and consciously switched gears from thoughts of Hugh to Keith Kelly.

"Oh, call me Sadie," she said, closing Hugh's file and moving the entire stack off her lap and onto the couch in order to stand and shake Richard's hand. "I appreciate your coming."

"I appreciate your giving me the chance to come," Richard returned.

Sadie smiled and indicated that they sit at the small table next to the couch. Richard followed her lead, pulling out one of the chairs opposite her.

"I hope it wasn't too difficult to get this information," Sadie said as she angled the laptop toward him.

He shook his head. "If Dad was trying to hide something, I think it would have been harder. As it was, I found the program open on his secretary's computer when she left for lunch and was able to track down the log-in information without much trouble."

As he spoke, he pulled a piece of paper from his pocket and set it on the table. He began typing on the computer. Sadie scooted her chair closer to his so she could look at the screen with him. Within seconds, a calendar popped up. Richard used the track pad—quite deftly, Sadie noted with a twinge of envy due to her slow adaptation to new electronic devices—and almost instantly they were scanning through the days before and after Jim's death.

The day of Jim's funeral was filled with appointments. A few days later, there was a note with the words "Send intent to buy to Sandersons." Sadie could only assume that referred to the letter that had May so mad. She felt her mouth tighten at the lack of sympathy from a man who had once counted Jim Sanderson as a close friend.

"Dad was in California the day Jim died," Richard said, pointing at the day five days prior to the funeral. Whereas most of Keith's days, especially work days, had up to half a dozen things written in the tiny square, the space for July 16 only said "San Jose."

"And didn't get home until the next day," Sadie commented as she moved forward on the calendar, noting "2:36 Delta" and "Dinner at country club."

"He was meeting with Jepson," Richard said. "They keep having all kinds of bizarre questions. We've been negotiating the merger for almost four months. Dad went down there to try to get them to pick up the pace."

Disappointed not to have found more, Sadie scrolled through the other days on the calendar. The man led a busy life, though he did manage to fit in a game of golf at least once a week.

"I learned something else," Richard said.

Sadie looked up at him and read the hesitation in his expression. "What?"

"That contract with C-Spec—the one Jim accused Dad of working up before the split?"

"Yeah," Sadie prodded.

"Jim was right."

Sadie narrowed her eyes. "Your Dad started pursuing that contract when SK Systems was still together?"

Richard nodded. "Hugh had run up a company credit card. Dad found out about it around the time he first got his foot in the door with C-Spec. Apparently Jim already knew about Hugh's debts and was trying to pay down the balance before Dad realized what was going on. Dad flipped—he's very financially responsible—but Jim refused to fire Hugh and said he'd pay off the card ASAP. Dad decided not to tell him about the C-Spec contract and insisted Hugh be removed from his position as a supervisor. Jim refused. Eventually, they went their separate ways over it."

"And your dad continued working the C-Spec deal."

"And felt completely justified in doing so. In his mind, Hugh was a liability, and Jim bailing him out made Jim a liability, too. Say what you will about my dad and the way he treats people, but he's a good businessman. Hugh was bad for business, and Dad wasn't going to sink with him."

"But you didn't know this at the time?"

"I knew Hugh had a gambling issue, and I knew my dad wanted him out of SK. I didn't know about the credit card debt, or that Dad was courting C-Spec while it happened. If he hadn't had C-Spec in the wings, I think he'd have stuck it out with SK and watched Hugh a little closer. Knowing he had a deal that would allow him to start his own company made the prospect of leaving more attractive."

"Does May know about the gambling?"

"I told her," Richard said. "When things started falling apart with us and she sided with her dad, I told her what I knew." He held Sadie's eyes.

Was that why May didn't want to talk about her family? She'd known that Hugh's history would catch Sadie's attention. She thought about the envelope Hugh had taken out of the mail. Could it have been a credit card statement he didn't want his sisters to see or some other debt in his father's name?

Sadie looked back at the online calendar, processing the possibilities as she scanned Keith's appointment book. Could she really trust what Richard had to say? She couldn't deny that the pieces fit, but Keith was his father. Was he really willing to offer up his father on a platter? Then again, he was offering up Hugh as well.

"It sounds like your dad told you all this pretty easily today," she said. "After ten years, does it seem odd he'd be so forthcoming?"

Richard shrugged. "Hugh responded to Dad's offer to buy out S&S, but Hugh wants a position with the company after the buyout. Not supervisory or anything, just a part-time floor man to help with the manufacturing transition. Dad hasn't said yes or no to the proposition, so I simply pushed him on it. This is what he told me."

"He doesn't want Hugh to work for him?"

Richard shook his head. "He's determined that Hugh won't. . . . Only he hasn't told Hugh that yet."

Suddenly, a name jumped out at Sadie from the calendar.

Jim S. @ Karri's @ 12:15

The date was two weeks before Jim's death. Could it be another Jim S.? Doubtful.

"Did you know they'd met for lunch?" Sadie asked, pointing to the computer screen.

Richard shook his head, and Sadie didn't skip a beat.

"Hugh was at dinner last night to talk about the purchase negotiations, wasn't he?"

Richard nodded.

"Was Hugh working with Keith before Jim died?"

"I don't think so. Dad sent the letter to Jim's kids after the funeral."

"But it looks like Keith had lunch with Jim two weeks *before* that letter should ever have been a consideration."

Richard looked back at the computer. "You're right. I don't know what that was about. Dad and Jim haven't talked for years."

What if Keith had met with Jim to discuss the potential purchase of the atomizer? If Jim refused, but then something happened to Jim, Keith would have had another chance.

"What was it that Keith wanted from S&S so badly?" Sadie asked, placing her hands on her knees and leaning back into the chair. "Why, after ten years, was he suddenly so interested? He has strong feelings against Hugh, and he's done well on his own. So why write the letters at all? Why deal with the family of his former partner in the first place?"

"Do you really mean, why kill Jim?" Richard asked.

Sadie hadn't meant to be so obvious, but, yes, that's what she'd meant. What was Keith's motivation for buying S&S? Could it also be a motive for murder?

Richard leaned back as well and crossed his arms. "I don't think he had anything to do with Jim's death."

Of course you don't think that, Sadie realized. Would he really have met with Sadie if he thought his father was guilty of murder? However, there was still the unexplained lunch date.

"What if he proposed some kind of reconciliation to Jim, and Jim refused?"

Richard shook his head. "What if Hugh was in debt again and needed Jim's inheritance in order to pay it off?"

Sadie had been thinking along those same theory lines, but didn't want to voice her growing suspicions of Hugh to Richard. "But why is Kelly Fire Systems even interested in S&S? What's in it for your dad? He doesn't sound like the kind of guy who would do something unless it was in his own best interest. I read the letter he sent to the Sanderson kids. It was cold and to the point; there was no residual warmth laced into it. He wants S&S. Why?"

"Well, there was that new atomizer," Richard said, but she could hear the doubt in his tone.

"Your father seems like a pretty confident man," Sadie said. "And pretty convinced of his own . . . worth." Sometimes it was hard to choose the right words. "One atomizer? I mean, I don't know much about the components of what you guys do, but it seems like a lot of effort being expended over one particular part, especially when things are obviously so intense with the Jepson deal. Something doesn't fit."

A puzzled expression crossed Richard's face. "You're right," he said simply, lifting his hands up slightly. "I don't know what it is, but I know my dad didn't kill Jim to get it." He paused. "Maybe he just wanted to win. Maybe even with Jim gone, buying S&S feels like he's won once and for all."

"Hasn't he already proven that?" Sadie asked. "He's done a lot better than S&S since they went their separate ways." Suddenly Sadie remembered something May had said. She'd said the new atomizer had made a splash in the industry, that Hugh was having a hard time keeping up with orders. Could the atomizer have been big enough that in time it would have helped S&S catch up with Kelly Fire Systems? Could Keith have felt threatened somehow? She didn't want to share those thoughts with Richard, though. He was defending his father tonight—not Keith Kelly's character, necessarily, but he certainly didn't believe his father capable of murder. She didn't want to push him and risk missing out on valuable information.

They sat in silence, contemplating their lack of knowledge. After a few seconds, Sadie had an idea.

"Do you think you could find out what that lunch with Jim was about? What if you just flat-out asked him what he wants from S&S? You could even say you heard about the lunch date with Jim—he won't know where you heard about it, and you don't have to tell him. But there has to be a reason he's working this hard to get S&S, and you've already set the groundwork by asking about the split with Jim. Maybe if we know why Keith wants S&S, some other things will fall into place."

Richard let out a breath. "He hates it when I ask him direct questions like that. He always assumes I'm questioning his ability to make good decisions. Even today, he was defensive with my digging into his reasons for splitting with Jim."

"Maybe you *are* questioning his ability to make good decisions," Sadie said with a slight shrug. "But as CFO, you deserve to understand his motives for buying S&S, especially in the wake of that lunch he had with Jim. A lunch that you knew nothing about."

"That's a good point," he said, but didn't sound any more excited about the prospect.

Behind them, Sadie heard the swish as the front door of the hotel opened. Probably someone checking in late; the hotel didn't seem particularly full tonight, which she was grateful for since it meant that she and Richard had been able to talk in private despite being in a common area of the hotel.

She turned to look at Richard, planning to ask him when he could have that discussion with his father, when a flash of red hair caught her eye. She looked over Richard's shoulder and froze.

May stood ten feet away, her eyes wide and her mouth open as she stared at the two of them with an expression of utter disbelief.

CHAPTER 35

Sadie jumped to her feet, the chair screeching in protest as she shoved it backward. "May," she said quickly.

At the sound of May's name, Richard also stood and turned. The three of them stared at each other in silence. May's eyes lingered on Richard for a few moments, but then she turned on Sadie, her eyebrows pulled together.

"What are you doing?" Her tone was understandably accusatory.

"I . . . uh, he's helping me determine what happened to your father."

May's eyes narrowed. "He's Keith Kelly's *son*. He's not going to help you with anything."

"But he is," Sadie hurried to say, her heart racing. "He got access to Keith's calendar and—"

"You're fired," May snapped, causing Sadie to pull back. "I want you out of Portland first thing tomorrow morning."

"May, please," Sadie said, taking a step toward her. "Let me explain. See, I followed—"

"I don't want to hear it," May screamed—really screamed—

silencing Sadie once again. Tears rose in her eyes, and Sadie just wanted to die.

After all she'd learned about May's history and her life, Sadie had betrayed her, and while she wanted very much to justify her actions, right now she could only see it the way May was seeing it.

"I came to you because I needed help," May said, her voice ragged with sorrow. "I needed answers, and I couldn't trust anyone to help me find them. I trusted *you*. And you went to . . ." She looked at Richard, who was standing with his arms at his sides and a stunned look on his face. "You went to *him* of all people." She pulled herself up, and the tears overflowed as she looked at Sadie again. "I try to give people the benefit of the doubt, Sadie, but I have a hard time trusting people. And now I'm reminded why." She raised a hand and wiped at her eyes, shaking her head. "I can't believe I thought it was fate that led me to you. I can't believe I've made such a fool of myself again." Her chin was trembling, and Sadie felt tears rising in her own eyes for having hurt this woman who had already suffered so much.

"May, I'm so—"

"Where are my dad's files?" May interrupted, looking around the table. Her eyes landed on the stack of files, still in the original folders, lying on the couch. She hurried to them and gathered them up, holding them against her chest. "Is this all of them?" she demanded. "Are there any more?"

Sadie tried to swallow the rock in her throat and shook her head slowly. "That's all of them—the copies and everything," she said, hearing her own voice catch.

May looked at Richard one last time, then turned on her heel and hurried toward the door.

Sadie was frozen, but her chest was on fire, and her brain buzzed with the attempts to figure out what had just happened and how she could fix it. Finally, as May got closer and closer to the hotel door, Sadie's feet began to move.

"Wait," she said, taking a few hurried steps toward May's retreating back. "Please let me explain." May had to know why Sadie had done things this way. If nothing else, she had to make sure May understood what was going on with Hugh. She noted a bewildered desk clerk poised at the edge of the front counter as though unsure whether to insert herself into the drama or not.

May didn't turn around, but pushed through the door, taking quick steps to the curb. She looked both ways and then hurried across the street for the parking lot.

"May, please," Sadie said after pushing through the door as well, leaving Richard and the desk clerk behind. She was glad to be wearing sensible shoes today. May was nearly at her car before Sadie managed to catch up with her. She put a hand on May's arm, and May turned quickly. Too quickly for Sadie to comprehend the open palm coming at her face. She managed a small yelp just before May slapped her, snapping Sadie's head to the side. The parking lot spun as intense heat and pain rushed through Sadie's head.

"Him?" May said in a hoarse whisper. Her expression was tight and her chin quivered. "You went to *him?*"

"He came to *me,*" Sadie said, swallowing as she raised a hand to her throbbing cheekbone. "I followed Keith to a restaurant last night. Richard followed me back from the hotel and confronted me."

"And you told him I think his father is a murderer? Do you have any idea what kind of risk that creates for me?"

Sadie hadn't thought about that at all, in fact. Had she put May at risk? "I'm so sorry," she said. "I . . . he . . . he was helping me."

"Right," May spat. "Richard Kelly is simply another version of his father, and I can guarantee that anything you've told him goes directly back to Keith." She closed her eyes and shook her head, more tears running down her blotchy face. "I can't believe this is happening," she muttered, raising her free hand to her face. "I can't believe—"

"May," Sadie said, touching her arm again.

Once again, May's free hand shot out, this time stopping at shoulder height while Sadie ducked and raised her hands to protect herself from another assault. She clenched her eyes closed. "Hugh was at the dinner last night, too," she said quickly, latching on to the only thing she could think of that might change the direction of the conversation.

She opened one eye, though she was still cringing. May's hand was still poised, but she was watching Sadie. Waiting. Sadie hurried to take advantage of the moment. "I didn't know it was Hugh until he came to the house today," she said in a rush. "He took something out of the mailbox this afternoon and hid it in his waistband before bringing in the rest of the mail. Richard says Hugh wants to sell his percentage of S&S Suppression—that's what the dinner meeting was about. But your dad had lunch with Keith two weeks before he died, and Richard doesn't know why." She paused and sucked in a breath before she passed out, allowing herself to straighten slightly. "The last thing I wanted to do was hurt you, May, and I'm so sorry to realize that's exactly what I've done. But please know that wasn't my intent; I was trying to get to the truth and using any opportunity I could to get to it. I haven't ruled Keith out, but there are other things to consider. You might need to decide if you want Keith's head on a platter or the truth. You might not be able to have both."

May lowered her hand, but her expression didn't relax. For a moment Sadie hoped that she was softening, that she was able to see the reasoning behind Sadie's assertions. The hope was short-lived.

"You're fired," she said again, turning and taking the last few steps to her car. She glanced at Sadie briefly before sliding into the car and dumping the files on the passenger seat. Just before she slammed the door, she added, "I never want to see you again."

CHAPTER 36

Sadie wiped frantically at her own tears as she entered the hotel lobby, having lost all control of her emotions following the confrontation. Richard stood near the front door and gave her a sympathetic look. "I didn't think following you would help. Are you okay?"

"No," Sadie said, embarrassed to choke out the word, but unable to hide the absolute devastation she felt. She raised her hand to cover her trembling chin and walked past him without looking.

"I'm really sorry," Richard said from behind her.

Sadie sniffled, shaking her head as she wiped her eyes again. "It's not your fault. It's mine. I knew she'd be upset when she learned I'd talked to you."

"She confirmed what I told you about us, then?" Richard asked.

"Lois did—her neighbor."

"What are you going to do now?" he asked, looking out the front door again.

Sadie was sure May was long gone. Every thought of May made her insides clench. She'd never been yelled at that way, never been *slapped*, for heaven's sake. Thinking about it caused her to raise her hand to her cheek again.

"I'm going to get some ice," Sadie said, heading toward the table to retrieve her laptop. "I'll figure out the rest of it in the morning."

"Do you still want me to talk to my dad?"

Sadie stopped and lowered her hand. What *was* she going to do now? Leave Portland, like May told her to, and just forget about all of this? Could she really turn her back on everything she'd discovered? She didn't feel close to any kind of breakthrough; quite the opposite—her brain was boggled with information, none of which seemed all that relevant as to who did, in fact, kill Jim Sanderson—assuming anyone killed him at all. But could she turn her back on the things she *had* learned? Was she simply a head to hire and fire, or was she personally invested enough to pursue this on her own—against May's wishes?

"Honestly, Richard," she said, meeting his concerned eyes. "I don't know. You heard May. I've been . . . fired. She wants me to leave Portland."

"She's angry," Richard said. "She'll calm down."

"It's been ten years, and she's still pretty ticked at you."

Richard looked down. "Well, that's true."

"I don't know what I would have done differently, but it sure seems like there should have been another option. Something I should have done that would have allowed me to make this less painful for her." She groaned again at the memory of May's face, of her words, of the absolute shock and disappointment of her expression when Sadie had first looked up and found her standing there. Oh, to rewind the whole thing and meet with Richard somewhere else.

She gathered her computer, glancing at the couch where the files used to be. If May looked through them before she put them away, she'd find Hugh's information. She'd know Sadie had gone through her dad's personal files. She closed her eyes and took a deep breath to calm the firestorm of emotion raging in her chest. Then she turned to Richard, who looked as defeated as she felt. His arms hung at his sides, and his hair was disheveled. She forced a smile she hoped would make him feel better. "I'm so sorry you were here for that," she said. "I'm sorry that I wasn't able to arrange that face-to-face meeting with May. At least, not the kind you were going for."

"I'm just . . . sorry," Richard said.

Sadie let out a breath. "Why don't I call you in the morning, when I know for certain what I'm going to do about all this, okay?"

Richard nodded. "Okay."

He walked her to the hallway where the rooms started, and then they said their good-byes.

When Sadie entered her room a minute later, she put the laptop on the bed full of equipment and then fell facedown on the other bed, whimpering into the coverlet. She couldn't get the look on May's face out of her mind. The last thing Sadie had wanted to do was hurt her. But she had. And she couldn't undo what had been done.

Was there, however, a way to make it right? Was there anything she could do to make it better?

Find the answers, she said to herself. If she offered May the truth, May could make an informed judgment rather than one based on her emotional reaction to Sadie having met with Richard . . . and her breaking into the filing cabinet . . . and asking too many questions about her family.

Sadie suspected that any answer other than proving Keith Kelly had killed Jim Sanderson wasn't an answer May wanted to have, but it felt wrong to leave the situation undone and unfinished. If Jim Sanderson had been murdered, the killer deserved to be brought to justice. May deserved to know the truth—even if it wasn't the truth she *wanted*.

Sadie had no delusions of absolution. She'd hurt May and didn't anticipate that anything she did would make that better. Rather, she feared it would make things worse. But she wasn't ready to go down with the ship. She didn't feel good about leaving Portland with so many loose ends.

With a sigh, she went into the bathroom and turned on the shower. She began unbuttoning her blouse, but then paused. Was that the phone? She hurried out of the bathroom and to the hotel phone, pausing only a moment before she picked up the handset. Would May have reconsidered and come back to the hotel to talk to her?

"Hello?"

"Sadie?" a familiar voice said on the other end of the line, but it wasn't May's voice. "It's Jane. We need to talk."

Sadie gripped the hotel phone. "How did you know I was here?"

"I have my sources," Jane said. "I really need to talk to you. Can I come to your room?"

"To my room?" Sadie repeated, trying to make sense of this.

"Yeah, I'm in the lobby. I can be there in about twenty seconds."

CHAPTER 37

P erhaps it was exhaustion that made her agree to let Jane come to her room, but as soon as Sadie hung up, she shifted into hyperdrive and began stashing boxes and equipment in the closet. Everything inside her told her to use extreme caution when dealing with Jane Seeley.

When she heard the knock—an eight-knock rhythm—she took a deep breath. *I'll let her say what she came to say, but I'm not inviting her to sit down,* Sadie determined as she moved toward the hotel room door and pulled it open.

Jane stood there, grinning broadly. Her red skinny jeans matched her lipstick and Converse sneakers. The shirt she had on was white with a rainbow stretched across the front. Her fingernails were purple. As soon as the door was open all the way, Jane entered the room and walked straight for the first bed.

Sadie knew she was scanning the room, looking for anything that might give her information Sadie wouldn't offer.

"What are you doing here?" she asked, remaining by the open door.

"You invited me," Jane said with a smile.

Sadie felt her eyes narrow. "Not what are you doing in my hotel room, what are you doing in Portland?"

Jane's smile faded, and a trace of insecurity crossed her face. Sadie didn't trust it and therefore refused to react.

"I'm trying to make amends," Jane said, fiddling with the tassel on the big purse she had under one arm. She met Sadie's eyes. "I really made a mess of things, didn't I?"

"You want my forgiveness?" Sadie refused to let Jane be in charge of this conversation. She crossed her arms over her chest.

"Yes," Jane said.

"Fine. You're forgiven."

Jane scrunched her nose. "I'd rather you meant it."

Sadie sighed. "You can't play with people's lives and expect that they will trust you; life doesn't work that way." Her words gave her own conscience a zing. Had she played with May's life?

"I know," Jane said. "But I am really sorry about all this and . . . it's just that . . . " She took a breath, and then spoke quickly. "They're talking about having Ms. Jane take on a couple more writers. They think I'm losing my edge, that I'm getting tired. I didn't realize that they own the column, not me, so they can bring anyone else in at any time, which is exactly what they're thinking of doing. I had to do something big. Something that would prove once and for all that I wasn't just a columnist, but that I could get the *big* stories, ya know?"

"So you thought you'd pump up your feature reporter skills by becoming a muckraker at my expense?"

"I've been watching you," Jane said, giving Sadie a hesitant look. "Almost since the first time we met. I knew about Florida months ago; I read up on the case and talked to a detective down there. I know what you did. I've looked into Eric Burton too—he's a player, by the way—and Pete Cunningham, who I might try to hook up with myself if things don't work out between the two of you. I know about your daughter and her fiancé. And about Shawn and the precarious position of his scholarship. I know it probably sounds crazy, but I feel like I know you, Sadie, like we're friends."

Sadie blinked, trying to keep her expression neutral. In reality she was completely creeped out by Jane's admission. "You're a stalker," she summed up. One unlocked door, and Sadie would be murdered in her bed!

Jane's eyes went wide. "No, I'm not a stalker," she clarified. "I just . . . I find you fascinating."

Sadie took a step backward and pulled open the door a little wider. "Get out of here," she said.

Jane sighed but made no move to leave. Instead, she folded her arms over her chest defiantly. "Okay, I get how that sounds, but I'm not here to hurt you, and I really didn't mean for the article to be so negative. I'd had a fight with my editor, and I needed something sharp, something intense. I *might* have gone around him to get it in the paper, and I *might* have taken things too far. I might even have regretted it later. But it happened, and I was written up for it. I might lose my entire career over this. I've learned my lesson, Sadie."

Sadie stamped out her rising sympathy before it got too far. Jane did not deserve Sadie's compassion, but no sooner had she thought that then she remembered that everyone deserved some kind of compassion.

"And you want me to feel sorry for you?" She didn't like hearing the softening of her tone. She wasn't really falling for this, was she? "It's called consequences; reaping what you sow. It's the law of the harvest. They talk about it in the Bible—you should read it sometime."

"I've read the Bible," Jane said. "It also talks about forgiving your enemies, blessing those who hurt you, and who—"

"Despitefully use you," Sadie finished for her. "I know the passage."

They stared at one another. "Seriously, Jane, why are you here? I forgive you, or at least I will forgive you at some point, and I am sorry that your bad decisions might cost you your career. Does that make you feel better?"

Jane frowned. "I want to help you."

"Help me with what?"

"With your case."

Sadie laughed out loud, surprising herself. She slapped a hand over her mouth. It took a few seconds for her to recover and lower her hand. Yes, this was Jane Seeley—a woman who had set Sadie's life on its ear—but Sadie was embarrassed by her own rudeness. "You want to help me with my case?"

Jane nodded, her eyes hopeful. "I'm a reporter, and I have all kinds of sources, databases, and journalistic wiles that I can use to help you. How do you think I found you here or learned about Shawn's school issues—I think he should stay in, just so you know. I can help fill in the blanks for you, Sadie. Round out what you need to know about Sharla-May Sanderson and her father's death."

Jane knew about Jim's death!

She continued. "I may have completely ruined my career as a journalist, but after following your escapades these last few months, I've realized there are other opportunities out there, other ways I can use my skills. You're going into investigations; I can do that, too. I can be your wingman—or wingwoman." She was fully animated, now, with a full smile and bright eyes that almost made her look like a different person. She stopped and grinned at Sadie, her expression so hopeful that Sadie felt herself considering Jane's offer.

For about two seconds.

It only took a brief stroll down memory lane, looking at the encounters the two of them had had up to this point in their relationship for Sadie to realize how ridiculous it was for her to even consider trusting Jane. And yet, Jane seemed so sincere in this bizarre offer that Sadie hesitated to give her a smack down.

"I need some time to think about this," Sadie said, feeling like an idiot for not giving this the gravity it deserved. "I have *very* few reasons to trust you, Jane, and I'm dealing with some extremely sensitive things right now."

Jane nodded. "I saw Richard Kelly leaving as I arrived. Sharla-May won't like you meeting with him."

For the second time in five minutes, Sadie was shocked by what Jane knew, but she couldn't show it, couldn't let her surprise give Jane the upper hand, even though she couldn't figure out how in the world Jane knew about Richard when Sadie had found him quite by accident. She was grateful Jane hadn't arrived in time to see May's dramatic exit, so she took a few seconds to try to decide what to do next. In the end, all she could think of was to stall.

"Where are you staying in Portland?"

"Well, here, at the hotel," Jane said as though Sadie should have guessed that. "I'm on the third floor."

Sadie nodded slowly, but the creep-out factor doubled. "I need to think about this," she said again in a cautious tone. "Can we meet in the morning?"

Jane's smile got even bigger, and she nodded, looking like a little girl desperate for approval. For an instant, Sadie wondered if Jane hadn't been exactly that kind of little girl once upon a time. She'd told Sadie about her half-sister—Beautiful Becca, Jane had called her. Jane was not so much beautiful as she was intense, and Sadie could imagine a girl like that driving her parents crazy. It made her sad to think about it, but it was just speculation; she needed to not get carried away. It wasn't always a good thing to have such a compassionate heart.

"How about eight o'clock?" Sadie said.

"For breakfast?" Jane asked.

"Sure," Sadie said. "Breakfast would be good. They have a pretty good one here at the hotel."

Jane headed for the door of Sadie's room, pausing on the threshold of the open door. "Thanks for listening to me," she said, sounding a little bit embarrassed. "Oh," she pulled open her purse and removed a piece of paper. She held it out to Sadie.

"What's this?" Sadie said, taking it cautiously.

"The pathologist's report for Jim Sanderson. The coroner often requests a pathologist's examination for unattended but unsuspicious deaths. The report is used to determine the cause of death, but it's an internal-type document, not one the family would necessarily get a copy of unless they asked for it, which few people do. Consider it an olive branch." She closed her purse and smiled one more time. "On the back I wrote down some basic notes on research I did for medications and such that could cause a heart attack that might be undetectable based on the testing they performed on the body."

Sadie's head snapped up, and she opened her mouth to ask how Jane knew that they suspected a heart attack–inducing medium, but realized the ramifications of her saying that out loud. She closed her mouth and turned over the paper, briefly scanning the list of eight or nine items.

One of the items was insulin, another was diuretics. There was also something called calcium hydroxide, as well as a few things she thought were prescription medications. It was a rough draft of Jane's thoughts, and they weren't complete. Clearly, Jane wanted to make sure Sadie had something to ask her questions about.

"I'll see you in the morning," Jane said before Sadie could come up with anything else to say.

Sadie caught sight of Jane's knowing smile before she disappeared through the door, leaving Sadie with her thoughts and the paper in her hand.

CHAPTER 38

Sadie studied the pathologist's report for nearly half an hour. May had been mistaken; the coroner *had* done a partial autopsy, which supported the cause of death as being a heart attack. They'd also done a toxicology report. Jim had had a glass of wine with dinner, but besides that, nothing other than his heart medication showed up. There was really nothing here to support an accusation of murder. Then she flipped the paper over to Jane's notes. She'd said these were things that could have been undetected based on the tests that had been run.

Sadie considered her options. She didn't trust Jane. Even though part of her wanted to, she didn't, and while the pathologist's report was interesting and Sadie was glad to have it, she knew it would be foolish to believe anything Jane said after the history she had with the feisty reporter. But . . . what if Jane was sincere? She'd managed to find out about Florida, and Shawn's school, and Sadie's life, not to mention Jim Sanderson's death. Jane had skills to do what Sadie couldn't.

It was an exciting possibility to have someone navigate the more twisty points of research, but the temptation didn't negate the possibility that this whole thing could be Jane's way of getting a story. How could Sadie know for sure? After a few minutes, she realized that she couldn't know for sure. Besides, Sadie had already taken too many liberties that had hurt May, and she didn't dare take anymore.

Forty-five minutes later, Sadie had packed up her equipment and made a new reservation at a hotel across town. From the Internet site, it didn't look like it had the charm of the Mark Spencer Hotel, but she'd pay cash this time and hopefully stay a step ahead of Jane until Sadie was ready to leave. Jane's offer still tingled in the back of her mind, but it was not a decision Sadie could make without lots of time to think it through. As tempting as it was to have Jane continue researching causes of death and look up the histories of people of interest, Sadie couldn't forget the story about the turtle who gave a repentant scorpion a ride across the river only to be stung halfway across.

"What did you do that for?" the turtle asked the scorpion as they were both drowning.

"It's just my nature," the scorpion replied.

Sadie didn't want to be a stupid turtle about this, but she could relate to the turtle wanting to believe that the scorpion had changed his ways. If Jane was actually what she claimed to be, things could really open up for Sadie; Jane could access information, help her line up the facts, and fill in the blanks. But this was May's life, May's pursuit for truth. Sadie couldn't hand that over to someone who might exploit it, who might drown them all.

After sleeping—sorta—for a few hours, Sadie got up and began taking her things out to her car, watching closely for Jane to appear around a corner and catch her escape. After she'd loaded up her car, she went to the front desk and checked out, much to the desk clerk's confusion. It was the same clerk who had witnessed the altercation in the lobby and parking lot. She was probably glad to see Sadie go, but that made Sadie feel kind of bad too.

"You have a very nice hotel," she said, hoping to assure the clerk that Sadie wasn't leaving because of poor quality. "I'll be sure to come again another time. You and your staff do an excellent job here."

"Thank you, ma'am," the woman said as she gave Sadie the final receipt, which Sadie tucked into her wallet for her records.

She took a final look around the hotel lobby, then headed outside and into the heavy cool air of early-morning Portland. The next leg of her journey had begun.

At ten minutes to eight that morning—after Sadie had managed another few hours of sleep—she sent Jane a text message explaining that she still needed more time to think about Jane's offer. She'd let Jane figure out that she wasn't at the hotel anymore.

Jane texted back a minute later.

I understand. I can wait.

It wasn't the response Sadie had expected, and it made her uncomfortable to be surprised by this woman. Knowing what she was dealing with was far more comfortable than trying to guess at Jane's motives.

She moved on to the next item on her list: set up an appointment with Gary Tracey. This one felt risky—Gary was awfully close to May—and yet she had an open invitation from him to talk, and without many other people to get information from now, it was hard to ignore the opportunity. Her gut told her it was a good idea; then again, her gut *hadn't* warned her that May would track her down with Richard last night. She called Gary's phone number from the card but only got his voice mail. She left a message and asked that he call or text her about meeting today.

On the way back to the airport—she wanted to turn in this car and get a new one so that she'd have a complete separation of expenses for on-the-job versus on-her-own—her phone rang. She clenched her teeth. She hated not being able to answer her phone and wondered why she hadn't invested in a Bluetooth when she'd bought all that other equipment. It could be Richard with information he'd learned about the lunch meeting between his father and Jim, or May, offering her another chance. It was a relief when she heard the chime that indicated a voice message; at least she'd know what the call was about.

As soon as she pulled into the rental car lot, she picked up her phone to see who had called. It was Pete, and a shiver rushed through her as she called her voice mail. She hadn't planned to speak to him until she returned to Garrison and was eager to know what had changed that plan.

"Good morning, Sadie. At the risk of setting a pattern each time you go out of town, I noticed this morning that you received a cell phone citation in Oregon. I know that we've both made it very clear that what you're doing there is none of my business, but I . . . well, I'm worried about you. I hope you're okay. I know you weren't planning to call me until you got back to Garrison, but if you wanted to call and give me an update, I'm not opposed to that."

Not opposed? Sadie repeated as she pressed the button to delete the message. Not opposed? Oh, what an infuriating man he was! She threw the phone back in her purse and pushed open her door. "Not opposed," she muttered as she headed toward the rental car office.

It felt as though she was at odds with everyone—except, apparently, Jane Seeley.

"Focus," she said to herself as she pushed through the glass doors. She could think about Pete later—Jane too—but she had a limited amount of time to make sense of the information she'd already learned and couldn't risk distraction. If May found out what she was doing, it would become even more complicated. There was no room for Sadie to get lost in her personal issues. Professional investigators had to put their personal lives on hold all the time. Unfortunately, Sadie was feeling less and less professional by the minute. She didn't even have a client anymore. But one thing she couldn't deny was that when she'd agreed to take this job, she'd felt that it was the right decision. After everything that had happened since then, staying and finishing what she could *still* felt right.

With a heavy sigh, she approached the counter, where a round-faced young man was waiting for her. She was officially changing the game she'd come here to play. Everything would be different now, and it made her feel very vulnerable and out of sorts. Focus was good, but confidence that she was doing the right thing would be even better.

CHAPTER 39

A n hour later, Sadie pulled up to Karri's—the restaurant where she and May had shared that first meal and where Jim had met Keith Kelly for a secret lunch more than a month ago. It didn't look like Karri's was open for breakfast, but there were two cars parked around back. She parked next to them and found the back door unlocked. She let herself in and paused on the landing of a split staircase. She walked up the steps until she entered a relatively small kitchen area, which had been expanded and commercialized since anyone had used this house for a residence.

"Hello?" she called out, taking timid steps toward a large stainless steel island.

"Hello," a woman called from somewhere to the left. "I'll be right there."

Sadie stopped where she was and waited for the woman to appear, which she did shortly, wiping her hands on a paper towel. The woman was tall and lean, with a green bandana tied around her dark hair that hung in one long braid over her left shoulder. She looked as though she might be part Hispanic, or maybe Greek. She had an open expression on her makeup-free face and swirling colors running the length of both arms. At first Sadie thought it was a shirt, then realized they were tattoos. She tried not to stare.

"Sorry," the woman said. "I thought you were my linen delivery." She threw the paper towel past Sadie and into the garbage can.

Sadie smiled as she put out her hand. "Are you Karri?"

"Sure am. And you are?" They shook hands briefly.

"My name's Sadie Hoffmiller. I'm sorry to bother you, but I wondered if I could ask you—or someone on your wait staff—some questions."

Karri's friendly expression didn't waver. "Questions about what?"

"Um, Jim Sanderson. He was regular patron here, I think."

The woman nodded. "Sure was," she said, her smile turning sad. "Who are you?"

Sadie had been prepared for this question, and while she couldn't believe she was doing it, she pulled the private investigator card Shawn had made for her out of her purse. Hopefully Karri wasn't familiar enough with a real private investigator license to know Sadie's ID wasn't official.

"You're an investigator?" Karri said after looking at the ID. She handed the card back to Sadie, her eyebrows raised.

Sadie quickly hid the ID in her purse again. She'd never hear the end of it when Shawn learned she'd actually used it. "I am."

"And you're investigating Jim?"

"Not Jim, someone else, but it pertains to Jim. I just need to fill in some blanks about a lunch he had here a couple of weeks before he died."

Karri frowned. "Jim came in a few times a week, but—" She glanced over her shoulder as something dinged behind her. The expression on her face showed her consideration of everything, and finally softened—a decision had been reached. "Um, those are my rolls. I'll do my best to answer your questions if you don't mind me working while we talk."

"Not at all," Sadie said, relieved that there would be something else to focus on so that the discussion wouldn't feel so formal.

"Thanks," Karri said over her shoulder as she headed toward another part of the kitchen. "We open in a couple of hours, and there's still a lot of prep to be done before then. Follow me."

They went around the corner and saw a young man with headphones on slicing vegetables, his head moving slightly to the beat of whatever was pulsing in his eardrums. He gave a little chin nod to them both when they passed, but immediately went back to his work. The smell of baking bread got stronger and stronger until they reached a double-door oven.

"You seem young to be the owner of this place," Sadie said, taking in how well Karri had used the limited space. Pans hung from the ceiling, and every portion of wall had something hanging from it or pushed up against it. "Did you always want to own a restaurant?"

Karri gave Sadie an appreciative smile as she pulled on a pair of oven mitts. "I sure did," she said. "Owning my own place has been my dream for as long as I can remember. It finally became a reality about four years ago when this place went up for sale. It was a great price but needed some updating in order to be up to code." She pointed at something on the ceiling with her eyes. Sadie looked up and noted the exposed sprinkler pipe.

Karri put the hot pan of what looked like multigrain rolls into a rolling cooling rack. Sadie could see the tips of sunflower seeds poking out of the rounded domes as well as a smattering of oats along the surface. "Jim gave me a great price on a fire system in exchange for two lunches a week for a year, and he's never stopped coming in, even when he had to pay. He's been very good for business too, bringing in friends and associates on a regular basis."

"I was here with his daughter the other day," Sadie said.

"Jolene?" Karri said with an excited smile.

"No, May. She lives in Ohio."

"I haven't met her," Karri said. "But Jolene used to come in a few times a month with her dad. How's she doing?"

"She says she's doing well," Sadie said, and though she doubted that was true, she didn't want to spread gossip.

"Good," Karri said, removing her oven mitts. She moved toward a big plastic tub of what looked like butter and picked up a scoop that sat next to it. There was already a cookie sheet full of little paper cups set out; Karri started putting a scoop of butter into each cup. Sadie was itching to offer her help, but didn't want to come across as too forward. Instead she continued talking, "I had the salmon and mushroom pasta. It was wonderful."

Karri's smile stretched even bigger. "That's one of my favorites, but I have to admit it was inspired by nothing other than tuna casserole."

"Well, it was nothing like any tuna casserole I've ever had," Sadie said. "It was delicious. And the blackberry crumble—well, it made this whole trip worthwhile."

"That recipe belonged to my grandmother," Karri said, "so I can't take all the credit, but I'm glad you enjoyed both of them. I try to mix up the more creative fare with some basic home-cooked goodness so as to not pigeonhole myself in any one type of cuisine. Anyway, what did you want to ask about Jim?"

Oh, right—Jim. Sadie opened her purse and removed the photo she had used to identify Keith Kelly a couple of days earlier. "Do you by chance remember Jim having lunch with this man?" She held the picture out to Karri, who furrowed her brow as she paused in her butter-scooping task to give it a quick look. She frowned slightly. "I don't spend much time at the tables," Karri said. "I could ask my wait staff when they come in, but that's not for another hour."

Sadie tried to hide her disappointment.

"What's so important about this guy?" Karri asked. "Like I said, Jim brought people here all the time."

"Oh, it's probably a long shot," Sadie said, tucking the photo back into her purse. "But he was Jim's former business partner who, according to Jim's family, hadn't had contact with Jim for years. However, I recently learned he'd had lunch here with Jim a couple of weeks before Jim died."

Karri paused, and then leaned forward slightly. "Two weeks before?"

Sadie noticed the slightest narrowing of Karri's eyes.

"Can I see that photo again?"

Sadie quickly complied, and this time Karri stared at it for several seconds. "I *do* know that guy, then," she said, not sounding pleased. She handed the photo back to Sadie. "He came in with Jim and ordered the soup of the day, but he sent it back twice because he said it was cold. I made a point to take it out to him personally the second time, to make sure he was happy, and he was really rather rude about the whole thing. He's much better looking in that photo."

Sadie was encouraged. "Yes, that sounds just like Keith Kelly. You don't remember anything else about their meal, do you? Any idea what they were talking about?"

"Jim wasn't happy," Karri said. "I can tell you that much. At first I thought he was just embarrassed by his friend sending the soup back, but then I realized there was something else going on. The tension between the two of them was intense, and he had a bunch of papers on the table. I was worried that this guy—Keith, right?—I thought he was an attorney or something and that Jim was having some trouble."

"Why did you think that?"

"There was a profit and loss statement on the table. I didn't recognize anything else, but I'd never known Jim to eat with someone he didn't like, and it was a pretty serious topic, whatever it was they were talking about."

Sadie opened her mouth to ask another question when she suddenly put two and two together. She'd assumed that Keith had been the one to instigate the lunch, but they'd eaten at Karri's, *Jim's* favorite restaurant. Duh! The lunch hadn't been Keith's idea at all.

"One other thing," Karri said, drawing Sadie's attention again as she continued scooping butter. "The soup wasn't cold. He was posturing."

"Posturing?"

"Making a statement," Karri explained. "Kind of like when a skinny girl orders a salad on a date, I know it's early in a relationship. When a couple shares a dessert, there's no doubt that they are comfortable with one another. And when someone makes a big deal about paying for dinner with a hundred-dollar bill, it's to show off."

Sadie understood. "And when a man sends hot soup back to the kitchen twice, he's dominating the situation."

Karri pointed her butter scoop at Sadie. "Exactly. This Keith guy finally agreed to tolerate the soup, and I left them to their business. I never saw the man again. Jim and I never talked about it."

"Hello?"

They both looked toward the sound of a man's voice, then Karri wiped her hands on her apron. "The linen delivery. Can I help you with anything else?"

"No," Sadie said, fumbling in her purse for the mini-notebook she always kept there. "But thank you for your time; this helps me a great deal. If you remember anything else, could you give me a call? I'll write my cell phone number down and just leave it here on the counter." She was already scribbling down the digits.

"You bet, and I hope you'll come back and eat with us again while you're in town."

Sadie smiled. "I don't even need the invitation, thank you."

Once back in her car, Sadie turned her key in the ignition in order to get the AC going and jotted down some notes on what she'd learned from Karri. After she'd gotten all the words out of her head, she read them over again, absorbing her discovery. Jim had issued the invitation for Keith to join him at his favorite lunch spot, which suggested that *Jim* had issued some kind of proposal to Keith Kelly; something May insisted never would have happened. Sadie had to repeat it a couple of times to really let it settle. This changed things—a lot of things.

She called Richard. It went to his voice mail, and Sadie reluctantly left him a message about what she'd learned. At the tail end of her recap, she had an idea and hurried to invite him to lunch at Karri's that afternoon. She didn't set a time, just asked him to call her as soon as possible. Just before she said good-bye, her phone vibrated slightly, indicating that she'd received a text message. She hung up her phone and then toggled to her inbox.

I'm ready when you are! Give me a call, and you'll be on your way to the financial independence you've always dreamed of. G.T.

It took her a moment to realize G.T. must mean Gary Tracey.

She wasn't looking forward to meeting with him, but with such limited options, she knew she had to take advantage of any opportunity. Plus, if Gary had returned her call, it meant that he must not be aware of the falling out she'd had with May. Without debating too much, she called him back.

"Hello," she said into the phone. "This is Sadie Hoffmiller; I just got your—"

"Sadie, Sadie, lucky lady, I'm so glad to hear from you." He didn't give her a chance to respond. "After I got your message, I was able to reschedule some things this morning so that you and I could have a chance to talk about the glorious potential you have through some financial restructuring. I made you a priority and am at your service."

Sadie clenched her teeth but pulled all her determination together so as to assume the role she now needed to play—interested investor. "Well, that's wonderful," she said, hoping she sounded sincere.

"I'm glad it will work for you," he said. "What time would you like me to come to the house?"

The house? Oh, he meant Jim's house, where he assumed she was today, helping May pack up the house. "Actually, could I come to you?"

"To me?" Gary asked, a little too surprised.

"Yes, do you have an office or something?" She tried to think of a reasonable excuse for why she didn't want to meet at Jim's, but nothing came to mind, and she didn't want to stumble over an improvised reason so she bit her tongue and kept her mouth shut, not an easy thing for her to do.

"Well, sure," Gary said. "I just, well, I don't usually meet with clients there."

Him not wanting to meet at his office made Sadie even more

determined to do just that. "It's just that Jim's house isn't my home, and with everything May has going on, I'd rather not infringe on her with my personal business."

"May won't mind at all," Gary said. "And we won't disturb her one way or another, so if it's all the same—"

"It's not all the same to me," Sadie cut in, then took a breath to calm herself and slow down her words. "I would not feel comfortable meeting at the house, but I'm eager to discuss this with you at *your office*." She tried not to feel bad about being a bully. "I'm afraid I must insist."

"Um, well, of course," Gary said with forced solicitousness. "Whatever you're most comfortable with."

"Wonderful," Sadie said. "Give me your address, and I'll be right there."

He proceeded to give her the address, and she punched it into Dora. His office was about fourteen miles away, which would, hopefully, give her plenty of time to determine how she wanted to handle this. She wished she'd done the same background work on Gary that she'd done for Keith, but last night had not turned out as she'd expected. She hated that she was going to the meeting unprepared and wondered if she should stop at a coffee shop with free Wi-Fi and see what she could find online. A quick glance at the dashboard clock rendered that option a moot point—she didn't have even five extra minutes.

Could she ask Jane to help? Should she? Part of her really wanted to—it would give Jane a chance to prove herself and help Sadie out of a bind. Unfortunately, she wasn't ready to trust anything of any real significance to Jane.

As Sadie slowed down for a red light, she had another thought. Her brother, Jack, worked for a real estate company. He was an accountant, but their office was across the street from a title company they worked with quite often. Title companies, she'd learned from her book on how to be an investigator, had access to all kinds of personal information—far more than Sadie could get on her own. She bit her lip, but could feel the excitement building. It was a long shot, but no longer than meeting with Gary in hopes of solving a murder. It was all about baby steps.

CHAPTER 40

After she pulled up to the office building, which was a square, brick building with water stains coming down from the rather ragged rain gutters, she dialed Jack's cell phone number, frowning when it went to voice mail.

She left the message that she was in somewhat desperate need of some background information on a forty-something-year-old man name Gary Tracey, married to Jolene Tracey and living in Hillsboro, Oregon.

"I know this is last minute, but it might be a matter of life and death. Please call me back ASAP! That's Gary Tracey. T-R-A-C-E-Y. Thanks, Jack." She hung up and hoped he would sense her urgency.

She got out of her car and cast her eyes up to the sky. What had been a partly cloudy morning was turning into an overcast afternoon. She would welcome a rainstorm—who knew when she'd get back to the Pacific Northwest and its famous rain—but she would prefer to enjoy the rain when she could be indoors. For now, the overcast skies seemed to simply trap the humidity, and she felt her skin tingle in anticipation of a full-body sweat.

The glass door creaked when she pulled it open, and the breeze caught the door, requiring her to wrestle it closed, which only made her sweating situation worse. Inside, she surveyed the interior. The tiles along the edge of the foyer, away from the traffic area, were three shades lighter than the middle sections. Some plastic plants had been added several years earlier, perhaps to provide a cozier look, but had apparently been forgotten about, since they were bent and dusty.

There was a plaque on the wall with the names of the building's occupants spelled out with little pushpin letters, though a few letters had fallen to the bottom of the glass case. On the top floor, there was an adult probation office—Adult P obation, according to the directory—and an empty office currently F r Lease. On the main floor, there was a medical billing office and a suite titled Tip-Top Transport. No King Me or Tracey Enterprises or Tracey Investments anywhere. Had she come to the wrong place?

"Mrs. Hoffmiller."

She looked up to see Gary coming toward her with a wide smile on his face. She had to give him credit for acting as though he was in class-A office space any businessman would be proud of. He reached out his hand and she put out her own, which he covered with both of his as though they were lifelong friends. "I'm so glad you could make it," he said warmly. "Right this way."

She followed him down a short hallway, separated from the other hallway by a set of restrooms, and through a door with vinyl lettering that read Tip-Top Transport. The office was quite bare, with an economical desk and chair, a whiteboard on the wall behind the desk, and a single filing cabinet in the corner. There were two chairs opposite the desk.

As Sadie sat in one of them, she noticed the dry coffee pot on the filing cabinet and the overall lack of . . . anything. She wondered if there was a box full of the typical office clutter behind the single door to the right of the desk. Either Gary rarely came here or he had cleared out the office before she arrived. When she finally met Gary's eyes, she realized he'd been watching her inspect the office. She smiled brightly to ease his concerns, but he burst in with an excuse before she could assure him she was fine.

"My top priority in everything I do," he began, "is to put everything I can back into my customer's best interest." He spread his arms wide and leaned back in his chair. "I could spend thousands of dollars on artwork and executive furnishings, but to what end?" He leaned forward. "I have no need for pretense; the fact is, I'm blue-collar, just like you."

Sadie fought back explaining to him that she had her master's degree in elementary education and that blue-collar people didn't make a living taking other people's money, but she understood he was trying to butter her up, so she didn't argue the point.

"I'm not out to make false promises or tell you that I can make you a millionaire; that's not my job. My job is to give you the financial security you need in order to ensure your very best possible future without risking what you already have. Therefore, trying to seduce you into trusting me by dazzling you with excess is completely counterproductive to who I am." He placed a hand on his chest. "I am who I am, and my life is dedicated to making other people's dreams come true."

He finished and grinned again.

"Well, thank you," Sadie said, feeling almost dirty to even pretend to believe him. "Tip-Top Transport—is that the car dealership you mentioned yesterday?"

"No point in owning two offices when one can do the job for both."

Sadie wondered if there even was a dealership or if this was all there was to Tip-Top Transport. "Makes sense," she said.

"I knew you were my kind of girl when I met you yesterday—a real salt of the earth woman."

Sadie nodded, her annoyance at his empty flattery making it harder to keep the smile on her face. She could feel it becoming more plastic by the minute. Her phone rang, and she apologized while she dug for her purse. It was Jack. "Sorry," she said. "I really need to take this."

"Go ahead," Gary said solicitously.

"Thanks," she said, then took a deep breath and stood up. She walked to the end of the office and kept her voice low. "Hi."

"What's wrong?"

"Nothing," she said lightly. "You got my message?" Maybe she should go into the hallway in order to have some privacy, but a quick glance at Gary showed he was busy with his iPhone and not paying her any attention.

"You said it was a matter of life and death. Are you okay?"

It took a moment for Sadie to figure out why Jack was so anxious; then she realized he thought she meant *her* life or death. "Oh, I'm fine, it's not like that." Gary may not be paying her much attention, but she still needed to be careful. "If you could take care of that, I would be forever in your debt."

"You're acting weird."

She smiled wider. "That would be great," she said, hoping he'd catch on.

"I ran into Pete Cunningham this morning, and he said he hadn't talked to you for awhile. What's going on?"

"Yep, the sooner the better."

Jack was quiet, and when he spoke next, his voice was softer. "You're not alone."

"Oh, no," she said with a chuckle. "It'll be fine though."

"But you're okay?"

"Yes," Sadie said, making sure her tone sounded sincere.

Jack paused a moment before he spoke. "Gary Tracey in Hillsboro?"

Sadie almost sighed out loud—he was going to help her. "Yep."

"You know there are probably two thousand men with that name in the US alone."

"Thanks again."

Jack sighed. "You owe me."

"You bet."

She hung up a moment later, relieved that Gary was still texting—or playing solitaire, she couldn't be sure which.

"So," she said, returning to her seat and pulling her chair up to the desk. "Where do we start?"

For the next fifteen minutes, Gary gave her an overview of his investing prowess, inserting questions about her financial situation between compliments toward himself. Sadie was cautious about what she told him, keeping everything but her home and her retirement to herself. He explained how she could borrow against her home, invest the money, and make back the loan amount plus interest *plus* a fifty-percent profit to pay off the mortgage in less than ten years.

"So, basically," Sadie said, trying to clarify, "I would use a portion of the loan on my home to pay the mortgage payment and increase my monthly income until the investment began to pay off."

"Precisely," Gary said with a nod, clasping his hands on top of the desk.

"And how long would it take for the investment to start paying off?"

"A year to eighteen months, tops," Gary said.

"And what exactly would you invest the money into?"

"Well, your investment would be rolled into an up-and-coming business, giving it the launch it needs to really make an impact, while assuring you cutting-edge marketing."

Sadie nodded. "So, what, exactly, would that up-and-coming business be?"

Gary paused. "Well, you'll forgive me for being just a little bit coy." He paused to laugh at his coyness. "But until I have an agreement between the two of us, I really can't get into particulars. In the interest of my other investors, of course, I need to protect the specifics so as not to inadvertently tip my hand and create my own competition."

So, he wanted her to get a loan on her house and invest the money with him without knowing what it was she was investing in. The whole thing had *scam* written all over it.

"That makes sense," she lied, nodding. "Um, how much would you need?"

"Well, we have tiers," he said, spreading his hands like a magician showing that they're empty before he pulls a raccoon out of his sleeve. "Platinum is two hundred thousand dollars."

Sadie's eyes went wide. "Two hundred thousand dollars!"

He put his hands up, palms facing her. "Gold level is a hundred thousand, and Silver is fifty thousand. Keep in mind, the more you invest, the more you make over time."

"That's a lot of money," Sadie said.

"It's all about the future," Gary said. "You've earned this money through the equity in your home; it belongs to you. Why hold it there, waiting for your children to inherit it, when you could be using it yourself to live a better life?"

His comment about inheritance reminded her why she was there in the first place. She nodded, not wanting to scare him off, but needing to get to the heart of things. She didn't have time to waste and was anxious about how much time she'd already spent. "Did Jim invest in this?" she asked, watching Gary closely when she mentioned his father-in-law's name. She wasn't disappointed. Gary's shoulders tightened and his lips thinned.

"Jim was a good man," Gary said. "And, yes, we did a couple of transactions together."

"With this program?" Sadie asked.

"Um, no. He invested in a business I owned several years ago."

"And it was successful?"

Gary's eyes narrowed, and his smile wavered. He paused, and then his expression changed, almost to the point of making Sadie pull back in surprise. Instead of becoming more uncomfortable, Gary suddenly was relaxed, and his smile returned to its full brilliance. "Very successful," he said. "Jim and I were both businessmen, and he had the utmost confidence in my financial abilities. I miss him greatly."

Sadie tried to keep the puzzlement off her face. Jim had gone to rather extensive pains to keep Gary from inheriting anything from his estate, which, in Sadie's mind, meant there had been some trust issues between the two men.

In the next instant, however, she understood. Jim was not here to counter anything Gary said. Sadie had agreed to meet with Gary, which meant he probably didn't think May had said anything about him—assuming May knew. Jim seemed to have kept certain things from his children. As far as Gary was concerned, whatever bad blood he'd had with Jim had gone to the grave. Literally. Beyond that, con men had a seemingly inexhaustible amount of arrogance. Even if Gary had told May the truth, he probably felt up to the task of convincing Sadie it was a misunderstanding.

Sadie feigned a sigh and put a hand to her own chest. "That makes me feel a lot better," she said. "From what I know of Jim, he did not make financial decisions of that caliber easily."

Gary smiled, perfectly at ease with his lie. "No, he didn't. In fact, I credit the recent success of his business with the things he learned through our work together."

"I wonder how things will go now, though, with him gone. I assume Hugh will manage the day-to-day operations at S&S?"

Gary shifted and shrugged his shoulders. "I assume so. He's the natural choice to take over."

"Doesn't Jolene inherit part of the company too, though?"

"Yeah, like thirty percent," he said, not hiding that this wasn't what he wanted to talk about. "Now, about your—"

"This must be such a difficult time for your family," Sadie said, one of the few sincere comments she'd made during the last hour. "I imagine thinking about the business is a difficult task right now."

"It's certainly not on the top of our list," Gary said.

Sadie hurried on, afraid he would try to redirect again. "Do you think they'll sell? The three of them, I mean."

"I suppose it's a possibility, though, as I said, it's low on our list of priorities."

"If it sold, though, you'd have cash instead of the company as an asset. Easier to invest."

"Of course, but for now Hugh is simply managing Jolene's portion."

"That does seem to make the most sense." Sadie nodded in agreement. "Is there a formal contract between Jolene and Hugh?"

"What for?" Gary said, betraying his annoyance. "He knows she's in no position to do much right now."

"Well," Sadie said, trying to keep on track, "May told me about the offer from Keith Kelly to buy out the company—is that something you've considered?"

Gary watched her closely, and she could fairly read his mind as he tried to figure out why she was asking about these things. "I'm sorry," she said, sitting back. "I'm being nosy. I was just curious, what with all your business sense, if you were helping Hugh with any negotiations. I get the feeling he wants to sell, but I don't want to pry, and of course I don't want to upset May by asking questions that are hard for her to consider right now. She doesn't have the expertise you do and would have a harder time thinking about these issues, I imagine."

Apparently, she'd said something right. Gary relaxed and shrugged as though to display his confidence. "Actually, I have had some discussions with Hugh. Jolene and I have talked about selling out to Hugh completely—maybe trading him our portion for his part of the house. It's a premium piece of real estate right now and ought to be able to make a tidy little profit once it sells. Of course, nothing is final, and it's best not to discuss any of this with May right now. She's had a difficult time with Jim's passing, and we're all being careful about upsetting her."

"Of course. Jim's death was a tragedy, but I imagine it will be a boon for your business. I mean, considering Jim's other assets and Jolene's portion of them. It's funny how it works out that way sometimes, loss and increase cycling together." It was a version of what Lois had said last night—rebirth in the wake of tragedy.

Gary was looking at her a little too closely, and she sensed she'd gotten too far off track.

"Did I mention my late husband left me with some money?" Sadie offered as a truce.

Gary immediately brightened and leaned across the table. "Really? How much?"

The admission about more money basically started the conversation over again, and Sadie went into autopilot, nodding intermittently and hoping her eyes didn't look as glazed over as they felt. She thought about what Gary had said about Jolene trading her portion of the business for the equity in the house. If Hugh were looking to sell his portion of the business to Keith, he had two-thirds to bargain with instead of the one-third he'd have otherwise. Had he talked to May about selling him her portion of the business as well? Once he had it all, he would have full power to make whatever future decisions he wanted to.

Sadie couldn't help but wonder if Hugh would kill for the chance to dig himself out of another financial mess. Jim had rescued his son before and lost Keith in the process of one of those rescues. If Hugh had approached Jim in need of financial help, would Jim have bailed him out again? What if Jim wouldn't do it this time? What if *this time* Jim told his son to grow up, not calculating the level of Hugh's anxiety and fear, or that Jim's assets may have been Hugh's only way out.

"So what do you think?" Gary said, all smiles again. "Are you in?" He pulled open a drawer and began shuffling through papers. He pulled out a half-sized desk calendar along with some other papers—things that had probably been on the desk and shoved in the drawer during the clean fest before Sadie's arrival—and finally pulled out a photocopied agreement of some kind. He pushed it across the desk toward her.

"I just need you to fill this out so I can begin gathering the financial information we need to generate the official documentation."

Sadie looked at the form and realized it was a release of information request. She imagined he planned to send it to her banks in order to verify her account information. Her phone rang again. The rudeness at taking another call was intense, and almost enough for her to let it go, but her internal anxiety was rising, and she could use a minute to calm back down. She apologized while she reached into her purse a second time.

Gary's smile wasn't quite as sincere as before, but she knew he wouldn't argue when the carrot of her money was dangling before his eyes.

It was Richard, and she felt her heart skip a beat. She hoped she could pull off another careful phone call.

"Hi," Sadie said into the phone, trying not to get her hopes up.

"I got your message. Lunch would be great. I've got some really interesting things to tell you."

"Oh, good," Sadie said. "Me too."

Her gaze flickered to Gary, who had pulled out his phone and was typing in a text message.

"You mentioned Karri's." Richard said. "It seems appropriate. I've got a conference call in a few minutes, but my role will be a small one. I shouldn't have any trouble being to Karri's by noon, but I'll text you if I'm running late. I think you'll be very interested in what I figured out."

A tremor ran through Sadie. He'd learned something important about Jim and Keith's lunch; she could feel it.

"Perfect," Sadie said. "I'll see you in an hour."

He hung up, and Sadie put the phone away. Gary was still

occupied with his phone, and Sadie scanned the desk, looking for anything that might give her more information.

Her eyes stopped at the desk calendar he'd removed from the drawer. By leaning forward slightly and turning her head just a little, she could make out some of the information written there. There were lots of little things—lunches and conference calls—but her eyes were drawn to a similar event written in pink marker every Thursday in August: "Jo to Prov. 3:00." Prov? Did that mean Providence, where Jolene received her cancer treatments? The other commitments were in a scratchy, decidedly masculine scrawl, but this one was in bubbly lettering, which gave away the fact that Jolene had likely been the one who'd written it in. Sadie thought again about the hospice website and wondered what was making Jolene give up hope; her treatment schedule seemed pretty intense and optimistic.

Sadie paused. Hadn't Jolene said she was finished with this round of treatment? Yet, according to the calendar, she had two more treatments this month.

"So, where were we?" Gary said, slipping his phone out of sight and not seeming to have noticed her interest in the calendar. "Ah, yes, the agreement," he said before Sadie could respond. He tapped the paper he'd put in front of her and moved it a little closer, his smile looking more and more radiant by the second. "Once we get that filled out, we're good to go."

"I just need to talk to my brother," Sadie said, pulling the card she'd kept up her sleeve all this time.

"This isn't the kind of decision you want to leave up to someone else," he said, his smile faltering and his expression hardening. "Like I said, and no disrespect to your brother, but family members aren't always the best people to go to in times like this. What we're doing here is an intricate investment; not everyone is willing to be open-minded enough to truly grasp the concept."

"I understand," Sadie said with feigned regret. "But he has financial power of attorney over my accounts." She folded the paper in half and tapped it against his arm. "But, believe me, I know how to take a stand when I need to, and I plan on having a very serious discussion with him about this."

"He has power of attorney?" Gary nearly deflated at the news. "You didn't mention that."

Sadie raised her eyebrows. "I didn't?" She made a face. "Do you have any other information I could show him about your company? A brochure or something to show him it's legitimate?"

"Um," Gary said, pulling open the drawer but not even bothering to riffle through the papers. He looked up at her, and she could tell that his smile was forced now. Apparently not getting a poor old lady—or in her case, a rich, not-so-old lady—to sign over her life savings in under an hour had soured his mood. "We're back to the privacy issues of the investment."

"Oh, right," Sadie said, snapping her fingers. She stood up and tucked the paper into her purse. "I've got your card, so I'll be sure to call you as soon as I talk to my brother."

Gary stood too. "And do you know when that will be?" He looked at his watch and made a face. "I made this time for you today, but I don't want you to get the impression that my time isn't at a premium. I wouldn't be able to pull the same tricks as I did today if we needed to meet a second time."

Tricks, Sadie thought. Interesting choice of word. She crossed her fingers and held them up. "I'll just have to hope for the best, then."

Gary forced another smile. She turned to the door, and he

hurried to open it for her. "I'll look forward to hearing from you," he said, but Sadie knew that *he* knew he'd lost his chance. No brother in his right mind would let his sister step into a pile of manure like he'd just proposed to her.

As she paused at the threshold of the office, she gave Gary a long look as sadness rose in her chest. Jolene had been so sweet about her husband when Sadie had talked to her last night, so grateful for him in her life. Gary, on the other hand, gave no impression that he even cared about Jolene. Maybe his detachment had something to do with the loss of his firstborn son. Or maybe watching Jolene's family members die one by one throughout their marriage had hardened him to the point that he didn't trust himself to absorb the emotions in front of other people. Or, maybe he was a narcissist.

"Good luck to you and your wife at this difficult time," Sadie said, every word heartfelt and sincere. "I really do wish you both the best, and I hope you and Jolene enjoy that cruise."

CHAPTER 41

Sadie arrived at Karri's fifteen minutes early and stared out the windshield, trying to determine how to fill the time until Richard arrived. The sky was grayer, and the wind was picking up, swaying the treetops and whistling around her door. Meanwhile, Sadie's thoughts were also picking up in a storm of questions as she considered the things she'd gleaned from her conversation with Gary. If only Jack had that background information!

She couldn't say for certain that Gary was a weasel, but there was something very weasely about him, and he'd talked to Hugh about selling their percentage. If only Sadie could ask May if Hugh had said anything to her. Could that be the reason for the tension between the two of them at Jim's house yesterday? May had said Hugh thought she was crazy to think their father had been murdered—was Hugh hiding something? Protecting himself? Could Gary be manipulating his sick wife into the most financially advantageous position? There wasn't enough information one way or another, but she knew she was getting closer and was more anxious than ever to fit the pieces together. She could smell it almost as well as she could smell Karri's lunch special once she opened the driver's door—chicken and citrus of some kind.

She pushed through the front door, squinting as her eyes adjusted to the darkened interior. She explained to the hostess that she was meeting someone and followed the woman to a table painted bright yellow near the far windows. As Sadie passed the kitchen, she looked in and waved at Karri, who was mixing something. It took a moment for Karri to recognize Sadie, but she smiled and lifted a hand for a quick wave back. Sadie felt better to be in a familiar place and was eager to hear what Richard had learned from his father.

"Can I get you anything while you wait?" the hostess asked, sliding the day's photocopied menu in front of Sadie once she'd sat down in the antique dining room chair.

Sadie opened her mouth to order a Diet Coke when the dessert tray across the room caught her attention. "Do you have the blackberry crumble today?"

"We do," the waitress said with a nod.

Sadie smiled up at her and handed back the menu. "Don't judge me for having dessert first."

The woman smiled and nodded, leaning in slightly. "You and me both," she said, then took the menu and turned away.

Sadie opened her purse, pulled out her notebook, and began writing down the disconnected thoughts she had about what she'd learned and the questions they inspired.

Gary's a scam artist—Does he have any convictions?
Dumpy office—What's his financial situation?
Hugh taking Jolene's percentage—Does the trust allow that?
Cancer treatments every Thursday—Is Jolene really getting
    better?

She tapped her pen on the questions, studying them. There was a connection there that she wasn't making. What was it? What was she missing? She could feel it hovering like a mosquito, inviting her to swat at it, but she couldn't connect with it, whatever it was.

"I'm so glad you came back."

Sadie looked up as Karri slid a serving of blackberry crumble in front of her. It was topped with fresh whipping cream and sprinkled with a little cinnamon. She couldn't be sure, but she thought it was a bigger portion than what she'd had yesterday. She smiled at Karri. "You're spoiling me," she said.

Karri shrugged and slid into the booth across from Sadie. "It's what I do."

"And yet you're a size six," Sadie said, picking up her fork.

"Stress is a pretty good workout," Karri said. "And if you're looking for a good workout, open your own business."

"That bad, huh?"

"Could be worse," Karri said with a casual shrug.

Sadie took the first bite of the dessert and let the flavors and textures mingle in her mouth. "This is so good," she said after she swallowed. "Some of the best crumb topping I've ever had."

"And probably the easiest recipe you've ever heard of," Karri said.

"I suppose asking a chef for her recipe is considered bad form, isn't it?"

"I'm not a chef," Karri said with a laugh. "I just love food." She leaned forward. "It's equal portions of oats, flour, brown sugar, and butter."

"That's it?" Sadie said, putting down her spoon. "You just cut it together?"

Karri nodded. "I add a little salt, a little cinnamon, and just a touch of lemon zest, but that's it."

"I'm flabbergasted," Sadie said. "You've just proven my point that good food doesn't have to be complicated."

"Absolutely," Karri said. "Hey, I also remembered something after you left."

"Oh?"

"It's not what you were asking about—lunch with the cold-soup man—but I got to thinking about Jim and remembered another lunch that stood out to me. I don't think it had anything to do with the other stuff, though, so it's probably not important, but—"

"I'd love to hear about it," Sadie said. "I'm trying to put some pieces together, so I'm not after anything specific. What was this incident?"

"Another lunch. Like I said, Jim came in quite often. A few days after the lunch with that Kelly man, Jim came in with his son."

"Hugh?"

Karri nodded. "See, they usually got along really well, but there was something wrong that day. I remember because I'd been a little worried about Jim after the lunch he'd had with that Kelly guy. He was so withdrawn and obviously stressed out. Anyway, he wasn't much different when he came with Hugh. I make a point to say hi to my regulars, but we were too busy for me to leave the kitchen when their meals came up, so I brought out their check instead. They were arguing."

"About what?"

"I don't know. They were both real intent, but with their voices low as though no one would know they were arguing if they weren't loud. I stopped a couple feet away from the table, hoping they'd notice me. Hugh said something I couldn't hear, and then Jim suddenly leaned across the table, pointed at Hugh and said he'd ruined him."

"Hugh had ruined Jim?" Sadie asked.

Karri nodded. "I think that's what he meant. Jim saw me standing there and put his hand out for the check, slid a fifty inside, and told me to give the change to Hugh. Then he looked at Hugh and said it was the last handout he was ever going to give him. He stood up and stormed out."

Sadie put her hands in her lap, suddenly not hungry. "Wow," she said.

Karri nodded. "I know, right? They both apologized for it later, but—"

"Both?"

"Jim came in the next day and was real embarrassed. He said it was a bad day, and he was sorry for behaving like that in my restaurant. It was real sweet."

"And Hugh apologized too?"

"After the funeral," Karri said. "He came a few days later and said how horrible he felt about the argument and how he hoped I wouldn't hold it against him."

"Did you know Hugh well?" Sadie asked. It seemed odd he'd return weeks later to apologize for something.

"He's the one who installed our sprinklers, and he came in a few times a month—usually with Jim. It was nice he made things right with me; I'm sure that after Jim died, Hugh felt horrible about that argument. It's funny how something tragic like that can suddenly make the things we get mad about seem small."

Sadie nodded. "That's an excellent point."

"Well, I best get back to work and let you enjoy that crumble," Karri said as she stood. "I'm glad you came back in. I'm afraid I got busy and couldn't find that number you gave me, and then Jim's daughter didn't know when she'd be seeing you next so I worried you wouldn't get my message."

Sadie's mouth went dry. "Jim's daughter?"

"Yeah," Karri said. She stood up and adjusted her apron. "When I remembered about the lunch with Hugh, I called Jim's house, figuring since you were friends with May that was a good place to start." She smiled, unaware of the pit in Sadie's stomach. "Anyway, I'm glad it all worked out."

"Yeah," Sadie said, her tone flat even though she tried to force a smile. "Me too."

"The blackberry crumble is on the house," Karri said as she turned away. "My treat."

"Thank you," Sadie said, but Karri was too far away to hear it.

Sadie looked down at the dessert that she had no appetite for—well, not as much as she'd had when she first ordered it anyway. Her stomach rumbled, reminding her that she hadn't had a reasonable meal all day.

She picked up her spoon and cut another bite. The crumb topping broke apart, causing the entire crust to crumble, and as she put the bite in her mouth, she reflected on how similar this whole situation with Jim Sanderson's death had become. She'd covered her bases, learned little details about the people in his life and the possible motivations that may have ended his, but many more things were crumbling even as other pieces came together.

Hugh was in debt.

Keith was out of town when Jim was killed.

Hugh was now trying to sell to Keith.

For a moment she wondered if Keith and Hugh could have been in on it together. The idea made her sick—Hugh was Jim's son!—but he was also an addict. Addicts were a personality type unto themselves.

Her phone dinged to signal she'd received a text message, and she dug the phone out of her purse, freezing for a moment when she saw that it was from May. Heat rushed up her neck and into her face. Karri's phone call meant May would know Sadie was not only still in town, but still working the case. Sadie didn't know if she could handle any more negativity right now, but she took a breath and opened the message.

I need to talk to you. Can you come over?

Sadie wasn't sure if she was relieved or not. She'd been nervous to open the text message for fear it would be full of angry words; could she stand that same anger face to face? And yet, could she refuse to go talk to May? Even if the idea made her want to curl up in a ball and rock back and forth in a corner?

She took a breath and replied.

I can be there in an hour.

The response was immediate.

Okay. You might beat me, but I'll be there soon.

Sadie looked at the text message and wished she could divine May's mood and intentions. Still staring at the phone, she took another bite of the crumble, barely tasting it this time.

Someone slid into the chair across from her, and she remembered that she was waiting for Richard. She looked up and almost smiled before she realized it wasn't Richard. The blackberry flavor disappeared from her tongue, and she swallowed as Keith Kelly looked back at her with a serious expression, his eyes almost cutting in their intensity.

CHAPTER 42

For a few seconds they both just sat there. Sadie's stomach was in her shoes, and sweat trickled down the back of her neck as she tried to formulate how to handle this situation.

Be confident, she told herself as she put the spoon down next to her dessert.

"Mr. Kelly," Sadie said, as though she'd expected him along. She hoped she didn't have any blackberries in her teeth. "It's a pleasure to meet you."

She put her hand across the table. His grip was firm, so she increased her own, which caused him to grip her hand even harder. Inside she winced, but she kept her cool and noted his attempt at besting her. Finally, he let go, and she dropped her hand under the table, flexing it a few times in an attempt to work out the ache in her joints.

"I'm not here to play games or act under pretenses," Keith began, his intense blue eyes boring into her. "You've asked my son to look into my personal affairs, and I resent it. You need to—"

"I'm sure you do resent it," Sadie cut in. "But your resentment is misplaced."

His left eye twitched, and she hurried on.

"Where's Richard?"

"He's been detained."

"Is he hurt?"

"How dare you ask that," Keith said, leaning forward slightly as his eyes narrowed. He placed both hands on the yellow tabletop. "Of course he's not hurt. He's my son."

"Who is suddenly not dancing to your tune." She raised one eyebrow. "Must be hard for you to stomach—him suddenly questioning you."

Keith took a breath, presumably to calm himself. "What do you want with Richard?"

"Nothing," Sadie said easily. "He's simply helping me put a puzzle together." She had an idea. Wondering if it would work, she pushed the blackberry crumble to the side. "Now that you're here, you can save me the trouble. What was the purpose of your lunch with Jim Sanderson on July first?"

Keith blinked in surprise. He moved as though to stand. "I'm not going to be interrogated by you," he said. "Richard may have tripped over himself to share my personal life with you, but I have no motivation to do so. I came here to tell you to back off." He stopped mid-threat, and Sadie noticed the slightest lowering of his eyebrows as though he'd just realized something. "You're here about Jim?"

Ah, he didn't know as much as he thought he did. "What? You think I'm with Jepson?" Sadie said, remembering how Richard had jumped to that same conclusion.

Keith said nothing, which was as good as an agreement for Sadie.

She leaned forward and took the upper hand. "I'm not with Jepson. I've been hired to look into the death of Jim Sanderson, and your name came up. Richard is helping me, yes, but he's not my only source of information." She was, of course, referring to his website and other public databases, but she hoped her ambiguity about what kind of sources she had used would unnerve Keith.

"What do you mean you're looking into Jim's death?" Keith said, totally thrown off. "He died of a heart attack."

"Not everyone thinks that heart attack was natural," Sadie said.

"And *my* name came up?"

"You wanted his atomizer," Sadie said simply. "And he wouldn't sell it to you."

Keith blinked, and Sadie watched in fascination as first shock and then anger lit his face. "You think I would . . . kill him?" He pointed his finger at her and clenched his teeth together as he spoke. "That's slander, and I'm calling my attorney."

"The same attorney who drafted up the letter of intent to be sent to Jim's heirs after the funeral? The letter in which you sug-gested that they sell you the entire business?" Sadie's knees were shaking. This man was powerful, and even if she wasn't showing it, he scared her.

Keith was once again taken aback, and Sadie, once again, used his surprise as her way in. She realized that she really didn't believe Keith had anything to do with Jim's death. But he might be the only other person alive who knew what that lunch was about, and the reason behind the meeting might very well lead her to the real killer.

"If you weren't desperate for the atomizer, then perhaps you can explain to me why events happened the way they did. Why did Jim Sanderson invite you to lunch for the first time in ten years, two weeks before he died?"

Keith took several deep breaths. He didn't seem to be a man who got thrown off his game like this very often.

"Look," Sadie said, anxious to get to the meat of the conversation. "I'm not out to get you; I'm out to discover the truth. If you can help me, then I don't have to ask Richard questions, and you don't have to worry about what I believe. You're not the only person I'm looking into, but I will tell you that your history with Jim makes you a very interesting person. Help me or don't, it doesn't really matter, because I'll find the answers. If you had nothing to do with Jim's death, then save me, Richard, and you the trouble of us having to entertain the possibilities."

"Richard thinks I could have done something to Jim?" Keith said quietly after several seconds.

"Not really," Sadie said. "But he didn't know anything about the lunch." However, Sadie remembered that Keith's secretary had noted the lunch on his calendar, which meant it wasn't *entirely* secret. She quickly threw that detail into her approach. "And while I realize you weren't hiding the meeting, Richard was surprised to know nothing about it. I would be thrilled to tell Richard that he has nothing to worry about and that his father is as trustworthy as ever." Based on results, however, Keith had never been all that upstanding in the trust department, but Sadie wasn't going to get very far with a comment like that.

After Keith digested what she'd said, he nodded. "Jim asked me to lunch. It wasn't my idea."

Sadie did a little victory dance in her head, but tried to look impressed with the information. "Why?"

Keith took a breath and exhaled slowly. "He wanted to sell."

"The atomizer?"

Keith shook his head. "The whole business."

Sadie was unable to hide her surprise. "The whole business?" she repeated. May had said Jim's dream was to have his children run the business together. He'd worked so hard to recover after the split that it was hard to believe he would suddenly want to sell. But Karri had seen financial documents on the table when Keith and Jim had had lunch.

"Why would he do that?"

"Hugh was racking up debts faster than Jim could pay them off," Keith said, leaning back in the chair and folding his thick arms over his thick chest. He was dressed in a powder-blue dress shirt with a buff-colored linen jacket.

"Like last time?" Sadie said.

Keith nodded. "I told Jim back then that if he simply stepped in and saved Hugh from the mess he'd made that it would happen again. And I was right. Hugh is in more trouble than ever this time. And not just with a company credit card he fished out of his dad's wallet. He's got bookies calling the office. And someone tried to run him off the road a few days before Jim made the lunch date. Whatever Hugh's gotten himself into is big."

"Big enough that Jim was willing to sell S&S to pay off Hugh's debts?"

"Hugh's an addict, and just like a drug, gambling requires more and more to get the same high. Here Jim had worked his whole life to become who he was—a brilliant engineer on the cutting edge of our industry—and Hugh was flushing it away on basketball and poker games."

"That's where the profits from the new atomizer were going," Sadie said, gluing together the pieces of information she'd spent the last two days gleaning. The company was finally having success, and Hugh was getting sicker because of it.

"Jim was out of fight," Keith said. "His daughter was dying, his son was drowning in debts and addiction, and he was calling uncle.

He believed if he sold the business, he could pay off Hugh's debts and get him into a treatment program as his very last attempt to save Hugh from himself. He said he wanted to retire—maybe go to Ohio to be with May after Jolene passed away—but he knew he couldn't trust Hugh with the company. Selling it was his only option."

Poor Jim, Sadie thought. For an instant, she pictured him laying in bed, overwhelmed with the trials of his children and coming up with this plan. Sadie wished she could have met Jim Sanderson. He seemed like a very good man. "Were you interested in buying?"

Keith looked down, and Sadie sensed that he wasn't proud of his answer. He uncrossed his arms and lined up the silverware on the table. "I was very interested," he said. His tone, however, was flat.

"But?"

His glance flickered to hers before returning to the silverware. He made a minute adjustment so that the handles were perfectly parallel. He looked like Shawn when Shawn knew he'd done something wrong. "But I wanted Jim to sweat it out a little bit." He dropped his hands into his lap.

Sadie shook her head slightly. His old friend had come to him in desperate circumstances, but Keith's pride had made him hold out. Now Jim was dead. Sadie didn't need to say anything to rub it in.

Keith continued. "I harangued him on how he'd handled Hugh all these years and how this was exactly what he deserved. I said he should have forced Hugh to get his act together back when we were in business together. I said that I wasn't interested in inheriting whatever reputation Hugh had given the company and that I couldn't see any reason why his problem should be mine."

"How very kind of you," Sadie said, unable to help herself. She braced herself, but he just looked at her with sad eyes.

"Indeed," he said. "How very kind of me." He paused for a

breath. "I told him I'd think about it and then I met with my attorney. We started working on how to facilitate the purchase. It was bad timing for me—I had Jepson on the hook, and they were proving to be a bunch of nervous Nellies—but I wanted S&S and, though I'm sure it's hard to believe, I wanted to help Jim."

"You just wanted him to know you held all the cards. No pun intended."

"When you've played politics as long as I have, it's a hard habit to break. When Jim died, I felt horrible." He shook his head. "I really think that we could have been friends again. I was going to offer him a consulting position with the company so that he'd be able to keep his hand in the industry and make a little money. I'm slowing down too, and I really hoped that we could put everything behind us." He shrugged. "Maybe he'd want to take up golf. We never got to that point." There was nothing insincere about the regret in his voice. He had lost a dear friend twice: first, ten years ago because of Hugh, and now because of his own stubbornness.

"So you contacted his kids after he was gone in order to fulfill Jim's wishes," Sadie said. She placed her clasped hands on the table and leaned forward slightly. There were still many unredeemable qualities about this man, but she was sympathetic for his regret—a regret he had no way to remedy.

"Hugh can't run that business," Keith said. "He's got a good head for the mechanics—he probably could have been an engineer himself if he'd had the discipline to go to school—but he'll run that company into the ground within the year on his own. After Jim died, I felt I owed it to him to at least try to buy the company, but he'd told me his kids had no idea he was meeting with me. I knew they'd probably think I was a liar if I tried to convince them of Jim's interest in selling out, but I hoped that maybe they would sell without me having to tell them Jim had given up."

"And Hugh's the only one who responded."

Keith shook his head slowly, still holding Sadie's eyes. "Jolene's husband, Gary, called last week."

"But Gary doesn't get ownership."

"I know, and the last thing Jim wanted was for Gary to have any part in anything, but with Jolene so sick, Gary said he was negotiating on her behalf."

Sadie thought back to the living trust that had stipulated that Gary was to get nothing. But Jolene was still his wife, and she was ill. Gary saw himself as a savvy negotiator; no doubt he thought he could convince Jolene to sell. No doubt he was right; Jolene fairly worshipped him. Suddenly, something Keith had said earlier in their conversation came to mind.

"You said Jolene was dying," Sadie said, remembering how Jolene had said she was getting better. "Did Jim tell you that?"

Keith nodded. "Leena had beat the cancer her first time around." He closed his eyes and took a deep breath. "But Jim said Jolene wasn't going to be as lucky. I made the comment at lunch that treatments had made so much progress since Leena, but Jim had little hope. Jolene wanted to take an Alaskan cruise with her husband and son before she died. I don't know if you know Gary Tracey, but the man is a financial nightmare. They've never had two nickels to rub together. If not for Jim helping them out all these years while Gary played with his stupid get-rich-quick ideas, they'd have nothing."

"But Jim didn't have the money, did he?" Sadie said. "To pay for that cruise."

"Jolene asked for a loan, an advance on her inheritance, and it was when Jim started looking into his options that he realized Hugh had maxed out their line of credit with the bank and run up two more credit cards, not to mention his own personal lines of credit. Jolene was pretty upset when he told her he couldn't do it. I don't think he told her why, but he said it had been a few days and she still wasn't talking to him, which was more than he could stand."

"He was awfully open with you at that lunch," Sadie said after a thoughtful silence stretched between them for a few seconds. A slight ticking had begun in the back of her head, and she glanced at the notes she'd written down. An equation was formulating, but she wasn't sure what it was. "I guess that surprises me, what with how things had been between you two."

"Even with all the issues between us, I knew his history better than most people. For good and bad, Jim loved his children, and they were destroying him."

"Jolene didn't get cancer on purpose." Sadie defended, not sure what he meant by his comment. "I'm sure his inability to help was wrapped up in his own grief." The ticking in her head continued.

Keith shook his head. "Probably, but he was losing her all the same, and it felt like he was losing her twice as much to have her angry with him."

Losing her, Sadie repeated. *Losing her* . . . All of a sudden, the locks clicked into place in Sadie's mind. She sat up straight and felt a rush of heat tingle up her spine, causing her to shudder.

"What?" Keith asked, watching her closely.

Sadie opened her mouth to let it all tumble out, but stopped herself as May's face came to mind from last night. *"Him?"* she'd said. *"You turned to him?"* That had been in reference to Richard, but Sadie had no doubt she would feel the same way about Keith.

"I'm so sorry," she said, putting her notebook away and fumbling for her keys. She wished there was time to get her blackberry crumble put in a to-go box, but time was of the essence. "I need to go." She looked up, realizing she owed him something for what he'd given her, even though the discovery she'd made had her stomach in knots. "Thank you, Mr. Kelly. I hope you know how helpful you've been. You did right by Jim in the end, and I'll be sure his family knows it."

She stood up, but stopped when he put a hand on her arm. His expression tightened. "Where are you going?"

"To talk to May."

"May? Is that who you work for?" The words came out like a hiss. "She's the one who thinks I would hurt Jim?"

Sadie pulled back on her arm, but Keith's grip simply tightened. "Mr. Kelly," she said calmly. "You need to let go of my arm."

"If I'd known you were working for May, I wouldn't have said any of those things." His grip was getting tighter. Sadie could break the hold with a simple twist-and-pull move—first lesson in self-defense—but she was interested in what he had to say. "*That's* why Richard was helping you? To help her?" He growled low in his throat, and all the compassion and regret he'd shown disappeared. Sadie wondered which persona was the real Keith. "That boy has less sense than a bucket of rocks."

"He loves her," Sadie said. "Doesn't that count for something?"

Keith narrowed his eyes. "He'd have never reached his potential if I hadn't gotten him away from her. Look at her family, look at the way her father gave up everything to clean up behind his children. There is no way to make a man of yourself when you attach yourself to people who will pull you down."

Sadie had had enough. She twisted and pulled her arm toward her, breaking his grasp and stepping back so she was out of reach. "Mr. Kelly, you're a brilliant businessman and have done well for yourself, but you've missed out on a lot of the good things in life. Jim Sanderson's heart may have been too soft to reach his potential in the business world, but he died as a generous man and that counts for something."

She turned and left the restaurant, her whole body tingling in fear that he would follow her, demanding an altercation, but she made it to her car unscathed. The breeze had turned to a wind, blowing her hair into pure chaos in the process.

As she pulled out of the parking lot, she finger-combed her hair into place and thought back to the last thing she'd said about Jim having died a generous man. Had he died because his generosity had run out? Sadie hoped not, but there was too much for her to ignore. She was glad she'd had a few bites of her blackberry crumble to help her through the next half hour.

How would she tell May that her brother and sister had the strongest reasons to want their father dead?

Blackberry Crumble

6 cups fresh or frozen blackberries (or any kind of frozen berry)
2 tablespoons flour
3 tablespoons sugar
½ cup butter
½ cup flour
½ cup rolled oats
½ cup brown sugar
½ teaspoon nutmeg
½ teaspoon cinnamon
¼ teaspoon salt

Preheat oven to 350 degrees. Mix berries, 2 tablespoons flour, and 3 tablespoons sugar together in large bowl. Spread in an 8x8 pan. In a mixing bowl, combine remaining ingredients; adjust spices to taste. Use a pastry cutter to cut ingredients together until pea-sized crumbles form. Sprinkle over the top of the berry mixture. Bake for 45 to 55 minutes or until crumb topping is browned. Let cool slightly. Serve warm topped with vanilla ice cream or whipped cream, if desired. Serves 6.

Note: Karri recommends adding a little lemon zest to the topping. Sounds delicious!

CHAPTER 43

Sadie had driven about half a mile when her phone rang. Scanning for cops as she waited for a light, she pulled her phone out of her purse, her entire chest tight with anticipation. When she saw it was Jack calling, she put on her right blinker and answered it. "Hang on just a minute," she said. "I need to pull over."

She set the phone down, glad no members of law enforcement had seen her breaking the law again, and turned right when the light changed. She pulled into the parking lot of a pharmacy and shifted into PARK.

"Sorry about that," Sadie said. "It's against the law to talk on your cell phone while driving."

"Is everything okay?" Jack asked.

"Well," Sadie started, trying to decide what she should or could say. "Everything is . . . complicated." She looked at the clock and felt anxiety rush through her—she needed to talk to May. "Did you find him?"

"Believe it or not, I did—well, we did."

"We?" Sadie asked.

"You're not dating this guy, are you?"

Sadie let out a breath. "No, Jack, I'm not dating him." She was dating Pete—well, maybe.

"So who is he?"

"Just tell me what you found out, please. I'm in a hurry."

"Okay, okay," Jack said. "In a nutshell, the guy's a crook. He's got at least seven judgments against him. Most of them have to do with leases he didn't pay and things like that, but he sure knows how to play the system. He's used about six different names—Tracey Gary; G. Tracey; TG Gary—they're all versions of his name but have allowed him to get away with an awful lot of stuff. He served nine months in jail a few years ago for fraud."

"I knew it," Sadie said.

"So, will you tell me who he is now?"

"Oh, he's just some guy who wants me to mortgage my house and invest it in one of his schemes."

Jack was silent. "If you're not happy with the investments I've—"

"No, no," Sadie said. "I also think he might have been involved in the death of his father-in-law. Knowing he has a history of being a deadbeat shores up that theory."

"You're investigating another murder?" Jack asked. "That's why you're in Oregon?"

"Well, kind of," Sadie said, squirming. "Anyway, I better go."

"Does Pete know you're up there?"

"Yes," Sadie said, feeling the mood drop. "He knows."

"And he's not happy about it, is he?"

"Not particularly." Sadie shifted into reverse. "Can we talk later? I really do need to go."

"Are you in trouble?"

Sadie groaned. She was the older sibling and hated it when he played big brother. "Thank you for your help," she said. "I'll call you later." She turned off the phone in the middle of his protest and dropped it in her purse as she pulled out of the parking space. Gary was an ex-con who hadn't learned his lesson and obviously didn't care who he hurt with his scams. It fit perfectly with what she'd deduced at the restaurant: if Jolene had died before Jim Sanderson, Gary would have inherited nothing. Jolene's portion would have gone directly to his son—Jim's only living grandchild.

Sadie pulled back into traffic but continued reviewing things in her mind and playing devil's advocate with the details. Hugh was up to his ears in debts he couldn't pay. That could be a motive for murder, except that Jim was trying to sell the company to pay off those debts. But Hugh didn't know that. With Jim gone, his estate was caught up in being settled according to the terms of the trust. The children had already received some money: May could afford to pay Sadie, Hugh hadn't been beaten by thugs, and Jolene and Gary had booked that long-awaited cruise. But Keith made it sound like Hugh's debts were immense. The first disbursement maxed out at $10,000. That wasn't enough to get Hugh out of trouble?

The rock in her stomach was getting heavier, and she took a breath, hoping it would help her find the strength to do what she had to do. She wished she had all the answers, that she had access to the personal files so she could look for proof of whatever investment Jim had made with Gary. She was all but certain that was why he'd been cut out of the will. Maybe that was why Gary went to jail? If only all the information were wrapped up with a bow and complete.

Her phone rang as she was driving, and she picked it up long enough to see that it was Richard, making her wonder why Keith had come to the restaurant instead of Richard. As much as she wanted to talk to him, there was no time; May deserved to know what she'd learned before anyone else did.

Ten minutes later, Sadie pulled up to Jim Sanderson's house and immediately noted that May's car wasn't in the driveway. Apparently she'd beaten May home.

"Oh, biscuits," Sadie said, letting herself out of the car anyway. The wind had picked up even more, and she noted that the clouds were dark. The coming storm was taking the edge off the summer heat instead of trapping it, but the wind required Sadie to continually brush her hair from her face. She nearly put her keys in her purse before catching herself and slipping them in her pocket instead. It hadn't done her any favors to keep them on her person, but it made her feel better to know she was following proper etiquette. She'd determined that a lot of police and investigative technique was based in paranoia. The collar of her shirt blew up against her cheek as she climbed the steps to the side door, and she smoothed it down, trying to turn into the wind so that it didn't wreak so much havoc with her toilette.

At the top of the steps, she tried the door handle; it was locked. Her pick set was in her purse, and she reached for it but then paused. Was she really going to break into Jim's house? It was illegal, unethical, and . . . wrong. Pete had made a point of telling her not to do this very thing. Sadie had assured him she wouldn't, and she'd already picked the filing cabinet. Sadie clenched her teeth and made a fist with the hand inside her purse.

Reviewing the trust document would help her gain confidence in the conclusions rushing through her head. She wanted to know more about Jolene and more about the lunch date with Keith. What if Jim had some notes about his plan to sell the company that she could use to help prove what she had learned from Keith? She wanted to call Providence and ask about Jolene's treatments to verify her prognosis.

Sadie's stomach sank when she thought about Jolene. What if Jolene was part of this? What if it wasn't just Gary who was after the money? Jolene had stuck by him through his jail time and judgments. She'd given her father the silent treatment like a petulant teenager because he couldn't finance a final vacation. Would she have been a part of her father's death in order to secure her inheritance for her husband? The thought made Sadie ill, but also increased her desire to try to get inside the house.

On top of everything else demanding her attention, Sadie wondered about Jim. He had done what he thought was best for his children. Did he somehow know what was happening now? What would he say if he did? What would he want Sadie to do about it?

Surely all the missing pieces were just beyond that door, and now that she knew more about what she was looking for, she would know better where to look. But she couldn't break in. She couldn't. She took her hand out of her purse and let out a breath, both proud and disappointed in herself for lacking the determination to do whatever it took to get the answers she wanted. Who'd have thought a moral compass could be so aggravating?

"Hello there."

Sadie turned, tucking her hair behind her ear again as she looked across the street. Lois waved at her, then looked both ways and crossed the street, heading toward her. Sadie moved down the steps, grateful she hadn't gone in with Lois watching. Maybe having a moral compass wasn't so bad. She met Lois at the end of the driveway.

"How are you, Lois?" Sadie said politely, wondering if May had told her about their confrontation at the hotel. Lois's face was kind and open, however, and Sadie tried to make herself relax.

Unfortunately, she was so tightly wound that it was nearly impossible to let go of the tension.

"May's out," Lois said. A gust of wind pushed her hair flat on the side, showing her pink scalp beneath her fluffy black hair. Lois raised a hand and attempted to coax her hair back to its former shape.

Sadie looked at the door again, her anxiety rising. "She texted me to come and meet her."

"She's been gone for some time," Lois said.

"She did say I might beat her here." Sadie let out a breath. "I just hoped I wouldn't."

"Tell you what—why don't you come over," Lois said, nodding toward her house as the wind gusted past them again. Sadie squinted against the dust that came with it. "My living room gives me a bird's-eye view of the house. It's unusual for us to get a storm like this in August, but all the more reason to hide indoors for a few minutes."

Sadie wasn't in the mood for small talk. Then again, Lois had given her some good information last night, and Sadie did need to talk to May as soon as she arrived. The wind blew up some dirt, hitting Sadie's legs with dozens of painful pings. "Actually, that would be really nice."

CHAPTER 44

"Make yourself comfortable," Lois said as they entered through the front door of her meticulous home. She waved Sadie toward the living room while she crossed to the entryway of the kitchen situated toward the back of the white-and-peach decorated house. Sadie could see into the doorway enough to make out some cabinets and a microwave. "I'll be but a minute. Do you like lemon tea?"

"Lemon sounds wonderful," Sadie said, taking inventory of the room. Everything was micro-coordinated, down to the tiniest detail. There was a velvety-looking sofa made of a darker orange upholstery, and a floral arrangement on the coffee table with a glass top that must be murder to keep clean.

"So, what was it May wanted to talk to you about?" Lois asked, pulling open a cupboard.

"I'm not sure," Sadie said, nervous about that very thing. "How long has she been gone?"

"She left about an hour ago," Lois said, opening and shutting another cupboard somewhere in the kitchen. "I expect she'll be home any minute, especially if she told you to meet her. May's a very reliable person that way."

Sadie nodded. "I'm sure she is."

She walked to the picture window, verifying that she did indeed have a full view of Jim Sanderson's house. She'd make sure to keep it in her line of vision for the duration of her visit. The first few raindrops streaked against the glass. They'd come inside just in time.

As she turned away from the window, a flash of red outside caught her eye, and she turned back to get a better look. A red car was parked a few houses down the street. She squinted, but it was too far away for her to see anything but the color, which stood out against the gray sky behind it. Something about that car bothered her, but she didn't know why. Yes, it was the only car other than Sadie's parked on the street, but was that enough reason for Sadie to be so interested? She looked at the car again before realizing that her anxiety was transitioning into paranoia. She forced her attention away.

"Do you have grandchildren, Lois?" Sadie asked, moving toward a wall of pictures and trying to keep her nerves in check.

"Seventeen, if you can believe it," Lois called back from the kitchen. "Three of them live in Astoria; the rest are out of state. I've got eight great-grandchildren as well. Thank goodness for webcams and Skype."

Sadie nodded, looking at the matching frames that reflected back numerous smiling faces of people whom Sadie assumed were Lois's children and their families. She pulled her phone from her purse and quickly texted May to tell her that she was waiting for her at Lois's house. "I bet you're a wonderful grandma," Sadie said after she put the phone away. She hoped May hurried home.

"The best," Lois answered, laughing at her comment. "And I make sure to remind them of that fact as often as possible."

Sadie scanned the photos, starting at the top left of the fifty-year march through Lois's life. There was a sepia-toned wedding photo of a young woman with her hair in a bouffant hairdo and curls beside each ear, pressed up against a young man in uniform. The next photo was a headshot of the same girl with a nurse's cap on her head, the hair not quite so flamboyant.

"You're a nurse?" Sadie asked.

"I was," Lois called from the kitchen. "I haven't had a license for several years now. I don't want anyone making me work. I still help out friends now and then, though. At my age, acquaintances are dying all the time." Sadie heard tea cups clink against saucers and glanced out the window again. The car was still there. But why wouldn't it be? It probably belonged to whoever lived at the house it was parked in front of.

Her phone dinged, alerting her to a new message. May had texted her back.

I'm on my way.

Sadie hoped she wasn't texting and driving, that wasn't safe—not to mention possibly illegal. She didn't respond in order to be sure she wasn't part of the distraction.

Sadie thought about what Lois had said about being a nurse. She was ready to see if she could fill in some of the blanks without tipping her hand too much. It was just Lois, but Sadie wanted to make sure she didn't betray May's trust any more than she already had by giving up too much information. "You know," she said carefully, glancing into the kitchen, "Jolene was looking into hospice care yesterday."

Lois was framed in the doorway. She poured tea into the cups.

"Was she?" Lois asked.

She didn't sound very surprised to hear the news.

"May seemed convinced Jolene was getting better," Sadie said.

"People are entitled to their secrets," Lois said. "I'm sure Jolene had her reasons for keeping it to herself."

"But she told you?"

Lois glanced up at Sadie. "Those Sanderson kids needed more of their mother than they got, and I've done my best to make up for that. They all come to me with their troubles."

"I don't know how May will handle Jolene's death," Sadie said, her heart heavy with the confirmation that Jolene wasn't going to beat her cancer like her mother had.

"She'll handle it like we all do," Lois answered. "It will be hard, but eventually she'll come to terms with it. I'll help."

But was an elderly family friend enough? Without Jolene, May was left with Hugh—and he was in no position to take care of his baby sister. Another wave of trepidation washed through Sadie, and she turned back to the window. Talking to May about all of this might be the hardest thing she'd ever done.

The rain had turned from a sprinkle to a downpour, and she watched the droplets bounce up as they hit the asphalt. Sadie looked through the blur of rain which had dropped a curtain over the view outside the window and found herself staring at the red car again.

Red.

Red.

Did she know someone who drove a *red* car?

Gayle drove one, but hers was more of a burgundy color. Then she remembered that Jane had a red car.

Instantly Sadie's eyes went wide, and she leaned forward. *It couldn't be!* There was no way Jane *drove* all the way up here. But she did have a cute little red compact that looked an awful lot like the car parked on the street. The rain prevented Sadie from being able to see whether anyone was inside, but her stomach tightened. *Of course* Jane would come to Jim's house after Sadie blew her off this morning. She'd have suspected that Sadie would end up here eventually. The tightening sensation turned to steel.

What if Jane confronted May about what she knew, and what if May thought Sadie was trying to sell a story? What if another article popped up next week about Sadie and her murder-magnetic personality? What if Jane found out Sadie had been fired from her first job? What if May suddenly found her tragic circumstances in the public domain? Sadie almost couldn't breathe for the anger and fear that gripped her as the possibilities rushed through her mind.

Why couldn't Jane just leave well enough alone?

Sadie had no sooner thought the words than she realized May felt exactly the same way about her. She'd told Sadie not to look into her family matters, and Sadie hadn't left well enough alone either. Sadie was being a hypocrite to judge Jane so harshly for doing what Sadie herself had done. Would she learn her lesson this time? Would Jane?

Sadie let out a deep breath, reminding herself to stay focused, and looked back at the photos, desperate for distraction.

The next two rows of photographs showed the march of life: from newlyweds to young parents to harried adults with four teenagers either smiling or scowling at the camera. When the youngest child looked to be sixteen or so, Lois was suddenly a single parent.

The smiles looked heavier, and two of the older children had been joined by spouses. A single grandchild sat on Lois's lap, and Sadie remembered that Lois had said she'd been widowed twice.

Her eyes went back to that first wedding picture. Those two young people in the frame had no idea what was in store for them. Sadie's heart was heavy from all the loss she'd heard about over the last couple of days. *No one is spared heartache,* she thought, but she still had no explanation for why some people experienced more than others.

The distraction wasn't working, and she felt her gaze pulled back to the car, despite the fact that she stubbornly refused to move her head. What was Jane doing out there? Was it really Jane at all?

"Bart," Lois said from behind Sadie, causing her to startle. She hadn't heard Lois approach.

"Your first husband?" Sadie asked after overcoming her surprise. She looked back at the sepia-toned wedding photograph. The more she looked at it, the more the young woman looked like Lois. Even the groom, Bart, looked familiar somehow.

"Here's your tea," Lois said.

Sadie accepted the dainty tea cup from Lois and put her purse down on the coffee table behind them so that she could use both hands for the tea. Lois moved the purse from the table to one of the chairs placed nearby; Sadie wondered if she'd missed a rule of etiquette that suggested purses weren't meant to go on tables. But Lois didn't seem offended and just smiled at Sadie.

"I put extra sugar in it. I figured you were probably having an extra-sugar kind of day."

Sadie smiled and nodded, but as soon as she looked out the window again, her eyes locked on the car. Had it moved closer? The rain was heavier, and it was hard to tell for sure, but it looked like the car had moved up a car length along the curb. She felt her heartbeat increase in anticipation of Jane's next move. And then she told herself, again, that there were millions of little red compact cars in the world and that she was jumping to conclusions.

Sadie turned back to the photos and raised the tea to her lips, taking a sip that startled her with its zing. A little bitter, but well-compensated by the extra sugar Lois had added. It heated her whole body as it traveled down her throat, and she felt herself relax—finally. She needed this. She needed to take a step back from the tension she'd been drowning in since facing May last night.

"Wasn't he cute?" Lois said, sipping her own tea. "We were married twenty-seven years."

"He was a good husband?" Sadie asked, thinking of Gary Tracey, who seemed ambiguous about the fact that his wife was dying, and who may also have had motive to kill Jim Sanderson.

"The best," Lois said. She went on to describe the kind of man Bart had been: kind, hardworking, and generous. They'd traveled to Cannon Beach every summer with the kids and loved to sail—something Lois still enjoyed with friends. Sadie continued sipping her tea while trying to keep her mind away from the red car.

"I guess my only complaint," Lois said a couple minutes later, "would be that he never could understand what a hamper was for when the floor was so much easier."

"They're never quite perfect, are they?" Sadie smiled, noting a funny feeling in her stomach. She hadn't eaten well today. That, coupled with her current state of anxiety, must not be agreeing with the tea. When she looked out the window again, the little red car was definitely closer. Now it was parked in front of the house just east of Jim Sanderson's. There was someone in the driver's seat, but the only detail Sadie could make out was a spiky-haired silhouette.

It was enough.

The driver was Jane, and she was slowly moving closer and closer. Did she know Sadie was in Lois's house? Sadie clenched her teeth together and wondered what she should do.

"No, they aren't perfect," Lois continued while Sadie tried to keep herself calm. "But he was a good man overall. A good husband and father. He died of Lou Gehrig's disease two days after his fiftieth birthday."

Sadie turned to look at the other woman, her heart brimming with sympathy as she tuned back into their conversation. A man from her church had died of Lou Gehrig's disease a few years ago. Sadie had brought in meals once a week for the last few months of his life to help ease the burden on his wife who had to watch him slowly lose all of his faculties week by week.

"I'm so sorry," Sadie said. "It's a horrible disease."

Lois nodded, still looking at the photos with a tender expression. "You never think it will happen to someone you love. When it does, all you can hope for is that they don't suffer too much. If you're lucky, you can help spare them a little."

"Spoken like a true healer," Sadie said, smiling at the other woman. As a nurse, Lois likely understood the frailties of the human body better than most and had committed herself to easing the suffering of people. It was a beautiful thing to realize that not everything and everyone in the world had ill motives for what they did.

Sadie looked at the car again. What were Jane's motives? Why was she here? Sadie reflected on what Jane had said last night about wanting to help and not simply being here for a story. At least Sadie could take consolation in having been right about the choice not to trust the reporter. It wasn't much, however, since she feared Jane was going to add complication to an already highly complicated situation.

Sadie looked back at the pictures and placed a hand on her stomach. She really didn't feel very good. "Is that your s-second husband?" Sadie had to take a breath midsentence as she nodded toward a picture of an older Lois and another man, this one balding and thick around the middle. It looked like they were in Hawaii, since they were both wearing leis around their necks.

"Charlie," Lois said, taking another sip of her tea as Sadie did the same.

Sadie blinked rapidly, finding it hard to focus her eyes on the next line of photographs—wedding portraits of Lois's children, she assumed. Man, her lack of sleep from the night before and her intense all-day tension was catching up with her at the absolute worst moment. She needed to be in tip-top condition to deal with May and, possibly, Jane. This was not the time for the stomach flu!

She scanned the photos, trying to keep her focus, when they landed on the last photo in the lineup—a 1980s wedding, complete with big hair and light-blue tuxedos. Sadie stared at the bride. She looked like May . . . No, it looked more like Jolene from the family photograph over the fireplace at Jim Sanderson's house.

Sadie knew the families were close, but to display Jolene's wedding photos? Sadie turned her interest to the groom, Gary Tracey, and felt a different kind of heat rush over her. Her eyes snapped back to the sepia wedding photo of Lois and Bart, then back again as she compared the physical features of both men—both the same age, same build, same coloring. In a matter of seconds, Sadie looked through the lineup of family photos she'd skimmed through earlier, specifically noting the third child—a boy with sandy-blond hair; a boy, who as he aged, looked more and more like his father; a boy who was the man standing next to Jolene in the wedding photo.

She turned to Lois, who was watching her with a strangely intent expression on her face. Sadie's head was feeling wobbly. "Gary is your son?" she said, and as soon as the words left her lips, all the nebulous details that had been swirling around the hypothesis she'd been putting together snapped into place.

"Yes. He's my third child," Lois said, sipping her tea and looking at the photos. "Didn't you know that?"

"N-no," Sadie said, stunned by this tiny piece of information and all that it might mean.

Gary was Lois's son.

Lois was close to the Sanderson family.

Lois was a nurse.

No . . . it was impossible . . . but . . .

The sound of chirping birds captured Sadie's attention—May's ring tone? She blinked hard to clear her eyes as Lois set down her tea cup and pulled a Blackberry from her pocket. It looked just like May's phone. Sadie looked up from Lois's wrinkled hand to her even more wrinkled face that began weaving back and forth slightly in Sadie's suddenly blurry vision. Her teacup seemed to tip out of her hand in slow motion.

Oh, biscuits, she thought as her mind started swimming. The tea cup spun in the air, the liquid arching out in a brown rainbow.

Pete's words came back to her, telling her that she didn't have the right training to take on this job. Would she get the chance to tell him she was sorry for not listening?

Chapter 45

"You told May about my concerns about Hugh," Lois continued while Sadie simply focused on keeping up with the older woman's words. "I was helping her empty out closets while she spent half the morning trying to verify account balances and learn who Hugh might owe money to. She set up an appointment with the trust attorney this afternoon and didn't notice her phone wasn't in her purse when she raced out the door. It's really a shame you added to her worry by implicating Hugh in all of this, Mrs. Hoffmiller. Don't you think she's had enough to make peace with?"

Sadie doubled over and immediately put her fingers down her throat, knowing she had to get the tea—and whatever had been mixed into it—out of her system. She gagged and coughed as she heaved tea onto the carpet. She knew her body had already digested most of it, but she had to try. As she straightened up, the room began to spin.

"That better not ruin my carpet!" Lois said from somewhere to the left. Footsteps retreated, but when Sadie looked up, she couldn't focus enough to see where Lois had gone.

She reached out to grab something to steady herself with, and although she could see the edge of the coffee table, her hand seemed to move through it as though it were a ghost. She felt herself falling to the side, still grasping for something to help her regain her balance.

Then a hand reached for her. Instead of helping steady her, however, Lois pushed her out of the way. Sadie stumbled for a few steps, still bent over, until she was able to stop—barely managing to keep herself upright by bracing her hands on her knees and keeping her center of gravity low by remaining bent over.

"Tea is one thing, but vomit? The key is to clean it up as quickly as possible, before the acids can absorb into the carpet fibers," Lois said. Was she scrubbing the carpet? "If you were one of my grandchildren, I'd give you a lickin' for making a mess like this."

"You killed J-J-Jim," Sadie said, still blinking furiously in an attempt to regain her sight. She couldn't formulate the words and tried to take a deep breath, even though it didn't feel like she could fully inflate her lungs.

"It wasn't fair, what Jim was doing to those kids," Lois said from somewhere above Sadie. "Causing Jolene to worry over Gary at a time like this." Her voice sounded strange, like she was getting further away. "Bart didn't believe in life insurance, so I was left with four kids and a nursing degree I hadn't used in twenty years. It wasn't fair for me, and it isn't fair for Gary. I'm not about to sit back and let that happen."

Sadie stared at the carpet, her chest heaving for breath. She thought of her cell phone in her purse, but she couldn't focus enough to even see the table, let alone walk to the chair next to it. "But . . . but Jim?" She thought back to the conversation they'd had last night. Lois had said beautiful things about the rebirth that happens after tragedy. Sadie had been touched by the sentiment. And yet . . .

"I ease suffering for the people I love," Lois said, her voice harder to hear than ever.

Sadie tried to lift her head to see where Lois was, but the whole room was spinning. Nausea started bubbling in her stomach

"Jim was turning a cold heart toward his children," Lois said. "He refused Jolene the one thing she needed most—reassurance that Gary would be okay when she was gone. It was the only thing she wanted, the *only* thing, and Jim refused because of his own personality conflicts with Gary, who has had a very rough go of things himself. It hasn't been easy for Gary to put up with Jim all these years. And then for Jim to hurt Jolene like this? Well, that was all he could take."

"He c-came to you," Sadie said, trying to follow along. "Gar-ry came t-to you for help."

"Of course he did, I'm his mother," Lois snapped. Sadie couldn't tell if she was still scrubbing the carpet. Her disembodied voice seemed to be everywhere, and Sadie had lost sight of Lois somewhere in the spinning room. "I did everything I could to persuade Jim to change the trust. He told me to butt out and mind my own business. Butt out? As if I weren't a part of this family!"

Sadie felt her fingers begin to tingle. She couldn't succumb to whatever was in that tea. She had to get herself out of this, but how? Pete came to mind, and along with the image of his face blurring in her thoughts was the reminder of the lesson he'd given her about keeping her keys . . . in her pocket! If she could get to her car, she wouldn't need her purse.

But where was the front door?

"I fight for the people I love, Mrs. Hoffmiller. I always have, and I always will."

Sadie reached for her pocket, but the movement threw off her balance, and she had to brace her hands on her knees again.

Lois kept talking. "I've been kicking myself for answering all those questions you asked me last night. After how hard I'd worked to keep Jim from making a mess of things, then you stepped in and made a bigger mess. Do you have any idea how much you've hurt my Jolene? My Sharla-May? I need to clean up the mess you've made and . . . " Her voice drained away.

Sadie could only hear whispering or rushing wind, as though she had seashells held up to both ears. She reached toward her pocket again, slow and careful . . .

The room continued to spin, and Sadie was halfway to the floor before she realized she'd lost her balance and was falling. The impact was probably harsh, and she felt a twinge in her shoulder, but it was as though she were wrapped in bubble wrap. She strained to keep her eyes open, but her eyelids felt so heavy. If she could get to her car . . . but she couldn't stand. If she could get to her phone . . . but Lois wasn't going to let her anywhere near her purse. And then her thoughts latched on to something else.

Perhaps her only hope.

Jane.

CHAPTER 46

Sadie could feel her mind slipping, begging for unconsciousness, but she fought it with everything she had, which wasn't much.

She had to get Jane's attention. But she was paralyzed and on the brink of unconsciousness. *Speak!* she commanded herself, but she couldn't open her mouth. *Move!* But her body didn't respond expect for a tremor in her arm, which was trapped at a weird angle beneath her body. If only she could kick something or scream or somehow make herself noticed. But she could feel nothing, could sense nothing nearby she could knock over, assuming she could gather the strength. But then she felt something in her hand—the hand of the arm that was in such an odd position. The hand that was restrained. Was she lying on her hand? Was she on her side?

And then she remembered. She'd reached into her pocket for her keys.

Keys!

Lois's voice droned on in the background, but Sadie couldn't spare the energy to listen to the words. Instead she put every ounce of everything she had into moving her fingers. The sensations were muted, but she felt the smooth plastic of the key fob. Somewhere on that fob was the panic button that would set off the rental car's alarm and alert Jane to her situation.

But her thoughts were slipping away from her. Blackberry crumble and peace roses flitted through her mind, soon followed by avocado-green appliances, turquoise tortilla chips, and her concerns about Shawn's next semester. Her thoughts became more and more vague, and even though she tried to focus on whatever it was she'd needed to do with her hand, she was barely hanging on to consciousness.

Food carts and macabre donuts spiraled through her mind. What was she trying to do, again?

Airplanes and blow dryers and Pete. And with Pete, the thought of keys. Keys! That's right, she was trying to set off the alarm. Pete had prepared her for this. She could do it. She could muster the strength she needed, despite the fact that her hands and feet were almost completely numb.

She focused on the plastic in her hand, feeling for the rubbery button. As soon as she felt a change of texture, she pressed. Nothing. Had she not pressed hard enough? Or was it the wrong button? She pressed again and then moved her thumb to the side. Another change of texture; she pressed again. Nothing. She could feel her lungs getting stiff, and tears began to threaten as she considered what would happen if she didn't hit the right button, if Jane didn't come to her rescue. She moved her thumb again as her thoughts turned to bicycles and strawberries, dreadlocks and bacon.

Another button and another push.

This time she heard the blaring of a horn. She drifted away for a moment, and then she heard something else as consciousness waved and kept her present a little longer. Was someone knocking?

No, banging!

She blacked out, but didn't know for how long before she surfaced again. She heard more movement, more voices, and then words she couldn't understand, and finally a voice she recognized.

"Boy, oh boy," Jane Seeley said from somewhere above Sadie's face.

Sadie sighed in relief. She felt a hand on her face that told her beyond the words and beyond the last five minutes that she was really going to be okay.

"You sure know how to keep things interesting, Sadie. I've already called 911. Hang in there, okay?"

She was safe.

Jane had saved her.

The feel of the key fob was gone, Jane's voice faded, the blaring of the horn disappeared, and then there was nothing.

CHAPTER 47

Someone was calling her name, and Sadie forced her eyes open. Three ghostly images of Jane's face moved in and out of one another, like that magic trick where someone hides a ball under one cup and then moves them around so you don't know which cup is which.

"Mumh huff fum."

"Don't talk," the three Janes said, shaking their heads in unison. "You've got an oxygen mask on."

Sadie blinked, aware of the jostling beneath her and the fact that she was lying flat on her back. It took a few seconds to realize she was in an ambulance, and the idea panicked her. She tried to sit up, but two strong hands pushed her back down.

"Don't get up," a male voice said. "We've got an IV in place, and it's helping move things through, but don't push it."

Sadie nodded, then looked at Jane again, realizing she might be the only person here with answers.

"She put something in your tea," Jane said, seeming to read Sadie's mind. "I found a mortar and pestle in the kitchen with some kind of pill crushed into it. The cops are getting it tested, but they think it was simply a sedative to make killing you easier. That lady had a syringe of something in her pocket; they think she'd have stuck you with it once you were fully out."

Sadie concentrated hard on the words. Lois tried to kill her? It didn't make sense . . . and yet it did.

"The car alarm was genius," Jane said. "I couldn't see much, what with the rain and everything, but I knew you were in trouble when the horn starting blaring."

"Wuff nob comflop." Drat, she'd forgotten she couldn't talk.

"Don't try and talk, Mrs. Hoffmiller," the paramedic to her left said. "Just relax. You're going to be fine."

"Did you know Gary Tracey, Jolene Sanderson's husband, is Lois Hilbert's son from her first marriage?"

When Sadie nodded, Jane continued. "The police were talking about it when we left." She shrugged. "I didn't even think to dig into the old lady across the street." She harrumphed, as though disappointed in herself. "I got so caught up in how Jim Sanderson was killed, I kinda skipped out on who would have wanted him dead."

Sadie nodded at the irony; she'd done just the opposite.

Jane let out a heavy sigh.

Sadie pulled her eyebrows together to silently ask what was wrong.

Jane smiled and reached down to push Sadie's hair off her face with surprising tenderness. "This would have made such a great story," she said wistfully.

Sadie felt all her concerns about Jane's motives descend again. But did Jane just say *would have*?

"I know what you're thinking, Sadie," Jane said. "You still think that's why I'm here—for the story, huh?"

Sadie didn't nod, but she didn't need to. Of course Jane was here for the story. That's what Jane did—she exploited situations for her own gain.

"I told you I'm looking for something different," Jane said. "And I'm going to prove it by not writing a single word about any of this."

Sadie narrowed her eyes. There was more than one way to "get" a story.

Jane read that thought too—which was starting to get creepy. "And I won't sell it or give it to anyone else either, even though it could get me my place back at *The Post*." She leaned down, allowing Sadie to focus on her face for the first time. "We could make a heck of a team, Sadie," she said as the ambulance started to slow. "Think about it while they pump you full of charcoal, okay?"

Unfortunately, it was absolutely impossible to think about anything other than charcoal for the next few hours. By the time the doctors told Sadie she could go, she was completely exhausted and still trying to wipe the black ring away from her mouth. According to the ER doctor, she hadn't been given a fatal dose of the medication, and the vomiting had gotten most of it out of her stomach. Of course they still had to charcoal her and run an IV. She probably could have fought to stay at the hospital overnight, but she would rather spend the night in her new hotel room. Tomorrow she'd meet with the police, and then . . . then she didn't know what she was going to do.

It was almost ten o'clock at night when Jane escorted Sadie out the front doors of the hospital. Sadie sat on a bench; she was exhausted. Although the rain had stopped, the darkened sky was heavy with the combination of moisture and summer heat. Sadie's scalp tingled as her sweat glands woke up and went back to work.

Jane leaned against a column as though waiting for someone.

"Where's your car?" Sadie asked after several seconds.

Jane reached into her purse and pulled out a pack of cigarettes. Sadie tried not to make a face. "I left my car at Jim Sanderson's so I could come with you in the ambulance," she said, putting a cigarette between her lips and digging a lighter out of the pack.

"So, you called a taxi?"

Jane looked at her and grinned that mischievous grin that made Sadie so nervous. "Not exactly," she said, the cigarette bobbing up and down.

The sound of a car engine caused Sadie to turn her head to the right as a pair of headlights swept into the pick-up area of the hospital. She was confused until she heard the transmission shift into park and the driver's side door open. On the other side of the car, Pete's head rose up, and his hazel eyes gave her a good look before he shut the door and came around the back of the car.

Sadie immediately began smoothing her hair and wiping at her mouth again. "You called Pete?" she hissed, looking at Jane, who inhaled sharply on the cigarette, hollowing her cheeks as she sucked in.

Jane blew out a steady stream of smoke. "Oh, come on, you're thrilled he came for you."

Well, when she said it like that, Sadie *was* touched, but still, she looked like death warmed over right now.

"Sadie," Pete said, causing her to look up at him from where she sat on the bench.

"Pete," Sadie said, not sure how to act. Things hadn't been exactly warm between them these last few days, and here she was, having escaped death . . . again . . . after going against his advice . . . again.

Instead of helping her to her feet, he sat next to her on the bench and looked up at Jane. "Thanks for calling," he said. "I think I can take it from here."

Jane nodded and started walking away.

"Wait," Sadie said, causing Jane to turn back as she took another drag from her cigarette. "Where are you going?"

"I'm in Portland," Jane said, as though that was answer enough. She pointed her face toward the sky and exhaled the smoke. "These are my people."

"Your . . . people? You're from here?"

Jane grinned. "I should be. The least I can do is my part to keep Portland weird, ya know?"

"It's getting late," Sadie said, well aware that she sounded like an overprotective mother.

Apparently, Jane thought the same thing. "I'll be okay, *Mom*." She smiled. "And don't worry, I'll be in touch." She waved with her free hand as she melted into the parking lot on her way toward . . . wherever it was she was heading toward.

"You have very interesting friends," Pete said.

"I do seem to be putting together quite a menagerie," Sadie said. She turned to look up at him and managed to push all her thoughts about Jane away for the moment. "You came to Portland."

He smiled. "I came to Portland."

"To take care of me?"

"Yes."

"You didn't have to come," Sadie said, asserting her independence and not certain that she liked the idea of being rescued. "I'm okay."

Pete took a deep breath and looked at her long and hard. "Are you trying to tell me you don't need me?"

"No," Sadie said quickly. "I'm just saying . . . I don't want to be a complication in your life, Pete."

"You're not a complication," he said, lifting a hand to tap her nose. "You're a silver lining."

Sadie couldn't hold back the tears that filled her eyes at the unexpected comment, and words failed her completely. But how was she supposed to trust that? It had only been a few days since she realized he'd been hiding their relationship from his kids.

"You were right when you said I *had* moved on, Sadie. I know you understand better than most people that Pat will always be my first love, the mother of my children, and the woman I have always believed to be my soul mate. But she's not here anymore, and my heart is wrapped all around *you*. If nothing else, this situation has shown me how silly it was to try to pretend my feelings for you weren't something that changed my life." He took another breath, and Sadie suddenly realized that his hand that had been on her knee was now holding her hand. "I won't pretend that these things you keep finding yourself in the middle of don't make me crazy, because they do, but you've filled in the nooks and crannies of my life, Sadie, and I can take the adventure you can't seem to stay away from if it means I also get the meaning you bring into my life every day."

Sadie sniffed, ever so indelicately. "Aren't you getting tired of us starting over all the time? We've been here before and—"

"We've never been here," Pete said. He leaned back on the bench, putting his left arm across her shoulders and drawing her toward him slightly. She couldn't help but melt into him. "We've never been to Portland."

Sadie smiled at his attempt to lighten the moment. "I meant that we've been *here* before—at a crossroads in our relationship. I thought we'd already reached this understanding."

"And now we've reached another one," Pete said. He faced her again. "I can't control you or tell you what to do, and I need to learn to stop trying. And you need to find a way to follow this drive you have without endangering your life. Do you think you can do that?"

"You won't tell me not to do something?"

Pete shook his head.

"And your kids?"

"Are okay."

Sadie blinked at him and then raised one hand to his face. "This is a lot harder than I thought it would be," she said quietly. "But I want it to work, I really do."

He smiled, his eyes crinkling as he leaned forward and placed his forehead against her own. "So do I, Sadie. Maybe we have been here before, but if all of this is part of the process of getting us to somewhere even better, if all these potholes and tangents are part of us working out the bugs and gaining assurance of where we want to be, then it's not wasted time, right?"

"Method to the madness," Sadie whispered, feeling the intimacy of the moment. She lifted her mouth toward his, wanting very much to seal the evening with a kiss.

"Exactly," Pete said, his breath whispering against her lips. "Does it matter how we get there so long as we arrive?"

Well, when he said it like that . . .

CHAPTER 48

"So, your dad found out about our lunch and stuck you on a conference call so he could take your place at the restaurant?" Sadie said two days later as Richard was driving her to May's house. They were almost there.

"Yep," Richard said. "I had no way to get out of the call, and I couldn't find my cell phone because he'd locked it in his office."

"Cell phones are tricky things," Sadie said, reflecting on how Lois had used May's phone to lure her in. "And how are things between the two of you now?"

"I had a lot to say when he got back, and no more reasons not to say it. I've agreed to stay on through the Jepson merger and the acquisition of S&S, but I've told Dad I need some distance. I need to have my own life. He says he understands, but I'm keeping my hand at the level of my eyes, and I'm going back to school so that by the time I leave the family business, I have what I need to make a new start." He pulled up to the curb of Jim Sanderson's house.

Sadie tried to swallow her nervousness and rolled her shoulder, which was decidedly stiff after her fall. She'd have to go back to her doctor this week to see if she'd done anything serious.

"A lot of changes coming your way, then," she said.

Richard was watching the house. "I'm ready for change," he said thoughtfully. "I'm ready to be the man I should have been before now. I hope she'll believe it."

Sadie hoped so too. A quick glance at Lois's house on the other side of the street didn't reveal much; the average passerby would never know that the woman who so painstakingly tended her peace roses winding through the trellis was also a killer.

Sadie pulled her thoughts away from Lois and looked at Jim's house again, gathering her courage. She'd spent Friday talking to the police, Saturday enjoying the sights with Pete—he'd gotten his own room at Sadie's hotel and returned her rental car for her—and now it was time to head home. She was still recovering from the near overdose, and she was anxious to see if Jane would be true to her word. So far nothing had shown up in the papers other than a small piece about Lois's arrest.

Regardless of what might happen next, however, Sadie couldn't leave Portland without talking to May.

Richard shifted into park. He'd been eager to be a part of this when she'd called him that morning. More importantly, he'd agreed to do it her way.

"Give me a minute and then come up, okay?"

Richard nodded as he wiped his palms on the thighs of his jeans. A car passed on the left—Pete's rental—and pulled to the curb ahead of them. After this meeting, she and Pete were heading to the airport. Sadie didn't feel ready to return to Garrison, but there weren't any other options left. At least she and Pete were returning together.

"I'm so nervous," Richard said, ducking slightly to peek out of the passenger window at the house that held a lot of memories for him. "I feel like I'm in high school all over again."

Sadie smiled and patted him on the arm as she opened the passenger door. "You'll be fine."

Sadie shut the door behind her and said a little prayer as she tapped up the front walk in the mini-heeled sandals she'd purchased yesterday from a boutique on 11th Avenue. Once on the porch, she knocked lightly and took a step back. She really hoped this would work. If not, she might be making an even bigger mess—if that was possible.

She heard footsteps approaching, and she braced herself for May's reaction. The door opened, and May just stared at Sadie. May's eyes were swollen and her face puffy, further testifying of what the police had already told Sadie.

"Can I talk to you?" Sadie asked.

May blinked and stepped aside with a look of resignation on her face.

Sadie looked over her shoulder and held up three fingers to signal how long Richard should wait. He nodded as Sadie stepped over the threshold. She left the door open a few inches and scanned the living room for May, spotting her sitting on the end of the couch. Sadie sat on the other end, facing May, who was staring at the outdated family photograph on the wall above the fireplace. The photo that had been taken before her mother died. Sadie wondered if May was reflecting on how much she'd lost since that photo had been taken. It must feel like everything.

The room was full of boxes, some full, some partial, attesting to the fact that life as May knew it was over; all of her sanctuaries were gone.

"Jolene was hospitalized early this morning," May said while

Sadie tried to remember the opening lines she'd practiced. "Apparently all of this was more than she could take. She hasn't eaten since she found out about Gary and Lois. She's in and out of consciousness, and I'm too upset to go see her. I don't want to make it worse."

"I'm so sorry," Sadie said. "I had—"

May cut her off. "Hugh's agreed to go into treatment, and Keith Kelly has agreed to pay off Hugh's debts as part of the purchase of S&S." She looked at Sadie with heavy eyes. "I guess Keith will end up with my father's legacy after all."

Tears spilled over and began trailing down May's cheeks as she looked down at her hands in her lap. "I've worked hard all these years to keep my faith in a loving God alive, Sadie, but I'm not sure I want to believe any more. I'm not sure it's worth feeling abandoned by one more person."

Sadie blinked quickly to keep May's face from blurring through her own falling tears.

"Why did you hire me, May?"

May didn't answer, allowing Sadie to clarify her question. "You could have hired another PI up here. Someone who knew what they were doing. Why me?"

May shrugged.

"Didn't you tell me you felt drawn to me?" Sadie offered. "Didn't you feel like I was the person who was supposed to help you?"

"This is *not* what I wanted," May said, looking up at Sadie quickly and waving her arm through the air. "I didn't want any of this."

"You wanted truth, and you wanted closure. I can't imagine what it feels like to face this all at once, but I've been asking myself why I came—especially after I hurt you so badly." Sadie forged ahead, even though her voice quavered. "And the only answer I can come up with was that I was *supposed* to. I felt it before I called you back that very first time, and I believe you felt it too." She took a deep breath. "I'm so sorry, sweetie. I'm so, so sorry this happened."

May dropped her head into her hands and gave into the sobs that had been rumbling below the surface since Sadie had first come inside.

Sadie slid closer to her on the couch, unsure if the other woman would accept her comfort but willing to try. She put her arms around May's shoulders. May resisted at first, but when Sadie put a hand on her hair and attempted to pull her closer, May crumpled into her, desperate enough for comfort to accept it from anyone, even the woman who had forced her to face things she didn't want to. She was so different from the confident woman who had approached Sadie at the Latham Club dinner. The last few days had peeled back her layers, and she seemed more like a girl than a woman right now.

A moment later, Richard poked his head into the doorway. Sadie waved him out before May could see him and put up two fingers for two more minutes. Sadie lifted May's head from her shoulder, and pushed her tear-drenched hair from her face so that she could look her in the eye. "There's one more thing," Sadie said. "Something important I need you to hear."

May pulled back, and Sadie hurried to assure her that it wasn't bad. Sadie slipped her hand into her purse and removed the digital voice recorder she'd taken with her during her first meeting with Richard. She'd already cued it to the part she wanted May to hear and pressed PLAY.

Sadie: You're in love with her.
Richard: Have been since I was fifteen years old.
Sadie: You have children.

Richard: I do.

Sadie: Are you married?

Richard: Not anymore.

Sadie: What happened between you and May, then?

Richard: I'll tell you everything. I'll answer every question you
have about my father, but I need you to promise me something.

Sadie: What?

Richard: I need to be face-to-face with May at some point.
Promise me. Promise me you'll help me see her. It won't be
as easy as it sounds.

Sadie: Why? Is she afraid of you?

Richard: Yes. No one has hurt her the way I did.

Sadie: Hurt her?

Richard: I broke her heart to the point that I don't think she'll
ever forgive me for it, but I have to tell her how wrong I was
and how truly sorry I am for everything.

Sadie turned the voice recorder off, and May closed her eyes as
though unable to listen to any more. Sadie held the younger woman
by the shoulders until May opened her eyes again.

"Richard Kelly loves you," Sadie said. May began to pull away,
and Sadie shook her slightly. May met her eyes, more tears leaking
over. "I understand why you don't want to risk being hurt again, and
no one can blame you for that. People aren't perfect, and Richard
certainly wasn't, but he's grown up and become a man who, I believe,
deserves the chance to make things right." She kept talking to May,
realizing she was advising herself as much as she was sharing her
thoughts. "Life is too short to not be loved, May. You *deserve* to be
loved; you deserve to be cherished."

May looked away, shaking her head. "Too much," she whispered, raising a hand to wipe at her tears.

"Too much what?"

Her face crumbled. "I don't want to leave anyone behind. I can't carry that responsibility."

Sadie felt her throat catch. "That's why you left Portland in the first place, wasn't it? To ease out of the connections you had to people and protect yourself from pain—not just Richard. Everyone."

May's shoulders pulled inward, but she didn't answer with words.

"It didn't work, did it? When your dad died, it hurt just as much, maybe worse, than if you'd stayed."

"If I'd been here," May said, "maybe I could have done something and kept Gary and Lois from . . . " She shook her head, unable to finish.

Sadie didn't have an answer for that. May was not responsible for Jim's death; May couldn't have stopped Lois any more than she could have prevented Hugh's gambling or Gary's greed or Jolene's cancer. May had nothing to do with any of that, but Sadie wanted to focus on the future rather than trying to help May make sense of the last several weeks. There would be time enough for her to work through the past, but right now Sadie felt as though May were standing on a precipice, facing the decision of what to do next. She was broken and hurting, and Sadie hoped that that equated to an openness that might help May see things differently than she'd chosen to see them these last ten years.

"May," Sadie began, "you've experienced more loss than anyone I know, but would you have chosen against having these people in your life in the first place if you knew how it would end?" Sadie had faced that question herself. If she'd known she would lose the love of her life, would she have married Neil at all? She had found her answer—a resounding yes that no longer hurt to say—but May had to find her own answer to that question. Sadie hoped May would trust herself to answer it honestly.

"No," May said, but it came with another sob. Sadie understood that she didn't want to *not* have had her parents and brother and sister and aunts and nephew; she just didn't want to hurt anymore or cause that kind of hurt for anyone else. That was something else Sadie could relate to, though not quite on May's level.

"Maybe you can let Richard make that same choice instead of counting yourself out so easily," Sadie said, rubbing May's arms as she spoke. "Richard was there when you lost your mother, and he's been in the shadows through your father's passing and this whole unbelievable mess that's followed. Is there any possible way you can trust him to make the best decision for himself? Can you believe, even a little bit, that regardless of what may come, his life might be better for having had you in it?"

May dropped her head, her tears overflowing and dripping into her lap. "I don't know if I can do that," she said with a sob. "I don't know."

Sadie pressed her lips against May's forehead, wishing there was a way to send all her feelings of love and tenderness directly to May's broken heart. May was a *good* woman, and with all her heart Sadie wanted her to find joy.

"You have so much to give," she whispered into May's hair. "And someone who wants to love you."

Movement caught her eye, and Sadie saw Richard step inside. He'd apparently been counting down those two minutes and was unable to wait even a second longer. She looked at Richard's questioning glance and answered with a slight nod that it was a good time for him to come in. Sadie was aware that she was taking a huge risk of making everything worse by orchestrating this reunion. Yet, somehow, she felt that May was ready—ready to let someone else help her pick up the pieces, ready to have something to live for.

Richard knelt next to May, and Sadie felt May stiffen when she realized he was there. She didn't look at him, but she didn't move away or yell or slap him either. Sadie took both of May's hands in her own and squeezed them slightly, willing May to open her heart just a little more. She wanted to point out that Richard had two healthy, happy children May could love if she felt unable to risk having her own and that he'd sacrificed all his security to help Sadie find Jim's killer. She wanted to convince May that it was a *logical* decision for her to take this chance, but it was May's heart that needed to believe.

Richard kept a comfortable distance and didn't try to touch her right away. "May," he whispered.

Sadie felt May stiffen even more. She squeezed May's hands again as Richard continued.

"I am . . . so sorry," he said, emotion causing his voice to tremble. "I know that's not enough. I know those words in and of themselves can't fix anything, but I am so, so sorry. Hurting you is the biggest regret of my life." He sniffed, and May lifted her head, ever so slowly.

She looked at him, her tear-streaked face and swollen eyes reflecting fear and hope and everything in between.

"It seems as though I've been in love with you all my life," Richard continued. "I beg you to give me another chance, to let us find happiness together—a happiness neither of us has found on our own."

"I don't know if I can do that," May said, shaking her head. "I just . . . I feel so . . ."

Sadie could think of several words that could work: alone, abandoned, betrayed, overwhelmed, hopeless, sad.

May dropped her head again, but Sadie could feel her resolve softening. With small movements, she removed her hands from where they covered May's.

Richard saw what she was doing and shot her a grateful look as he placed his larger hand over May's small and shuddering ones. May didn't pull away at his touch.

"Let me love you, May, the way I should have the first time," he whispered, raising his other hand to touch her face. "Please."

For a moment May was still, and then another sob broke through and she moved ever so slightly toward Richard.

It was all the prompting Sadie needed. She slipped off the couch, and before she could take a step, Richard slid into her place. Just as May had crumpled into Sadie's arms minutes earlier, she melted into Richard, allowing him to hold her, allowing him to wrap his arms around her and bury his face in her hair as the sobbing began anew.

Sadie wiped frantically at her eyes as she walked toward the door. Before leaving the room, she took one last look at them, just in time to see May wrap her arms around Richard's shoulders, holding him as tightly as he held her. Sadie closed the door silently behind her and wished them all the happiness they had never known.

Once on the porch, Sadie kept her hand on the doorknob but leaned back against the door, letting out a breath and willing away some of the lingering fear and tension that had taken hold of her neck and shoulders. Not all things broken could be fixed; Sadie knew that from her own experience with loss and with life in general. She'd been reminded of the same thing in spades as she'd watched the depth of human suffering this week and tried to comprehend the evil that could rot men's—and women's—souls. And yet, as the sun came up every morning, as the roses bloomed every spring, she was reminded again that there was healing even in a world so full of confusion and pain. There was hope. There was love.

And love, above all things, was worth the battle.

She started down the steps and smiled at Pete, who had stepped out of the car, watching her approach.

"Good?" he asked when Sadie was close enough to hear him.

"I think so," Sadie said, continuing forward until she could link her arms behind his back and look up into his face. "I'm sure glad that life comes with second chances."

Pete's arms snaked around her back as well. "So am I," he said, leaning down for a kiss—soft and perfect.

Sadie pulled back enough that she could still feel the barest touch of his lips against hers. "I love you, Pete Cunningham," she whispered, wondering why she'd held back so long on saying those words. It had seemed like he should say them first, but why?

Pete smiled and tapped her nose with his. "And I love you, Sadie Hoffmiller. I love you, too."

Second-Chance Baked Potato Soup

½ cup butter

½ cup flour

5 cups milk

4 to 5 large, leftover baked potatoes, peeled and mashed (or 3 cups mashed potatoes)*

1 teaspoon salt (don't be afraid to add more to taste)

½ teaspoon pepper

4 green onions, chopped and divided

12 slices bacon, cooked, crumbled and divided

1½ cups shredded cheddar cheese, divided

1 (8-ounce) package sour cream

Melt butter in a heavy kettle over low heat. Add flour, stirring until smooth. Cook for about 1 minute, stirring constantly.

Increase heat to medium and gradually add milk, stirring constantly until mixture is thick and bubbly.

Add potatoes, salt, pepper, half of the green onions, half of the bacon, and 1 cup of cheddar cheese. Cook until thoroughly heated. Stir in sour cream (add extra if necessary for desired thickness).

Serve soup with remaining portion of onions, bacon, and cheese sprinkled on top. Serves 6.

*To make soup from scratch rather than with leftovers: Wash raw potatoes and bake in the oven at 400 degrees for about 1 hour or until done. Be careful not to overcook them and make them too mushy. Let potatoes cool before cutting. Scoop out insides of potatoes and set aside. Then follow the recipe using the freshly baked potatoes.

Acknowledgments

In 2009, Deseret Book sponsored me on a book tour throughout the western United States with my friend Julie Wright (*Cross My Heart*, Covenant, 2010). Along the tour was my first and only visit to Portland, Oregon, and I knew immediately I wanted to set a book there.

I came home, toiled and whined far more than was warranted, and eventually handed the book over to my publisher. A big thank you to that Deseret Book team who made this a reality: Jana Erickson (Product Director), Lisa Mangum (editor, and author of *The Hourglass Door* series, Shadow Mountain, 2009–2011), Shauna Gibby (designer), and Rachael Ward (typographer).

Thanks, too, to my sisters, Cindy Ellsworth and Crystal White, who joined my friend Melanie Jacobsen in the pre-reading phase of this book—and boy, was it rough when it went to them! Thank you to Tawnya Gibson and my cousin-in-law Alisa Watson for some of the Portland weirdness I was not getting on my own. And thank you to Gregg Luke (*Blink of an Eye*, Covenant, 2010), who gave me some medical facts that, while they didn't all end up in this book, have been saved for later use, they were *that* good.

Once again, I couldn't have done this without my test kitchen bakers: Annie Funk (Annie's Triple-Berry Summer Salad), Michelle Jefferies (Loaded Bread Dip), Don Carey, Danyelle Ferguson (Second-Chance Baked Potato Soup), Laree Ipson, Megan O'Neill, Whit Larsen, Sandra Sorenson, and our newest member, Lisa Swinton. Thanks goes out to Luisa Perkins for making up the Salmon and Wild Mushroom Casserole recipe for me and my good friend Cindy Voorhees, who also donated the Marvelous Bran Muffin recipe. Without the help of such wonderful cooks, I could never pull this off. Thank you, guys.

Thank you to my family, friends, and fans who have loved Sadie and sent me notes about how much they've enjoyed the series. Every one of those notes adds a drop to my lamp of motivation, and I so appreciate every thought that is shared. Thank you to my "girls": Annette Lyon, Heather Moore, and Julie Wright. They become increasingly more important to me every year, both in writing and in life. Thanks, gals, for "getting" me.

Thank you to my fabulous writing group: Nancy Campbell Allen (*Isabelle Webb, Vol. 2*, Covenant, 2011), Becki Clayson, Jody Durfee, and Ronda Hinrichsen (*Trapped*, Walnut Springs, 2010) for reviewing the first fifty pages again and again, only to miss the ending every time. I'm blessed to have your friendship and your patience as well; Sadie would not be who she is without you.

Thank you to each of my children for their patience, but also for their enthusiastic support. One day they will know how hard it is for me to choose how to spend my time, but for now they simply know that my writing is important to me and therefore important to them. It is my greatest hope and prayer that the sacrifice is worth it and that my support of their talents and passions equalizes the strangeness I bring into their lives. Someday the words might run out and the ideas may run dry, and I am grateful to know that should that change come to pass, I will always have you.

Thank you to my husband, Lee, who has believed in me every step of the way. He is the answer to so many of my questions, the strength to my many weaknesses, and the soft place I'm always eager to return to. Thank you, Lee, for reminding me every day that I "fit" and for giving me a life where I can spread my wings and see just how far I can fly.

For all of this, a final thank you to my Father in Heaven, for giving me the measure I'm trying to live up to, for helping me find the words when I feel abandoned, for taking the words when I've abandoned something else, and for leading me to the understanding that there is a plan for each one of us, and that every gift, every passion, every opportunity we face in life is here to make us better and happier and closer to Him.

Enjoy this sneak peek of

pumpkin Roll

Coming Fall 2011

CHAPTER 1

"So, what's the difference between a sociopath and psycho-path?" Sadie Hoffmiller asked as she put the last plate in the dishwasher.

Pete Cunningham, Sadie's boyfriend—though that was such a juvenile term—looked up from where he was replacing a hinge on the flat-fronted cabinet. "One starts with an S and the other starts with a P," he said before going back to the task at hand—one of the two dozen items from his self-imposed honey-do list. They were in a suburb of Boston, watching Pete's grandsons while Pete's son and daughter-in-law, Jared and Heather, spent five days in Texas, where Jared had just accepted a residency following his completion of medi-cal school at Boston University.

"Funny. I meant in a psychological way. How are the disorders different from one another?" She sat down on one of the cheap kitchen chairs that went with the cheap kitchen table; Jared and Heather had been poor college kids for ten years, during which time they'd had three children. The din of little boys playing in the other room was at a moderate level, giving Sadie and Pete a rare chance at adult conversation.

Pete turned the final screw and stepped back to shut the cabinet, which now hung perfectly. "This question wasn't inspired by my grandchildren, was it?"

As if waiting for an invitation, three redheaded boys, graduating in height from tallest to shortest, ran into the kitchen. Kalan, the oldest, darted behind Pete, while Chance and Fig—a nickname somehow derived from Finnegan—held plastic swords above their heads, trumpeting a war cry in pursuit of their brother. All three boys had taken off their shirts to further emphasize their warrior physiques as only a six-, four-, and three-year-old could.

"Get 'em, Grandpa! Get 'em good," Kalan yelled.

Sadie smiled as she watched the show; it was her favorite—Grandpa Pete.

After using a series of karate chop actions to fend off the blows, Pete grabbed the plastic blade of one sword and then the other.

"I cut your hand off!" Chance yelled, tugging at his sword.

"Hand!" Fig repeated, pulling on his sword as hard as he could.

Pete lifted both swords until the boys had no choice but to let go. They stared at him with angry pouts.

"Gib it back!" Fig demanded.

Pete hadn't stopped smiling. "I can't."

"Yeth you can." Fig held out his hand. "Gib it back!"

"It's almost time for bed." Pete put the swords on the counter behind him.

All three boys immediately began whining in protest.

"If you get ready by yourselves, we'll have dessert before story time."

Sadie lifted her eyebrows, and Kalan yelled, "Dessert!"

"Ice cweam!" Fig yelled.

"Not ice cream," Pete said, pulling open the refrigerator door. "Aunt Sadie made a Pumpkin Roll."

"Bread?" Chance asked, crinkling his nose and sticking out his tongue.

"Not bread—cake," Pete said as he pulled out the platter of rolled cake with cream cheese filling.

"Cake!" all three boys said at once.

"But you've got to get ready for bed first," Pete said, lifting the platter out of their reach and looking to Sadie for help.

She turned to Kalan. "Will you help your brothers put on their pajamas?"

Kalan was only six, but he understood what it meant to be the big brother, so he grabbed each younger boy by one of their arms and began pulling them out of the room.

"Are you sure cake before bed is a good idea?" she said. It was after eight o'clock, and the dessert was supposed to chill for a few hours—it had barely been two.

"What's the fun of having Grandpa stay over if you can't have cake right before bed?"

It was hard to argue with such logic.

"I should have asked you first, though, it's your cake," Pete said, holding the platter with both hands as though trying to determine what to do with it now. "Sorry."

It was easy to forgive. Sadie stood up from the table and kissed his cheek. "You're a fabulous grandfather," she said, pointing for him to put the platter on the table while she headed for the newly re-paired cabinet to retrieve some plates.

"I don't know about that," Pete said, setting down the platter and watching her busy about the kitchen. "This may turn out to be the longest five days of my life."

Sadie laughed and grabbed a knife to slice the roll. "Haven't you ever played Grandpa full-time?"

"No," Pete said, moving to the sink to wash his hands. "Pat went a few times when the kids went on vacations or had babies or whatnot, and we had Brooke's kids for a weekend here and there, but I haven't been called upon since Pat died."

Sadie looked up at the casual mention of his late wife, liking that he was becoming more comfortable merging his old life with the new possibilities of their relationship. "Well, then, I'm glad I could be a part of this new experience," she said. "And rest assured, you're doing wonderfully—cake before bed notwithstanding." She grinned at him as she carefully sliced the cake.

"I appreciate the validation," Pete said with a nod, leaning against the counter as he dried his hands with a dish towel. "Even if I don't really deserve it."

Sadie carefully lifted each spiral of cake and cream cheese filling before putting it on a plate. A moment later, Pete's arms snaked around her middle and his lips pressed against her neck, sending a tingle down and then back up her spine. She turned in his arms, holding the knife out to the side so as not to appear threatening.

"I couldn't have done this without you," he said in a tender voice. "Aunt Sadie is amazing with these kids."

"I'm glad it worked out," Sadie said. She'd been very uncomfortable with the idea when Pete had first invited her. Staying in the same house didn't seem right, and her reputation had already suffered some painful blows in recent months. But the more she considered the possibility, the more she wondered why she cared so much what people thought of her. She *was* a woman of high standards, and the people who truly cared about her knew that. A phone call with

Heather had assured her that the boys could share one room, which would leave a guest room for Sadie.

It had been nice to have so much uninterrupted time with Pete, and she'd always loved New England in the fall. They had arrived two days early so the boys could get used to them before their parents left for Texas. "It's been fun getting to know Jared and his family from the inside-out," she added, looking up at Pete and trying not to get lost in his hazel eyes.

"And they love you," Pete said. He leaned in for a quick kiss before eyeing the knife still in her hand. "Maybe I should let you get back to work before one of us gets hurt."

Sadie laughed and turned back to serving.

Pete pulled out a chair. "So, why the interest in psychopaths and sociopaths?"

Sadie shrugged, but easily made the shift in the topic of conversation. "I caught part of a *Law & Order* episode the other day. They seemed to be using the two terms interchangeably in the show."

"Well," Pete said, folding his arms over his chest, "they're both antisocial personality disorders, which means they function 100 percent on what they want."

"So, that means they have no moral code, right?"

"Not necessarily," Pete said. "Many of them still live by a moral code, but only because it gets them what they want. Generally, a sociopath is classified as such because they exist on the fringe of society; they don't fit in very well with normal people. A psychopath, on the other hand, has an uncanny ability to mimic the way normal people act. Neither of them has a conscience—but one group can pretend that they do."

"Are they all violent?" Sadie asked.

Pete shook his head. "Not necessarily. Many of them live

relatively normal lives and are contributing members of society. Once their disorder turns malignant—meaning it escalates to the point where they're aggressively acting on their most base instincts— they become dangerous, which is where I end up coming in."

"That's scary," Sadie said. "To think there are people with no conscience living their lives amid the rest of us."

Pete nodded. "But, like I said, they aren't all criminals. Some of them find ways to control people and situations to their liking without breaking the law. Pat was involved in the PTA for years, and I'm pretty sure there were a few psychopaths involved in that organization."

Sadie smiled as she moved to the table and put a fork on each plate. Pete knew so much about so many things. Then she paused. "Shouldn't the boys have been back by now?"

Pete cocked an ear toward the doorway. "I hate to interrupt them if they aren't screaming . . . Wait."

Sadie heard it too. Whispers. She and Pete shared a quick look and then bolted toward the doorway. Sadie reached it first and came up short when she saw the three boys kneeling on the couch and peeking over the back in order to look out the big picture window. They were in their pajamas, she noted with relief, but were obviously intent on something happening outside. She looked over her shoulder at Pete, who was standing directly behind her, and he shrugged.

Slowly, they moved into the room, Sadie veering to the left side of the couch and Pete toward the right. They leaned forward to look out the window, and Sadie scanned the street to figure out what the boys were looking at. After a few seconds, she spotted a woman across the street, digging in a flower bed outside the house . . . in late October . . . at night. And she wasn't using a trowel to worry out some dead flowers—she was using a spade and making a pile of dirt on the sidewalk that led to the front door.

"Who's that?" Sadie asked Kalan, who was closest to her.

"Mrs. Wapple," Kalan said quietly.

"What's she doing?"

"Being weird," Kalan whispered.

"Does she do weird things a lot?"

Kalan nodded and folded his arms over the back of the couch, resting his chin on his hands. "We like to watch her when Mom turns off the TV."

"She's a witch!" Chance said.

"Witch!" Fig repeated.

Sadie's eyes flickered to the large cardboard cartoon witch on the wall—one of a dozen decorations Heather had put up in preparation for Halloween next week.

"I think she's just . . . digging," Pete said. But Sadie knew he found it strange as well.

"Mr. Forsberk's dog pooped in her yard and she cast a spell on it and it got hit by a car," Kalan said.

Sadie flicked a look at Pete, inviting him with her eyes to help her out. He didn't get the cue. "I feel bad for Mr. Forsberk's dog," Sadie said, "but unless Mrs. Wapple was driving the car, then it was probably just a very sad accident."

"It wasn't," Kalan said, still wide-eyed and sincere. "It was a spell. Mama even said."

"Your mom said it was a spell?" Pete asked for clarification.

"Well, no," Kalan said. "But she did say Mrs. Wapple is a witch."

"A witch!" Fig said, loudly this time, and began jumping on the couch. Apparently, his interest had waned. "A witch, a witch, a witch."

Pete tried to shush him, and Sadie once again launched into a defense of the poor old woman digging across the street. Then Chance pointed out the window, his mouth open. Sadie followed his gaze and was startled to see Mrs. Wapple facing them, standing on the sidewalk that ran parallel to the street rather than on the walkway leading to her house. The streetlight down the block illuminated the gray hat made of some type of coarse fabric on her head, and the long dark hair that fell in frizzy waves past her shoulders. As they watched, Mrs. Wapple lifted her hand and began drawing pictures in the air with her index finger.

"Okay, boys," Sadie said, ushering them off the couch. "She's just a silly old lady. And there's cake in the kitchen, so let's eat."

"Cake!" Fig shouted as he bounded off the couch. Chance and Kalan followed, though Kalan kept looking back over his shoulder. Pete finished herding them into the kitchen, and soon the boys were arguing about which piece of cake was the biggest.

Alone in the living room, Sadie hurried to the side of the window near the floor lamp, but before she pulled the blinds closed, she turned off the light, hoping it would make her less visible. Then she looked at Mrs. Wapple one last time. The woman was still on the sidewalk. Still staring, with her finger still pointing toward the house. No, not the house—pointing at Sadie.

Sadie swallowed and pulled herself a little further behind the heavy curtains. But she didn't take her eyes off the strange woman outside.

Mrs. Wapple lifted her hand so that it was pointing at the sky, and then she closed her fingers into a fist. Still staring in Sadie's direction, she punched her hand upward at the precise moment that the lightbulb in the lamp next to Sadie exploded with a pop. Sadie jumped out of the way as a thousand tiny shards of paper-thin glass tinkled to the floor.

"What was that?" Pete asked, stepping into the doorway that led to the kitchen.

Sadie looked at him. "The lightbulb exploded," she said, refusing to consider the coincidence that it had happened at the same time Mrs. Wapple punched her fist over her head. She looked out the window again, but Mrs. Wapple was gone.

She wasn't on the sidewalk; she wasn't digging in the garden. She was gone.

Sadie felt a strange tingling sensation wash over her skin like a chilled breeze as Kalan's words came back to her: *Mama says she's a witch.*

Good thing Sadie didn't believe in that kind of thing.

ABOUT THE AUTHOR

Josi S. Kilpack grew up hating to read until she was thirteen and her mother handed her a copy of *The Witch of Blackbird Pond*. From that day forward, she read everything she could get her hands on and credits her writing "education" to the many novels she has "studied" since then. She began her first novel in 1998 and hasn't stopped since. Her seventh novel, *Sheep's Clothing*, won the 2007 Whitney Award for Mystery/Suspense, and *Lemon Tart*, her ninth novel, was a 2009 Whitney Award finalist. *Blackberry Crumble* is Josi's thirteenth novel and the fifth book in the Sadie Hoffmiller Culinary Mystery series.

Josi currently lives in Willard, Utah, with her wonderful husband, four amazing children, one fat dog, and a varying number of very happy chickens.

For more information about Josi, you can visit her website at www.josiskilpack.com, read her blog at www.josikilpack.blogspot.com, or contact her via e-mail at Kilpack@gmail.com.